MURDER ONE LOVES MURDER TWO

GK DAVENPORT

1

Marc floored the pedal, making the tires of his Jeep squeal as he drove his truck toward the remote Caldwell homestead.

At the top of the hill, intermittent beacons of red light flashed against an orange sky. Men in jumpsuits, latex gloves, and plastic booties swarmed like hornets in the gauzy morning shadows, electrifying every nerve in his body. He scrambled from the Jeep, ducked under the flimsy barrier, and sprinted toward the sheriff.

JP jerked his head in the general direction of Marc's parked vehicle. "Get back in your car and wait till I'm finished here, Whitcomb."

Marc flinched at his buddy's curt dismissal. "Arrogant little SOB," he muttered.

He tightened his scarf against the brisk October wind and drifted toward the Caldwell house, a pristine two-story home, nestled in a ridge of rolling hills. He stumbled into the garage. A gas can streaked with fluid rested on the splintered remains of a doorframe. Smoke tongues licked the walls. The stench of gasoline fumes and charred wood saturated the air. Marc coughed and wheezed as his chest constricted.

He hurried to the backyard to escape the acrid odor of scorched rubble. Eyes closed, he took a deep breath and exhaled, counting from one to five until the tightness eased.

When his eyes opened, he was not alone. A solitary woman followed his movements closely. Her interest waned quickly, and she resumed her stoic pose.

"Whitcomb, damn it, get over here," JP hissed.

Marc shook off his preoccupation with the woman and hurried toward a short, barrel-chested sheriff leaning against the pasture fence.

"About time," Marc said, irritated. "What was so important that you had to call me in the middle of the night? Jessie's ticked."

"It wasn't the middle of the night . . . and Jessie's always ticked. Now, what the hell are you doing here? This is a crime scene, not a circus. You know the law, Counselor."

"Come on, JP. There is law, and *there is law*. This is Brule, not Tulsa. And you called me, remember?"

"I said we needed to talk . . . not follow me here, damn it. Now, shut up before you get me fired. I'll catch up with you later."

"Okay, I'm leaving, but tell me who the woman is." He pointed across the yard.

JP shrugged. "I don't see anyone."

"Over there!" Marc nodded in her general direction, but when he turned, she was gone.

"I don't see any woman." JP shook his head. "But if it was a prissy blonde, she's the victim's widow."

Marc squinted through the sun's glare and glimpsed the back of the woman's head as she disappeared down the dirt road on foot, her long blonde tresses dancing in the wind.

Marc's focus shifted. "Who's the victim? Last I heard, no one lived here. Old Man Caldwell died, and his widow is staying with some relative."

"Yeah, that's right. It's their boy," JP said, grabbing Marc's elbow and shoving him toward the road.

Marc pushed his glasses up on the bridge of his nose. "Do you... have any idea who did it?"

"I have my suspicions." JP stopped and dug the toe of his boot into the dried grass. "Kinda points to Jimmy Don Allen."

Marc grimaced. Devin's best friend couldn't be a murderer. Jimmy was a clean-cut, likable young man.

"Are you . . . Are you sure?" Marc stammered, his mouth dry.

"And Jimmy didn't do it alone," JP said as he pushed him toward his Jeep. "Like I said, we'll talk later."

Marc slung his arms free from JP's clutch. "We'll talk now. Spit it out. What are you saying?"

"You need to talk to your son," JP said through clenched lips. He pivoted toward the house, took two steps, and paused without turning. "Listen. As one friend to another, your boy has a problem."

Marc watched the little piece of shit in uniform retreat toward a bunch of important-looking men. He, Marcus Whitcomb, had pulled every string in the county to land that job for JP, and the little turd was accusing his son of murder. He spat and ground the dirt with the heel of his shoe. This needed fixing fast before JP damaged more than his reputation.

Marc crumpled into a heap against the steering wheel, wadded up with fear. *No way. Not Devin.* His fingers trembled as he dialed Devin's number.

"Hello. This is Devin. I'm not home right now, but please leave a message."

"This is your dad. Call me," Marc said, then slung his phone across the passenger

seat and pointed his Jeep toward Harper's Café.

The entrance to the tired little diner at the end of the block was surrounded by pumpkins, hay bales, and a lumpy old scarecrow. *Fall, an appropriate season for murder*, Marc thought as he fought to open the door against the brisk fall wind.

"You're late, Counselor." The shout-out drew his attention to a group of men at the back. Familiar faces engaged in animated conversation, the clatter of dishes, and the smell of frying bacon surrounded him.

"Yo," he said, waving in their general direction. Marc smoothed the wrinkles in his shirt, brushed aside the wayward locks of hair, and took a deep breath.

Marc approached the customary table. He understood these men, the ones who monitored the heartbeat of this tiny central Oklahoma town. They all descended from "Sooners," the homesteaders who jumped the gun on the 1892 land run and entered the Oklahoma Territory at night to stake the best claims. The power of old blood and money could not erase the fact that they all—including him—sprouted from "cheater" seed.

Hank Walton headed up the table. The burly rancher, with his unruly crop of red hair, filled the space of two men. An avid storyteller, he stretched his tale like taffy. To his right, Johnny, the mayor for seventeen years, nursed a steaming cup of coffee. Skip, the local coop manager, and Ross, the district judge, rounded out the group. Marc usually enjoyed his membership in this elite circle, but today, his mood felt as tarnished as the lacquer-yellow haze of the dingy café.

"Have a seat." Hank motioned toward an empty chair. "Thought we might have to send a posse for you."

Marc laughed with the others. As he slid into his chair, he battled the pounding in his chest that lingered from toxic fumes in the Caldwell garage and nerves. He tucked his hands in his pockets to squelch his nervous habit of fidgeting with his glasses, but his stuttering presented a more significant challenge. Best to keep his mouth shut today.

The waitress's slender frame hovered above Marc's shoulder as she tapped her pencil on her order pad. "The usual?"

Marc grunted in an affirmative as he scanned the familiar faces, all laser-focused on Hank's latest story.

Marc observed Hank's performance as if watching a mime, deaf to the sounds around him. Images of Devin and Jimmy scrolled through his head. *Marc's twins rode bikes and shot BB guns as children, but Devin read books and rescued puppies. Was Jimmy a helpless pup that needed saving? Could that be what dragged his son into this mess?*

Hank finished his story, and snorts of laughter jerked Marc back to the present. Judy slid a plate of sizzling bacon, two eggs with creamy yolks, and biscuits smothered in sausage gravy in front of him. She moved methodically around the table, balancing hot platters of grease and carbs. No dummy, Judy scratched out a living for herself and her boy waitressing. She heard things. He made a mental note to visit her later.

Marc noted subtle changes among his childhood buddies. *Had they heard anything about Devin? Maybe not. Hank was his usual dynamic self, but something felt out of kilter. September 20, 2015, could be a life-changer.*

The café clamor began to crash like cymbals in Marc's ears. He sopped up the last bit of gravy with his biscuit, finished his coffee, and pushed back from the table. He would wait for JP in his office.

"Wait up, buddy." Hank's rock-hard fist landed on Marc's shoulder. "I'll walk you."

"Sure," he said, resenting the intrusion.

"Quite a commotion at the Caldwell place." Hank's offhanded delivery didn't mask his implication. Marc dodged the question with a simple nod.

"Funny, I could've sworn I passed your truck heading out that way this morning."

Marc shrugged in feigned indifference. "I took some papers to JP."

"Paperwork and crime tape. Hmm. Interesting." Hank toyed with him. Annoyed, Marc stepped up his pace but couldn't shake him. "By the way, how's that boy of yours? Haven't seen him around in a while."

"I have three boys, Hank. Which one?"

Marc stifled his urge to bolt and run. The twins played high school basketball with Hank's son, and Hank had seen them at Tuesday night's game. His oldest son, Devin, lived in Tulsa, leaving little doubt about which son Hank singled out.

"Jimmy Don's friend."

The hair on Marc's neck bristled. "What's on your mind?" He slowed his gait, waiting for an answer, fighting a queasy sensation that crept from his stomach to his throat.

"Easy, Marco. We've been friends for a long time." He spoke with an unusual intensity. "Always there for each other, if you know what I mean. Remember when I lost Patty?" Marc nodded and waited. "By my count, I owe you one."

Marc recalled the twisted mess surrounding Patty's death. Lightning sparked wildfires across dry grasslands in the middle of the night. Hank got into his tractor and took off to plow a firebreak. Patty had followed him. She stood too close, and her foot caught between the hitch and the disc. Hank dragged his wife halfway across the field, mutilating her body beyond recognition, her screams drowned out by the roar of the tractor engine.

Rumors spread that Hank did it on purpose. Patty had inherited the land from her folks; he was the sole beneficiary upon her death, and whispers of divorce had swirled for months. But the night was dark. Emotions ran high.

Marc didn't question Hank's version of the incident but stepped in, killed the scuttlebutt, and managed the legal garbage. Hank survived the commotion unscathed.

"Today? You owe me one . . . today?" Marc asked with sarcasm.

"Cut the crap. Your boy's in trouble, and we both know it."

2

Marc doodled strings of letters on a legal pad as he waited for Hank to finish gawking around the office. His mind flipped from past to present like shuffling a deck of cards.

He possessed every attribute required of a great trial attorney except one - his emotions. He couldn't forgive himself for being naïve, inexperienced, or just plain stupid. His first year at the University of Oklahoma had been a disaster. He slept through morning classes and cut out after 3 p.m. for Eskimo Joe's Bar and Grill to meet up with his buddies.

It took some hefty string-pulling to overcome his failing grades. Upon graduation, his dad, a masterful puppeteer, secured a prestigious internship for him with Smith & Noble, Attorneys at Law. He married a prominent client's daughter, had a son, and landed a spot on the defense team for a highly publicized murder trial.

Everything was great until it wasn't. He fumbled the ball, and the defendant got the death penalty. It cost him his job and wife within a year, leaving alcohol as his only cheerleader. He embraced liquor with both fists. His father rescued him from the ashes again and built a law office in Brule for the two of them.

Leather-bound books lining the wall behind his mahogany desk and the sweet aroma of cigars evoked memories of a father who believed in him. His practice of the last twenty years in the tiny town of Brule didn't require emotional commitment. He rolled through real-estate transactions, land transfers, and frequent DUIs without a dent in his psyche. Brule had very little crime, but when trouble found him, Marc withdrew to this sanctuary to hide. Today was such a day, but there was one problem. Hank had followed him.

"Nice place. Never been back here before."

"Thanks," Marc grunted, tapping his pencil on the desk, impatient for Hank to state his purpose.

"Nervous, my friend? No need. A smart man like you shouldn't have any problems. You managed my little situation quite well."

"And what is this . . . situation?" Marc swallowed.

Hank drew back, surprised. "Devin and Jimmy . . . Didn't JP tell you?"

Marc's pencil stopped. "JP couldn't wait to get rid of me. When did *you* talk to him?"

"I called him right after I passed you this morning and told him about Devin and Jimmy."

"Told him what?" Marc expected his usual paralyzing anxiety to well up. Instead, his chest filled with the urge to beat the crap out of Hank.

"He and Jimmy pulled into the Caldwell place last Friday. I saw 'em when I checked the cattle tanks on my quarter next to their house."

"That was three days ago." Marc was puzzled at the lapse of time between Hank's alleged sighting of the boys and the murder reported today.

"The man's been dead for three days," Hank said. "I thought you knew." Red flags exploded. The forensic team couldn't have completed canvassing the crime scene, and labs don't work that fast.

"Are you stating facts or conjecture?" Marc said in his lawyer's voice.

The burly rancher stood to leave. "Look, I'm offering my help, but if you don't want it . . ."

Marc calculated the risk of alienating the most powerful man in town. He could blow Hank and JP out of the water for their legal infractions, but he couldn't afford to make enemies . . . yet.

"What are you proposing, Hank?"

"Let this go down easy. The way I see it, Jimmy killed the man, and Devin got bamboozled, tricked into assisting or something like that."

"My boy's innocent," Marc said, slamming the desk with his fist.

"Spoken like a true father." A smirk flitted across Hank's lips. "Your boy runs at the back of the pack. I watched him grow up, and he's a follower. I can get him probation if he pleads guilty to accessory . . . and he agrees to be a witness for the prosecution."

Hank spoke the truth about Devin. He never started trouble, but he inherited his share from his friends—nothing serious, the usual kid stuff. Hank had the clout to pull off a plea deal. He had his hands in the back pocket of every judge in the county, but the price was Devin's reputation.

Hank wanted Marc to forfeit the game before he took the field. *Why?*

"I need time . . . to digest everything. But I'm curious. What's your stake in this?"

"No stake. I'm helping two friends."

"Me and who else?"

"Madeline Caldwell." Hank drew to full height and puffed out his chest.

"The widow? Is she involved? With the death, I mean?" Marc watched Hank's face for a reaction.

"Hell no." Hank's eyes blazed fire. "But I don't want to see her dragged through the mud. Let's make this quick and easy."

"She's a friend?"

A full-blown grin spread across Hank's face as he tipped the brim of his Stetson. "Don't take too long, buddy boy," he said over his shoulder as he sauntered out of the room.

Marc reached for the phone and dialed. "Hello. This is Devin . . ."

That damned answering machine. He grabbed a pencil and stabbed a Big Chief tablet, ripping it to shreds. With a quick swipe, he wadded the mutilated pages of the tablet into a ball and tossed them into the trash. He took a deep breath and exhaled as he counted to five.

His secretary, Nancy, peeked through the door. Concern clouded her brown eyes, hiding behind sensible glasses. "Are you all right?"

"Yeah." Marc shrugged.

She hovered for a moment, smoothing a strand of gray hair that had escaped from her bun. "Do you need anything? I'm going to the courthouse, but it can wait."

"Yes," Marc answered. "I want you to find out what you can on David Caldwell. Who inherits his land, how many children, living or dead? Dig up everything you can find, down to their shoe size."

"Is that all?" she laughed. Relief flooded her matronly face.

"No. Cancel any appointments I have for the coming week, and don't schedule any new ones."

"What about the stuff stacked on your desk?" Marc sensed her disapproval. She hated his sloppy piles of work papers.

"Finish what you can, and I'll review it. We'll run off the emergency fund Dad left me for a while."

"I'm sorry I asked," she said with a slight huff.

For the first time today, he flashed a grin. What would he do without her? "I'll be out the rest of the day. If Jessie calls, tell her I had to run to Tulsa to meet with a client."

Marc passed the one-hour drive to Tulsa by replaying his strange encounters with JP and Hank. He rotated snatches of their conversation around and around in his brain like squares of a Rubik's Cube. Hank planted the seeds of Devin's guilt with JP and spread a protective wing over the victim's widow in rapid succession . . . within hours of the discovery of the body.

Marc tortured himself with questions that had no answers. He needed a copy of the police reports as soon as possible.

Traveling east on Hwy 412, he dodged the westbound commuters during rush hour, but when he turned on 244 South, traffic pelted him from every direction. Marc darted across two lanes and hung a sharp left at the next exit. He spotted his son's car parked in the drive of an old Craftsman-style duplex near the courthouse. He bounded up the steps to the small, tailored portico and knocked. Before long, Devin's tall, lanky frame filled the doorway.

"Dad," Devin said with surprise and a little concern. "Come on in."

"Why don't you lease an apartment a little easier for your old man to find?" Marc laughed, throwing his arm across Devin's shoulder. He found it easy to joke with his oldest son. Devin's spontaneous hug lifted his spirits. A few sane words from his boy should straighten out this whole murder gibberish, and he could be on his way home to Jessie.

"I phoned you several times this morning. Why didn't you answer?"

"I turned the ringer off to get some work done. What's up? Is Mom okay?"

"Yeah . . . everything's okay." Marc studied the blond-haired man with agate blue eyes. His chest ached with pride. His son had transformed from a tenderhearted five-year-old into a zealous advocate for juvenile offenders. He worked with Jimmy as a youth guidance counselor at the Madison Youth Center. Both were fine young men.

"There's talk that you and your friend were at the Caldwell place last Friday night. Is that true?" Marc swallowed hard, easing the lump in his throat.

"No." Devin's eyes darted about the room, avoiding contact.

His son lied.

"No, what? No, you weren't at the Caldwell place, or no, Jimmy wasn't at the Caldwell place? Which is it?"

"I wasn't there."

"But Jimmy was?"

"I can't believe you drove here to ask me about Jimmy's whereabouts on Friday night." Devin's face flushed red.

"A murder occurred at the Caldwell ranch, and you two are persons of interest." Marc slumped back into the leather couch. He had expected a simple explanation to end the whole thing, but the conversation was spinning in the wrong direction.

"It's a damn lie. I haven't been near the place!" Devin shouted.

"Get Jimmy over here. We need to talk to him."

Devin's fiery flush paled. "He's gone . . . to Sallisaw."

Marc reeled with the implication. Jimmy found sanctuary with his Cherokee people.

"How do you know that?"

"I took him."

"Don't talk to anyone without me present, son." Marc grabbed his coat and headed out the door.

On the long drive home, he mulled over the consequences of murder on tribal grounds. The Supreme Court decision on the 2020 McGirt v. Oklahoma case restored vast swathes of Eastern Oklahoma to the Native Americans, casting a net of tribal rule over a substantial portion of the state. Jimmy's fate fell under federal jurisdiction. Oklahoma courts had no authority.

Marc headed straight to his office and called Jessie to tell her he would be working late. He pulled a dusty binder titled "General Guide to Indian Jurisdiction in Oklahoma" from the top shelf and flipped through its pages. The specialized field of Native American law was foreign to him. The journey began tonight.

The bridge across Indian Creek led smack dab to the middle of Cherokee country. The Caldwell homestead was on tribal land, no doubt about it. Marc leaned back in his chair and rubbed his bloodshot eyes.

The killing occurred on Native ground. Jimmy fell under federal authority. JP would have to collaborate with the tribe to bring him in. But Devin was fair game. *This bloody mess just got complicated.* Marc slammed the book shut, turned off the lights, and headed home.

He craved a drink . . . a stiff one to soothe his nerves. He tiptoed into the house and down the long hall to his office. Four drinks later, the amber liquid numbed his senses as he slipped into a fitful sleep on the recliner.

3

"Jessie, have you seen my gray tie?" Marc barked in a panic.

"Quit bellowing, honey. I'm right here," Jessie rounded the corner with an armful of folded laundry. A long black ponytail swayed with purpose against her tawny skin as she marched toward the closet. "I'm sure it's right where you put it."

"I'm sure it's right where you put it," he parroted as he rummaged through a basket of loose clothing in the corner of the closet.

"Why don't you wear this one?" Jessie dangled a blue paisley tie under his chin.

He hated that tie. It looked like a hippie headband, but at this point, what difference did it make? He couldn't afford to be late.

"I still don't understand why you think you have to attend that man's funeral. You didn't even know him." Her intense brown eyes challenged him.

He wasn't sure why. Curiosity? The morgue held the body for ten days after the autopsy. Rumor had it that the widow refused to claim the body. Or maybe because a perpetrator might attend a memorial service to admire his handiwork. The reason why escaped him.

"I've met the victim's mom." This spur-of-the-moment answer came as close to a non-lie as Marc could muster. He had physically run into David's mother at the Venture Grocery once when their carts collided in the produce aisle.

"Don't forget the twins have a basketball game tonight." Jessie gave him a quick peck on the cheek as he headed out the door, leaving the soft scent of Shalimar perfume on his shirt. *Damn, she's beautiful.*

The service would be in Rosston, twenty miles by county road. Marc pushed the speed limit. If he wanted a back-row seat, he needed to show up early. The back seats fill first at a funeral. A smattering of cars parked around a tiny country church erased any hope of sneaking in unnoticed. Getting lost in a handful of people would prove difficult.

Marc missed his chance for the back pew, so he ducked his head and moved toward the aisle seat in the third row. A memorial pamphlet, thrust into his hands by a middle-aged woman at the door, offered a welcome diversion while he waited for the service to begin.

David Caldwell was a handsome fifty-two-year-old man with a generous smile, perfect teeth, and dark-brown hair. Hell, he should be grilling in the backyard and playing ball with his grandkids. Instead, he was in a pine box, surrounded by the musty fragrance of potted lilies and yellow mums. Marc shivered. Funerals creeped him out.

The mellow moan of an organ filled the room as the family entered through a side door. An older woman led the procession, flanked by two younger women. Her lips quivered as she fought to hold her tears in check, stumbling twice before reaching the front pew.

Marc craned to see the faces of the two young women. Neither resembled the woman with the long blonde hair from the crime scene. He gawked at the meager congregation—no trace of the mysterious widow.

The minister began. The two young women dabbed at tears, while David's mother sobbed, lifting her arms above her head as if pleading with God. Her cries grew louder. The preacher's face grew redder. He wiped his forehead with a handkerchief.

With the final amen, the old lady jumped from her pew and faced the congregation.

"The sons of bitches killed my son!" she screamed, flailing her arms about. She fell onto the pew, heaving. "They killed my boy. They . . . killed . . . my . . . son."

"Shhhh, Grandmother. It's okay." A petite dark-haired woman grabbed her grandmother's arm. A forceful shove sent the young lady sprawling at Marc's feet, making him the bullseye of attention.

Whispers and accusing looks shot through the crowd and landed on him. "The father . . . accomplice . . ."

"Are you all right?" Marc asked, extending his hand to help her.

"I think so," she said as she smoothed her skirt. "Sad, isn't it? Her whole world revolved around my dad."

The second woman clasped both arms around David's mother and pushed her toward the exit.

Mourners continued to file out of the sanctuary. With a shake of her head, the young woman turned to Marc. "I'm Danielle Caldwell," she said, extending her hand. "Just call me Dani."

"Marc," he answered politely, squelching the impulse to ram through the lingering crowd and escape. "I'm . . . I'm sorry about the loss of your father."

"Were you a friend?"

Marc pushed his glasses up on his nose and stuck his hands in his pockets. He hated lying. "You might say that."

"Thanks for coming." A sincere smile dimpled her cheeks.

"Sure thing." An awkward pause followed. "Please accept my . . . my apologies, but I've got to run. My boys have a game tonight, and my wife will kill me if I'm late."

Once free of the church and its people, Marc bolted to his truck. He had no business at the funeral. Throwing the Jeep into reverse, he backed up and sped away. The road hummed under his truck's tires, easing his feelings of guilt with each passing mile.

Three oddities twirled in his mind. He did not see the blonde woman JP identified as David's widow, the obituary did not list a wife, and the burial took place ten days after the state released the body.

He needed to find the answers, but first he had to get to the twins' basketball game.

The funeral had drained the life out of Marc, but this game wasn't optional. Jessie made that clear. He spotted his wife, decked out in the team colors, in the front row of the bleachers. Her black hair fell loose around her face, framing her sculpted cheekbones. The classic profile of his Cherokee wife never failed to trigger a rush of pride.

"Scoot over." Marc nudged her to the center, glancing at the scoreboard. He had missed a few minutes of the first quarter. "Looks like we're ahead."

Jessie erupted from the bleachers with the rest of the crowd, wildly cheering a three-point shot by her son.

"Wow. John's on fire. Did you see that?" she shrieked.

Marc's mind was in a funeral fog. He had no idea what she was talking about. "Did I see what?"

"Aren't you watching the game?"

"It's been a long day," he answered with a weary sigh.

Marc tried to follow the action up and down the court, but his brain didn't engage until his eyes locked on the young woman from the funeral, waving in his direction from the opponent's bleachers. *Crap, she's the last person I wanted to see tonight.*

The sharp blast of the final buzzer and Jessie's elbow in his ribs jerked Marc back to the present. "Did you see that last shot?" Jessie screamed, turning to Marc.

"Sure did," he lied. Marc jingled the change in his pocket, impatient for a quick exit and a shot of bourbon. "I'll catch you at the house." He gave his wife a quick pat, then vanished into the frenzied crowd. He would wait for the family at home.

"Great second half, boys." Marc clapped John on the shoulder and tossed Robert's hair when they swarmed the front door.

"You see that three-pointer I made in the fourth quarter?" John, the go-getter of the two, never missed a chance to crow.

"Sure did, son."

"Well, did you see who set him up to make that shot?" Robert countered.

"Anyone coulda done that," John said.

"Enough already. Finish the debate tomorrow on who outdid whom. Off to bed now," Jessie barked with a military flare.

John and Robert saluted behind her back and flashed twin grins. The boys called her Sergeant Jessie.

"Are you coming to bed?" she asked Marc, heading up the stairs without waiting for an answer. The question was rhetorical.

MARC DID his best work in the wee hours of the morning. He filled a glass with Jim Beam whiskey, added a splash of water, and retreated to his tiny office. The first shot blunted the pinging of his frazzled nerves, and the second muffled the white noise in his brain.

With the third Beam and water, the random conversations with JP and Hank crystallized into one intriguing thought. Hank claimed he saw Jimmy and Devin while checking cattle on his land bordering the Caldwell ranch. He was lying. Indian Creek

dried up with the drought, and the parched grass was unfit for grazing. There were no livestock to check. The thin veneer of trust he'd had in Hank disappeared.

Marc shuffled through a mess of papers on his desk until he uncovered a clean sheet to scribble on. "1. Hank's cattle 2. update from Nancy 3. haircut." Satisfied he had captured the essence of the day, he rested his head on the desk and let the fourth drink do its magic.

"Breakfast is ready." Jessie punched him on the shoulder.

He pulled himself upright and nodded. A bowl of oatmeal, a slice of dry toast, and a cup of hot coffee did nothing to lift his spirits. He missed Harper's crispy bacon and gravy-soaked biscuits.

"Pass the sugar, please."

"I thought we decided to cut down on sweets." Jessie cast a look of disapproval over the top of the newspaper.

"Don't start with me this morning. Hand me the damn sugar." The instant he spoke, he regretted it, but she could be maddening.

Marc swallowed the pasty oatmeal and gulped the tepid coffee. He lacked the energy to make amends.

Jessie broke the silence. "What's wrong with you? You've acted like a maniac for the last two weeks."

"I know . . . sorry."

"Sorry's not good enough." Her half-moon smile didn't light up her eyes. "You're keeping something from me. Does it have anything to do with the young lady who was looking for you at the game?"

"What lady?" Marc's voice cracked.

"She said her name is Dani."

"W-what did she say?" Marc stammered.

"Ask her yourself. Here's her number." Jessie tossed a credit card receipt with a number scratched on the back toward him. "At least you have good taste. If you ask me, she's quite attractive but a little young."

"What the hell are you talking about?"

"I saw her trying to get your attention at the game, and you ran out like a scalded cat. Is she the reason you're never home? On the rare occasions when you are home, you hole up in your office and drink."

Her words hurt more than a slap in the face. He had never been unfaithful. Ever. His anger spewed out before he could stop it. "Maybe if you didn't run the house like a drill sergeant, barking orders at me as if I were one of the kids, I would come home more often." The second the words came out, Marc realized he had screwed up.

Jessie's eyes glazed. "Keep your secrets. Whatever they are. Better yet, stuff them in that bottle of Beam you hide in your office."

Marc didn't mean what he said, yet he had sliced her to pieces because he couldn't stand to utter Devin and murder in the same breath. If he said it aloud, the possibility would become real, and he couldn't deal with it.

4

Towering skyscrapers punctured the Tulsa skyline as evidence of the city's newly found wealth. Once a scrappy little cow town with a population of 200 people in the late 1800s, Tulsa exploded like a geyser with the first oil strike in 1901. The population surged to 72,000 by 1920, and it had swelled to over 400,000 by the last census.

Marc, once addicted to Tulsa's pulsing energy, had no use for her now. He turned into the nearest parking garage, took a ticket from the attendant, and began an endless spiral of right turns to reach the top level. Vehicles, lined up like bullets in a magazine, reeked of gasoline fumes and tire rubber, evoking memories best forgotten. With a shake of his head, he focused on the task at hand: meeting Dani, the lady from the funeral.

Dani lived in a loft two blocks from the parking facility. Marc had no choice but to walk the remaining distance. He paused before the BOK Center, a tall building with towering concrete pillars. Twenty years ago, he would have entered through the revolving door, caught an elevator to the eleventh floor, and entered the law offices of Smith & Noble, Attorneys at Law, to begin a day's work. Today, the very thought sickened him. He shrugged it off.

Marc pushed through eight-foot double doors into the foyer of a 1920s warehouse converted into upscale apartments. Large expanses of brick and glass framed the chic interurban décor of the lobby. It possessed every modern amenity except an elevator. He climbed three flights of stairs and took a left as Dani instructed, arriving at Suite 104, winded by the effort.

A petite young woman with a playful pixie cut, dark eyes, and fair skin answered the door. She resembled the nice-looking man on the memorial pamphlet.

"It's you," Dani gasped, stepping back from the door. "I'm sorry. I had no idea—"

"That the man at the funeral was Marcus Whitcomb, the lawyer?" Marc finished for her. "I should have mentioned that when I called you."

"Right," she laughed. "I went on a wild goose chase to track you down . . . per Grandmother's instructions. And there you were. You were kind of stingy with your last name at the service."

"I'm here, but barely. Little out of shape." Marc fought to catch his breath. "Those stairs are brutal."

"Grandmother would agree with you," she giggled, making him feel old. "Have a seat, and I'll get you a glass of water."

Marc glanced about the apartment. Crocheted doilies and porcelain figurines on oak end tables looked dumpy and dated under the soaring ceiling with exposed air ducts.

"Grandmother's stuff." Dani placed a glass on the table and laughed. "Quite a combo."

Marc nodded, embarrassed that she'd read his thoughts.

"So your grandmother lives with you?"

"Yes, but she's with her sister this afternoon so that we can talk."

"I'm a little puzzled. Why didn't you call the office? I'm listed in the phone book."

"Two reasons, Mr. Whitcomb. First, I don't like people knowing my business. Second, you've done work for my family before." Her eyes narrowed as she watched his reaction.

"I hate to disappoint you, but I have no recollection of performing services for any member of the Caldwell family."

"I'm not surprised you don't remember, but it's true. You prepared the deed to Grandmother's ranch fourteen or so years ago."

"If you want the deed updated, make an appointment with Nancy. I'd be happy to assist." Marc struggled to hide his disappointment. He had gone through a lot of nonsense for a deed.

Dani walked to the desk in the corner of the room and returned with three tattered diaries. "I don't need help with a deed. I need help getting Grandmother's farm back . . . from Dad's *grieving* widow."

Marc's heart thumped; his temples throbbed. Counting to five twice, he regained his composure. This could be big.

"Do you have any idea who did it?" He fought to control his voice.

"Who did what? The murder? I didn't know we were talking about Dad's murder." Dani studied Marc's face. "There are rumors, but small towns lie, and I am unconvinced. My dad wasn't the man he appeared to be. Grandmother's diaries reveal a side of him that differs from the world's perception. Take these and read them. That's all I'm asking."

"Why?"

"The people my grandmother mentions might surprise you. Please. I'll pay for your services."

"That's all? You want me to look over the diaries?"

"Yes," she said with a wink. "And don't worry. Grandmother writes wonderful things about you."

Marc's mind clicked through the ethical ramifications like a Rolodex. She asked for help concerning her grandmother, but his son had been implicated as an accomplice in her dad's murder, a fact that didn't seem to trouble her. A possible conflict of interest existed, and he could be disbarred if he tiptoed too close to the line.

Dani's steadfast gaze pushed him toward this questionable alliance.

"I'm sure I'll enjoy the experience." His answer sealed the dubious pact that could ruin his career.

"Maybe. Maybe not."

"Either way, no charge . . . and no promises. Consider this a favor. My schedule is tight this week. I'll get back to you." Marc had crawfished out of a total commitment, but the girl and her grandmother Ruby's journals hooked him. He had skirted ethics in his local practice, but this alliance made him nervous. He closed the door behind him and breathed a sigh of relief, leaving his ethical qualms trapped on the other side. But most of all, he was thankful the stairs pointed downward.

On his way home, he dropped by the office to instruct Nancy on a land deed for a local farmer. She knew more about the preparation and enjoyed pecking out the details on the keyboard, a task he found tedious. Her data assimilation skills served him well, but her pace proved maddening. The information he had requested about the Caldwell case hadn't materialized, and she got testy when he asked. Someday, a stack of files would appear on his desk, alphabetized and color-coded to perfection, but today wasn't the day. With Nancy launched, Marc headed home. A tall glass of Jim Beam and three intriguing diaries needed his attention.

Poking around in an old woman's diaries seemed like an invasion of privacy, but Dani had asked him to read them. He placed her journals on the corner of his desk and fixed a drink. All reservations disappeared after polishing off the second Beam and water. He opened the oldest, *The Story of Ruby*, and chuckled. The title sounded like a biblical odyssey.

AUGUST 25, 1967 – Is it wrong for a mother to love one child more than another? David is a perfect twelve-year-old. Dark eyes. Dark hair. Like my people. Tony says he guesses I can't control my feelings, but I'd better not show them.

August 26, 1967 – How can two brothers be so different? Jack is a pale, blond, blue-eyed, frail version of my father-in-law. David has enough gumption for both.

August 27, 1967 – That kid can sweet-talk me into anything. What

David wants, David gets. The little suck-up. We both know it, but it works. Ha . . . It pays to be the baby.

August 31, 1967 – Tony's complaining again. Says I'm spoiling David. says I give him everything he wants. Maybe I do. But what's the harm? Tony's so hard on him that I have to even it out.

September 7, 1967 – Shit hit the fan today. David took ten dollars from his dad's billfold. Tony took the belt to him and left welts on his butt. I could have killed him. David only took the money to buy me a present for my birthday.

MARC LEANED back in his chair and crossed his arms above his head. What did any of this have to do with the murder? The warmth of the liquor soothed his tired body as he fanned through the remaining pages of book one. Another drink might help clarify this motherly tripe. Ruby adored her youngest and tolerated Jack.. Simple. He moved on.

THE STORY OF RUBY, Book Two

January 12, 1990 – Jack had another dialysis treatment today. Things aren't looking good. His arms have huge knots from the tubes, and he's lost so much weight he doesn't even look like himself. They're doing surgery in the morning. He might not survive with his one remaining kidney functioning less than twenty-five percent. All I can do is cry. I don't know if my tears are for Jack or me. Maybe both. I feel so guilty.

"MARC, DINNER'S READY." Jessie's voice broke the monotony of his reading assignment. Grilled chicken breasts with boiled carrots sounded like a boring diversion from Ruby's log, but he was hungry.

Marc glimpsed himself in the mirror as he rose from his desk. Spider-veined eyes and sallow skin told a story his wife hated. Jessie despised his drinking. He detoured to the hall bath, brushed his teeth, and combed his hair. Not perfect, but better.

"Where are the boys?"

"Late ball practice," she muttered as she placed a steaming platter on the table.

Marc watched Jessie move about the room with a coldness directed at him, and it hurt. He hated it when she withdrew from him.

"Look, I've been a jerk, and I'm sorry."

"I've told you. *Sorry* doesn't cut it."

"It's the damn Caldwell case," Marc blurted out. "Satisfied?"

"What Caldwell case? I heard it's still under investigation." She leaned toward her husband, her interest trumping anger.

"Right." Marc grimaced. He had made a blunder, and his wife picked it up.

"Right, what? How would you be involved if they don't have a suspect?"

Marc slammed his fist on the table. "Damn it, Jessie. I need some space." His outburst unleashed her rage.

"I can arrange that." She threw her oven mitt on the table and stomped off.

"Wait, honey." Marc jumped to his feet. "Sit down . . . please." She stopped but kept her back to him. "According to JP, Jimmy Don Allen is the prime suspect."

"Jimmy? That's crazy."

"Well, it gets crazier. Hank said he spotted Devin at the Caldwell place with Jimmy on the day of the murder. JP also said Jimmy had help and insinuated my son might be involved."

"Why did you hide this from me?" Anger shadowed Jessie's face.

"I wanted to tell you, but . . ."

"But?

"I'm afraid there might be some truth to it. I talked with Devin. He drove Jimmy to Sallisaw on the day of the murder."

"That makes him guilty?"

"Could make him an accessory," Marc said and sighed.

"Let me remind you that Devin is *our* son." She touched Marc's shoulder and began to massage his muscles, easing the tension that had built up over the past two weeks.

Jessie was his second wife. Marc's first wife abandoned him and Devin when he left the prestigious firm of Smith & Noble. His ex had no use for a small-town lawyer making small-time money. Jessie was Devin's first-grade teacher and made a great effort to draw him out of the shadows cast by the loss of his mother. Marc believed his attraction to her hinged on Devin, but it was more than that. The warmth of her compassion washed over him like a soothing balm.

"I need your help." Marc's voice broke. He couldn't keep her out of it.

"I know." Jessie's eyes pooled with sympathy. "We'll leave in the morning. I'll call Grandpa Duke and tell him we're coming."

"Let's get moving." Marc threw his suitcase and Jessie's three into the Jeep. Jessie slid into the passenger side and checked her makeup in the visor mirror.

"For heaven's sake, we're going to Tahlequah, not Tahiti."

"You're going to Tahlequah. I'm going home. That's an enormous difference," she said, flipping her hair. He flashed an amused grin.

He landed a prize when he married Jessie. Too bad her family didn't feel the same about him. Two trips to her hometown during their twenty years of marriage were two too many.

He had forgotten the beauty of southeastern Oklahoma. Tall green cedars clutched the ground between slate-gray boulders on the gentle hills of Sequoyah County, a mountainous region straddling the Ozark Plateau to the north and the Ouachita Mountains to the south. Marc took a deep breath, exhilarated by the purity of this rugged country.

"Did you bring your inhaler?" Jessie broke the spell.

"Yes, sergeant." An asthma attack was inevitable. Never if, but when.

"Good. Now, turn south at the next junction."

"We have navigation, dear." How many times must he remind her?

"And it never works near Tahlonteeskee. Trust me." She refused to admit that the old Cherokee capital had ceased to exist in the early 1800s, when the Indian nation's center of gravity shifted to Tahlequah. Tahlonteeskee was little more than a blip on the radar sitting on private land near Gore. There was no way that bump in the road would appear on navigation.

"Turn right there." Jessie pointed at a dirt road whizzing by in a blur.

Marc slapped the steering wheel. "You can't say 'turn right there' as I'm passing the road."

"Make a U-turn and go back, then. I thought you saw it on your navigation thingy," Jessie said, waving her finger at the screen as she slumped back in her seat.

He clenched his teeth, drawing his lips into a thin line. Ten miles of fussing with Jessie added to his dread of facing his in-laws.

Two hills and one dirt road later, the Waite homestead appeared in a clearing. Well-to-do by local standards, the spacious stone home would fit any urban setting if you removed the guinea fowl strutting about the yard and a slump-backed Jersey cow in an adjacent pasture. Jessie scampered from the Jeep, ran to her mom and dad, and wrapped them in a big bear hug.

"Agilisi. Agiduda," Jessie squealed, turning to an elderly man and woman waiting patiently in the shadows. These proper Cherokee names for "grandmother" and "grandfather" evolved into Lisi and Duke long ago, which pleased the aging couple.

"Get over here, Marc," Jessie's dad said, flashing a broad grin. He opened his arms wide and drew Marc in for a quick hug and slap on the shoulder. Her dad, a short, squat man with mischievous dark eyes, opened the door for Marc to ease in. "Relax. Mama will warm up before long."

"Haven't seen you in a coon's age." Mama Waite had her claws out. "I almost forgot our Jessie had a husband."

Lisi moved toward Marc with the tentative steps of an elderly woman.

"Come, tell us how we may help you," Lisi said, beckoning him with her hand. Her kindness loosened the knot in Marc's chest.

Marc watched as Duke and Lisi moved toward the house. According to Jessie, the purple shawl draped about Lisi's shoulders symbolized wisdom, and Duke's corn-bead necklace represented the tears the Cherokees shed along the trail from Georgia to Oklahoma.

Marc hung back and fiddled with the luggage, fighting to rein in an unfamiliar emotion. This family, steeped in tradition and honor, transported him to another place and time. He felt unworthy to sit at their table.

Marc carried the luggage to the bedroom and stopped in front of the mirror. His six-foot frame forced him to crouch to catch his reflection. Graying temples added a distinguished touch to the familiar face. Except for his slight paunch, he had changed little over the years, and most considered him handsome. Even Lisi had called him a good-looking man, but after twenty years of marriage, Mama Waite didn't believe him worthy of her princess. Marc sucked his gut in and threw his shoulders back. He must not appear a slouch to Jessie's mother.

"Jimmy? Jimmy Don Allen?" Mama's incredulous outburst meant Jessie had shared the awful news.

"And they believe Devin was an accomplice," Marc said as he entered the kitchen.

Duke leaned close to his wife and began to speak in the tonal language of the Cherokee, Tsalagi, his voice resonating like the melodic chirping of a mockingbird. One of 2,000 fluent speakers of the dialect, Duke spoke in his native tongue, sharing his thoughts only with Lisi before turning his attention to Marc.

"Have they arrested Jimmy?" Duke asked.

"No, the sheriff thinks he's hiding somewhere in Sequoyah County, farther south. Devin drove him to Sallisaw and dropped him off on the night of the murder. They haven't spoken to Devin either." Marc cringed at the mention of the connection between his son and Jimmy.

"Bait." The simple utterance came from Duke as a smile creased his tawny, weathered skin.

"Bait? What do you mean? Who's bait?" Marc found the statement ludicrous.

"Jimmy. They need you to find him. Are you sure he killed the man?"

"I know what the sheriff told me." Marc slapped the counter in frustration. "Look. I'm not privy to all the pieces of the investigation."

"What do you believe?"

Marc shook his head. "I don't think Jimmy, or my son, is capable of . . ."

"Then we have work to do. This sheriff you speak of uses you to find Jimmy before they bring your son in. They're banking on Jimmy's cooperation because of their friendship."

"Bullshit."

Mama stretched to her full height as she glared at Marc. "Jessie, tell this man we don't speak to elders in such a manner."

"Marc meant to say he doesn't understand." His wife gave him the evil eye, daring him to speak another word.

Marc understood two things: He needed their help, and he had stepped into a cow patty. Bullshit was a term of endearment in his circle, but that one little expression sent the entire family into an uproar . . . except for Duke.

"Let him be." Duke's stern order stopped Marc's mother-in-law's tongue but left her scowl intact. "This man is trying to save his son. I would do the same." He turned to Marc. "Tomorrow, we will spring the trap and see what we catch."

Marc had no idea what he meant.

"What do we need to do?" Jessie blurted, anxious to bolt out of the gate. Duke cupped her face with both hands. "*We* will do nothing."

Disappointment spread across Jessie's face.

"Marc and I will head out to the Bottoms in the morning." Duke stepped into the utility room, picked up a bucket, and headed out the door.

"Where is he going? We just got started." Marc gawked as the man made his way to the barn, steady and vigorous despite his age. Clad in blue jeans and a plaid shirt, he dressed like any other rancher in southeast Oklahoma except for a long gray braid down his back and a beaded necklace.

Jessie laughed. "*You* just got started. *He's* finished. Besides, it's five o'clock and time to milk Buttercup."

5

Duke roused Marc from a deep sleep at five o'clock the next morning, careful not to wake Jessie. He grabbed a thermos of coffee, two cups, and a sack of biscuits from the counter. "The sun will be up soon. We'd better hit the road."

Still groggy, Marc dressed and followed Duke to the Jeep.

"You drive." The elderly Cherokee man tossed Marc the keys he had plucked off the dresser.

Marc slid behind the wheel. He had plenty of gas in the Jeep and an abundance of curiosity. Adrenaline and hot coffee kicked his energy level into high gear.

"Where to?"

"Paw Paw Bottom," Duke answered.

"I have no idea where that is."

"No problem. I scouted for Crazy Horse at the Little Bighorn. I'm sure I can find the Bottoms." Duke burst out laughing.

"But that was over a hundred years . . ." Marc stopped and laughed with hesitation. He got it.

"Go east on Interstate 40 and turn right on Old Hwy 64, past Muldrow. After that, it gets tricky."

"What's at Paw Paw Bottom?"

"With any luck, Jimmy," Duke answered, then fell silent. The miles clipped by in slow motion, stretching the thirty-minute drive into an eternity.

"Turn off on the next county road and head south. In a few miles, we'll cut back to the left. Somewhere along the way, we should run into E 1160."

Marc wound through the belly of the Ouachita Range, a mountainous ridge snaking through the center of Texas and across southeastern Oklahoma, before curling its tail into the heart of Arkansas. Angry streams rushed between weathered boulders to the fertile bottomland of the Arkansas River. The brilliant red of Caddo maples and the yellow fire of lacebark elms flamed across the rugged hilltops. Below, a wall of green eastern redcedar, loblolly, and pinyon pine, capped by a blue-domed sky, soared above the narrow road, swallowing the Jeep whole.

"Beautiful—and worthless unless you like to fish or hunt," Duke mused in a brooding tone.

Marc nodded in agreement, uncertain of Duke's meaning.

"Turn at the next left and pull off the road. We will need to walk a ways."

Marc angled into a bar ditch and parked in a small clearing. The Indian summer sun teased an unseasonably warm, humid day. Sweat beaded under the collar of Marc's khaki coat as he navigated the steep hill to the river basin. After a short walk, he spied the remnants of an old settlement along the banks of the rushing Arkansas River. The muddy ribbon of water gutted most of the structures, but a few ravaged brick walls remained.

"You think Jimmy is here?" Marc struggled to control his doubt.

"He's here. Sit with me behind the rock and wait. You will see."

The muggy air along the riverbank compressed Marc's lungs. He fought to breathe as he sucked two puffs from the inhaler, waiting.

"Look." Duke stood and pointed across the river. "Jimmy's launching from the far bank heading our way."

Marc squinted through the glare of the sun. Sure enough, a person resembling Jimmy navigated across the roiling water, landing on the beach not a hundred yards away. The man shimmied the canoe onto the shoreline and walked to a rambling structure with a full stringer of fish. Marc started to rise, but the older man pushed him down before he could get to his feet.

"Wait," Duke said, "a man reasons better on a full stomach."

Exactly, Marc thought, nibbling on a dry biscuit washed down with tepid coffee, drooling at the thought of Jimmy's meal of fresh fish.

"Now." Duke stood and approached the column of smoke rising above the ruins.

When they rounded a lone brick wall, Jimmy stared at them with eyes as dead as the fish on his stringer.

"We need to talk, boy," Duke said. Jimmy did not flinch. Instead, he motioned at the platter of fried blue catfish balanced on a nearby rock and went about his business.

"Thanks." Marc reached for the plate piled with the golden-brown filets. With a quick swat, Duke knocked the fish from his hand.

"What the—" Marc stopped speaking, silenced by the scowl on Duke's face.

"Do you know why we're here?" Duke asked. Jimmy nodded. "Want to tell us what happened?"

Silence.

"Did you do it?"

Silence.

"How long can you hide without being caught?"

Silence.

"Look, boy. We're here to help. You've met Mr. Whitcomb. He's come all the way from Pawnee to help you."

Jimmy cast dull black eyes at Marc and shrugged as he squatted by the fire, shoulders hunched like a cornered animal. His hand trembled as he poked the dying embers with a stick.

Duke's voice softened. "Son, I've known your family clear back to your great-great-granddaddy. Good people in their way."

Jimmy stirred, agitated by the remark. "I don't know you, mister. And as for Mr. Whitcomb, I've only met him a few times. But if you go back with my family like you say, then you understand. I shot Mr. Caldwell because the old dog deserved to die."

The unemotional confession turned Marc's stomach. His son couldn't be as cold-blooded as this man, yet they were friends.

"Anyone privy to your whereabouts?" Duke quizzed.

Jimmy's eyes hardened. "Not unless you told."

Duke took a deep breath, his patience exhausted. "Get your affairs in order. We'll be back tomorrow morning."

Jimmy nodded. Duke spun on his heels and headed up the hill. A deal between the two had been struck that Marc couldn't wrap his head around.

"Hold up!" Marc shouted. "I have a few questions for our friend here."

"Not now," Duke answered.

"What about Devin?" Marc shouted.

Jimmy flinched, and Duke kept walking.

Marc stared at the dark-headed young man, lean and bent like a sapling in a strong wind. He wanted to spit on him and hug him at the same time. Duke returned and grabbed him by the elbow, ending his quandary.

"Tomorrow." Duke tightened his grip, pinching Marc's flesh hard as he continued his march toward the Jeep.

"Whose side are you on anyway? He's the only one who can clear my boy, and you let him go."

Duke stopped and leaned close to Marc. "You think Jimmy's word would clear Devin?"

"Maybe," Marc whispered. The trek up the hill had robbed him of breath, and doubt weakened his answer.

"Jimmy could have disappeared from the face of the earth . . . but he didn't." The old Indian resumed walking.

"But you let him go." Marc jumped into the Jeep, slammed it into drive, and sped down the narrow back road, his anger boiling. "What were you thinking? The little turd will be long gone by morning." Marc jerked the steering wheel to dodge a raccoon.

"Slow down. It won't help Devin if you kill us both."

"I'm heading straight to Tahlequah and reporting him. They'd better pick him up tonight, or we've wasted our time."

"The boy lied," Duke countered.

"He barely spoke."

"His actions lied. Did you watch him look toward the ground when he told us the old dog deserved to die? He spoke with his tongue, not his heart." Duke kept an eye on the road as Marc fumed. "Take I-40 W to OK-82 N if you want to go to Tahlequah."

Marc began to simmer down. His heart was so heavy he couldn't think. He wanted to help his son, not whirl about like a Tasmanian devil.

"Go on. I'm listening." He expected Duke to resume his diatribe on Jimmy.

"I'm hungry. Sallisaw is up the road, and I sure could use some Wildhorse Mountain BBQ."

Marc had whiplash from the sudden change of subject, but Duke would speak when he was ready, and not a moment sooner.

Wildhorse Mountain BBQ was a backwoods café with dingy menu boards and hodgepodge seating. Duke beelined to the counter to place their order as Marc hung back, sulking about the morning's chain of events.

"Two orders of chips, a couple of Coors, and two pulled-pork sandwiches, one with the *hotter-than-hell sauce* and the other with *baby* sauce," Duke said and laughed, as did every patron within earshot. All eyes turned to Marc, branded with the handle of newbie.

"Very funny." Marc resented being the brunt of Duke's joke. He ate his lunch with a wordless pout.

"Let's go." Marc rose suddenly and headed toward the door, leaving his half-eaten sandwich and wrapper on the table, not waiting for Duke to follow.

Marc heard the crunch of gravel in the parking lot as Duke sprinted up behind him.

"Wait up, Kemosabe." Duke slapped a hand on Marc's shoulder, bringing him to a stop. "Sorta tough when you don't fit in, isn't it, son?" Duke squinted in the sun and nodded toward a road not much wider than a path. "Hop in. Let's head up there."

Marc followed an asphalt road until it turned into a graveled county lane. "Where to now?"

"Keep going."

Gravel pelted the Jeep as dust tornadoes spun from the tires of a farmer's truck barreling down the road ahead.

"Now. Pull over." Duke got out of the vehicle and stood on the side of the road. He pointed toward the roof of a modest dwelling at the bottom of a ravine. "Jimmy's folks live here."

Marc walked to the edge and peered into the steep chasm. The woods crowded the bungalow between towering trees, threatening to reclaim stolen ground. Chipped paint on pressed wood siding exposed rotted fiberboard. Tar-paper patches were visible between sparse shingles.

"Wow, I wouldn't have guessed since Jimmy always presented himself so well." Marc paused, stepped back, and took a hard look at his friend. "So what?"

Duke had messed with his mind all morning, and Marc's patience wore thin. *Why can't the old man spit out what he's thinking? Why does Duke glide beneath still waters, never breaking the surface with his thoughts?*

"Wait a minute. You can stop selling 'cause I'm not buying. I don't care how poor he was. It's no excuse—"

"I'm not selling anything but the truth about Jimmy. You must understand your enemy . . . as well as your friends."

Exasperated, Marc said, "The man confessed, and my son's involvement hangs in the balance. If the sheriff finds out I talked to Jimmy and we let him go, it won't go well for Devin."

"Jimmy's lying about the whole thing." Duke climbed into the Jeep. "It's getting late. If you intend to turn Jimmy in, we'd better get going."

The two men rode in silence for miles as Marc retraced the route back to the interstate. He had to decide whether to trust Duke's intuition or make tracks to the authorities. The choice hinged on Duke's answer to one question.

"Jimmy said, 'But if you go back with my family like you say, then you understand.' What did that mean?"

The older man took his time answering. "Listen with the spirit of a Cherokee and not with the passion of a father."

Marc nodded, Duke's meaning escaping him once again.

The aging Cherokee began to speak. "Before 1890, when the tribes condemned an Indian to death, they allowed him thirty days to go home and fix his affairs. He went without guard, arranged all earthly matters, and said goodbye to his friends and family. When he returned at the appointed time, they shot him. No man failed to appear for his execution . . . Jimmy will be at the Bottoms in the morning."

Duke didn't address Jimmy's innocence, but the story moved Marc. He headed the Jeep in the direction of the Waite home.

6

The sun dipped low in the west as they pulled into the drive. Jessie and Lisi sat in the two rockers on the front porch as Mama prepared the evening meal. Marc's stomach grumbled at the savory aroma of battered pork chops, steaming cabbage, and sweet corn. He plopped his weary bones into a chair beside his wife as Duke headed to the utility room and out the back door to attend to Buttercup's needs.

"Any luck?" Jessie asked.

"Tomorrow will tell, but I think so. Duke's a hard man to figure." Marc removed his glasses and rubbed his eyes.

"He's experienced more in his eighty-four years than we ever will," Jessie said as if that should explain everything. "Better put your glasses in your shirt pocket before you lose them."

If her last comment rubbed him the wrong way, he didn't let on. "At least Duke's beginning to warm up to me. He called me Kemosabe."

"Kemosabe? He called you Kemosabe?" Jessie placed her hands over her mouth to hide her giggling.

"Yes. Why? Doesn't that mean 'friend'?"

"It means 'trusty scout,'" Lisi said with a poker face.

"In Cherokee?"

"No, in Tonto and the Lone Ranger," Jessie smirked.

Not amused, he made a quick exit. "I need a whiskey and water."

Jessie followed. "Spill. What happened today?"

"We found Jimmy, and he straight-out confessed to killing the man. No emotion." Marc dug the Jim Beam out of his suitcase and headed to the kitchen for ice. "Duke insisted we leave Jimmy alone until morning. No telling what we'll find when we get there. He might take us both out like he did Caldwell."

"Don't be silly. You're afraid he will be gone, aren't you? Don't worry. He will be there." Jessie trailed behind, not missing a beat.

"How did Duke know where to find him?"

"He didn't. I told him. Jimmy and I powwowed when he and Devin came to visit. He mentioned that his great-great-grandfather on his dad's side was an intruder on Indian lands. Spent most of his time in Paw Paw Bottom."

"Another mystery solved," Marc said with sarcasm.

"Don't make light of it, Marc. Those riffraff and outlaws were money-grabbing trash who took over our lands. Does my attorney husband need more proof to understand what happened? Do I need to talk paleface to you?" Jessie teased, then left the room, returning with a yellowed newspaper clipping from *The Telephone – Tahlequah Indian Territory*, 1890.

Marc skimmed the article, then threw the paper down in disgust. "Enough. I get it. Does this mean that Jimmy's great-great-grandfather acquired tribal status on the Cherokee lands?"

"Not tribal status, but he 'legally' stole parcels of our land for the paltry sum of five dollars, with the blessings and protection of the government to boot." Jessie's voice faded. "I'd call him a blood-sucking leech."

Marc sat in awkward silence. He had tapped into a vein of resentment that needed to bleed out. *Why had he never noticed?*

"What about the Caldwell clan? Were they intruders?" Marc asked. He had studied Oklahoma history, but somehow these "minor" points didn't make it into the books.

"So many homesteaders joined in the land runs. Who would know where they came from? Free land attracted all kinds, good and bad."

"Typical government stupidity," Marc muttered. He had no use for the rambling, disingenuous promises of politicians and recoiled with a pang of guilt. His own family participated in the land runs, which were nothing more than legalized theft of Indian land.

"Jimmy told Duke, 'If you knew my people, you would believe I killed Caldwell.' That's not an exact quote, but it's close. Then Duke told me Jimmy lied about being the killer. Make sense of that."

"You're asking me a question I can't answer. Jimmy identifies with the Cherokee, and Duke says the boy has 'a tribal soul.'"

Marc fixed himself another drink and collapsed into a recliner.

"I'll join you." Jessie reached for the bottle of Beam.

A warmth spread through Marc. Jessie seldom drank and hated whiskey. As they sipped on their drinks and talked until the wee hours of the morning, the distance between them melted like snow in the winter sun.

"What did Duke mean about Jimmy having the soul of the tribe? How does anyone know someone else's soul?"

"I'll tell you, but I'm not sure you will understand." Jessie looked at Marc in earnest. "Did you ever listen to Jimmy with your eyes?"

"With my eyes?"

"Yes, there's pride and defiance in Jimmy's eyes. He resents the taint of intruder blood."

"I've never spent much time with Jimmy, but this is crazy talk. Listen with your eyes?" Marc laughed.

Jessie grabbed her empty glass, shot him a *go to hell* look, and headed toward the kitchen.

Marc's belittling carved another hairline crack in Jessie's armor. Shame crept over him. Whiskey had robbed him of the power to control his mouth. The kitchen went dark, and he heard Jessie's footsteps click down the hallway and up the stairs.

"Wait, honey. I was . . . I didn't mean . . ." Marc stumbled toward the bedroom, relieved that Jessie hadn't locked the door.

Duke bounced him out of bed early the following day. Both men moved in quickly, preparing to deliver Jimmy to the authorities and prevent him from giving a damning confession. It wouldn't be an easy day.

Marc's head pounded from a hangover, making it difficult to sort out his behavior last night. He hated the term "mean drunk," but no other description applied. Jessie's indifference toward him grew with each episode, and he feared she might reach a breaking point. But she didn't understand. He would quit drinking when this nightmare was over.

Marc groaned inwardly. If Jimmy had disappeared in the night, Marc would have lost his only hope to clear Devin.

"Do you think he went home?" Marc asked with a hint of nervousness.

Duke shot him a quizzical look. "You mean to his mother's house?"

"Yeah."

"I don't think so."

"What about cleaning up his affairs? I thought you said he would go home to do so."

"Don't be so literal, Marc. Jimmy's home is Paw Paw Bottom. The affairs he needed to deal with are in his head."

Duke showed no signs of concern. Fifteen more miles and they would have the answer.

Smoke from a fire along the water's edge curled into the predawn sky. The silhouette of a young man in a white T-shirt and jeans danced in the flicker of flames. Jimmy glanced in Duke's direction, then continued about his business.

"Ready?"

Jimmy finished packing his knapsack, doused the fire with water from the river, and headed toward the Jeep. Duke grabbed two fishing poles leaning against a log and followed, leaving Marc to bring up the tail end. Everything happened as Duke said it would. Marc shook his head in amazement at the seamless apprehension of a suspected killer.

Tahlequah rested in the foothills of the Ozark Mountains. The capital of the Cherokee Nation was part of a new settlement in Indian Territory founded after the forced march on the Trail of Tears. Tribal lands had complex rules of engagement under which these Native Americans held dual citizenship, one with the Cherokee Nation and the other with the United States. Marc relied upon Duke to navigate the unfamiliar territory of Indian law.

"There on the left." Duke pointed to a modern brick building off Muskogee Avenue. Marc parked in the visitor's parking and began to follow his two companions into the Cherokee Nation National Services office.

Marc's zeal to turn Jimmy in waned. It could spell the beginning of Devin's demise. If Jimmy held to his confession, his son would also appear guilty. Deep down, Marc believed his son was innocent, but his intuition about Jimmy had missed the target. Once the wheels began turning, there would be no going back. Duke put his arm on Jimmy's shoulders, and both stood a little taller as they marched toward the uncompromising halls of criminal justice. The dark-haired, fresh-faced Native boy leaned into the slender frame of his Cherokee elder, siphoning the strength he needed to place one foot in front of the other.

A memory tugged at Marc . . . a story Jessie shared long ago about the Rite of Passage of the Cherokee. A boy must spend the night in the forest alone, blindfolded. Cries for help were forbidden. If he survived the wild beasts in the darkness, he became a man.

With each deliberate step, Jimmy walked like a boy on the verge of manhood—his Rite of Passage had begun on the banks of the Arkansas last night.

A young officer staffed the desk in the austere foyer. Jimmy shifted from one foot to another. Duke motioned for him to take a seat by Marc and began speaking to the man. The officer disappeared around the corner and returned with an older gentleman of higher rank. With the decorum of a tribal chief, Duke began to converse in Cherokee with the senior officer for an extended period.

Marc squirmed, unaccustomed to legal exchanges he couldn't

understand. The young man beside him folded his hands in his lap and stared into space, waiting. Marc could not read guilt or innocence on Jimmy's face. When Duke's conversation ended, he signaled to Jimmy to follow the man. The two disappeared down the hall.

"We are finished here," Duke said as he strode toward the door.

"Wait. Shouldn't I go with Jimmy? He might need a lawyer," Marc said with concern. Yesterday, he wanted him locked up. Today, he tried to protect him. His emotions flew all over the place.

"Are you registered with the Tribal Bar Association?"

"No." Marc never studied tribal law, and it was too late now.

"No matter. The tribe wouldn't let you near Jimmy anyway. You're the father of the alleged co-conspirator. Remember?"

Marc felt cheated. Jimmy hadn't made a peep during the drive from Paw Paw Bottom to Tahlequah despite his attempts to get the young man to talk. The opportunity to quiz him about Devin evaporated, and now the tribal circle cut him off from any communication. He, like the rest, must wait. There was nothing left to do but leave.

"What happens now?" Marc asked as he fired up the Jeep. He hated not being in control.

"Now?" Duke's eyes remained fixed on the road ahead. "You need to worry about your own. Your sheriff brought Devin in for questioning."

"How would you know that?" Marc and Duke had been inseparable since daylight.

"The officer, the one who spoke Cherokee, told me. He called the Pawnee County authorities the minute his deputy told him Jimmy turned himself in, and a warrant was issued for Devin's arrest."

"So Devin's been picked up?"

"That's what I understand. They wanted Jimmy locked up before they made a move on Devin, and the quickest way to nab Jimmy was through you. Pawnee County has no authority on tribal lands. It could have taken years to bring Jimmy in."

The old Indian was right. Duke, with Marc's help, sprung the trap on Jimmy and caught his son in the same snare.

Marc wagged a fist in Duke's face. "Why did you lead me to

Jimmy if it meant Devin would be crucified? You're the reason my boy is in jail."

"You're wrong. This matter must be dealt with before Devin—or you—do something stupid. I haven't changed the outcome; I've only changed the process. Devin, guilty or innocent, must meet this head-on."

"I see. You think this is Devin's Rite of Passage . . . or something like that," Marc said sarcastically.

"No, Kemosabe. It's yours."

7

"Damn it, JP. I thought we were friends." Marc's rage bordered on hate.

"Not when it comes to murder. You should appreciate that more than anyone," JP answered with a nonchalant shrug.

Marc's face flushed with anger. "You've known Devin since he was a kid. This whole thing is crazy. My son never met the man."

"Yeah, I know your boy, but I still have a job to do. Hank saw those two together the morning of the murder. Left me no choice but to bring him in."

"Sure took your sweet time to fill me in. You went stone-cold silent on me."

"I gave you a heads-up as a friend. And you almost cost me my job by running out to the Caldwell place like a fool." JP leaned back in his chair and pushed his hat back. "I've said enough. Your boy's got an attorney. Best talk to him."

"Where's Devin?"

"Pawnee County Jail."

Visiting hours at the jail wouldn't start for another two hours. Marc waited in the Jeep, watching the dashboard clock tick off the minutes until the doors opened. For the first time in his life, he completed an official application to see an inmate. He produced his ID, passed through the metal detector, and then proceeded to the visitation center under the watchful eye of an armed guard. A sheepish smile dimpled Devin's cheeks as Marc approached.

"Damn it, Devin. I told you not to speak to anyone without me present," he said before he could stop himself.

"Relax, Dad. Hank got me a great attorney who said I wouldn't be here long."

"Hank? How did Hank land in the middle of this?"

"I called him when I couldn't reach you. Where have you been?" A touch of blame crept into Devin's voice. He had let his son down.

"Where's this attorney located?"

"He's with Smith & Noble, some high-powered criminal defense firm in Tulsa."

"I'll make an appointment to speak to him."

Devin shook his head. "Not necessary. I've got this." The calmness of his voice was chilling.

Marc pushed one more time. "His name?"

"No!" Devin shouted so loudly that a guard approached. "Stay outta this."

"Problems?" the guard asked, his eyes glued on Marc.

"No problem here, sir. I am leaving."

Marc stood and stared at Devin. The law firm he left in disgrace held his son's life in its hands. To believe that Jimmy's surrender to authorities in Tahlequah, Devin's arrest, and Hank's arrangement for a lawyer from his former firm was a coincidence stretched the limits of Marc's imagination. Duke had warned him. Jimmy was the bait, and he had triggered the tripwire to snare his own son. Marc trudged back to his Jeep, struggling to find the energy to keep moving. The whole thing played like a nightmare. Lost in a dark tunnel, he ran toward the light. Then bam. The door slammed shut.

He needed his mind to shut off, to go silent so that he could rest. Beam and water would do the trick. The Jeep found its way home on autopilot, delivering Marc to the dark recesses of his garage. Marc made his way into the house and down the hall toward his tiny office, his steps echoing in the hollows of his soul.

"I'm home!" Jessie called as she entered the back door. "Can you help me with the groceries?"

Marc heard her footsteps as she tracked to and from the garage, followed by a thud on the kitchen counter. After the fourth round, the door shut, and Jessie's footsteps clicked down the hall toward his office.

"Didn't you hear me?" she said. "I needed help. What's the matter?"

Marc was sprawled out on the couch, bleary-eyed and sloppy drunk. The Beam had unleashed the demons that were destroying him. Jessie grabbed the bottle and hurled it across the room, shattering it into a thousand pieces that glistened like diamonds on the dark tile floor.

"That's it, Marc. I'm done. Devin needs you, and all you can do is crawl into a bottle and hide."

Jessie stormed out of the room. Marc heard her rummaging through the bedroom closet and banging drawers, the staccato click of her heels headed toward the garage. After a moment, she returned.

"Your bag's in the Jeep. I'll drive you to your office." She tossed the office keys in his direction. "You can sleep it off . . . downtown."

Tonight played like a rerun. When Marc got drunk, she got mad, but she had never packed his bag. With great concentration, he staggered to the Jeep and fell into the back seat. A seat belt stabbed his ribs, and the pain of their conversation robbed him of sleep. Jessie's forgiveness had reached its expiration date. He must change or lose her.

Marc woke the next morning, dry-mouthed and sweaty, with a sharp shoulder punch from Jessie. He and the Jeep were still in the garage.

Jessie placed a bowl of oatmeal and a slice of toast before him, then busied herself with loading the dishwasher. "I can't do this anymore, Marc. I lied to the boys and told them you went to the office early this morning, but they know. Everyone knows."

"I'm sorry."

"I know," she said, dropping her hands to her side. "You're always sorry."

"Seeing . . . Seeing my son in jail . . ." The ugly stammer crept upon him.

"This is the last *last* time. If you can't do it alone, get help. Whatever it takes, make it happen." Jessie slammed the last plates into the dishwasher, then turned to face him. "I mean it."

Marc leaned against the shower wall, letting the hot, steamy water cascade over his aching body, but the cleansing he needed was not born of water. He had to find his way before he lost Jessie.

Marc found her in the bedroom. "I'm going to see Hank." He extended his hand and prayed she would take it. After a moment, she slipped her hand in his and nodded. "If I can't beat this, I promise to go to rehab."

"I love you, but no more do-overs. The stakes are high for everyone, especially Devin." She forced a smile that made him sad. "Now, get out of here and find out what Hank can tell you."

She deserved better. They all did.

The breakfast crowd had cleared out, leaving only the gang at the back table. Marc spotted Hank's red hair towering a head above the rest. Marc had avoided his friends since his conversation two weeks ago, and this reunion soured his stomach.

"Come back here and join us, buddy boy," Hank called as if nothing had happened.

"Long time no see," Johnny chimed in.

Marc's discomfort eased as he slid into the remaining empty chair, surrounded by the familiarity of his childhood pals. For a moment, he felt he belonged again.

"Judy, bring a cup of coffee for my friend and refresh mine while you're at it." Hank waved his hand in Judy's direction. "Tough break with your kid."

"Heard they have that Allen boy in custody. Once he starts talking, your boy should be in the clear." Johnny offered his two cents' worth with the confidence of a small-town busybody. "You gonna represent that Indian kid? The judge here will take care of Devin. Right?" The mayor slapped Ross on the shoulder.

Ross rolled his eyes. "I won't be anywhere near the trial. I'm too close to the case. The state will appoint a judge and a prosecutor. You'd best stick to mayoring, Johnny. This is above your pay grade."

Banter bounced around the table until it landed in JP's lap. "Slow down, boys. Let me set the record straight for ya. Jimmy's trial will be in Muskogee County. Ross won't be the judge. The tribe will take Jimmy under their wing. That'll be a fight from hell, and ol' Marc here won't be able to touch him."

The rah-rahing about the table shut down like a flipped switch. The five men glued their eyes on JP, waiting for him to continue. The sheriff puffed his chest, cocksure and ready to crow.

"What do you think this means for Marc's boy?" Johnny sounded concerned, but Marc knew his motive was a good piece of gossip he could swap with the farmers at the local coop. "I bet the Allen kid will take a plea and do his best to nail Devin."

"Shut the hell up. Your bullshit is too deep for my waders." JP pushed back from the table. "Best I steer clear of you boys until this thing is over." He tipped the brim of his hat and made tracks for the front door.

The thought had crossed Marc's mind days ago, but hearing it aloud made the possibility real. The only thing Marc knew for sure was his head pounded from his binge last night, and the scuttlebutt flying around pinched his chest like a vise. Time to go home after he got what he needed from Hank—the name of Devin's attorney.

"I want to thank you for finding a lawyer, Hank," he said with difficulty.

"Forget it. You would do the same."

"What's the name of Devin's attorney? I want to see where we're heading with this thing."

"Mike Halley with Smith & Noble."

Marc knew Mike well—too well. He and Marc had partnered on the case Marc had fumbled. For Devin's sake, he would swallow his pride, but the prospect of dealing with his ex-partner sickened him. His one consolation was that Mike was the best criminal defense attorney in the state. But hell, Hank knew his story. Why would Hank pick his worst enemy to defend Devin? He never should have confided in Hank. Marc motioned for Judy to bring him his check.

"Here you go," she said as she slid the tab under the edge of his cup.

He laid a ten-dollar bill on the table, more than enough to cover the coffee, and stuffed the check in his pocket.

8

Marc opened the door to the small bar in his office to find bottled water in place of his Beam. The liquor cabinet was one of numerous changes to his sanctuary—as was the decluttered desktop, empty trash baskets, and the scent of furniture polish filling the room. He chuckled. Jessie had cleaned up his act single-handedly.

"Marc, did you look at this?" Jessie waved a wad of paper in his direction. "I found it in the wastebasket by the front door."

"That's the check from Harper's this morning."

"Did you look at it?"

"No."

"Judy wrote you a note."

"Let me see." He snatched the crumpled tab, smoothed the edges, and read the note scribbled across the bottom: "Can we talk soon?"

Jessie's attention to detail impressed him. If an ant crossed the floor with a breadcrumb, she would nail its ass and demand the little bugger put it back.

"Do you still want my help?" Jessie asked in a hesitant voice. Their relationship, as fragile as eggshells, demanded permission asking. Marc hated it, but his wife dictated the rules of engagement.

"Sure, but at this moment, I need—"

"A drink?" she asked, raising an eyebrow.

"An aspirin." They both smiled. It was a start.

Jessie handed Marc an aspirin and water before landing in a chair across from her husband. "Where do we begin?"

"The first thing on the agenda is to meet with Mike Halley, the attorney Hank hired for Devin."

"You want me to go with you?"

"Nope. I'd rather you meet with Judy. Find out what she has to say, then drop by the office and see if Nancy's made any progress on the Caldwell information. Bring anything she has with you."

"I'll call Judy and make a plan." Jessie's eyes glimmered, but Marc struggled with what was ahead. The thought of meeting the man who had ruined his career as a defense attorney loomed before him —a mountain he had never wanted to climb.

"I'm turning in," Marc said. "Tomorrow's a big day."

He rose early the next morning, showered, and shaved. He chose his best suit and shirt for his visit with Halley, hoping to erase the image of the small-town lawyer he had become, but the man in the mirror disappointed him. His attire didn't hide his lack of confidence. His former law partner would sniff his weakness a mile off, but he had no choice. He would bow his neck and challenge the headwinds of his fears.

By ten o'clock, the morning traffic had thinned, and navigation of the one-way streets proved easier. Marc pulled into the downtown parking garage and headed to the top level, where he had a bird's-eye view of the BOK Tower—twenty years had not changed the beauty of the massive skyscraper looming above the bustle of East Second Street. Drawing a deep breath, Marc marched toward his past.

"I'm here to speak with Mike Halley."

The receptionist appeared disinterested. "Your name?" she asked in a well-modulated voice.

"Marc Whitcomb. Mike knows me."

Her fingers flew across the keyboard, searching for his name. She paused and studied the screen for a moment. "Do you have an appointment?"

"No." Marc shifted from foot to foot.

"I'm sorry. Mr. Halley is not free today. You may wish to make an appointment. I have an opening three weeks from this Thursday."

"It's urgent. I have to see Mike today." A surge of panic ripped through his body. He knew the drill. She had found his name on a "no access" list. Halley had blocked him.

"I would be happy to put you on a waiting list in case we have a cancellation." Her politeness irritated him.

"Forget it." Marc's mind raced to figure out how to reach Mike. The foyer stood empty. If memory served, Halley's office would be the first one on the right. He stepped toward the elevator, paused, and then pivoted. With or without an appointment, Mike would see him today.

Marc barged through the door to find Mike at his desk, a phone to his ear.

"Let me call you back," the short, balding man in a dark-blue suit whispered into the phone. "Come on in. Hank said you might be coming by." Mike stood and extended his arm for a handshake. The clammy grip of his well-manicured hand repulsed Marc.

"Please. Have a seat," said the stocky man with a slight lisp. "Coffee? Water? Or something stronger?"

Mike Halley's nod to Marc's drinking habits stung. "Let's cut through the pleasantries and discuss Devin's case."

"Have you talked to your son?" In true lawyer fashion, Mike regained control of the conversation.

"Not in a day or two," Marc said, growing uneasy. "Fill me in on the police questioning and the status of the crime report."

"My client requested that I not share his circumstances." He tilted his chin and looked down the barrel of his nose. The sanctimonious little lizard was brushing Marc off.

"Your *client* is my son. I'm sure he wasn't referring to me."

"On the contrary, your son named you."

Adrenaline-fueled hate pulsed through Marc's veins. *How did his son become involved with a murder and then shut him out? Something was off with the situation, but Mike held the trump card of attorney-client privilege. Arguing served no purpose.*

Marc rose from the chair with deliberate reserve. "I appreciate your time."

"Look, Marc. I'm sorry about all this, but you understand the rules." Mike Halley said the proper thing, but there was no soul in it.

"I sure understand *your* rules," Marc said as he inched toward the door. Like a pardoned prisoner, he needed to escape the stifling confines of Mike's office.

The morning had been a disaster, but Marc couldn't surrender. Dani had hinted at some special revelations in her grandmother's diaries, but he hadn't found the time to read them all. He could cut to the chase and save time by quizzing Ruby in person. Two blocks and forty-five stairs later, Marc arrived at Dani's apartment. He rapped on the door three times before it opened the width of a security chain. An owl-like eye peered at him through the crack.

"Ruby? Marc Whitcomb here."

"What do you want?"

"I was hoping to visit with Dani. Is she home?"

She slid the chain from the latch and swung the door wide open. "You can talk to me."

Dani had made it clear that her grandmother was off-limits and would view this as an intrusion. At this point, he didn't care. He would grab any straw blowing in the breeze.

Ruby, a tiny woman, folded her arms across her chest and gave him a good once-over. When she finished her assessment, she let out a hearty chuckle.

"Those stairs wouldn't be so bad if you lost a few pounds," she snickered.

"My wife would agree with you." Marc blushed, self-conscious about his weight.

"You're not fat all over, only around the middle. Exercise would do the trick."

"I'll keep that in mind."

"Sit before you fall over. I'll be right back." Her candor embarrassed and amused him.

Ruby shuffled to the kitchen with steps as dainty as the figurines on the end tables. Her pink silk blouse illuminated her silver hair, curled about her face like a bonnet, framing her startlingly blue eyes and fair skin. A light dusting of blush and lip gloss added the finishing touches to the attractive older woman. Marc marveled at not having noticed at the funeral, but grief was ugly. She returned holding a small plate of cookies and a glass of water as if entertaining guests for an afternoon tea.

"Fig Newtons won't hurt you," she said, patting his hand.

The apartment was too hot, his brow was sweaty from climbing stairs, and he hated Fig Newtons.

"Thank you," he said, balancing two cookies on a napkin. He washed the dry crust and fig jelly down with a swig of water. When his tongue functioned again, he braved his question. "What happened to your son?"

Ruby stared out the expansive windows, scanning the Tulsa skyline.

"Do you remember when David took me on a cruise?"

"No, ma'am." *Where did that come from? Why would she ask me that? We just met.*

"He paid for everything. Wouldn't let me spend a dime," Ruby said, beaming.

"Very generous." Marc's compliment fell flat. *This could be a long afternoon.*

"Can you believe his wife booked an expensive cabin for them, while Dani and I stayed in a cramped box on the lower deck? My granddaughter was sure mad because she was stuck with an old lady." Ruby reared back and laughed in self-deprecating amusement. "But the trip was lovely. David always treated me like a queen."

Marc squirmed. He didn't have time to reminisce about a man he had never met. He glanced at his watch.

"I'm sorry. I have an appointment. Please tell your granddaughter I stopped by and will call later."

"Sit down, David. You're not so busy you can't spend a little time with your mother."

Marc eyed Ruby. She believed he was her son.

"Ma'am, you have me confused with—"

Ruby leaned back. "Don't argue with me. I raised you better than that."

Marc struggled to follow the twisted path of her conversation. "My apologies."

"For what, dear? You can't help what Madeline does."

"David's wife?"

"Your wife."

"Okay," Marc said in surrender, unsure what she was talking about. She spoke in circles like a crazy woman, and something about the wife festered in her. He, whether as Marc or David, was knee-deep in her story.

"Why are you angry with Madeline?"

"I don't like the way she treats you. You know good and well that's why I moved out."

Marc wrestled with the ethics of pursuing the conversation. He trod on dangerous ground, but the compulsion to help Devin overshadowed his hesitation.

"You never told me."

"I told you over and over. Madeline's mean, and you won't admit it."

The image of the frigid woman at the crime scene emerged. He had sensed a chilling aloofness about her.

"Tell me again. I promise to listen."

She rose from her chair and tiptoed down the hall, opening the doors to the rooms as she went.

"All clear. Madeline's gone." She leaned in and whispered, "She locks me in my room when you're not home."

"That sounds like elder abuse," Marc said before he could stop himself.

"What's this about elder abuse?" Dani asked.

Marc cringed as he turned to find Dani, arms loaded with

groceries, standing in the front hall. *Had she heard enough to catch me pretending to be David?*

"Ruby and I were visiting. I hope you don't mind," Marc mumbled.

"I do mind, Mr. Whitcomb. May I speak to you . . . alone?"

"Certainly," Marc said with fake assurance. He lifted the bags from her arms and followed her to the kitchen.

"In case you haven't guessed, Mr. Whitcomb, my grandmother is in the early stages of Alzheimer's. Do you have any idea what that means?"

"Yes, and please call me Marc."

"Taking advantage of my grandmother makes you a scumbag. You violated my trust. I have several names for you, Mr. Whitcomb, and not one of them is 'Marc.'"

"Please, I know what you're thinking, but I came to see you. Ruby insisted I come in. It never crossed my mind that she would assume I was her son."

"Did it cross your mind that I wouldn't approve of you interviewing my grandmother in my absence?"

"Yes, I confess it did, but I want you to understand that I never intended to mislead Ruby."

"But you did."

"For my son's sake." Marc turned away, ducking his head. "I'll go now. It won't happen again. No need to see me out."

Marc grabbed his coat and briefcase and made a hasty exit, the click of his steps taunting him as he descended the stairs. *How could I have been so stupid?*

"Wait," Dani called after him. "Come back."

Marc stopped, torn between leaving after his shameful behavior and returning for more chastising.

"Come back," she called again. "Please."

He sat down on the bottom step and waited for her. Never in his career had he stooped so low. He deserved whatever Dani chose to shoot at him.

The dark-haired girl with a pixie cut and teary brown eyes slipped beside him. "My grandmother's memory is worse since Dad died. She looks at me sometimes and says, 'Did something happen to David? I feel like something terrible has happened to David.' If I tell her Dad is dead, she grieves all over again as if it happened yesterday. If I tell her he's fine, she looks for him. What am I supposed to do? Then you come along and stir it all up again."

Marc shifted his attention from his own hurting to hers. He hadn't considered the effect of the murder on anyone but his son.

"So she believes he is alive?"

"Sometimes. The doctor calls it time-shifting, and the worst times are when she does remember."

"How often does this happen?"

"Depends. My dad's death has triggered long bouts of living in the past."

"I apologize again for adding to your problems." Marc grabbed the stair rail and pulled himself to his feet. "I'll be on my way."

"Before you go, I want you to understand something. My dad was the only one who *wasn't* a victim."

"Strange words from a daughter."

Dani took a step back and shrugged. "Perhaps. Until we find the murderer, we won't know who the real victims are, will we?"

Marc's lips curled into a quizzical smile as he contemplated her words. "May I visit Ruby again? We may have more to gain from the past than the present."

"I'll think about it." She retreated up the stairs, leaving him a tiny thread of hope.

Mile markers clicked by as heavy traffic dive-bombed across the four-lane highway, but it didn't faze Marc. He replayed the day's events like a broken record. *Halley has built a wall between me and my son. Why? He couldn't harbor resentment toward me and accept Devin as a client, and the very idea that my son has rejected me is absurd.* Rewind and play again.

The blast of a horn jolted Marc from his trance. He jerked the wheel to the right, turning back into his lane, as his mind switched gears to Ruby. She despised Madeline, the evil daughter-in-law, and he wanted to find out why. Spouses ranked high among the suspects, and Madeline seemed to him a prime candidate. Ruby said she was mean to David.

Marc knew two things about Madeline. She had called the sheriff when she found her dead husband, and according to Ruby, Madeline had locked her in the bedroom. These events did not add up to capital murder. He had lost his mind and fought to turn the volume down on the endless internal chatter. A Beam and water, at this point, would silence the noise, but he didn't dare.

The Jeep's headlights illuminated his wife, who sat snuggled in a bright-colored afghan on the front porch. The ochre wrap warmed Jessie's face like a sunset, a comforting sight for his frazzled mind.

"Did you learn anything?" She slipped her arm through his.

He gave her a gentle squeeze and a half-hearted smile. "Yes, I learned that Fig Newtons won't hurt me and exercise would fix my paunchy stomach."

"What?" Jessie chuckled. "Sounds like your day was more productive than mine."

"Follow me. I'll tell you all about it. But first, I need a drink. Do we have any root beer?"

Jessie threw her arms around his neck and gave him a peck on the cheek. "Yes, but no Fig Newtons."

9

Marc's meeting with Mike Halley had scorched him like a hot July sun, and the balance of the day had proven futile. He prayed Dani would come through and allow a second visit with Ruby. Jessie hadn't fared much better. Judy's big news amounted to petty gossip. She saw Hank and Madeline dining in Tulsa last week, but both parties were widowed and had adjoining land interests. The straws Judy gathered wouldn't make a bale.

"How about Nancy? Did she have anything for you?"

"Not much. David filed the deed the day before his father passed away. Funny how the farm skipped Ruby."

"Did she tell you he presented it in person?" According to Dani, he prepared the transfer. If he had done so, he would have filed it then. Why couldn't he remember the Caldwell name?

"I think so, but she talked so fast I couldn't catch it all. It'll be ready next week. Ask her."

These circumstances smacked of manipulation, immoral but not illegal. Marc sifted through the tidbits. Anyone could prepare and file a deed. If Ruby and Tony had signed the deed without naming a successor, anyone who possessed the document could execute it, with one stipulation: The donor and the recipient must both be living at the time of transfer. David's timing was impeccable.

"Hey." Jessie slung her pencil across the room to get his attention. "What do we do now?"

"About what?" Marc had drifted.

Jessie sighed in exasperation. "What do we do to help Devin? Where's your head?"

"We can request a police report, but the information will be limited. The arrest record might be helpful, but the system restricts actual interrogations for legal reasons. I'm not saying I won't get them, but don't get your hopes up about their usefulness." Marc groaned. "My only hope is that Dani will allow me to see Ruby again."

"What about Jimmy? Duke says he's lying. Maybe we need to find out why."

"Agreed. But first, I want to see Ruby again."

Marc phoned Dani one more time to make his case for a visit with Ruby. She seldom answered, but when she did, she resisted his request with the tenacity of a bulldog.

"Hello." Dani's somewhat pleasant voice caught him off guard.

"Marc . . . Marc here," he stammered. "Look, I know you're trying to protect Ruby—"

"Stop right there. We've been over this. The answer is still no."

"I'm just asking you to consider it. We'll never get to the bottom of this without Ruby's help," he pleaded. A long silence followed. He sensed she was weakening.

"I promise I'll be careful. I wouldn't hurt Ruby for the world," Marc added.

"Maybe not intentionally, but you don't know her triggers," Dani countered.

"I know this: The more we can find out, the better chance she has of getting the farm back." Marc waited for a response, but none came. "You can coach me," he said, and crossed his fingers.

Dani couldn't argue that point. "All right," she said, sighing, "but I have one condition—and if you break it, I'll throw you out and lock the door. Do you understand?"

"Understood. What's the condition?" Marc would promise anything for one more chance.

"Never cross her timeline. If she's in the past, you're in the past. When she's in the present, you're in the present. Don't correct her. Otherwise, she gets stressed."

"Got it."

"I hope so. I meant what I said."

"May I drop by tomorrow morning?" Marc asked, pushing while she was in the mood to cooperate.

"Make it in the afternoon, and don't stay more than two hours." With a click, she was gone.

He had scored a victory.

"I did it. She said yes." Marc grabbed Jessie's hands and kissed her palms. "I promise, Ruby holds the key to this murder."

"What about Jimmy?" she asked again.

"We'll head out tomorrow evening from Tulsa as soon as I finish with Ruby."

"You're taking me to meet her?" Jessie's eyes sparkled with anticipation at the thought of meeting the spunky octogenarian.

"Not on your life. Devin could be out on bail. Swing by his apartment. He might listen to you." Marc watched Jessie wilt with disappointment, but he needed her help elsewhere. "Let's hit the road," he said, grabbing his keys.

Chapter

Jessie navigated the morning traffic while Marc fiddled with a flash drive, concealing a voice recorder.

"Say something." Marc pointed the recorder her way.

"Like what?"

"It doesn't matter."

"Have you lost your mind?"

"Forget it." Marc hit the play button. Scratchy voices repeated what they had just said.

"Perfect," Marc said, grinning.

Jessie raised an eyebrow. "I hope you know what you're doing. It's illegal to record someone without consent."

"Dammit, Jessie. Just drive."

She dropped him off at Ruby's apartment, and he began his ascent to the third floor. Marc rapped on the door. Soon, he heard footsteps. One watery blue eye peeked through the crack of the doorway before Ruby slipped the chain free.

"Dani's not here, Mr. Whitcomb," she said, formal and subdued.

"I'm here to visit with you. Look, I brought you cookies," Marc said as he handed her a package of Oreos.

A half-smile lit her delicate face. She fluffed the pillows on the couch and motioned for Marc to sit. "Tea?"

Ruby's smile wilted, and his smile faded with hers. Marc guarded against developing attachments to clients, but this woman pulled on him. He did not understand his relationship with her and did not want to find out. The thought that he was using her to save Devin bothered him.

"Here you go, son. Be careful not to spill."

The time shift occurred when she returned from the kitchen, just as it had during his last visit. Whatever the trigger, she had become his mom in the blink of an eye.

"Ruby, I want to record our conversations, but I need your permission. Do I have it?"

She flashed a broad smile and nodded.

"I need you to answer yes or no into the recorder."

"Yes. Of course, son."

Damn it! She called me "son." Click. Rewind. "Just say yes."

"You're worse than your father."

Click. Rewind. "Just say yes or no."

Ruby rolled her eyes and opened her mouth. "I . . ." Marc placed a finger on her lips.

"Yes or no."

"Yes."

"Why did you move out?" Marc stopped short of calling her "Mom."

"I told you. Madeline is mean to me when you're not home. She locks me in the bedroom."

For the second time, she mentioned that Madeline had locked her up.

"Why do you think she does that?"

"So I won't hear what she and that daughter of hers are talking about." Her indignation flared.

"Do you mean Dani?" Marc had no idea how many children David had. He should have done his homework.

"Not your daughter. Your wife's daughter." Ruby slammed her fist on the coffee table, rattling the delicate figurines.

Marc calculated the risk of pushing forward. Dani wouldn't let him return if she suspected he had upset Ruby, so he did a quick pivot.

"Did you enjoy the cruise?"

"It would have been better if you had left that bitch at home. And where did all that gambling money come from? Dani says you're stealing from me."

Marc had no answer.

"You didn't use to steal, son."

"I'm not a thief, Mom," he said impulsively. Ruby had suckered him into the moment.

"And Dani says you stole my farm." Ruby tilted her head and eyed him hard. "She doesn't lie, you know."

"How did I steal the farm? It's still there, isn't it?" Marc forced a laugh.

"Don't be a smart-ass. It's unbecoming."

The theft accusations caught him off guard. Dani must help him get his bearings soon. This thirty-minute conversation left him confused. He expected terrible accusations to be aimed at Madeline, but somehow found himself in the hot seat. There was no need to continue this madness.

"I must be going, but I'll see you next week."

Ruby's face drooped with disappointment. "I've made you mad. Now you're running off. I'm sorry."

He walked to the door, kicking himself with every step.

"I love you," Ruby called after him. He glanced over his shoulder and saw her tiny figure hovering in the doorway. He didn't respond. The afternoon had been screwed up. Madeline wasn't the only one who had treated Ruby poorly.

10

Marc meandered about the apartment commons until he found a bench, where he waited for Jessie to appear. With time to kill, he dialed Dani's number. No answer. A disappointing end to a disappointing day. He tightened the lapels about his neck and hunkered down to wait.

Late-November winds whipped around the brick structure, sending shivers through his bones despite his wool coat. Brittle leaves swirled at the feet of barren oaks while yellow mums, nestled in pots on apartment patios, did their best to lift the late-fall gloom.

Marc turned toward a commotion in the street. Crews in bucket trucks wrestled to mount Christmas wreaths on light poles in the blustering wind. *Thanksgiving is still a week away*, Marc thought. *Turkey Day has been pushed to the side.* He knew the feeling.

"Marc?" Dani walked up behind him and sat down.

"I tried to call you."

"I know," Dani said and laughed. "I have you in my contacts."

"How did you find me?"

"It's not magic. I manage these apartments, as well as others in the neighborhood. When you called, I had gone to check on Ruby, so I didn't answer, but I could see you."

"See me? Here?"

"Giant windows are handy, and few well-dressed gentlemen are in the courtyard this time of year." She laughed again. "You're cold. Let's go to my office."

A mug of hot coffee warmed his hands, and Dani's friendly disposition thawed his reluctance to quiz her about Ruby.

"Man, I jumped into deep water this afternoon."

"I was afraid that would happen." Dani's voice softened when she spoke of Ruby. "She lives in two worlds and moves at will between them. Grandmother's a complex lady."

Marc raised his hands in mock surrender. "Then help me understand her. She thinks I'm your dad and talks to me about things I know nothing about."

"I had hoped the diaries would give you what you needed," Dani said, shooting an accusing scowl his way.

Marc looked around the room, trying to think of one good reason why he hadn't read them all. None came to mind.

"You haven't read them, have you?" Dani's eyes sparked with anger.

"Parts."

Dani walked to the large window on the far side of the room, watching the steady stream of traffic three stories below. She spoke without turning to face him. "Grandmother's dog in this fight is a Chihuahua. She's up against a pack of hounds that will tear her to shreds for the little money she has left."

"I had no idea," Marc answered after a pause.

"Are you representing your son or that Indian boy?" Dani asked.

He pursed his lips. "The answer is neither, and the reasons are complicated."

Dani turned around. "Then I wish to retain your services for my grandmother."

"I can't take on a new client now. My son needs me, whether I represent him or not."

"My gut tells me we have a common goal."

"Who's in this pack?" Marc asked with hesitation. He knew better than to encourage her.

"Madeline, for one."

Marc calculated the implications. She offered an opportunity to dig into the dirty laundry of the victim's family, which may or may not touch on the murder. But so far, his current circumstances had yielded a big fat zero.

"What are you suing for?" Marc's curiosity reached new heights with the mention of Madeline's name.

"Elder abuse and theft of her farm and money."

"Oh, boy. That's too close to a line I shouldn't cross. If you're right about a common goal, then a connection to your dad's murder must exist."

She locked her puppy dog eyes on him. "All we need to do is get a proxy lawyer to file against the estate to freeze the assets until you are free. Please, please, please."

"Any attorney can handle this. Why wait for me?"

"Money. Grandmother has none. Pro bono attorneys are hard to find and are as weak as water. I'm trusting your fees will be reasonable." An impish grin dimpled her cheeks. "Besides, you owe me."

Dani had tossed a noose around his neck when she agreed to let him see Ruby. She just tripped the gallows, and he dangled midair.

"I'll make it work," he said with resignation.

"Great. I'll hire an attorney to file, but when Devin's case is settled, I want *you* to represent my grandmother."

"You think the courts will agree to postpone your case until Devin's is finished?"

"Yes, if the lawyers on both sides agree upon it. I'll instruct my attorney to accept any

date after the conclusion of Devin's trial."

"And what makes you think Madeline's attorney will agree to postpone?"

"Mike Halley's firm represents Madeline. I'd bet my life they will be glad to put it off, and I'm willing to take the gamble."

This petite young woman with pixie hair and chocolate eyes had devised a complicated scenario that might work. Marc would have no conflict of interest at that point.

"You've given this a lot of thought." Her logic both amazed and scared him.

"You would do as much for someone you cared about."

And more, Marc thought.

"I'm not sure about this cheap fee business, though. This case will require a lot of research."

"I promise you will get more than money out of this." She flashed a smile and winked, making her point clear. The keys to Ruby's kingdom dangled before him, and he couldn't resist the temptation.

"Okay. I'll take the case, but you must sign a written disclosure of the possible conflict of interest. I will attest my interests will not interfere with my representation, but you must acknowledge I've made proper disclosures." These meager attempts to whitewash the decision did little to salve his conscience. He felt dirty. Was it because he pushed the bounds of ethics, or did the alliance with Dani add an undercurrent to already troubled waters?

She reached into her purse. "Of course, but as I said before, our interests align. Here's a dollar for your retainer. The balance can be found in Grandmother's diaries."

"I'll be out of town next week for Thanksgiving, so let's meet the following Monday. In the meantime, find an attorney to file the initial documents."

"Everything is under control." Dani walked to the large bay window overlooking the parking lot. "I believe I see your red Jeep, complete with a female chauffeur," Dani teased. "Please tell your wife hello for me."

"You know Jessie?"

"Met her at the basketball game after you ran out the door."

She spoke with a taunting bite, and her attention to detail rivaled Jessie's.

11

"Any luck with Devin?" Marc blurted out as he slid into the passenger seat.

Jessie shook her head. "No, a neighbor said he hadn't seen him around. I went to his work, but no one had seen him since the arrest. He disappeared in a puff of smoke after Hank bailed him out."

"I bet Mike Halley knows where he is," Marc said through clenched teeth.

"Let it go. Right now, we have more important things to worry about."

Jessie drove in silence while Marc stared out the window. Darkness draped across the poverty-stricken hills of Cherokee County, concealing the rough cabins and single-wide trailer houses. He didn't miss the reminder of Jimmy's humble beginnings.

"Duke should be there by now." Jessie pulled into the Holiday Inn Express at Tahlequah. "Take the luggage and check us in. I'll park the car."

Marc spied Duke in the far corner of the lobby and motioned him to the front desk.

"I made reservations for a couple of rooms," Marc said to the desk clerk as he laid his credit card on the counter.

The clerk produced the keys, and the two men headed toward the elevator.

"Meet you at the bar in a few. Bet ol' Marc could use a drink," Duke said with a smile.

Alcohol of any kind sounded like a great idea, but he had fought the demon of abstinence for the past week and intended to win.

"No, thanks. Just come to our room when you're settled. I'll order something to be brought in, and we can catch up. Burgers okay with you?"

Duke shot Marc a quizzical look and shrugged. "Sure," he said and disappeared down the hall. Thirty minutes later, he knocked at their door.

"Come in," Marc called as he cleared his bags from the chair to make room for Duke.

"I'm not doing so great on my end. Hope you had better luck." Duke grabbed a burger and sat in the recliner in the corner. "Jimmy's not talking, won't accept visitors, and stonewalls his court-appointed attorney."

"Damn it," Marc muttered, tossing his sandwich on the plate. "What do you make of his behavior? Is it an Indian thing?"

"No, it's a man thing." Duke's calmness perplexed Marc.

"What do you mean?" Jessie asked.

Marc's hand shook as he reached for his glass of water. His nerves seared his skin like a red-hot poker. Life had spun out of control, careening through a darkness that threatened to swallow him. He had never needed a drink as badly as he needed one now.

"Marc, are you all right?" Jessie's voice broke through his haze.

"I'm fine, a little tired. Go on, Duke. What's this 'man thing' you're talking about?"

"Jimmy's clamming up to protect a woman at any cost," Duke spoke with an assurance that left little doubt about his meaning. "This woman must be someone he cares about more than himself."

"Why won't he clear Devin? Is he going to sacrifice his best friend for this person?" Marc asked. "It makes no sense."

"We don't know whom he's protecting or why. Don't assume Jimmy's motive proves Devin's innocence as an accomplice."

"I'm not listening to this crap." Marc grabbed his coat and headed toward the door.

Duke grabbed Marc's arm and pinned it behind him. "If you're too weak to stomach the truth, we are better off without you. Ignorance is dangerous."

Marc's knees crumpled beneath him as he slumped down. "My son is not a murderer," he whispered to the floor.

"Stop it—both of you!" Jessie screamed.

Duke turned toward Jessie. "Cowards wear a mask of denial."

Jessie's eyes brimmed with tears. She touched Duke gently, and he released his hold on Marc. "No one's a coward here."

Marc convulsed as he drew a deep breath. "Duke's right." His pleading eyes locked on the elder Indian. "I don't understand why Jimmy refuses to clear Devin."

"Simple. If Jimmy eliminates suspects one at a time, the last man standing is guilty. He has thrown a blanket of silence over all to protect the one."

"Where do we go from here?" Marc asked in the voice of a man who had lost his way. Deep down, he knew Duke spoke the truth.

"Tomorrow, we'll begin our search for the woman Jimmy values. I'm unsure if it's his mother, sister, grandmother, or girlfriend. When we find her, we will find the motive. Then Jimmy will talk." With a sharp look, Duke retreated to his room.

Marc sat on the edge of the bed, staring at an ice bucket with a plastic liner draped over the edge. "I'll be back," he said as he grabbed the container and headed out the door. He returned with a bottle of Jim Beam, two tumblers, and a bucketful of ice.

"Here." Marc shoved a glass toward Jessie. "I think we both need a drink. I'm calling Kings X until Devin is free. Okay?"

Jessie had used those two silly words to freeze the world and call a time-out until she could restore peace to battling siblings. Now, Marc needed the world to stop until he could catch his breath—a truce from the war within—and liquor was the only way.

"I don't need a drink, Marc," Jessie said, heavy with disappointment.

"That's nonsense. As I said, this is a brief break. It worked with the boys."

"Did it?" With cool indifference, she turned away from him. "Drink your booze. I'm going to take a shower."

"I'll promise to stop once this mess—" The slamming of the bathroom door silenced Marc's plea.

The whiskey surged through his tired body, drowning the hurt and confusion trapped inside. After the fourth drink, the ugly truth retreated to the far corners of his mind, leaving him spent.

"Duke and I have work to do tomorrow," he muttered to the empty room as he flopped onto the bed, fully clothed, and fell asleep.

The alarm went off at precisely 5:00 a.m., two hours before daylight. Marc rolled out of bed and rubbed his scratchy eyes. He banished the image of Jessie's hurt from the night before. *I'll make it up to her later.* The evening with Duke had been sobering. *Did Duke possess a sixth sense of the workings of the human psyche? Could this aged Indian read a person's spirit trapped in a mortal body?* The thought that Devin's freedom depended on Duke's primitive instincts seemed shaky, but if Duke was right, then Devin could be knee-deep in a cover-up.

"Good morning, Kemosabe," Marc said, smiling sheepishly when the elderly gentleman joined him.

"You'll soon be fluent in Tonto." Duke smiled and looked around. "Where's Jessie?"

"She's got a headache," Marc lied. She had slept on the couch, and they hadn't spoken since last night. "Tell me where we're going."

"Marble City."

Marc brought the Jeep around while Duke grabbed a couple of muffins and two cups of coffee.

"Go south on Hwy 82 for thirty or so miles. We'll end up in the center of town."

Marble City consisted of a row of dilapidated buildings, leaning on each other like a bunch of drunks. An abandoned two-story structure on the corner stood above the others, evidence that this small town once teemed with life.

"We're here. Now what?" Marc asked.

"Turn right at the next road, go about three miles until you see a ravine on your right, then pull over."

"This is Jimmy's house." Marc recognized the tiny hut at the bottom of the chasm. "Is someone expecting us?"

"If someone expected us, no one would be here. Wait in the car. I'll let you know when to come."

Two young children, coatless in the chilly morning air, chased a black-spotted pup around the yard. Duke paid no attention, threading his way through tangled weeds poking out of junk piles, as he inched down the slope. He knocked and waited. A plump, middle-aged lady answered, then disappeared into the house with Duke behind her.

Marc fidgeted with his glasses as he flipped through the radio stations. He usually led the charge, but today he had to rely on Duke's instincts to help Devin. Fifteen minutes dragged by before Duke reappeared and motioned for Marc to join him.

Marc expected the same disarray inside that surrounded the home's exterior. Instead, worn furniture shone with fresh polish, and not a speck of dust dared touch the shelves filled with family pictures and Native art. He wiped his feet vigorously, afraid to track the spotless floor.

Three women sat on the couch like blackbirds on a fence, ready to fly.

"Marc, meet Mary Thomas, Jimmy's mother."

Mary had the handsome features of a classic Cherokee woman, except for her fair complexion. She smiled and extended her hand.

Duke nodded at the woman in the middle. "Susan is Jimmy's grandmother." She made no move to welcome him but acknowledged his presence with a glance.

"And here we have Bernice, Jimmy's great-grandmother." Bernice acknowledged him with a grunt, never dropping a stitch as she continued to knit.

"I've met your son, Mr. Whitcomb. He's a good boy," Mary said, surprising Marc. "He comes here sometimes with my Jimmy to hunt and fish."

Whose kid is she talking about? He had never known Devon to like the outdoors in any fashion. Now he learns his son traveled a hundred miles to do just that.

Duke took control of the conversation. "Jimmy is a fine man, too, but somehow these two have managed to find trouble. That's why we're here. Have you spoken to Jimmy?"

"Refuses to see me," Mary said, struggling to hold back tears.

"Do you know of any reason he would want to kill Caldwell?"

She shook her head. "He didn't."

"But he takes the blame," Bernice interjected. "He's protecting Ken, that no-good husband of yours."

"That's a lie!" Mary shouted. "You know nothing."

"You say it's a lie, but it's true." The old woman continued knitting without looking up.

"Shut your mouth or leave my house."

"I owned the land you stand on. I will not be leaving," Bernice said. "We have kept quiet too long, and Jimmy is paying the price."

"My husband pays the bills," Mary hissed.

The clinking of the knitting needles stopped. "We exist on the royalties of my land allotment . . . and I *will* tell."

The matriarch turned to Duke. "Her husband, Ken, works in construction when the mood strikes him. He took a job in Hugo last month and had a run-in with the hiring manager." Bernice shot Mary a defiant look, daring her to interrupt. Mary returned a glare but made no effort to interfere.

"David Caldwell hired and fired for Broce, Inc. Ken and his buddies went to work for him." Bernice turned to Mary. "He should have read them papers before putting his John Henry on the dotted line."

"What did he sign?" Duke probed.

"That Caldwell man had them sign an agreement to rent from him if they wanted a job."

"Was that bad?"

"Very bad. Caldwell bought an old two-story house in his wife's name and divided it into tiny boxes he called rooms. A grown man could touch both walls if he spread his arms. Fifteen men shared two bathrooms. Most of the time, the water didn't even work." Bernice's voice rose with the telling.

"His wife was as mean as he was. She put worn-out coin-operated washing machines in the basement with a rope strung wall to wall to hang their wet clothes."

So the prissy Madeline Caldwell was a slumlord. Her "me before thee" attitude could go a long way in Ruby's filing on Monday. He had dealt with landlord disputes in his career, and they all fit this scenario in some fashion. This tidbit would not be admissible in court, but understanding his adversary would help him squeeze the lemon.

"Ken should have refused to pay," Marc offered.

"Not that easy. No rent, no job. Ken signed the papers, and Caldwell deducted the rent from his pay. Those people charged double the rent of most places in town."

David Caldwell had committed extortion, to say the least.

"When Ken and his pals got their first paycheck, there was hardly enough to cover their bar tab. That's when they started making plans."

"Plans? What kind of plans?" Marc asked.

"They were gonna teach him a lesson."

"Did Ken have access to Jimmy's car?" *Hadn't Hank spotted Jimmy's car on the day of the murder near the Caldwell place? From a distance, he might have misidentified the driver or the passenger. Maybe he had assumed.*

"Mary's always borrowing Jimmy's car for one reason or another, then lets Ken drive it."

"I believe we have what we need." Marc was excited to find a man with a motive and opportunity.

"Good for you, Mr. Whitcomb. My son confessed to a murder he didn't commit, and now you want to convict my husband too." Marc cringed at the bitterness in her voice. His joy had heightened her pain.

"I only want the truth, and I'm sorry if it implicates your husband."

"Liar. Get out of my home."

Marc backed toward the door, as anxious to leave as she was to have him gone. Duke didn't budge.

"Do you believe your son is guilty?" Duke queried gently.

"No." She trembled as she forced the words through tears streaming down her face.

"Neither do I." Duke paused, then asked, "Did Jimmy have a girlfriend?"

"Let's go," Marc said, hovering in a partially open door. He had the answer he was looking for. Why wouldn't Duke turn loose of the crazy notion that a woman was at the center of this murder?

"He's been seeing some girl for the past few months, but I only met her once."

"Her name?"

"Amber Browning . . . or Brownrigg. I'm not sure."

"What can you tell me about her?"

"She's a child, not a woman. Clung to Jimmy the whole time they were here."

"Anything else?" Duke asked, pushing for any clue that might motivate Jimmy to kill.

"She has two kids, three if you count her. That's all I know. The last thing Jimmy needed was another man's kids."

"Have you heard from her?"

Her eyes flitted about the room before coming to rest on his. "No, and I hope I don't."

"We need to be on our way, Duke. Nice to meet you, ma'am. Sorry it couldn't be under better circumstances." Marc fidgeted, impatient to be on his way.

Mary shot him the evil eye. She had no more use for him than she did for Amber.

"I'll be waiting in the Jeep." Marc ducked out the door and made a hasty retreat up the slope of the ravine.

Duke slid into the Jeep twenty minutes later. "Drive," he ordered. Marc spun his tires, spitting gravel. "Damn it, Marc. You've got to slow down."

Marc dropped his speed. "Better?"

"I wasn't talking about your driving. You need to rein in your reckless rush to judgment."

"What are you talking about? Bernice laid it out for us. I'll get a hold of JP and tell him the whole story."

"You don't know the whole story."

"Jimmy is protecting his old man. How much plainer can it be?" Marc's rebuke sounded harsh, but his last nerve throbbed with this nonsense.

Unperturbed by Marc's outburst, Duke kept his eyes on the road as he spoke in his usual devil-be-damned manner. "Ken is not Jimmy's father. Mary hooked up with him three years after Jimmy left home. Best I can tell, the only one in the family who can tolerate Ken is Mary."

"How do you know all of this?"

"I spoke with Mary after you left. That way, you couldn't screw up the entire day."

Marc ignored the dig. "What about the car? Jimmy loaned it to Ken all the time?"

"Jimmy loaned it to his mother. I doubt he knew she let Ken use it."

"So what? It doesn't matter if Jimmy knew or not." His retort sounded weak. Duke's counterpoints had dampened his high spirits. He had acted rashly with all the assumptions he'd made. He did need to slow down. His habit of running with the surface current led to him losing a high-stakes trial at Smith & Noble. He couldn't afford to make that mistake again.

"Mary has spoken with the girl."

"She said that? Well, there's another surprise."

Duke grew quiet, offering no answer.

"I'm hungry. Let's stop by Wildhorse Mountain BBQ," Marc said, breaking the awkward silence. "This time I'll order."

A faint smile lifted Duke's hollow cheeks as they pulled into the parking lot.

Marc marched up to the counter. "Two bags of chips, two Coors, and two pulled-pork sandwiches with *hotter-than-hell* sauce on *both*, please."

A full-fledged grin flashed across Duke's tawny face. "Keep this up, and you'll be a man someday."

"Where do we go from here?" Marc asked, fighting the fire in his throat. Water didn't quench the burning sensation of the habanero pepper sauce on his tongue.

"We must find out about the girlfriend."

"Any idea on how to make that happen? Devin and Jimmy won't talk." Marc didn't share Duke's conviction about a woman as the root cause of murder.

"Check out the people he worked with. They might know something. In the meantime, I will see what I can pry from Jimmy's attorney. I don't hold much hope in that arena, but he, too, speaks fluent Cherokee. The club is small. He might let his guard down with me."

Duke leaned over and touched Marc's shoulder as they approached the Holiday Inn. "I wouldn't waste my time on this Ken thing. Granny hates his guts. Let's find the woman."

"We'd better head to the house. The twins are probably there by now," Marc said as he dropped Duke off at his car, killing the discussion about this elusive woman. "I'll grab Jessie and be right behind you."

12

The scent of cinnamon and ginger from Lisi's golden pumpkin pies melded with the earthy aroma of sage cornbread dressing in the oven. *Heaven. Pure heaven*, Marc thought as he watched the twins drifting toward the kitchen, hoping to sneak a taste.

"Outta here, you little beggars," Mama Waite teased, flipping a tea towel in their direction. Lisi smiled and slipped each boy a cookie before shooing them out of the way.

An hour later, the table was loaded with turkey and all the trimmings of a traditional Thanksgiving feast. Marc piled his plate high, avoiding Jessie's watchful eye. Today, he intended to break out of diet prison and answer to his warden later. When his belly was full and his plate empty, he pushed back from the table.

"Many compliments to the chef . . . or chefs," Marc said, winking at Lisi. "Now this old man needs a nap."

"Not so fast, mister," Lisi said, laughing. She walked to the pantry and returned with her famous duty jar, which had chores written on tiny squares of paper, ready to be drawn.

Moans, groans, and loud laughter erupted as each learned their duty. The twins scored by clearing the table. Lisi and Mama Waite landed the coveted job of putting away the leftovers. Marc's lot fell to dreaded dishwashing and Duke to the lesser evil of drying, leaving Jessie to put away stacks of clean dishes. After outlandish negotiations to trade jobs, Duke's hilarious finger-pointing at a pan that failed inspection, and wild accusations of sandbagging, the rowdy bunch eventually produced a spotless kitchen.

The day had been picture-perfect . . . except for Jessie's mood. Her aloofness loomed like a dark cloud. A simple sadness crept over Marc. Years of family fun, the laughter of three generations of women, and the boyish antics of his ornery twins on holidays past were lost. Why had he avoided Jessie's family? Work? Other commitments? Or his love of drinking? He knew the answer, and his sadness deepened.

Tomorrow, he and Jessie would return to Brule, where he could bury his regrets in Devin's problems.

Business at Harper's was slow on the Saturday after Thanksgiving, but he could count on the gang being there, providing the perfect opportunity to corner the sheriff. Marc rose early, slipped on a pair of jeans, and tucked in the tails of his shirt. He checked his appearance in the bathroom mirror. The paunch around his belly had flattened with Jessie's toast-and-oatmeal diet, and the man in the mirror looked haggard and drawn. This whole ordeal had sucked the life out of him.

Marc spied Hank and JP sitting at the large table in the back. He summoned what few crumbs of resolve he could muster, squared his shoulders, and negotiated through the diners.

"Look at you. You've lost, what, maybe ten pounds?" Hank's booming voice filled the café.

"As our honorable mayor Johnny would say, the wife's got me on a diet." He spoke with a lightness he didn't feel.

"Pull up a chair, Marco." JP slid a chair in his direction and hailed Judy for a round of coffee.

"I need to talk to you, JP. Ask a few questions about the investigation." Marc kept his delivery low-key.

"You know I can't tell you anything not in public records." JP leaned back and crossed his arms over his chest.

"Relax. We'll keep it in the public domain. I haven't had a chance to get a copy." Nancy sent a stack of papers containing the police report to the house yesterday, but he wanted to get a read on JP.

"In that case, I guess it won't hurt to talk about it." JP glanced at Hank, looking for approval, then turned back toward Marc.

"Did anyone, besides Hank, see Jimmy or Devin drive on the Caldwell property the Friday of the murder?" Marc asked.

"Not that I know. But Hank here saw 'em when he was checkin' cattle, and his word is good with me."

"What time?" Marc directed his question at the burly rancher.

"Sometime early morning. Why? Are you playing detective now?" Hank's defensiveness did not surprise Marc since his friend didn't like to be challenged and hated to be wrong. Marc must approach Bernice's story in a manner that would let them off the hook for overlooking the real killer.

"It's hard to see at daybreak. Perhaps you made a mistake, Hank. It would be easy enough to do. Hell, at our age, we're lucky to . . ." Marc stopped and sighed. Hank wasn't buying. He had no choice but to dive in and spill Bernice's story to his disinterested audience.

"So you think it was Ken and his buddy in Jimmy's car?" Hank asked.

Marc nodded, relieved he understood.

"Only two problems, buddy boy. Jimmy confessed, and the car didn't belong to Jimmy."

"Then whose car was it? And, by the way, Devin hasn't confessed."

"Read the files, Marco."

"Your son took a plea bargain. End of story." Hank slammed Marc's last hope on the floor and stomped on it. "He'll get two years with credit for time served and a five-thousand-dollar fine. Pretty light for a murder. You've got Mike Halley to thank for that."

"I have *you* to thank for railroading my boy, you son of a—" Marc's heart pounded.

"Hold on, Marco. I found Devin an attorney while you gallivanted about looking for that Indian boy."

"And you know that how?" Marc hadn't mentioned his first trip to anyone.

Hank's face burned bright red. "I'm done."

"This isn't over." Marc slammed his fist on the table and glared at the men he once called friends. "And when I get to the bottom of this, I'll—" His tongue locked. Mike Halley and Hank had sealed Devin's fate, and he could do nothing about it. How had he become a spectator in his son's battle? He fumbled his way to the door and navigated the few blocks to his office, where solitude and a bottle of Beam awaited in the library.

Two shots of whiskey began to take effect. Marc stretched out on the leather recliner in the corner with a bucket of ice and a fifth of Beam at arm's length. He savored each sip like a thirsty man in the desert. The pounding in his head diminished with each swallow.

When the door to the library opened slightly, Marc stirred but drifted off again, lost in the fog of sleep. Hours passed before he woke, fuzzy-brained and dry-mouthed, moaning as the memory of this morning's revelation swept through him like wildfire. Despite his throbbing head, Marc had enough sense to know he had fallen off the wagon, and it had run over him.

He stumbled to the office bathroom and found the spare toothbrush and comb he kept there for emergencies. If Jessie saw him like this, she would kill him. Except for his bloodshot eyes, Marc managed to erase the evidence of his drinking. He found an empty bottle of eye drops in the medicine cabinet. *Damn it.* He looked like hell, but would have to brave her anger. Jessie would have dinner on the table by now.

But there were no lights on in the house. No car in the driveway. Strange. Marc ran up the steps and straight to the kitchen. A note in Jessie's handwriting was on the counter.

"It's over, Marc. No more chances, The boys and I are going to stay with Mom and Dad. Please don't call. I can't deal with you right now. Jessie."

Marc lit the logs in the fireplace and stared at the flames flickering in the darkness. A partially decorated Christmas tree stood in the corner. With a click of the remote, Bing Crosby began to croon "I'll Be Home for Christmas," Jessie's favorite holiday song. A second click silenced the room. He read Jessie's note for the fourth time. His wife had left him. He tossed her note into the flames and walked to the pantry to scavenge for a bottle of anything with alcohol, but only bottled water, root beer, and cranberry juice lined the shelves. Then he remembered. Jessie bought a bottle at the hotel in Tahlequah. It must be here somewhere. He flew up the stairs, opened the closet door, and dragged out the suitcase. Jessie had tucked the large bottle of Beam in the pouch of the empty luggage.

She had packed the very liquor he would drink, but he knew a drink hadn't driven her away—a drunk had. The irony of the situation made Marc sad.

He held the whiskey tumbler at arm's length. The amber liquid muted the brilliance of the dancing flames. Angry with the total collapse of life, he hurled the fragile glass at the fireplace, smashing it into a million pieces.

Sunday rolled by with no word from Jessie, though Marc hadn't expected to hear from her. He didn't dress or read the paper. Instead, he paced the rooms, tortured by the emptiness. Twenty years, erased by a drink, was difficult to swallow. If only . . . If only what? He had been different?

Ruby's diaries stared at him from the edge of his desk. Start there. Start with Devin. Start today. He willed his hands to open the pages of Ruby's life.

November 27, 1990 – It's been two months since Jack died. Tony won't eat, and I don't have the strength to care. He looks at me like I'm the reason David's gone. Maybe I am. Maybe God is punishing me for favoring David.

November 22, 1990 – Thanksgiving Day. Ha. What do I have to be thankful for? A husband who won't talk to me? My dead son? And David won't quit pestering me about deeding the farm over. He wants it now, and Tony says there is no way in hell he will inherit the farm until we are both buried and gone.

Ruby's anguish mimicked his own. She had little left except broken people. Marc closed the book and went upstairs.

Monday's alarm sounded at 6:00 a.m., and Marc crawled out of bed, trying to muster the strength to meet the challenge of living without Jessie. He arrived at the office before 7:00, started the coffee, and rummaged through a stack of mail.

"You're here early. What's the occasion?" Nancy asked.

"No occasion. I have work to do." *How could he tell Nancy that Jessie had left him?*

"I heard about Devin's plea. That's a bummer."

"It's more than a bummer. It's wrong. Devin had nothing to do with Caldwell. Help me prove it?" Marc's pleading sparked Nancy to action.

"Of course. The papers I dug out for you might be a good place to start." Nancy, his no-nonsense savior with a gray bun and kind eyes, reported for duty.

Papers. Marc had forgotten about the legal stuff Nancy sent to the house. Jessie had placed them on his desk last Friday.

"I'll run home and get them."

"Let me. I'll call Jessie and let her know I'm coming by," Nancy said as she reached for her coat.

"She's not home."

"Later, then."

"Jessie's not coming home." He rested his hand on the desk to brace himself.

Nancy's eyes widened with comprehension. "I kept a copy of everything. Use these." She hoisted a bundle of papers from her bottom desk drawer. "Take a close look at the deed. It's on top."

"This deed has a filing date of January 6, 2010. The assignors were Tony and Ruby Caldwell to David Caldwell. Dani claims I prepared the deed, but I never met Tony. And Ruth just came into the picture recently. That's strange."

"Gets stranger," Nancy commented as she adjusted her black-rimmed glasses and leaned closer to the desk. "Look at the ink. Tom's and Ruby's signatures look faded, but the ink on the grantee and the notary lines is quite fresh in comparison."

"Dani told me I prepared the deed twenty years ago. Why did it take so long to file?"

"I couldn't find a copy of a will for Tony and Ruby, but the deed would supersede the will. Maybe Dani could help with that one."

Marc had confidence that if one existed, Nancy would have found it. No will had been filed.

"Do me a favor. Look through Dad's old files and see if you can find the Caldwell name. I suspect he's the Whitcomb Ruby remembers."

"I'll come dressed to work in that dirty basement tomorrow, but someone will have to help me move boxes!" Nancy called after Marc as he raced out the door.

13

Dani's phone rang five times before going to voicemail. Marc turned the Jeep toward Tulsa, hoping to catch her at work. At 4:00 p.m., he should miss the rush-hour traffic. With any luck, the apartment parking lot would be empty, sparing him a two-block walk from the parking garage. Marc climbed the dreaded three flights of stairs. After three quick taps, Dani opened the door.

"May I come in?"

"No," Dani whispered. "When Grandmother goes to bed, I'll meet you in the sandwich shop across the street. Give me an hour."

Frustration and hunger gnawed at Marc. He hadn't eaten a decent meal in three days, and his stomach rumbled in protest. The thought of a Reuben sandwich without a beer added layers to his bleak mood. By the time Dani arrived, his patience had evaporated.

"Let's talk about the deed." Marc skipped all pleasantries.

"What do you want to know?"

"The deed looks dated, but the grantee's signature is fresh. Any possible explanations?"

"Yes, but it's not a pretty one."

"Shoot."

"When you prepared the deed fourteen years ago, my grandparents had one living child, my dad. Grandpa didn't trust people... especially attorneys. He concocted the crazy idea of having a deed prepared and leaving the grantee blank. My dad could write his name in and record it at the courthouse when they both passed. Grandpa called it his 'dresser-drawer deed.'" Dani threw her head back and laughed without amusement. "You should know by now that my family is a bunch of paranoid loony tunes."

"When did your granddad pass?" This deed thing had an odor to it.

"January 7, 2010."

"Are you aware your father filed on January 6, 2010?"

Dani's face twisted in anger. "Yes, it was no secret my dad couldn't wait for them to die. He wanted the farm any way he could get it. According to him, old people didn't need money."

Marc remembered the picture of the nice-looking gentleman from the funeral and shook his head. What a contrast to the monster Dani described.

"So he helped himself to the deed?"

"Yes, on the day I brought grandmother home from the hospital." Dani hesitated for a moment. "Do you want the whole story?"

"Go on." Marc wanted to know everything.

"Granddad was in hospice care, and Grandmother had heart problems. Their house felt like a nursing home with hospital beds and smells of disinfectant. Lovely, right? When I got my grandmother settled in the spare bedroom, my dad roared up the driveway, slammed his truck in park, and ran to the desk in the den. I screamed 'What do you think you're doing?' when he started digging through Granddad's papers. I tried to block him in the hallway, but he shoved me aside and left with the deed in hand."

"He took the deed without your grandparents' blessing?"

"They were too sick to know what he was doing. The hospice nurse can attest to that."

"Did he attempt to tell them he took the deed?"

She leaned toward Marc, eyes glistening with pure hate. "Nope," she said through clenched teeth. "Not a word."

Marc pitied the young woman, who couldn't be much over twenty-six or seven. The loss of her granddad, the murder of her father, and caring for Ruby with apparent signs of Alzheimer's would crush most people. Dani took it in stride.

"One more question, and we'll call it quits for the night. Do you have a copy of your grandparents' will?"

"Grandmother does, but I will have to sneak it from her room. She clutches on to that paper with both hands, afraid someone will steal it . . . as if it matters now."

"See what you can find out about the will, and let's meet again on Friday." Marc summoned the tab.

"Make it after five. I'm slammed on Friday." Dani scooted out of the booth and left. He watched her glide through pools of light from the streetlamps and disappear into the night.

Marc spent the trip home sorting out the layers wrapped around David's death. Duke believed Jimmy lied about killing David, and his son had confessed to a crime that didn't make sense. The victim had multiple enemies, and the killer's identity was buried in lies. The common theme surrounded the deed. David must have needed access to money quickly and struck at the first opportunity. The farm, valued at around a million dollars, would heal a multitude of money problems.

Marc arrived home around midnight. Everything was as he had left it. The coffee table, littered with paper plates and an empty Beam bottle, offered meager signs of human habitation. Jessie would disapprove. He found a trash bag and picked up the litter. With the mess cleared, he headed to bed, where loneliness settled over him like a gloomy cloud, pushing aside any hope of sleep—*four days until Christmas, and no Jessie.*

He willed the thought from his mind and turned instead to Ruby's diaries, which lurked in his brain like a bad dream. He'd never finished them. A guilty conscience and the lack of comforting booze drove him to his office to take another stab at them.

Marc selected one titled *Book of Ruby*, which covered 1989-2015, the time frame of the deed preparation. The Whitcomb name should be somewhere.

February 23, 1998 – Tony and I went to see Murray Whitcomb today about a deed to the farm. That was a waste of time. My husband is so bullheaded it's embarrassing. He wanted the attorney to prepare a deed and leave it blank. Now, what kind of a deed is that? Mr. Whitcomb was very nice, but I could tell he thought we were idiots.

February 27, 1998 – Mr. Whitcomb called today to see if we had decided on an heir. Tony shouted at him over the phone to leave the damn heir blank. Mr. Whitcomb told him the deed was invalid without an heir. Tony really lost his temper then and informed him we would find someone else who knew what they were doing. Ha! Like Tony would know.

March 3, 1998 – Tony found an attorney who would prepare the deed like he wanted. I'm not crazy about him. His name is Mike Halley with Smith & Noble in Tulsa. That fancy name will cost a lot of money, but Tony says we will save more in the long run. Ha. Guess we'll be dead, so it won't matter.

Marc slammed the diary shut. Ruby remembered his father's last name, but Halley did the work that violated ethical standards. No wonder Caldwell didn't ring a bell.

14

Marc packed a bag and made reservations at the Hampton Inn. A Friday evening appointment did not fit his usual client agenda, but he had no real reason to return home. He missed Jessie like hell, and nights were the worst. Besides, if he stayed, he could drop by Devin's duplex Saturday morning and have a look-see.

Ruby must have heard Marc stomping up the stairs and greeted him at the door before he could knock.

"What do you think?" She twirled around in her blue shirtwaist dress and pearl button earrings for Marc's approval.

"You look like Grace Kelly," Marc teased as she floated about the room.

"Stop it," she said, laughing. "You'd better get ready yourself."

Dani stepped out of her bedroom, dressed to the nines in black boots, a white tank top with a red bandana, Levi's jeans, and a cowgirl hat as dark as her hair.

"Do I have the wrong apartment or the wrong date?" Marc made light of a confusing situation. He thought Ruby might have had one of her time-shifting thingies since her attire went out of style in the forties, but Dani's appearance ended that notion.

"Right apartment, right date. We're taking Ruby to Cain's Ballroom tonight."

"Ruby?"

"Yes." Dani winked and smiled. "When we go out, she thinks 'Grandmother' makes her sound old."

"And don't you be calling me 'mother,'" Ruby said, wagging her finger at him, "or people will think I'm Grandma Moses. Hurry, we don't want to be late."

"He looks fine, Ruby."

"Well, at least lose the tie and comb your hair," Ruby said.

"I don't dance." Marc squirmed.

"Don't be a party pooper." Ruby slipped into her coat and grabbed her purse. "Time to shake a leg."

Ruby's girlish enthusiasm sparked a glimmer of amusement. *Date night with Lucy and Ethel*, Marc mused as he removed his tie and smoothed his hair. One evening wouldn't kill him.

The Cain's Ballroom marquee displaying "Bob Wills & His Texas Playboys" branded the night sky. Men and women in their eighties—some with their spouses, many alone—waited with excitement for admission to the old dance hall. All were giddy with their seventy-year-old memories still fresh as the evening air. These people had fought on the battlefields of Normandy and worked in the war plants. They visited this ballroom to escape from the ugliness of World War II. A fleeting feeling of gratitude tugged at Marc, followed by a sense of shame. Ruby had invited him into her past, and he had begrudged the intrusion. With pride, he took Ruby's hand and led her through the mezzanine and into the great dance hall.

Ruby waved frantically toward a small table near the back. "Over there."

"You can't see the bandstand," Dani protested.

"I can hear, and that's good enough for me."

Marc scanned the walls lined with black fiddle-shaped fixtures. Single red bulbs illuminated photographs of famous musicians who had played at Cain's over the years. For a few short hours, ghosts of the Dust Bowl, the Great Depression, and World War II hid in the room's dark corners while these "Okies" of the thirties and forties danced the night away to timeless ballads. Marc inhaled the history and the spirit of these men and women.

Over a thousand people filled the hall as the band began to play "San Antonio Rose," the all-time favorite of every Bob Wills fan. Clapping hands and twirling hats erupted at the base of the stage while couples spun in wide circles, dancing the Western swing. Even Marc tapped his foot to the pulsing beat of bass guitars.

"I'll be back," Dani whispered in Marc's ear when the band took a break. "I'm going to say hello to some friends."

She disappeared like a wisp of smoke, leaving him alone to entertain Ruby.

"I met Tony here," Ruby said. Marc smiled and nodded. Tonight, he was not David.

"I worked a swing shift at McDonnell Douglas, welding on planes. Tony was a lonely soldier on leave. Somehow, we both ended up here on a Friday night," she said, laughing. "Fate, I reckon."

"LOVE AT FIRST SIGHT?" Marc asked. "Rosie the Riveter meets a soldier?"

"Oh, I fell in love with him straight away, but Momma disapproved. Tony's parents had immigrated from Italy. When Italy sided with Germany, she called Tony a Nazi. It didn't matter to her that he joined the army and fought for our side." Ruby leaned back and shot him a stern eye. "Hate is blind. Remember that."

"He . . . he must have . . . won her over." Marc stumbled, unsure of the proper reaction.

"Not an ounce. When the war ended, we eloped. Two broke kids and a dream. Ha. I guess it's how we all start." A wistful lightness had returned to Ruby's story.

"What did you do after the war?" Marc wanted her to keep talking.

"Tony went to work at the glass plant, and I waitressed. When the men came home from war, I lost my job at Douglas. Pretty rough for a while."

"Children?"

"Two, and both are dead." The dim lights of the ballroom did not hide the pain on her face. "Jack, my oldest, died twenty-two years ago."

"I'm sorry. That must have been hard." Marc winced at the triteness of his words.

"After my oldest son passed, Tony got cancer. Every penny of our savings went to bury David and care for my husband. It felt like someone had pulled the plug and my life was swirling down the drain. "

Marc marveled at the hardships this woman had endured. "How did you survive?" he asked.

"His folks died in 1996, two months apart if you can believe that. We inherited their house and farm. Life should have gotten easier, but the loss of his parents and our son left Tony not quite right in the head."

"I don't know if I could manage as well as you did." Marc reached out to touch her hand, but she withdrew.

"I didn't do so well. David pestered the life out of me. 'Give me the farm. Give me the farm.' He sounded like a broken record. Finally, my husband decided to prepare a deed to the farm to shut him up, but Tony left the name blank. Ha. One attorney warned us not to do that, but my husband wouldn't listen." Ruby raised both hands in surrender.

"And . . . ?" Marc leaned in. He needed her to continue.

"Ha. My youngest boy came running with his hands out and snatched it all."

"He abused your trust!" Marc said with disgust.

Ruby's enthusiasm waned; her voice weakened. "Yep, he stole everything. Everything. My money is gone, and I live off my granddaughter's charity. Not a great ending."

"I'm going to help you get some of that money back," Marc spoke with an assurance he didn't have.

"Good luck getting anything from Madeline." Ruby nodded toward the crowd several tables over. "Being a widow agrees with her."

Marc glanced across the room to see a woman with golden blonde hair and expensive clothing flash a dazzling smile at Hank. Next to him sat Mike Halley with his spouse. An unknown couple rounded out the group. Marc had dismissed Judy's tidbit about Hank and Madeline as nonsense, but it took on a troubling nuance tonight. This was no business lunch.

Marc stood. He had no desire to run into Hank and Mike. "Let's get out of here. Where's Dani?"

"I'm not leaving," Ruby said, patting his hand. "Relax, Madeline is too busy being important to notice us."

Marc slumped back in his seat. Ruby might make a scene if he tried to force the issue, and Dani was still out making her social rounds.

The iconic melody "Take Me Back to Tulsa" filled the hall as the crowd returned to the dance floor, leaving most of the tables empty. Hank and Mike Halley's wife took to the floor. Halley leaned close to Madeline, whispered as she touched his arm, and laughed. Their intimacy struck Marc as odd. David had died less than three months ago, but his widow had recovered in record time. Halley extended his hand to Madeline, and they joined the sea of dancers. His archenemy and Madeline, the woman Marc intended to sue, danced cheek to cheek. The realization that Ruby had little hope of winning her case against Madeline felt like a stomach punch.

The sinewy cry of steel guitars filled the room. "Faded Love" lured reluctant wallflowers onto the floor, providing the perfect opportunity to disappear, with or without Dani. Marc helped Ruby to her feet, offered his arm for support, and guided her to the nearest exit.

"Where are you two going?" Dani asked from behind.

"Home," Marc replied, then kept walking.

15

"What was your big hurry?" Dani asked after she settled Ruby for the evening.

"Didn't you see your stepmother and friends?" Marc countered.

Dani flopped down on the couch and shot Marc a defiant grin. "Yes, but we don't speak. I hate her, and she, for sure, hates me. I'm going to sue her ass, and she knows it."

"Big words. Hope you're ready for a fight. Did you happen to notice the people sitting at her table?" Marc appreciated her gumption, but she underestimated her opponents.

"I paid no attention to her or her friends."

"Let me point out the formidable Mike Halley and the wealthy Hank Walton. We will be lucky to make it to trial."

"I recognize those names from grandmother's diaries." Her smile disappeared.

Crap. He still hadn't finished all of Ruby's diaries.

"So you recognize the name of Hank Walton."

A cloud of concern crept into her eyes. "Yes, Grandmother mentions him more than the others."

Dani slipped her boots off and headed toward the kitchen. "Do you want anything to drink? This could be a long evening, so we might as well be comfortable."

A tall glass of Beam and water flitted across Marc's mind. "Water."

Dani handed him his drink and plopped down in a white leather recliner.

"Before we dig in too deep, I need you to answer a question. Is Ruby capable of taking the stand? Without her testimony, I'm not sure we have a case."

"No, she's not capable."

"Are you sure? She seemed lucid tonight."

"Good, isn't she?" Dani's eyes twinkled. "She can fool the best of them. It took me months to convince the doctors she had Alzheimer's."

Marc didn't find her answer amusing in the least. If Ruby couldn't testify, what did they have?

"If I had to label grandmother tonight, I would call it *showtimer's*, not Alzheimer's," Dani said and sighed as if tired of telling the story.

"Cut to the chase." The evening had taken its toll, and Marc had no tolerance for cuteness.

"I mean, Grandmother pulls it together in front of others," Dani answered defensively.

"So sometimes she's all right? When she wants to be, that is?"

"No, she puts on an act that can fool you unless you know her. It's not real, and she can slip back to her own reality with a single word."

"So, nothing she told me tonight is right?"

"You really don't get this Alzheimer's thing, do you?" Dani let out a long sigh. "Listen, her long-term memory is fairly good, but as she progresses, that will fade too. Her short-term memory slides around like a greased pig."

Marc's hope sank. Ruby appeared fine tonight. No one could predict the outcome if her case were to be heard a year from now.

Dani laughed as she blinked back tears. "Sometimes I wonder if I'm the one who imagines things, but when Grandmother asks, 'Exactly what is a screen door?' I know it's not me. The world moves too fast around her, so she pretends when she doesn't understand what's happening. Most of the time, she doesn't realize my dad is dead."

"Is that why she transfers to me? Pretends I'm her son?"

Dani shrugged. "I think so. Who knows?"

"I want to be upfront with you. If what you say is accurate, I'm afraid this case is an exercise in futility."

"What I'm telling you *is* accurate, and that's why my dad got away with stealing everything she owns." Her voice cracked, and she couldn't hide her tears any longer. "Please, don't give up until you see what I have."

Marc understood the desperation of trying to save someone you loved with the odds stacked against you. He couldn't give up on Devin any more than she could her grandmother. *We're both fools,* he thought. *Two Don Quixotes tilting at windmills.*

"What do you have?" He kicked himself the moment he spoke. Marc questioned his stamina to fight two battles, knowing he stood to lose both.

"I'll be right back." She disappeared down the hallway and returned, arms loaded with files and boxes.

"Here are Grandmother's bank statements from the last three years and a copy of all her CDs."

"How did you get your hands on these if David had possession at the time of his death?"

"Easy. After Dad died, I petitioned the courts for power of attorney to oversee Grandmother's business."

"So these are bank copies?"

"Better than that. I also called the insurance adjuster to assess the damage at the farm. They told me to make an itemized list of everything, take photos, and send them copies."

"That's highly unusual. The chain of command for the farm ownership would have followed the will. Were you a named beneficiary?"

"Dad didn't leave a will."

That statement could change everything. "You told me earlier that your grandmother had the will and you would try to get your hands on it."

"Can't find it. Maybe it was just a figment of Grandmother's imagination."

"Then, according to Oklahoma law, Madeline inherits half and you the other half. So you can tie up the farm sale. Perfect. Any other assets?" Marc felt a glimmer of hope.

"Dad's personal residence—bought with Grandmother's money, I might add—goes to the spouse. Madeline thinks she's getting the CDs too, but they're gone. Nothing is left. That leaves a few pieces of farm equipment for Madeline and me to fight over."

"Did the company send an adjuster?"

"Nope, I called my cousin to help me, and we did the inventory."

"And you took these records?"

Dani giggled. "Yep. The sheriff had removed the crime scene tape, so I figured the leftovers belonged to my grandmother and me."

Marc smiled. This girl had enough guts for both of them.

"Do you still have access to the farmhouse?"

"Yes."

"Would you take me there tomorrow?" Marc had wanted to investigate the property for the past three months, and Dani held the keys to the kingdom. She had hinted more than once that they might have a common interest, and he began to believe she was right.

"Okay, but there's not much to see."

"Great. It's late, and we have a big day ahead of us tomorrow. I'll pick you up at 8:00 a.m. Be ready." Marc hurried out the door, anxious to tackle the next day.

16

Marc felt giddy with the prospect of inspecting the crime scene without interference. Like a rummage sale on the third day, the good stuff had long disappeared, but if he looked hard enough, he might find something overlooked in the chaos. Any findings would be worthless in court, but maybe he would find something to alter the course of his search.

When he arrived, Dani was waiting in the parking lot with a smile and two large cups of coffee.

“I couldn’t sleep last night. This day means a lot to me.”

“What are you looking for?” she asked with polite curiosity.

“A four-leaf clover? A horseshoe? Anything that can stop this runaway train before it goes off the track.”

“That makes two of us. I can’t afford to hire a caretaker for my grandmother if her Alzheimer’s gets worse. It would cost a fortune, and I barely make ends meet as it is. Quitting my job is not an option.”

Wisps of her brown hair clung to her pale skin, giving her a rocker vibe. His attention drifted to the rearview mirror, where he caught his own reflection. A purplish-pink halo circled both eyes, puffy and sallow from lack of sleep. *And I look like a druggie. She and I are two doozies—losers with nothing left to lose.*

"Pull up next to the barn." Dani waved toward a weathered red structure behind the house. "No one can see us there."

Low clouds scudded across an overcast sky, spitting tiny droplets of freezing rain. The two dashed across the yard toward the Caldwell house, which appeared as cold and dark as the morning. Lifting his coat, Marc covered their heads as Dani fumbled to unlock the back door. "There," she said, throwing the door open and stepping in.

"Where's the furniture?" His voice echoed in the empty room.

"Dad sold it when Grandmother went to live with him and Madeline. She cried and begged him to let her keep a few things, but he laughed and said Madeline would never allow her old stuff in their new home."

The austere furnishings shocked Marc. A ladder-back kitchen chair and a battered end table holding an old radio were in the middle of the living room floor. Another chair was on its side, charred and broken, near a large burn hole in the carpet.

Marc continued down the hall to the utility room next to the garage entrance, ignoring the mice scurrying out of the splintered wood of the broken doorway. An old coin-operated washer and dryer in the utility caught his attention. He opened the lid, peeked in, then slammed it shut.

"Whose commercial washer and dryer?" Marc asked, pointing at the worn-out pair.

"It's another example of how my dad *cared* for his mother."

"You're kidding. Who owns this house now? Your grandmother?"

"No, it was part of the farm, so Dad owned it. Kinda makes me and my stepmother partners in this mess now." Dani's hollow laugh held no amusement.

Marc couldn't get his head around the twisted relationship between mother and son. "You're losing me. If your grandmother lived with your dad, why would she need a washer and dryer at the farm?"

"Dad dumped Grandmother here when she had a big blowout

with Madeline. Of course, she had no furniture since Dad sold it. He dug these two old chairs, that washer and dryer, and an old bed from his rooming house in Hugo out of storage and left her to fend for herself." Anger burned in Dani's eyes. "I would have shot the old dog myself if someone else hadn't beat me to it."

That thought had crossed Marc's mind. David Caldwell surrounded himself with people who preferred him dead, including his daughter. And he had heard Jimmy say those exact words. Was Dani the female he'd protected?

"Is the burn hole in the living room carpet where they found him?"

"Yes, whoever shot Dad in the temple doused him with gasoline and set him on fire."

Wow. Marc reeled from her revelation. Dani's version did not match the story swirling about Brule. Rumors of a single bullet to the head and a quick attempt at a fire in the garage summed up the murder story he had heard. But whoever killed David hated the man with a passion.

"Pretty stupid, if you ask me," said Dani.

"Why do you say that?"

She had revealed details that weren't evident from the scene. If she played a part in the murder, the more she talked, the greater her chance of making a mistake.

"First, fire can't burn a bullet hole out of a skull. Second, the house lacked circulation and couldn't sustain a fire for long. Third, fingerprints. Touching gas cans is risky business."

"Were there fingerprints?" Marc's attention was riveted on his young client. She possessed an understanding of the murder not found in public reports.

"Had to be. Two people and one pair of gloves. There are fingerprints somewhere."

Dani's lack of emotion struck Marc as odd, yet she exhibited genuine concern regarding Ruby. He would probe that subject on the way home. Right now, he wanted to make one more trip through the rooms.

"Did you get what you were looking for?" Dani asked when Marc joined her in the living room.

"Maybe. No. I'll be right back." Marc dashed to the utility room, removed a carpet piece from the old washer, and returned to the hole cut in the carpet.

"It's a match!" Marc shouted, doing a little dance. He ran back to the utility and rummaged for something to wrap the piece in. He found a plastic trash bag that would serve his purpose.

"Hold this open." Marc handed Dani the bag. "I want the contents of the washer."

"What for?"

"Hold it." Marc methodically placed pieces of carpet and pad from the washing machine into the bag.

"Done," Marc said and headed for the door.

"You're a strange one," she said as she hurried to keep up.

Marc threw the bag in the trunk and started the Jeep. On the ride home, an adrenaline rush pushed a million thoughts through his head.

"According to Ruby, Madeline had abused her, but from the looks of things here, David had treated her worse than his wife had. Who's the real villain?"

Dani stared out the window. The corners of her mouth drooped as if watching a sad movie.

"That's hard to answer, but I'll give it a shot. After my granddad died, my dad took my grandmother to live with them. He and Madeline had purchased a huge—and I mean, *huge*—home. I called to check on Grandmother, but they refused to put her on the phone, and I wasn't allowed to visit her either. I had no idea what happened in that house, but I knew Grandmother wanted to go home to her farm."

"This is hard, but it will get brutal if we pursue a case." Marc's sternness stemmed from his distress. He began again, striking a softer tone. "How did you finally connect with her?"

"Dad dumped her at the farm when she and Madeline butted heads again. Grandmother had no food and little money, but she did have her cell phone and the keys to the old Buick stored in the garage."

"So she called you?" Marc coaxed.

"No, she called Aunt Marie, her older sister, and invited her to spend a week at the farm." Dani burst into hysterical laughter. "Can you imagine?" she asked, gasping for breath between fits of giggling. "Grandmother, in her eighties, drives the old car to town and picks up Aunt Marie and two cartons of ice cream."

Marc laughed too, caught up in the ridiculous, bittersweet moment. The cleansing outburst released the tension that had held him hostage for months. Any sane person would have them committed, but he didn't care. His raw nerves needed the healing balm of laughter, rational or not.

"And?" he asked, pulling himself together.

"After a week, Marie went home and called her son. She told him that she and Ruby had two kitchen chairs and a radio. No TV. No food except ice cream. To make matters worse, the washer and dryer didn't work even when they put quarters in." Dani's giggle died. "The only words for that fiasco are elder abuse."

Marc agreed, but who had abused Ruby—Madeline, David, or both?

"Marie's son, Steve, contacted me. I drove to the farm and brought Grandmother to my apartment."

"Thanks. It helps to know the full story."

"You don't know the half of it."

Marc raised his eyebrows. "There's more?"

Dani tilted her head and smiled smugly. "When we get back to the apartment, I'll show you."

"Let's table it until next week. I'm heading to Tahlequah tomorrow, but I'll be back Tuesday. Does that work for you?" He wanted—needed—to see Jessie.

Dani nodded. "I've been sitting on this for a while—a couple more days won't matter."

17

Marc threw a bag in the Jeep and headed south to see Jessie. He burned with curiosity about Duke's progress, but the desire to see his wife consumed him. He had spent the holidays sober and hurting since she left two weeks ago. Christmas break would end on Monday, and the boys had to finish the final semester of their senior year. That gave him three days to mend things with her. The possibility of redemption waged war with the fear of rejection, leaving Marc emotionally spent by the time he reached the Waite home.

A string of vehicles lined the driveway, the whole clan accounted for, except Jessie. Her Suburban was missing. Marc parked and began a slow walk to the house. His mood was as gray as the frosty winter morning. He anticipated a less-than-pleasant encounter with his mother-in-law. Before he could knock, Mama Waite opened the door and planted her hands firmly on her hips, teapot-handle style.

"We've been expecting you. Jessie's in the bedroom." Marc couldn't gauge her feelings, but she didn't throw him out. She stepped aside to let him enter, then hurried back to her kitchen. The aroma of sweet cabbage and homemade rolls filled the house, making his stomach growl. He had grabbed a protein bar and coffee from a convenience store earlier, but the meager fare had worn off hours ago. He hoped Mama Waite would invite him to stay for lunch.

"Marc?" Jessie stepped into the hall.

Jessie's hair tumbled over her shoulders, spilling onto her green plaid shirt. Twenty years of marriage had not dulled the rush of excitement he felt whenever he saw her. Could he reverse the damage he had done?

"I was afraid you weren't here. I didn't see the Suburban."

"The boys went to town to fill up with gas. We're leaving this afternoon."

"May we talk?" Marc fought the impulse to beg.

"I don't think we have much to say." Her sternness scared him.

"Give me a chance to explain.

"I'm done, Marc. I've listened to you explain for years, and nothing has changed."

"This time is different. Please?" Begging crept into his voice.

"Yes, this time *is* different. I'm different. I can't do this anymore."

Marc stuffed his hands in his pockets and stared at the floor. His heart sank to his stomach. She meant it.

"I have gifts for the boys," he said awkwardly. He didn't know this Jessie.

"Wait until we get home. I gave them plenty . . . from both of us. No need to remind them you missed Christmas Day."

"What choice did I have?" Her words hurt, and his defense seemed weak now.

"None. You made that choice long ago."

"Where do we go from here?" he mumbled, dreading the answer.

"The boys and I are going home today so they can finish the semester. I'm filing for divorce the minute we send them off to college this fall."

Jessie turned and retreated to the bedroom, dismissing any further conversation. Marc followed, unwilling to give up. She ignored him as she packed the suitcase stretched across the bed.

"And in the meantime?" he asked, not expecting an answer.

"In the meantime, we will keep pretending we are happily

married for the twins' sake. I have tons of experience in that arena." She held her head high and spoke with unwavering resolve. "We'll start with lunch. The boys have no idea, and we'll keep it that way."

"I can't . . ." Marc started, then stopped.

Nausea replaced the gnawing hunger pangs. The muscles in his chest constricted, creating a vacuum in his lungs despite the damn breathing exercises. Life had smashed him like a bug for the second time in two weeks. Marc's first impulse was to turn and run, to leave the whole blooming mess and drink himself into a stupor, like he did when he left his old law firm years ago, but the stakes had risen exponentially. He must climb out of this hole or lose everything: his wife, the twins, and Devin.

"Have you told your folks?"

"Only that you couldn't make Christmas because of Devin, but make no mistake—my parents, Duke, and Lisi know." With a swift flip of her hair, she tossed him off like a fly.

"The boys and I are heading home within the hour. When can we expect you?" Jessie sounded like she always did: caring, calm, and polite.

"I'd like to stay a few days and work with Duke." They both needed space.

"Suit yourself." Her half-assed smile looked like relief to him. "Right now, let's get this charade behind us. Everyone is waiting."

The Waite clan gathered around the table, bubbling with laughter. Duke teased the twins while Mama Waite served large slices of coconut cream pie to the still-hungry boys. Norman Rockwell would adore this family. Marc felt jealous. A forced smile could not ignite a spark of joy in his heart. Jessie would be leaving soon.

Jessie gathered the twins and packed the car after she helped clear the noon dishes. Her indifference cut more than her cold, angry words. Marc leaned back in the rocker on the porch and watched the taillights of the Suburban leave the drive. The winter sun slipped behind scudding gray clouds, casting a gloom over the valley that matched his mood.

His craving for whiskey, ever present, became unbearable. One drink would clear his mind. One drink wouldn't hurt. Duke kept a bottle in the pantry, so Marc made his way to the kitchen, fingers crossed he'd find the prize. He plucked a bourbon decanter from the third shelf and turned to see Duke at the pantry door.

"Let me fix one for you." Duke lifted the bottle from Marc's hand and moved to the kitchen island. The clink of ice cubes hitting the bottom of the tumbler elicited a smile as Marc licked his lips in anticipation.

"I'll take mine on the rocks."

Duke shrugged. "That's a potent order."

"It's been a rough go all around. A drink will take the edge off."

Duke handed him the dark-amber drink. "Enjoy. It will end all your problems."

"I wish," Marc said. Duke's comment didn't sound like a joke. "If a drink could cure all my troubles, I wouldn't have a care in the world."

"This drink is strong enough to sterilize the ground you walk on. It will kill your marriage, send Devin to prison, and destroy what little self-respect you have."

Marc stared at his glass as he swirled the liquor—a whirlpool of ice tinkled against the sides like a wind chime in a gentle breeze.

"Jessie told you everything?" Marc asked.

"She didn't have to. I have eyes."

Marc shook as he set the drink on the table and cupped his head in his hands.

"Son, if I asked you to name all the things you love, how long would it take to name yourself?" Duke asked.

Marc hated the man he had become, one who had failed so many times and hid in the dark recesses of drunkenness. He grabbed the glass and threw it to the floor. The glass shattered, sending sparkling shards racing across the floor. Duke had cut to the core, and he hated him, too.

He felt Duke's gaze follow his every move, recording his trembling hands and pathetic brokenness. Tears welled in Marc's eyes, the final admission of failure. He had reached the bottom, and it felt amazingly comfortable—no more struggling to be more than he was, a broken-down loser.

"Love yourself enough to let us help you," Duke said, surprisingly sympathetic.

Marc nodded. He needed help. Tears streamed down his face, and he didn't try to stop them. When he raised his head, Duke was gone. The oppressive weight of emptiness surrounded him like a shroud. He sought refuge in the den and fell into an overstuffed recliner, where he huddled until the peaceful blanket of sleep overcame him.

"Let's go." Duke shook Marc's shoulder firmly.

Marc bolted upright, startled and disoriented by the surroundings. The older man stood above the recliner, looking down at him. He must have fallen asleep in the chair, and every muscle in his body confirmed his conclusion. His mouth felt like cotton, and his joints ached from the unwelcoming, makeshift bed. Exhausted, he fought to find the energy to move.

Duke shook him hard once again. "Rise and shine, boy. We've got work to do."

Duke had no intention of letting him off the hook. Any resentment Marc felt would have to wait. He stumbled to the shower and tried to scrub away the memory of yesterday.

The comforting smell of coffee and frying bacon filled the kitchen like a warm cloud, and his appreciation for Duke tingled in his chest. Could this older gentleman heal his body and soul?

"I apologize for last night, but the thought of losing Jessie drives me crazy. You said I needed to ask for help, so I'm asking. Please help me keep my marriage together."

"I'll help you mend your wounds, but you must win Jessie back on your own."

Marc drew back and looked at him. "What wounds?"

"As I said, my eyes can see. Learn to wash your hair in the blood of your enemies," Duke admonished.

"That's crazy. I have no enemies," Marc spat, but he knew that his enemies disguised themselves as friends, and he didn't challenge them.

"I can't help someone in denial."

Marc sat silently, doubting his courage to face the reality Duke demanded. Hell, he couldn't beat his craving for alcohol.

Duke grew impatient. "I'll be in the barn milking."

"Wait. Give me a chance," Marc implored, a feeling welling within him that solidified his commitment to fight for Jessie and Devin. "I can do this."

A broad grin spread across Duke's face. "Good. Anyway, I've already milked Buttercup, Kemosabe. Let's hit the road to Tahlequah."

18

The miles rolled by too fast for Marc. He had so many questions for Duke.

"Are we going to see the sheriff at Tahlequah? Does he have any more information? Will Jimmy talk to us?" Marc rattled.

"Yes, yes, and yes," Duke answered between chuckles. "The sheriff is slow-walking Jimmy's case to give us time to do a little research."

"Why would he do that?"

"The tribe protects its own. They are very law abiding, but honestly, don't trust palefaces. They want all the facts before bringing a case to trial."

"Can't say I blame them. Devin was railroaded into a false confession."

"Jessie talked a lot about Devin and mentioned several strange things."

"Like?"

"JP, your sheriff friend, brought Devin in for questioning on the same day Jimmy turned himself in. Wolves circling for the kill."

Marc had forgotten that connection. He had plowed all his energy into Devin's plight and lost this thread between the two incidents.

"Go on."

"Don't you find it odd that your friend Hank arranged an attorney for your son and picked the one who set you up at Smith & Noble?"

"That thought crossed my mind, but how did you know?" Marc asked.

Duke placed a hand on Marc's shoulder. "Jessie told me. Regardless of the state of your marriage, she still cares about Devin . . . and you."

"Okay, but what makes you think Mike Halley set me up?"

"Your wife gets credit for that. She's felt that way for years."

Marc thought he had buried the nightmare from Smith & Noble, but Jessie's take on it brought it to the surface. Was it his wife's loyalty, or did she sense something? Either way, his spirits rose with the thought she believed in him.

"Is that all?"

"No, Devin is blocking you for a reason—to protect someone, as Jimmy is doing. I am unsure if they are protecting the same person, but both act like human shields for a purpose."

Marc's head spun with all the twisted possibilities. He had lived in the pocket of petty local politics for twenty years, and now these small-town bullying tactics had morphed into threats of sizable proportions somewhere along the line.

"You say Jimmy is protecting a woman. I'm not ready to rule out his mother. Are you?"

"I haven't ruled out anyone yet."

"Fair enough. So it could be Jimmy's mother, his girlfriend, or . . ." Marc paused, but Duke's "blood" comment pushed him on. "Or David's daughter, Dani Caldwell."

"We have permission to talk to Jimmy if he agrees. I'm not sure he will."

"If he does by some wild chance, we must weave these names into the conversation and judge his reaction," Marc said with zeal.

Duke nodded and smiled. "Might work."

The junior officer they had met last time staffed the reception area of the police station. Marc and Duke announced their business and waited to begin the entrance ritual, provided Jimmy agreed to the meeting. The young man disappeared for a moment, then returned, signaling approval. He led them to a small room at the end of the hall, where they waited. The white walls, fluorescent lighting, and simple furniture evoked the coldness of a doctor's office, sterile and uninviting.

Jimmy's orange jumpsuit stood out against the white walls. His buzzed haircut, colorless complexion, and gaunt frame gave him the classic look of a prisoner. He avoided eye contact with Marc but made a connection with Duke. Marc understood the primal bond between the two and kept his distance, but he couldn't quiet his electrified senses. He stood ready to glean every crumb of evidence Jimmy might drop.

Duke eased into the chair beside Jimmy and leaned back, giving him space.

"Treating you okay, boy?" Duke asked.

"No complaints." Jimmy's eyes, black with indifference, held Duke's gaze.

"Your mother's concerned. I promised her a full report, so be truthful with me."

Jimmy didn't waver. "Tell her I'm fine."

"Do you have a good attorney?"

"Yeah." Jimmy's terse reply signaled he had no interest.in the exchange.

Duke's patience wore thin. "Jimmy, let me be blunt. Marc and I think you are innocent. Devin pled guilty to accomplice after the fact, and we think that's a bunch of hooey too. I don't know why you won't help yourself, but I'd certainly appreciate it if you could help him."

Jimmy winced. "Devin and I walk separate ways. He speaks his truth, and I speak mine. I can't help him." He bit his tongue to trap unspoken words.

"That's a coward's answer. You two are bound together and walk the same path." Duke's dark eyes hardened, but Jimmy refused to engage.

"Your words, old man. Not mine. Now leave me alone."

"Impossible, my friend. You don't own the truth."

"Dani believes in your innocence as well," Marc interjected.

A flicker of recognition flashed then faded as Jimmy leaned forward and placed his elbows on his knees. "I don't know anyone by that name."

By Marc's calculations, ball four crossed the plate. None of their inquiries scored.

"Do you have anyone you wish for us to contact on your behalf?" Duke fished for the name of anyone of interest.

"Nope," Jimmy muttered.

"Time's up." The jailer motioned for Marc and Duke to leave.

The two men walked in silence to the parking lot.

"That scored a big fat zero," Marc said as he started the Jeep. "But Jimmy is struggling with Devin's situation, and I'm sure he's crossed paths with Dani. This bears watching. I'll take it up with her when I get back."

Duke crossed his arms and leaned back in the passenger seat with a big smile on his face.

"What are you grinning about?" Marc asked.

"You're learning, son."

"If you say so," Marc said with a grin that matched Duke's.

"Go home tomorrow. Work on your family problems and this business with Dani. Did you check out Jimmy's girlfriend?"

"Damn," Marc muttered. He had forgotten all about that. "I'll get on it first thing when I get back. This time I won't screw up."

"I believe in you, Kemosabe. I'll revisit Jimmy alone. He seemed nervous with you in the room."

Marc left for Tulsa at daybreak, optimistic for the first time in days. His first stop in T-Town was the Madison Youth Center. He met with the staff to sift for information on Jimmy's personal life in the big town of Tulsa, but they had little to offer. Yes, he had a girlfriend. No, they hadn't met her. He gathered his notebook and headed toward the door.

"Mr. Whitcomb, wait a minute." A young woman with blonde hair and a fresh, youthful face flagged him down as she raced across the parking lot. "I remember something," she said, panting from the sprint. "But first, I want you to know how sorry I am about Devin. There's no way he had anything to do with a murder. If you see him, tell him what I said."

"What's on your mind?"

"Devin told me Jimmy's girlfriend was Amber Browning. I hope that helps."

"More than you can imagine," he mused. Marc learned that Devin knew her. He and Jimmy could be protecting the same person. Now, he needed to find this Amber Browning.

The phone book contained a dozen Amber Brownings, so he began the process of elimination. Seven were married, and two were no-answers, leaving three on the list. A quick drive-by in an elite neighborhood reduced the list to two. One resided at an apartment complex near Jimmy's home, so he stopped by the office. A sizable middle-aged lady with tattoos and blue hair peeked over her computer.

"Can I help you?" she said, sighing, clearly put out by the interruption. "All of our apartments are rented. Best I can do is add you to our waiting list."

"No, I'm looking for Amber Browning. Is she a tenant of yours?"

"Used to be. She moved out a couple of months ago." The woman glanced down at her desk, bored with the topic.

"Did Amber leave a forwarding address?"

"Can't give it to you. Privacy, you know." She popped her gum and went back to work.

The direct approach failed so he switched tactics. "I'm impressed you can remember an ex-tenant when people always come and go."

"That's easy. We're friends, both being single mothers and all." She preened at the compliment, which encouraged Marc to push harder.

"Single mother and a job—not easy for either of you." Marc's voice sounded so sincere that it startled him.

"We helped each other out. Since she lived across the hall, I took care of her kids at night, and she watched mine during the day. We made do."

"Did she work the night shift here?"

"Hell no," she snorted. "There are only four apartments, and I live in one. If there's a problem, tenants knock on my door twenty-four-seven. Most of 'em work for my boss anyways, like she did."

"And where is that?"

"The gentlemen's club down the street." She leaned back and crossed her arms. "If I were young and skinny, I'd work there too. Easier than this." She let out a belly laugh that shook everything around her. "I do all the work—keep the books and hire the dancers—while my boss rakes in the money. Does that seem fair to you, mister?"

Marc began to doubt this lead held promise. He couldn't imagine Jimmy paired up with a stripper and her kids, but he wasn't ready to turn off the spigot of information flowing from the blue-haired woman.

"She had the face and figure for it, but danced like a pelican. You shoulda seen her. The men liked her well enough, but she was a little loopy, if you know what I mean."

"I'm sorry. I guess I don't know what you mean."

"She acted like a child, wide-eyed and clingy with anyone she met, always trying to please. Folks took advantage of her. It didn't matter to her what they wanted as long as she was the center of attention."

Marc snapped to full alert. Jimmy's mother had described Amber in the same manner. This was the girl he was looking for.

"Listen, I need to talk to her." Marc's temples pounded with excitement as he landed his first real lead. Duke's instincts pointed to a woman, and he would produce her. Maybe.

The blue-haired manager popped her gum twice, ruminating before she answered. "Leave me your number. We'll see what happens." She rose from her desk and sauntered off. She was done with him.

Marc shrugged off his disappointment. He still had one more stop to make before he called it a day—dropping off the carpet samples at a private lab.

The lab work would cost a pretty penny, but he needed a professional opinion. Someone had stuffed the pieces into the washer, and the forensic team had overlooked them. Was it an oversight or intentional? He would find answers tomorrow, but tonight he would head home to Jessie and the twins to savor every minute remaining on a ticking clock.

19

An empty house greeted Marc. His heart sank like a rock as he rambled through the dark rooms and down the hall to his office. Jessie had taped a note on his computer. "Don't forget the boys are playing this evening at eight. Try not to be late."

What a relief. She and the kids were at the game.

Marc raced to the gym and nudged his way through the crowded foyer. Johnny, Hank, and JP huddled in the corner in their usual cliquish manner. He had once been a part of the inner circle, dissecting the lives of their neighbors, flexing power to move people around like pawns on a chessboard in the tiny kingdom of Brule. Thoughts from the past sent shivers down his spine as he pushed his way through the crowd toward the stands.

The hollow sound of basketballs thudding against the wooden court echoed through the gym as the boys warmed up for the game. He slipped onto the bleachers beside his wife. For the moment, the distance between him and Jessie disappeared. Tonight, they were a family.

"You're late," Jessie chastised him, but a faint smile lifted the corners of her lips.

"You know me. I almost forgot." Marc beamed at his wife,

enjoying her company, even if temporarily. "Thanks for the reminder."

"Junior and senior parents are meeting in the cafeteria after the game to make prom plans. Do you have time to join us?"

Marc nodded an affirmative. His answer must have pleased her. She began clapping and cheering for the twins with a vibrance he hadn't seen in months. He hated for the moment to end.

After the final buzzer, Marc found himself lost in a sea of prom moms, enduring endless conversations about "A Night in Paris" décor and snack trays ad nauseam. But he had to be there for both their sakes. Nevertheless, he heaved a sigh of relief when the last cheese tray had been assigned, and they could go home.

"We need to take the tree down," Jessie said after the boys had gone to bed. "Or leave it up until next year. What do you think?" she asked playfully. Her elevated mood encouraged him.

"I don't give a flitter what we do with the tree. I prefer to take you down."

Jessie sidestepped his embrace. "Nothing has changed, Marc. I'm leaving when the twins head to college." With her head back and chin tilted, she stared at him with icy eyes. "Let's make the best of it."

"Sure," Marc answered. "No problem." Jessie had years of practice pretending she loved him, but he was new at this. He headed to bed in Devin's old room, disappointed but not defeated.

Thoughts of Jessie stole Marc's sleep. In the wee hours of the morning, he surrendered to insomnia and climbed out of bed. He might as well get on the road to Tulsa to meet with Dani. Marc had lost a few pounds, making the stairs to her apartment easier to navigate. The spare tire he had carried deflated, leaving a well-contoured abdomen younger men would envy.

"Ready?" Dani chirped, anxious to reveal her secrets. "Grandmother's napping, so we have a little time, and we must be quiet."

"Almost. First, I have a couple of questions."

"Shoot."

"Do you know Jimmy Don Allen?"

"I've never met him, but I know of him. He's the one who killed my dad."

"But you never met him?"

"No. Why do you ask?"

"I went to see Jimmy in Tahlequah, and when I mentioned your name, I would have sworn he reacted as if he knew you."

"Fat chance. I wasn't allowed to go to my dad's house. I was persona non grata thanks to my stepmother, Madeline," she said with contempt.

Her answer puzzled him. "What does that have to do with Jimmy?"

Dani looked at him sideways. "He dated my stepsister, Amber, according to Grandmother. I thought you knew."

"Amber? Amber Browning is your stepsister?" A thousand possibilities flitted through his mind. "I knew Madeline had a daughter, but I didn't connect the last name, and I never would have guessed she was involved with Jimmy."

"Oh yes, Crazy Amber. That's what we called her." Dani giggled. "She's the real loony toon."

"Who's we?"

"Dev . . ." Dani sucked her words back. "Different ones . . . me, Dad. I don't know. Lots of people," she said with a shrug. Marc noted the sloppy save. *Was she about to say Devin?*

"Crazy enough to murder your dad?" Marc hoped he had found Jimmy's accomplice.

"Maybe . . . I don't think so," Dani answered in a deliberate, measured tone. "But she's crazy, so who knows?"

"What kind of crazy is she?" Marc asked impatiently. He had to know what Jimmy saw in this girl.

"Most of what I know about her comes from Grandmother. Like I said, after Dad married Madeline, I was not welcome. Period."

"How old was Amber when your dad married her mother?" Marc asked, his voice rising.

Dani placed a finger across her lips. "Shhhh. Let me check on Grandmother before we dive deeper into this. She gets mad when I talk about Amber. I don't like her, but Grandmother defends her because Dad did."

Dani tiptoed down the hall, peeked into Ruby's room, then crept back to the kitchen.

"Want a drink?" she asked, leaning through the doorway.

"Water, please."

Dani appeared with drinks and a platter of fig newtons and powdered donuts.

"Are you ready for the whole enchilada? 'Cause the only sugar-coating you'll get today is right there," Dani joked, glancing at the tray of snacks. "I've never shared Amber's goofiness with anyone. Never had a reason, but this is important."

Sitting cross-legged in the leather recliner, Dani took a big sip of red wine.

"Back to your question. Amber was ten, maybe eleven, when Dad and Madeline married. Skinny . . . my gosh, that kid was skinny. Her hair was matted. She looked like an orphan. I didn't fault Madeline. The girl was old enough to groom herself, but she wouldn't. She wanted her 'mama' to do everything for her." Dani paused, tracing her finger around the rim of her wine glass.

"Did Mama step in and help her?" Marc wanted to establish the dynamics between Amber and her mother.

"Not often. Seems to me that people are disposable to Madeline . . . unless she wants something. She executed her motherly duties when she wanted to make a good impression."

"That's half true," Ruby said from the shadows in the hall. "Amber has disinhibited social something or other, and Madeline is just plain mean."

Marc and Dani snapped around to face an angry woman wrapped in a bathrobe.

"I didn't mean anything by—"

"Hush. You don't know what you're talking about!" Ruby shouted. "That little girl told me about Madeline's plan to take my farm. That's more than you ever did for me." Ruby locked her eyes on Dani.

"Dad, not Madeline, stole your farm. I've told you that over and over," Dani said firmly.

"Out of my house!" Ruby screamed, pointing to the door. "I said, get out!" Ruby picked up a porcelain figurine from the coffee table and hurled it at Dani. The tiny ballerina hit the floor, breaking into a thousand pieces. "Look what you made me do!" she screamed, tears threatening to fall from her eyes.

Dani kneeled and began picking up the pieces. "I'll get you another one," she said, without glancing up.

"You can't. Momma gave it to me!" Ruby wailed.

"How about some ice cream? I bought your favorite today," Dani said gently.

"Rocky Road?" Ruby smiled. Dani had flipped the switch.

"Yes, and it's time to take our medicine. Come with me. I'll get your pills for you." Dani's demeanor was smooth and calm, as if Ruby's outburst had never happened.

Marc sank back onto the sofa, unsure whether to leave or wait for Dani to return. Ruby had a wild burst of rage at the funeral, which he had attributed to grief. But this outburst proved otherwise. He must arrange for Dani to be appointed friend of the court, allowing her to act on Ruby's behalf.

Marc checked his watch and called Jessie to let her know he would be home as soon as he wrapped up his conversation with Dani.

"Whew." Dani entered the room. "Another battle on the books."

"Is she like this often?" Marc asked.

"It comes and goes. Grandmother puts her best foot forward for strangers, so today surprised me. But the topic of Amber and Madeline can trigger her without warning."

"I'm not sure she's up to us going after Madeline in court."

"We've got no choice. I can't care for her much longer, and Madeline has all her money."

"Half of her money. Fifty percent belongs to you. That should be enough to take care of Ruby for a good while."

"No," Dani said, gritting her teeth. "I want everything that bitch and my dad took. The farm belongs to my grandmother . . . all of it."

Dani's tall order exceeded the money needed for Ruby's care. Her hatred demanded complete restitution. Marc grew weary of the merry-go-round of Ruby's troubles.

"Let me see if I understand this scenario clearly. Ruby moved in with David and Madeline. Madeline and Ruby fell out of sorts, and David took Ruby to the farm to live alone. Ruby's sister Marie joined her, and Marie told her son, who told you, that Ruby was living in the empty farmhouse, and you went to get her."

"Not bad for an amateur," Dani said, laughing.

"And your dad took a blank deed to the farm and assigned it to himself. After his death, the farm should pass to Madeline and you since he died intestate, leaving Ruby out in the cold. Your answer to the problem is to nullify the original transfer, right?"

"Right."

"Did I leave anything out?"

"No."

"Looks like you're fighting Madeline with a flimsy sword. As far as I can tell, besides being a bad daughter-in-law, Madeline appears to be an innocent bystander." Marc's confidence in the case nosedived.

"Let me finish. After Grandmother lived with me for a couple of weeks, she threw a fit to have her own place. She had plenty of money for her own place, so I helped her apply to an assisted living center. Everything looked peachy until the facility tried to verify funds." Dani paused, flashing a smug grin. *She had another shoe to drop.*

"Grandmother had no money or CDs in the bank. Zero. My darling dad controlled her bank account and paid her bills. He stole the rest of the money, sucking her account dry."

"Did your grandmother confront him?" Marc tried to sound interested, but David was still the villain.

"I did. I phoned Dad, and we had a shouting match. I called him a thief, and he called me a liar. When I hung up on him, he dialed

Grandmother, wanting to take her to lunch. That was his answer to everything. Get her alone and sweet-talk her."

"Did she go?"

"Yep. Dad schmoozed her and said he had moved her money for safekeeping. Blah, blah, blah. And she believed him." Dani's words boiled with anger.

"Misconduct points to David. Unless you have more, I've heard nothing that implicates your stepmother." Marc shifted uncomfortably and reached for his glass. He hated to tell a client they didn't have a case, but at this juncture, Ruby had little to stand on.

"Would it make a difference if I told you Madeline used the funds from my grandmother's CDs to buy her house? She signed all the checks for the purchase."

"Maybe."

"I had hoped for a better reaction. You're another Mike Halley."

"Mike Halley?" Marc exploded. She hadn't mentioned this before. "What did he say?"

"I went to him before I hired you. He told me my allegations were absurd. The minute he said he knew Madeline, I stopped talking. She can twist her stories tighter than a pretzel."

Marc grew quiet. Mike Halley had put a roadblock in front of Dani. He relished a chance to best his former partner.

"We need more. Do you have your proxy attorney lined up? It's time to file and start discovery. It won't be easy, and Ruby might not hold up as a witness, but we'll give it our best shot."

Dani jumped out of her chair and threw her arms around his neck. "Thank you. Thank you. Thank you," she cried through tears and hugs. "I told you I needed help." She cocked her head, leaned toward Marc, and whispered. "I'm sure whoever killed him had my grandmother targeted too."

"That's a big leap. What makes you think that?"

"A young cop involved in the investigation told me. He said the sheriff had expected to find two bodies since Grandmother's car was in the garage. No one knew I had taken her to my apartment."

"Your dad and Madeline didn't know?" Marc quizzed.

"I don't think so. Dad didn't know until I called him, and he took Grandmother to lunch. That was the day of his murder—Friday. He told Grandmother he would deal with Madeline on Monday, and she would move back in with them. In the meantime, he was going to the farm."

Marc's brow furrowed with concern. "Was your dad the intended victim, or a mistake?"

"Your guess is as good as mine."

"I'll stop by and visit with the young cop you mentioned. In the meantime, keep your doors locked. I don't like the direction of this story."

"Good luck finding him. JP, your sheriff friend, fired him. Convenient, huh?"

"Fix the lock so Ruby can't open it." Marc grabbed his hat and coat. Ruby, as a potential target, changed everything. Add a dash of Mike Halley, and the fight was on.

20

Ruby presented a considerable challenge. Her state of mind and moods twirled like a whirligig. A discovery petition would produce bank records, but would that be enough? They would also need the records for the purchase of David and Madeline's new home, new pickup, insurance payments on the house and farm, and property tax payments. The paper should provide a money trail, the only sword in this battle.

Marc called Dani to get her input on any additional sources of evidence. When it came to Ruby's business, she had the instincts of a bloodhound.

"Good morning," he said when she answered the phone. He did not wait for her to reply. "I am sending you some preliminary discovery questions your attorney will need. Read them carefully and add anything I might have overlooked."

Dani laughed and said, "Good morning to you too. I'll watch for it and get right back to you."

"Perfect." Marc didn't want to take Dani off track, but his curiosity got the better of him. "I'm going to switch topics for a minute. You don't have to answer my next question. You might find it too personal, but . . ."

"What's the question?"

"Why was your father's funeral delayed ten days?"

After a short pause, Dani answered, "Madeline refused to pay the funeral home for their services, and Grandmother and I didn't have the money."

"You've got to be kidding," Marc said and gasped. Madeline's lifestyle suggested she had tons of money, and when she discovered the body at the farmhouse, JP said she wailed like a banshee. But the image of the coolheaded woman Marc observed that morning in the backyard belied her grief. Which persona represented the real Madeline Caldwell?

"What's more, I had to beg her to release the body. Madeline finally agreed but made sure I understood she wouldn't spend one thin dime to bury him." Dani's voice trembled as she struggled to speak. Love and hate for her dad intertwined. He never knew which side of the spectrum would appear. Today, love trumped.

"Then how . . ." Marc stopped, hesitant to dig deeper.

"How did we pay for his funeral? Grandmother's sister, Marie, paid for it. And in case you missed it, Madeline didn't attend. Funny what grief will do to you." Dani's sarcasm was not lost on him. He had no answer except an awkward silence.

"Dad didn't deserve to be executed and set on fire like garbage." Dani burst into uncontrollable sobs. "And I bet she's never shed a tear, except when she put on that big act for the cops. She's destroyed Grandmother's life, my life, and . . ." Dani faded into quiet, weepy moans. "She's sitting pretty in her big house while Grandmother is a beggar. We both are."

She began to giggle hysterically, her emotions hanging by a thread. "I hope you remember that when you send our bill."

Marc wanted to reassure her that everything would turn out all right, but he lacked confidence in the outcome.

"Do you think Madeline had anything to do with this?" he probed.

"I don't know. Maybe. I think Madeline would shy away from

something as messy as a murder. Who would know with Miss Perfection?"

"Watch for the discovery questions, and we'll talk later," Marc muttered, ready to end the conversation.

Marc turned his attention to Amber. His guts told him she was the epicenter of the earthquake. The apartment manager had mentioned the gentlemen's club, so he would start there. He parked on the far side of the lot behind a row of squatty cinderblock buildings and waited. The club opened at 7:00 p.m., so he expected employees to arrive around 6:00. His bravado began to wane as the sun receded behind the skyline, dropping a heavy cloak of darkness. The seedy neighborhood, with ratty trash containers and broken streetlights, gave Marc the willies. Finally, two young girls, approximately twenty-two or twenty-three years old, crossed the lot. He jumped from the Jeep and stepped in front of them on impulse. They split in opposite directions and ran toward the back door, screaming.

"Wait!" he called. "I just want to talk." *Stupid, Stupid. Stupid*, Marc thought. *They think I'm a molester.*

"Pay at the door like everyone else!" the girl with pink and green hair shouted back.

Marc threw his hands in the air and shrugged, retreating to his Jeep. He made a lousy detective but couldn't involve the police in his wild-assed hunch. *Take it easy*, he cautioned himself as he rolled down the window. Ten minutes passed before a strapping young man strolled in front of his car.

"Sir, I'm looking for Amber Browning. Is she working tonight?"

"She's not here, and I don't arrange private appointments." He kept walking.

"Do you know her?" Marc asked.

"Look, buddy, find another Boy Scout. I tend to bar. I don't answer customer questions, and I don't help little old ladies across the street." He opened the back door and disappeared.

Strike two. Marc had better places to waste time. He rolled up the window and started the Jeep. A loud slap against the passenger door broke the eerie silence of the darkness. A slender blonde-haired woman in black leggings and an oversized hoodie plopped into the passenger seat.

"I'm Amber," she said. "You looking for me?" She squinted as she studied Marc's face. "Do I know you?"

Marc couldn't believe this girl had climbed into a car with a strange man and struck up a conversation. Dani, Ruby, and Jimmy's mother all mentioned her unusual behavior, but for the first time, he understood how uninhibited she was.

"No, we haven't met, but I wanted to visit with you about my friends Jimmy . . . and Devin.

"Okay. Makes sense. I'm Jimmy's girlfriend."

"So I've heard, and he needs your help. You know the trouble he's in, but he won't talk."

"Sorry, mister. Mother told me not to speak to anyone about that."

"But you do want to help Jimmy, right? Would your mother talk to me? I believe Jimmy is innocent, and Devin is no killer."

"Too bad about Devin," she said angelically. "But Momma won't talk to you either. And I'm to keep my mouth shut."

"Do you think your mother had anything to do with your stepdad's murder?" The bold question was a long shot, but he feared he wouldn't have a second chance to ask.

The question amused Amber. "Are you kidding? Mom would never get her hands dirty."

"She's not opposed to murder, only dirty hands?" Marc fought to keep the sarcasm out of his voice.

"Mom's a nurse. She would use a needle if she wanted to kill someone, and no one would ever know." Amber flipped her hair and smiled as if that settled the matter.

"You've talked about this with your mother?"

"Maybe . . . a little."

Marc pushed harder. "Did she have your stepdad in mind?"

Amber began to fidget and twist a stray lock of hair around her fingers.

"Look. I'm not supposed to be here—Mom's orders . . ." Another smile dimpled her cheeks. This girl's dazzling greenish-blue eyes shone with the innocence of a cherub.

Amber reached across the seat, took his hand, and gently squeezed. "Could you give me a ride home?" With startling ease, she spliced a conversation about murder with a simple request for a lift.

"I like you. I think we could be friends," she said.

Marc squirmed. This encounter made him uncomfortable.

"Don't you have a car?"

"I walked, but it's a long way. Besides, it's dark."

"Okay," Marc said with hesitation. "Where do you live?"

"Oh, I can't go home. Mom told me not to come around until things settle down. I'm staying at a friend's house. Turn left on Denver, and I'll tell you how to get there."

Amber's instructions led to a familiar neighborhood—his son's.

"There it is." Amber pointed at Devin's duplex.

"You live here?" Marc blurted.

"It's temporary. Devin said it was okay."

"You've talked to Devin?" Marc asked. The situation grew more bizarre by the minute.

"Mom talked to his lawyer, and Mr. Halley said it was okay with Devin."

Sanity flew out the window like a spooked quail. He struggled to digest the convoluted string that tied Devin to this case.

"Quick question. Jimmy said you have two children. Are they here?" That was a lie, and the question was insane, but he wanted to know.

"My kids are with my ex's folks," Amber said as she hopped out of the Jeep and tossed a wave. "Thanks for the ride."

Marc watched her slender frame as she walked up the sidewalk and disappeared through the front door.

Wow, Marc thought, *I'm in* The Twilight Zone.

He picked up his phone to call Jessie, praying she would answer. His anxiety reached panic level, and he needed her to talk him down.

"The person you are trying to reach is unavailable. Please leave a message after the tone." *Damn it.*

He tossed the phone at the passenger door and watched it slide over the edge of the seat. He began counting from one to five, repeatedly trying to calm himself.

21

Marc slammed the Jeep into park and bounded up the driveway to find Jessie sitting on the couch, flipping channels on the TV with the remote.

He couldn't take much more this evening. "Why didn't you answer your phone?"

"Because I left it in my car. Why? What difference does it make?" Jessie was in no mood to take his nonsense tonight. "Calm down."

"No difference, I guess." Marc let it go. He sensed this was not the time to squabble. "You've got to hear this," Marc said, huffing to catch his breath.

"Me first," Jessie said with an odd smile. "I've got news about Devin. He refused to sign the plea, fired Mike Halley, and is ready to talk . . . to you."

Hot tears stung Marc's eyes. He collapsed on the sofa, limp with the release of pent-up emotions.

"How? Why?" Marc asked, not caring about the answers.

"I've tried to see Devin every day since I came home, but he turned me away until today. He wouldn't talk at first, but he listened."

"What did you say to change his mind?"

"I'm not sure I'm the one who changed his mind, but I happened to be the one there when he did. Devin's shaken up but not stupid."

"What did you tell him?" Marc snapped, frustrated with Jessie's slow delivery.

"That there had to be a reason Hank stepped in and hired Mike Halley to represent him."

"You told him that?" Marc threw his hands in the air. "What in the hell were you getting at?"

"Shut up, Marc. Shut up if you want me to finish." Jessie turned her back to him. "All this business about Devin taking a plea and not talking to you started with Halley. There had to be a motive, and the only one I could think of went back to your tenure at Smith & Noble."

"What about Smith & Noble?" Marc cringed at the very thought of the trial that almost ruined him.

"I told Devin the truth about you and Halley."

Jessie had exposed his failure to the person he loved the most—his son. He slumped deeper into the sofa, numb with the thought.

"Come on, Marc. You've tormented yourself for over twenty years because you failed to present a piece of evidence to clear the man."

Marc struggled to speak. "Please, not today."

"Yes, today. I know you. You have a photographic memory. You would have remembered if you had seen that evidence during the first trial."

"I would now, but I was young then. Maybe I put it in my drawer and forgot about it."

"And maybe you didn't. Maybe they were planted after the man was convicted. When did you find the missing documents?"

"After the man had been sentenced to death."

"Exactly. It takes years to carry out an execution. You found them before the appeal. Wasn't this information presented then?"

Marc leaned forward, bent by the weight of a memory he wished to forget.

"I gave it to Halley, told him I had overlooked those papers and that we could use them." Marc never intended to share the step-by-step destruction of his life, and it hurt.

"Did he use them?"

"No."

"Why not?" Jessie asked, picking at the scab until it bled.

"Because they disappeared!" Marc screamed at the top of his lungs. "They disappeared, all right? He said I never gave them to him."

"And they couldn't be reproduced. How convenient for our Mr. Halley. A dependable witness gives a sworn testimony on their deathbed that would have cleared your client, and the papers went missing."

"It's not that simple." Marc shook his head.

"Who benefited, Marc? Halley?"

"Yes, Halley played his cards to benefit a friend."

"Who did Halley protect?" Jessie asked.

"The man they executed was Hank's cousin, leaving him the sole beneficiary of their granddad's estate."

Marc locked eyes with Jessie. "My real sin is that when I knew Halley wanted our client to take the rap, I couldn't . . . didn't stop him. I could've turned the magnificent Mr. Halley into the bar, court, or . . ." Marc's hands began to tremble as the color drained from his face.

Jessie sat beside Marc and put her arms around his shoulders. With a gentle rocking motion, she soothed him until the trembling stopped. "Why did you let Halley get away with it?"

"The truth is, I was a coward. I had been with the firm for six years and wanted to make partner, and my whole career hinged on Halley's recommendation. It was easy to rationalize. Maybe I overlooked the confession. Maybe I didn't understand Halley's strategy. I fell all over myself trying to find reasons to be wrong. But I knew deep down I should have had the courage to take Halley on."

Jessie pushed Marc away. *She hates me*, he thought with little emotion, and he couldn't blame her.

Marc put his elbows on his knees and drew himself upright. "I'm still a coward. I should have told Devin the truth long ago, but you had to do it. Now, the man I shielded has his hands around Devin's throat. If something happens to my son, the fault lies with me."

Jessie grabbed Marc and shook him hard. "Stop it. Halley told Devin that your incompetence caused an innocent man to die, so Devin did as he was asked to protect you—no more hiding. No more taking all the blame. Halley orchestrated the man's death, and you were a low-ranking pawn."

Marc lifted his head and straightened his shoulders. "You're right." A weary smile lifted the corners of his mouth. "I won't let him trap me twice."

Jessie smiled and nodded. "Now, what did you have to share with me?"

Marc related the story of the strange encounter with Amber. Jessie sat quietly next to him, absorbing every detail.

"I'll see Amber tomorrow and make no secret about Devin. If she knows I'm his mother, she might open up."

"Thanks," he said, taking her hand. This time she did not pull away. "It sounds like I need to get to the jail and help Devin out of this mess."

22

"Come on, son. Let's get out of here." Marc touched Devin's shoulder and nudged him toward the exit. The battleship-gray walls and dingy tile floors were too prisonlike for his taste. He posted the required $100,000 bond Devin had refused earlier and made tracks out of the courthouse as quickly as possible, his son in tow.

Marc resisted the urge to criticize his son for the pain he'd caused the family. The guilt of Marc's own hurtful actions over the past twenty years dwarfed Devin's wrongdoing. *Like father, like son.*

"You'll stay with your mother and me until this is settled."

Devin nodded and resumed staring out the window at the barren trees and brown fields along the highway. Miles passed before he spoke.

"I'm sorry, Dad."

"How—" Marc bit his tongue. He wanted to say, "How stupid could you be?" Or, "Do you know how hard it will be to reverse your willingness to plead guilty?" But lashing out at his son seemed cruel. "I know," he answered.

Jessie met them at the door and lavished hugs and kisses on her prodigal son.

"Get in here, you two. Dinner's ready, and I made your favorites." She bustled about the kitchen like a mother hen. The table, full of family and food, felt like a holiday celebration. Jessie saw to that and wouldn't allow the seriousness of the situation to spoil Devin's reunion, especially with the twins. The time to size up their battle would be after she cleared the dishes.

"You boys need to get after your homework, and don't forget to shower. I put clean sheets on your beds today." Sergeant Jessie dismissed the twins and turned to her husband and son. "Our turn. Let's get down to business."

Jessie's command of her domain comforted Marc. He understood her need to organize and control things that frightened her. She would beat her fears into submission and store them away.

"Devin, tell us what happened on the night of Mr. Caldwell's murder, and don't you dare leave the tiniest detail out."

"Yes, sir." Devin saluted Jessie and chuckled.

"Jimmy and I did go to the Caldwell farm early on September 18, but Mr. Caldwell wasn't there. No one was home. Amber asked Jimmy to drive to the farm and get a kitchen table she had stored in the barn. I went with him to help load."

"What time was that?" Marc asked.

"Early. Maybe 6:30 a.m. or so."

Marc placed a mental checkmark beside two items. The time matched Hank's story, and Dani had told him David had headed to the farm after lunch with Ruby.

"Why so early? That's a two-hour drive from Tulsa."

"I had to be at work by 9:00 a.m."

"And Jimmy?"

"He had the day off," Devin said with a shrug.

"Then what?"

"The usual. I went to work and then home."

"No other places?"

"No, I told you." Devin's voice had an edge, but Marc had no intention of letting up.

"When did you hear from Jimmy?"

"At 4:47 p.m.—I checked the time on my incoming calls."

"Where did he call from?"

"I don't know. I guess he called from Blackburn, that little town about thirty miles by dirt roads from the Caldwell place. That's where I picked him up that evening." Fatigue crept into Devin's answer.

Jessie studied his face. "Let's finish this in the morning. You look exhausted."

"No, we'll finish this tonight," Marc said gruffly.

"At least take a breather. I'll make coffee." Jessie hurried to the kitchen to brew a pot for the late-night interrogation, soon placing steaming cups in front of the two men. Devin wrapped his hands around the cup and took a sip. Marc ignored the offer and pushed forward.

"Was he alone when you picked him up?" Marc was particularly interested in the answers, since Hank had inherited a quarter section of land near Blackburn. The terrain in the area had deep ravines a nd rough pastures, making it a perfect place to ditch the evidence.

"He waited alone at some mom-and-pop convenience store on the edge of town."

"Describe his demeanor, son. Take your time. The answer is important."

"He looked like hell. Dirt covered his shoes and jeans, but the wind blew hard that day, so I didn't think much about it. His clothes smelled of gasoline, and one of his sleeves was torn. It seemed odd. Jimmy's a neat freak, but that night he looked ragged."

"Did he say why he was in Blackburn?"

"No. He asked me to take him to Sallisaw. Said he would explain later. I had a long day and didn't feel much like talking either."

"You rode together for over three hours and didn't say anything? Weren't you curious?"

"Not really. Jimmy's been different since he met Amber. I don't try to figure him out."

Marc feared Devin's trusting nature could take him down this time. Young, naive, and loyal—all bad traits when dealing with murder. His son's story was consistent with the one he had initially shared, providing little for Marc to go on. Tomorrow, he would travel to Blackburn and check out Hank's land. Trespassing seemed minor in the scheme of things.

"What do you know about Amber?"

"What do you mean? I know she's Jimmy's girlfriend. That's about it."

"How long have they been together?" Marc pressed.

"Jeez, I don't know. I'm guessing six months. Why?" He sighed with exasperation.

"Tonight, I'm asking the questions," Marc said firmly. "How would you describe their relationship?"

Devin rubbed his bloodshot eyes. "All right, I guess. I haven't seen much of Jimmy since they got together."

"That's enough for tonight, Marc." Jessie scooted back from the table, signaling the end of the conversation.

The weight of the day settled in. Exhaustion paralyzed him—time to call it a day.

"Clean sheets on your bed too," Jessie said, smiling at Devin. "I put a toothbrush in your bathroom and found you some clothes in the twins' closet."

Marc raised his eyebrows. While Devin was here, he and Jessie would be roommates. The thought brought him pleasure mixed with anxiety. After the day's events, he would be sleeping on the floor, but at least in the same room. Marc headed for the stairs, ready to turn in.

"I saw Amber today." Jessie tugged at his elbow. "Sit down and listen. It's good stuff."

Marc's weariness evaporated as adrenaline surged through him. He had forgotten Jessie's mission.

"Lay it on me. I need some good news." He patted her hand gently in a guarded expression of appreciation.

"I wouldn't call it *good* news," she said with emphasis, "but it does shed a different light on Amber's innocent demeanor."

Marc scoffed. "I hate to disappoint, but when I found out she stripped for a living, her innocence slipped a little in my books."

"I don't mean that kind of innocence. She's had a rough go of it."

"Like?"

"Amber married a man who ran hard with druggies and dealers. About a year ago, he and a buddy entered the Peppermint Lounge, a sleazy bar on Tulsa's north side. Her husband's friend started heckling an off-duty cop, slapping him, calling him names . . . you know the drill. Amber's husband grabbed the cop and held him while his buddy beat him almost to death. The cop survived, but he's paralyzed. Her husband and his friend were charged with attempted murder, and both went to prison."

Marc let out a whistle. Nothing about her actions or appearance suggested violence in her background.

"I take it she divorced him."

"Yes, but oddly enough, she's still close to his parents. They have her kids right now." Jessie laughed. "And you're not going to believe this, but his parents have drug records and are on probation for drug violations."

Marc shook his head. At this moment, he would believe anything. No one could make this stuff up.

"She reminds me of Ruby's figurines, all dainty and fragile, but when you peel back the layers . . . surprise. You find rock, not porcelain." Marc spoke with sadness, baffled as to why a young girl from a family with money would throw her life away on a bum and his druggie family. "I hate to hear she's dumped her kids too."

"You're reading too much into this. I didn't say she dumped her kids. She called her ex-in-laws multiple times while I was there, pestering for details about her children."

"Then why aren't the kids with her?" Marc asked.

"She took them to her ex's parents on the day of the Caldwell murder."

Marc leaned back and covered his eyes "What the hell? We keep dragging puzzle pieces out of the box, but we've got to start putting them together at some point." Marc cast a weary glance in Jessie's direction. "I owe you one, honey. You always come through."

"That's the funny part. Anyone can be her best friend if they give her any attention whatsoever. I guess I didn't set off any alarms, so she talked like a magpie."

"Did she talk about the murder?"

"Not yet, but I have a feeling she will."

Another half-baked lead. He craved answers, and Blackburn was the one weighing on his mind now. What business did Jimmy have in that dusty backwoods town?

"Would you go with me to Blackburn tomorrow? I could use help in scouring the canyons on Hank's place. I have a hunch we might find something of interest."

"Sure," Jessie answered hesitantly, "I'm still your best friend, no matter what."

23

Marc and Jessie set out at daybreak, streaks of golden sunlight blazing across the purple morning sky. A skiff of February snow from last night's flurries blurred the line between the shoulder and the road. Tapping his brakes to reduce speed, he navigated the narrow ribbon of asphalt through the rolling hills of Pawnee County before turning on the gravel road leading to the Caldwell farm.

Marc pointed to the west. "There's Hank's place that joins the Caldwell homestead. Tell me what you see."

"What do you mean? I see a pasture with brown grass and a few hills."

"What's missing?"

"I'm in no mood to play games." Jessie turned her back on him.

"Cattle are missing. Hank told JP he saw Jimmy and Devin early on September 18 while he was checking cattle on this quarter."

"That was months ago. Besides, all ranchers claim they're checking cattle, even when they're not. Makes them sound busy without doing any work.

"Very funny. But I'm telling you, no cattle were in this pasture in September, or all winter for that matter. The summer drought burned the grass to a crisp. Nothing for cattle to graze on since last June."

The gentle rolling hills gave way to miles of red-clay bluffs striated with limestone veins. Tall stalks of dry prairie grasses clung to the steep canyon walls, rippling in the gusty Oklahoma wind. Marc loved the raw beauty but understood that this rugged terrain could hide a multitude of sins.

It had been years since Marc accompanied Hank to this property. He hoped he could find the entrance. "We're almost there, so keep an eye out for a cattle guard with the letters HW welded to the gate."

Marc drove through a rusty metal cattle guard with yellow "NO TRESPASSING" signs plastered all over.

"We're trespassing?" Jessie said. The thought had not occurred to her.

"Yep." Marc aimed the Jeep toward the ridge that circled a deep ravine. The vehicle bounced across deep crevices eroded by wind and rain, inching its way to the top of the bluff.

"Ready?" Marc put the Jeep in park, then grabbed his binoculars and gloves.

Jessie tightened the scarf around her neck and donned a stocking hat. The wind and cold were killers this morning.

Marc stood on the crest and scanned the deep valley.

"Here, take these and look over there." He handed her the binoculars. A large mass resembling a charred car chassis rested on the canyon floor.

"Let's go," Jessie said, handing the binoculars back to Marc. "And take it slow. I'm out of shape."

Marc surveyed the charred Buick LeSabre. The tires had ruptured upon impact, leaving shattered glass on the ground. Blackened seat frames and a melted steering wheel testified to the burning inferno contained in the cab of the classic sedan.

Marc leaned in and took a picture of the VIN on the front windshield, then walked to the back of the car, snapping photos with his phone as he went. The partially open trunk exposed a black trash bag. He grabbed the plastic bag, worked it through the small opening, and then dumped the contents on the ground. A pair of women's tennis shoes and a blood-spattered T-shirt tumbled out.

"Jessie, look at this." Marc picked up a nearby stick, lifted the shirt, and held it for his wife to see. It appeared to belong to a female, a small one.

"We had better notify JP," Jessie said, shrinking from the bloody clothing.

"JP has no authority in this county. We'll go to the local authorities. I don't want JP or Hank to know about this until the site is secured. Now hand me your scarf."

"What for?"

"You'll see," Marc said as he gently removed her scarf. He placed it on the ground, then wrapped one shoe and a piece of the shirt he had ripped from the sleeve into a bundle. "What do you think?" he asked, holding the makeshift bag triumphantly in the air.

"I think we can't take these things," Jessie said. "That's tampering with evidence."

"They can add that charge to trespassing. What's one more infraction? Besides, I left them plenty."

Jessie hung back.

"Trust me, please. Something's off with JP and Hank, so I'm keeping this as insurance in case evidence disappears. Mike Halley taught me well."

"I don't know about this, Marc. What if they find out we were here?"

"They will know we were here when we report it. They don't have to know I lifted a couple of pieces if you don't tell them."

"And if they find out, then what?" Her words hung in the air.

"It could backfire. The crime scene integrity becomes compromised, and law enforcement would declare it a poison tree. None of the evidence would be admissible in court."

"And you're willing to risk it."

"Willing? No. Must? Yes. I've got no choice," he said as he headed to the Blackburn Police Station to report the abandoned vehicle. Marc wrestled with his obligation to the law, but he first must exorcize the torment of guilt screaming in his head. Tampering with evidence might cost him his license to practice and Devin's freedom —if he got caught. *Consequences be damned.* He did what he needed to do to protect his son. JP, Hank, and Halley attempted to wrap the case by pressuring Devin to plead guilty. Jimmy's confession would put the matter to bed, pronto . . . unless he broke the chain of corruption.

Jessie beelined to Marc's office the minute they arrived in Brule, so Nancy could run a VIN lookup while Marc paid a visit to Harper's Café to check the town's pulse. The Blackburn office had wasted no time in notifying JP, so shockwaves should be forthcoming.

The café had few patrons in the middle of the afternoon, but Marc could count on Hank, JP, and the rest of the gang when a gossip tsunami threatened. If the scuttlebutt had legal implications, Ross, the local judge, would also make an appearance.

Marc hung his hat and coat on a wooden peg and stooped low to catch his reflection in the mirror. His face had lost its puffiness since he gave up the Beam habit, and his waist had also whittled down a notch or two. No more bulges in his pinstriped shirt. He hated to admit it, but discipline looked good on him. As Marc straightened his shoulders and launched toward the familiar table, the lyrics from the Janis Joplin tune, "Bobby McGee," played on the jukebox. Marc grimaced. He, too, had nothing left to lose.

Expressions of surprise, even shock, greeted Marc as he approached the table. Johnny spoke first, stammering, "Y-you're looking good, considering . . . life's been treating you . . . Ah, hell, sit down." Johnny's smile seemed genuine despite the nervous chatter.

Skip motioned for Judy's attention. "Coffee and a cinnamon roll for my friend."

JP remained silent, but Hank spread his legs over two spaces and crossed his arms.

"JP tells me you paid my place a little visit this morning," Hank said with gruffness. "Can't you read? No trespassing signs are plastered all over the place."

Johnny and Skip recoiled. Hank was deadly serious.

"Relax, Hank. The wife and I were out for a little drive, and I didn't think you would mind."

"I'll be pressing trespass charges."

"Don't bother. Trespassing is a misdemeanor." Marc reached into his pocket and pulled out his billfold. "Here's five hundred. That ought to cover the fine, and it's worth every penny. The scenery was beautiful."

"Keep your money." Hank rose from the table. "I prefer to file charges and let a judge decide."

Marc flashed a grin at Hank. "Congratulations, my friend. You might win best of show in the liar's club. File away."

Hank stormed out the front door with JP on his tail. The war had started, and Marc fired the first shot. He stuck his hands in his pockets to keep them from trembling. Skip and Johnny stared at him like he had lost his mind. Maybe he had. Time would tell. Marc paid out and headed to the office. Jessie and Nancy should have an answer about the owner of the burned-out vehicle. He suspected it belonged to Ruby.

"Any luck?" Marc asked before the door shut behind him.

"Yes, and you're not going to believe this. The car is registered to Madeline Caldwell . . . not Ruby."

"I'd believe anything right now." Marc's mood brightened. According to Devin, he and Jimmy were in a pickup that morning, not a Buick LeSabre. This could clear his son.

"It's time to visit Jimmy. Fill him in. The truth will come out, with or without his cooperation. For his sake, I hope he picks the right path."

"I'm going with you." Jessie's cheeks flushed with excitement. "Jimmy's a good boy, and I can help."

"What about the twins?"

"Devin can step up for a few days. It's settled."

Marc felt a deep sense of relief. He depended on Jessie and needed a staunch ally.

"Call Duke and tell him we'll be there about noon tomorrow. See if he can get us in to see Jimmy."

24

Marc looked forward to returning to the Waite home. He had stayed there more often in the last few months than he had in the previous twenty years of marriage. Duke possessed an uncanny ability to cut through the static and connect directly with the heart of a situation. He marveled at the simplicity of this wise Cherokee man. Jessie possessed the same quality. He breathed a heavy sigh. In two months, he would lose both.

Mama Waite greeted them at the door in her customary apron, hands planted on both hips. She hugged Jessie, then reached for Marc and gave him a hearty squeeze.

"You've lost a few pounds," she said, pinching his waist. "I fixed a ham with all the trimmings to fatten you up again." Her warmth caught him off guard.

Marc ate until his belt buckle cut into his belly.

"Delicious, but no more," Marc said as he winked at Mama Waite.

"Coffee, then, so we can talk?"

"Yes, please."

Lisi picked up her knitting and began her work, ticking time with her needles like a metronome. Jessie's dad excused himself to plow the garden for spring planting, leaving Marc, Jessie, Mama Waite, and Duke to unravel the tangled threads of a murder.

Marc relayed the week's events: the burned-out Buick, Devin out on bail after firing his lawyer. Jessie shared Amber's story as Duke listened with an occasional grunt of acknowledgment.

"Amber is evil." Lisi did not look up as she spoke.

"Madeline is the evil one, if you ask me," Jessie said.

The clacking of Lisi's knitting needles picked up their pace in response.

"We cannot judge evil without understanding the deed," Duke admonished.

That sobered Marc. Motive. The answer was in the reason for the murder. Marc understood this, but Duke's compass put him back on course.

"When can we see Jimmy?" Marc asked.

"Tomorrow at 1:30 p.m. His lawyer will be present, so plan your questions carefully."

Duke pushed back from the table and headed to the utility room. He grabbed the bucket and motioned toward Marc. "Time to milk Buttercup. Care to join me, Kemosabe?"

"I believe I will," Marc answered, pleased with the invitation.

Marc followed Duke down a narrow path to the weathered barn where the Jersey waited. Buttercup's golden-yellow hide glistened in the sun like butter. The smell of sweet feed and fresh hay lured her to the stall, and Duke set about milking. Marc reveled in the simplicity of a life foreign to him, as the gentle cow nuzzled his hand with her wet nose.

"Be careful with Jimmy tomorrow. He is silent but not idle." Duke's warning came out of the blue.

"What do you mean? How could someone locked away in jail be anything but idle?"

"Jail mail. Jimmy communicates with someone through his mother. She carries notes for him. After today, I suspect that someone is Amber."

"How do you know this?"

"The deputy, the young man at the front desk, did a routine search of his mother's purse after her last visit."

"What did it say?"

"Murder one loves murder two."

"I'll be damned. That note should clear Devin and nail Amber."

At the very least, Jimmy's note was a confession to murder, and Amber was his accomplice. It fit Devin's version of events. He wasn't a party to the killing of David Caldwell. Relief spread over Marc like a balm. Devin's only crime was being a loyal friend.

"Maybe. I said I *suspected* the note was intended for Amber. We need more. The deputy tossed Jimmy's cell and found nothing else."

"Did he notify JP? That note might get Devin out of this hellish nightmare."

"He did but hasn't heard back from him," Duke answered. "You and I believe Amber was involved, but whoever it is, Jimmy is hell-bent on protecting them."

"Any suggestions on how I proceed tomorrow?"

"Talk to him about Amber. Let him know how great she's doing. Paint a picture of how happy she is. You get the idea. Make him understand he is protecting someone who's perfectly okay without him."

He truly washes his hair in the blood of his enemies, Marc thought, in awe of Duke's relentless plan of attack.

"What if she's innocent?"

"Jimmy is the one who is lying."

"One more question: Did Jimmy's mother identify the intended recipient?"

"No, she claimed she didn't know Jimmy had slipped the note into her purse. But trust me, a mother won't betray her son at any cost."

Marc drove to Tahlequah alone, rehearsing his approach all the way. Madeline's Buick and the blood-spattered clothing should absolve Devin, but a statement from Jimmy would seal the deal. He moved through check-in robotically, accustomed to the routine. The deputy led him down the hall to the standard visitation room. A man in a dark suit and blue tie sat next to Jimmy.

"John Kanoske." The man in the dark suit offered his hand. "Have a seat, Mr. Whitcomb. I represent Jimmy." His reserved manner and stiff handshake left little doubt about who would control the meeting. "I advised Jimmy against meeting with you, but he insisted out of respect for your son. Please keep it brief."

"Sure," Marc mumbled. Duke had mentioned that Jimmy's attorney would be present, but had not considered it a problem . . . until now. This Kanoske had the presence of a two-ton boulder.

"Before we start, I must know if you will serve as counsel for your son."

"Possibly." He and Devin had not discussed his representation.

"Our clients could be at odds in a courtroom, each trying to damage the other with their testimony. I don't need to tell you this meeting is quite unusual, and I will keep a tight grip on it. You understand, don't you, Mr. Whitcomb?"

Marc's heart sank. The opportunity to crack Jimmy with stories about Amber shrank to nothing. He inhaled deeply and counted from one to five to quiet his nerves.

"I believe that Jimmy and Devin are both innocent, and any information I seek will go toward that end. I have some news that may be of interest to you and your client. A burned-out Buick LeSabre, linked to Madeline Caldwell, was found in a pasture near Blackburn. Blood-spattered clothing was found in the trunk. It's at the lab now for testing, but I feel certain it will match David Caldwell's." Marc leaned back to give the two men space and watched Jimmy for a reaction. Except for a slight lift of his eyebrows, Jimmy remained aloof.

"Uh, Amber asked me to tell you hello. She . . . said to tell you she's doing well and that the kids are fine." Marc opted for a soft, direct approach, but his damn stutter had other ideas.

The attorney's stare bored holes through him, shaking his confidence. His delivery sounded like a Hallmark greeting card, and Jimmy's interest registered zero. Marc cleared his throat to ease the tightness.

"Jimmy, the deputy mentioned you tried to contact someone with a note that read, 'Murder one loves murder two.' Can you tell me who 'murder two' is?" Marc asked in desperation, not expecting any response.

Jimmy perked up and shot a big grin at Marc. "Sure, I'll tell you."

"Don't answer that question," Kanoske said, grabbing Jimmy by the elbow.

"I think he deserves an answer." Jimmy shook free and turned to Marc. "I wrote the note to Devin. We're a couple, you know."

Marc struggled to keep his composure. He didn't know his boy. Waves of shock reverberated throughout his body, rendering him helpless.

"You have your answer, Mr. Whitcomb. This meeting is over." The attorney snapped the lid of his briefcase shut with a loud clap. He stood and walked briskly from the room, pushing his client in front of him.

25

The afternoon weighed on Marc, making the drive back endless. He needed to talk to Duke to assess the repercussions of Jimmy's revelation and to steel his strength for the next battle.

Jessie ran to meet him as he pulled into the drive, her eyes wide with anticipation.

"How did it go?" she gushed. Her hair whipped about her face as she clutched at a flannel shirt too light for the frigid winter air.

Marc slid out of the Jeep, buttoned his coat, and stuffed his hands in his pockets to brace against howling February winds. A quick chill ran through him as he shivered from the cold . . . or his nerves.

"Not well. Jimmy barricaded himself behind his attorney, and I couldn't pry anything out of him. The next time we see him, he will be in court."

"I'm sorry." Jessie touched his hand.

Marc fidgeted with his keys, ignoring Jessie's offer of sympathy, but she stood like a guard at the door of the Jeep, refusing to leave.

"There's more. Spill."

"Jimmy wrote a note and asked his mother to deliver it." Marc groped for the best way to put it.

"Go on."

"It read, 'Murder one loves murder two.' I thought we had Jimmy trapped. If Amber were the intended recipient, Devin would be clear." Marc stopped talking and looked away.

"And?" Her question hung midair.

"And . . . and Jimmy said the message was for Devin. He said our son is gay." Tears gathered in the corners of Marc's eyes.

Jessie stepped back from the Jeep, eyes narrowed. "What's bothering you, Marc? Are you troubled that Jimmy pointed to Devin as his accomplice, or that our son might be gay?"

"That's unfair. Yes, I'm worried my son might be an accomplice to murder, and I hate myself for entertaining the possibility. Does it bother me that my son is gay? No. But why didn't he tell me?" Marc turned away from Jessie. "I don't know my boy, and that makes me sick."

"You aren't very approachable. Between your working and drinking, there isn't much room for the trivial pursuit of family."

Her scathing rebuke ripped the blinders off Marc. Jessie wasn't divorcing him solely due to his drinking problem. She couldn't take his absentee approach to their lives. Sobering up would not fix the marriage. It would take much more. This tidal wave swept away his last sandcastle.

"Where's Duke?" Marc asked.

Jessie pointed toward the barn and walked away.

"Got a minute?" Duke glanced at Marc, grunted, and motioned for him to sit down. "This was a day from hell."

"You look like a man who's taken a beating. What happened?" Duke asked.

Marc recounted the story from the beginning, rolling each detail about in his head, searching for a speck of hope. When Marc finished, Duke shrugged and continued milking without breaking his rhythm.

"You have nothing to say?" Marc asked, disappointed.

"When I speak, you do not listen."

"What are you saying? I did everything you told me to."

"I told you to wash your hair in the blood of your enemies. Instead, you walked in fear, and Jimmy sensed your weakness."

Duke's rebuke released an uncontrollable anger in Marc. "Who in the hell are you to judge me? You weren't there."

Duke turned a stone face toward Marc. "Do you want to learn to walk, or shall I carry you?"

That sliced deeper than the first statement. "Cut the crap and say what you mean."

"How did Jimmy act when he told you Devin was gay?"

"He kinda laughed—not an outright laugh but a huge grin. It amused him."

"If Devin were the object of the love note, Jimmy would not have answered you. Jimmy guards his secrets with his life, yet shares that one piece of information with a smile. I don't think so, Kemosabe. He threw you a bone you couldn't chew to stop your interference."

"So you think it was a ploy?"

"Yes. Ditch the words. Watch his actions."

The last twenty years had rendered Marc lazy, insulated from the primal instincts required to win. Duke pegged him. When he stuttered for the first time in months, Jimmy's attorney took control. Marc's failures, lined up like a string of dominoes, fell one after the other.

"You're right. I lost that round, but there will be another."

"You've lost nothing yet."

Marc kicked the dirt with his boot. *There he goes again. Talking in riddles.* "What do you mean when you say, 'wash your hair in the blood of your enemies'? I'm missing something."

"When you wash your hair in the blood of your enemies, you bring them to total defeat. They cannot rise again to harm you. Beware. An injured opponent will return ten times stronger." Duke smiled. "In paleface lingo, it means shoot to kill."

"That's kinda what I thought. So what am I doing wrong?"

"Jimmy is not the enemy. The system is. The prosecutor wishes to be done with this matter, and Jimmy is making it easy for them. Seek out Jimmy's attorney. Make him listen."

Marc drew a deep breath. He had sought simple answers to crack the case and magically free his son, but the truth was in a burned-out car and a bloody shirt.

Jessie had packed the car, ready to make tracks for home. Marc sprinted to the Jeep, steeled with new resolve.

"If Devin agrees, I'd like to represent him." Marc glanced at Jessie. "What do you think?"

"I don't know. You've not overseen a case of this nature in a long time." Lines creased Jessie's brow. "Are you sure you want to try?"

"I can do it." Marc slammed his fist on the steering wheel. "I could use a little encouragement."

"Okay. You can do this if . . ."

"If what?"

"You stay sober. Remember Christmas?"

Marc nodded. "I haven't had a drink in two months."

"I applaud your effort, but I don't know . . . You get so twisted up when it comes to Devin."

"All right, but think about it. In the meantime, visit Amber. Get close to her. Become her best friend. She's knee-deep in David's murder. I'd bet my life on it."

"How much time do we have?" Jessie asked.

"Three weeks until Jimmy's trial."

26

Marc spotted JP's cruiser across from the courthouse and made a U-turn. The lab work on the Buick should be back by now. He found JP alone in the break room, filling his coffee cup.

"Have a minute?"

JP jumped like a scared rabbit.

"As soon as my heart quits pounding." A scowl twisted JP's face, warning Marc to tread with care.

"Do you have the lab report from the old Buick?"

"Yeah. Came in this morning. I intended to give you a shout later today, but since you're here, I'll tell you. The findings don't look good for Jimmy or Devin."

"How's that?"

"Come to find out, Mrs. Caldwell owned the old junker, and someone took it around the time of the murder."

"Did she file a report?"

"No, Madeline suspected Jimmy had 'borrowed it.' He put his car in the shop that morning, and she figured Amber gave him permission to use it."

"What did they find?"

JP squinted and tilted his head back. "A shirt had Caldwell's blood. That was it, buddy boy." He omitted the fact that a woman's tennis shoes were in the trunk. JP lied, but Marc couldn't call him out without admitting he tampered with a crime scene.

"Looks pretty bad for Jimmy, but I don't see the connection with Devin."

"Easy. The people who own the convenience store in Blackburn identified your boy with Jimmy the evening of the murder."

Nothing could shock Marc now. This snake-infested investigation reeked of a cover-up.

"Guess I'll see you in court." Marc tipped his hat, signaling that the real war had begun.

The next step would be to pay a visit to the private lab in Tulsa.

Marc hung a right onto a narrow one-way street in Downtown Tulsa. LABCO, Inc., a private research lab squatting in a row of old brick buildings, resembled a pawn shop with iron bars on the windows. Five years ago, the owner had split from the herd of commercial labs and established an innovative, state-of-the-art facility. He attacked a project with creativity, leaving nothing to chance. The forensic team that investigated the Caldwell crime scene had gathered the routine information, but nothing about this murder fit a mold. Marc picked LABCO for that very reason. He needed a maverick.

"Hello," Marc called. The empty reception area did not surprise him. The owner worked solo and spent most of his time in the back lab.

Steve, a gray-haired gentleman in a stained white coat, strolled to the front. "Whatcha got for me today, buddy?"

"A tennis shoe and a piece of a bloody shirt."

"Caldwell case?"

"Yep."

Steve slipped on a pair of gloves and extended his hand. "Lemme see."

Steve rotated the shoe back and forth, plucking at the loose stitching. "Where'd you find this?"

"Found it and the shirt in the trunk of a burned-out Buick."

"That might explain it. Look here." He pushed a finger through the upper vamp. The stitching popped easily as the shoe began to fall apart. "These threads are bonded nylon six point six coated with beeswax. The heat from the fire melted the stitching."

"I could have figured that out on my own," Marc said and laughed, covering his disappointment.

"Guess you could have, but there's more. See these spots? Looks like a petroleum product." Steve lifted the shoe to his nose. "Smells like gasoline, but I need to run some tests to be sure."

"When will you have the results?"

"I can run the test on the shoe now, but I have no baseline for the blood. I can tell if it's human, but that's the limit unless you can bring me a sample of the victim's blood."

"Test the shoe. I'll wait." Marc had no way to obtain Caldwell's blood specimen. Besides, JP admitted the blood was Caldwell's. He could petition the courts for access, but could he explain why he needed independent testing without revealing he helped himself to the shoe and a piece of the shirt? Evidence tampering was a crime and could lead to disbarment.

Forty-five minutes later, Steve returned with the results. "The spots are gasoline, all right. But even more interesting, the glue between the thermoplastic rubber sole layers has dissolved, and the culprit is gasoline."

"What are the implications?" Marc asked.

"Whoever wore this shoe not only spilled gas on the upper vamp but walked in pools of the stuff, which makes perfect sense."

"Perfect sense?"

"The tread on the shoes transferred the accelerant to the carpet. As the fire burned, the accelerant left by the shoe pattern burned into the carpet." Steve slapped Marc on the back. "We, my friend, have a match to the carpet sample you dropped by earlier."

A woman had been present when David's body was burned . . . the woman Jimmy was shielding. Amber hadn't waited in the truck while Jimmy tried to burn the house down.

Duke had pegged this one, but where to go from here? JP omitted the existence of a tennis shoe and pooh-poohed the bloodied shirt. Marc had stolen the evidence and couldn't present it without incriminating himself. He could accuse JP of improper conduct, but that would add another battle to the two he was already fighting. The best chance he had was convincing Jimmy to come clean.

Marc phoned Jessie to check on her progress with Amber. She answered on the third ring.

"I'll call you back." The phone clicked.

Marc drove in circles for an hour, waiting for Jessie to call, his imagination on full throttle. Had she run into trouble? He took the Denver exit and headed toward Devin's duplex, determined to get Jessie out of this nonsense, when his phone rang.

"You won't believe what Amber told me. It blows everything wide open," Jessie said.

"Meet me at the park on Riverside Drive. And hurry."

Marc found Jessie sitting on a park bench surrounded by a bed of daffodils poking their noses through the damp soil.

"I think they've been tricked," she said, nodding at the tiny blooms.

"Tricked?"

"By the mild weather," she said. A faint frown tipped the corners of her mouth. "Winter will bare her cold, hard teeth again and bite their tiny blooming heads off."

"What are you talking about?" Marc asked, puzzled by her concern over a flower bed.

"I'm serious. Look at 'em. All hopeful . . . trusting Mother Nature. Then boom. Gone." The sadness in her eyes was real.

"Are you talking about the damn daffodils or us?"

"Both."

Her sadness spilled over to him, but he had to press on. "Tell me about Amber."

"She and her boyfriend, Jimmy, went to confront her stepfather about molesting her daughter," Jessie said in a calm monotone. "Amber said they intended to teach him a lesson. She said Madeline had left the children with her stepdad, David, and when she returned home, the little girl complained of her private area hurting."

Marc's head spun. His conversations with Dani had led him to believe the murder stemmed from greed, not passion. David Caldwell—child molester. The nice-looking gentleman in the funeral home picture didn't look like a predator, but they never did. Sick. How could anyone molest a little girl? If anyone hurt his kid, he might kill too. This scenario fit his son's personality to a tee. Devin had been a champion of the underdog since childhood. Any lost pup had a home with his boy. Amber would be no different. Devin's possible involvement lurked in the corners of his mind.

"Wait until you hear the last part. Amber said, 'I lost it. I had to put the old dog out of his misery.'" Jessie's excitement picked up speed, and his own emotions soared. A confession that matched Duke's assessment, Jimmy sacrificed himself for Amber.

"You were right about that girl. She's way too trusting. I told her I had stopped by to pick up some things for Devin. She offered me a Coke and said it was the least she could do for Devin's mother."

"Does she realize our son is going to trial for something she did?" Marc's voice cracked.

"Maybe to some degree. Amber trusts everyone, especially her mother. Every other word out of her mouth was Madeline this or Madeline that."

"She talked freely?"

"She acted friendly from the get-go. I don't think her mother has spoken to her since she dumped her at Devin's apartment. Amber craves attention." Marc detected concern in Jessie's voice that irritated the hell out of him.

"She would be the center of attention if she confessed." Marc hated the snide comment, but this young lady could destroy his life.

"Do you want to hear the story or not?" Jessie shot back.

"Sorry. Go on."

"Amber and Jimmy dated for seven months. Madeline was not a fan of her daughter's ex-husband, who went to jail for attempted murder, but she approved of Jimmy. From what she told me, she and Jimmy visited her parents frequently."

"One happy little family," Marc said.

"Stop it."

Marc nodded. He couldn't afford to tick Jessie off at this point. "I found it strange that Amber said her mother was a nurse and could kill him whenever she wanted to with an injection and that no one would be the wiser."

"She said the same thing to me. I even asked her if she thought her mother was involved in her stepdad's death. She told me Madeline didn't like to get her hands dirty," Marc said. "Anything else?"

"No, I didn't want to push too hard."

"Now for the million-dollar question: Where do we go from here?" The question was rhetorical. Marc watched the bicycle riders, enjoying the warm day as they sped along the park trail. "Twenty-five years ago, I rode my bike along the same path before . . ." His eyes were vacant, his mood melancholy.

"Do we need to contact JP about Amber's involvement?"

"I stopped by JP's office today. He denies finding any tennis shoes in the car. He lied. Why?"

Jessie turned to Marc. "For the same reason that Jimmy is lying. They're both protecting Amber."

"I think you're half right. Jimmy is protecting his girlfriend, but JP's got someone else on his mind." Marc knew JP well. He wouldn't put himself on the line unless someone directed him.

"I still say we confront JP. You have pictures, one of the shoes, and the bloody cloth."

"If I confront JP, I might as well kiss my ass goodbye. Time in prison is not appealing. And, my dear, you could be right there with me, especially if JP had anything to do with it."

"What do you suggest?" Jessie asked.

"Duke's suggestion. Not mine. You and I will see Mr. John Kanoske, Jimmy's attorney. First, see Amber one more time and squeeze her for anything you can. In the meantime, I will get the police report."

27

Marc stopped by the courthouse, procured a copy of the police report, and returned to the office. He intended to study every word until he had memorized it. JP had a mission, but he was no Einstein, and these documents might tell the story.

David Caldwell Crime Scene Report

At approximately 6:30 a.m. on September 20, 2015, Deputy Sheriff Robert Smith of the Muskogee County Sheriff's Office was directed to 1337 SCR, a Muskogee County, Oklahoma residence, regarding a dead, burned body. Deputy Smith arrived at the scene and ran into Madeline Caldwell, who was crying on the ground in the backyard. Mrs. Caldwell pointed to an open door leading into the house's garage. Deputy Smith entered the house and followed footprints to a badly burned body lying on the living room floor, a portion of its torso missing. Mrs. Caldwell later identified the victim's body as her husband, David Caldwell.

Chief Deputy JP Davis arrived at the scene, entered the residence, and saw the body of Mr. Caldwell lying on the living room floor. The house had a strong chemical odor, and the utility room floor was slippery and wet. Chief Deputy Davis observed shoe impressions burned into the carpet near the body and cut the impressions out for testing. Because there was a circular wound to Mr. Caldwell's head that Deputy Davis believed to be a gunshot wound, he called the Federal Bureau of Investigation for assistance.

FBI Agent Jenny Hoskins came to the scene that day and took photos of the property and damage. Agent Hoskins noted the door to the garage was open, and the doorframe was pushed inward and was not attached to the wall. The striker plate and screw were lying on the garage floor, and damage to the door indicated that it had been forced open. Agent Hoskins collected a glove on the garage floor and turned it over for DNA analysis. FBI Criminalist Bev Oldham extracted DNA from the submitted gloves and obtained a male DNA profile on one glove with a significant male component and a minor component on the other. FBI Criminalist Kyle Kennedy analyzed the profiles and determined that DNA and the principal component matched Jimmy Don Allen in all sixteen loci. The minor component was insufficient for comparison. Agent Hoskins noted the garage floor was covered with soot and a strong odor of accelerants. The lid was also missing from one of the gas cans found in the garage.

Inside the house, Agent Hoskins entered the laundry room, where the floor was slick and wet with liquid that had a strong accelerant odor. There was smoke damage on the walls and soot on the floor. Proceeding through a hallway toward the body, Agent Hoskins found the hallway did not have fire damage but had severe smoke damage and was covered with black soot. She located a bedroom on the south side of the hall and found open metal lockboxes on the bed. The living room was severely burned with severe smoke damage. Most of the burn was located in the center of the living room, where Agent Hoskins observed a severely burned wooden dining room chair, the body of David Caldwell, and a strong odor of accelerant.

The body was so severely burned it was missing some limbs, and there was a bullet hole in the right side of the victim's head. Because of the bullet hole in Mr. Caldwell's head, Agent Hoskins and other officers also looked for firearms, shell casings, and projectiles but never found any. Mrs. Caldwell noted that two pieces of jewelry—a solid-gold Cuban link necklace and a ring, gold with inlaid black diamonds—were also missing from the corpse.

Agent Hoskins continued to the kitchen, observing that the ceramic tile floor was slick, covered with a liquid, and had a strong odor of accelerant. Some drawers and cabinets were open, and the refrigerator was removed from the wall. On top of the counter, Agent Hoskins found a box and next to it a wadded piece of paper with a void pattern in the soot underneath it, indicating it was placed there before the fire. Agent Hoskins collected this piece of paper. The kitchen was severely damaged by smoke, with charring damage to some items, including the box of documents on the counter.

Concerning the outside of the residence, Agent Hoskins documented large tire tracks, consistent with a dually truck, which led north of the home to a line of trees. A charred blanket was lying on the ground beside the exterior propane tank.

State Fire Marshal Agent Terry Jones, an expert in fire investigation, arrived to assist. Agent Jones examined the property and testified there were pour patterns of an ignitable fluid from one end of the hallway (leading from the garage to the living room) to the other. A distinct hydrocarbon accelerant odor was also in the hallway, kitchen, and laundry room. The body was burned in an outline, and the way it burned (the amount of consumption of the body) indicated there was probably an ignitable liquid poured on the body. The pour patterns in the area of the body were consistent with his findings. There was no evidence that this was an electrical fire.

Agent Jones took the liquid samples on the kitchen and laundry room floors. FBI Agent Grant Rogers analyzed the samples and found that Item 1A contained an ignitable liquid in the heavy petroleum distillate class 2. Because the gypsum boards in the house held no residual heat, the fire must have occurred at least twelve hours before the arrival of investigators. As to why the house was not entirely consumed by fire, considering the widespread presence of accelerants, Agent Jones explained that there was a lack of continuity in the pour down the hallway. The home was well built with double-pane windows, and once the oxygen was depleted, the fire went out.

Forensic pathologist and medical examiner Joshua Langston testified that Mr. Caldwell died of a gunshot wound to his right temple. The bullet entered Mr. Caldwell's right temple, went through his skull, and exited the back of his head. Dr. Langston determined it was a contact gunshot wound due to the soot found on the skin and skull of Mr. Caldwell. Because no soot was found in Mr. Caldwell's airways, Dr. Landry determined that Mr. Caldwell was not breathing at the time of the fire and, therefore, was deceased before the fire occurred.

Several items in JP's report jumped off the page. The first concerned Madeline Caldwell. He did not mention Madeline walking away, leaving her car cordoned off at the crime scene. The second problem involved the footprints near Caldwell's body. They failed to mention the female shoe. The third and most troublesome issue was the dually truck tracks. The truck belonged to David Caldwell. Hank claimed he saw Jimmy and Devin in the old Buick on the morning of the murder. And Devin claimed they drove a small truck to load a kitchen table. Three vehicles and two people did not add up.

The fingerprint on the glove presented a different question. Amber told Jessie they went to see David to teach him a lesson in an impulsive act of anger. The gloves pointed to premeditation.

Marc put the report in his briefcase. He needed time to digest the contents. Jessie would be home from Tulsa soon, and he wanted to surprise her with dinner. He had not used his grilling skills in a long time. Brisk March winds blew from the south, making it hard to light the grill, but soon the embers glowed red-hot, perfect for a nice juicy steak. He tossed a salad and popped rolls in the oven. He hoped Jessie would be pleased.

Headlights flashed in the driveway. Jessie had made it home.

She made her way toward the house in the dark. The strain had slowed her gait, and her shoulders drooped. Beautiful, as always, but tired.

"Any luck?" Marc asked.

"Oh, Marc. That girl spills her guts on everything. I don't think her mother would want her near a witness stand."

"That sounds promising," Marc said, grinning.

"That girl's got a big problem."

"More than one," Marc mumbled. "Sit down. Dinner is on the table. Eat, relax, and tell me all about it."

Jessie flashed a weary smile at Marc. "Thanks, I'm starved."

Marc struggled to let her eat in peace. If he pushed, she would clam up. Jessie would talk when her mind cleared and not a moment before.

"I worry about Amber," Jessie said. Her opening volley didn't meet his expectations, but he kept his mouth shut. She never missed a detail, and they would come when Jessie was ready.

"I did some reading on people like Amber last night. Very interesting. I think she suffers from disinhibited social engagement disorder or something like that."

"You're right. That is interesting. I send you off as a detective, and you return as a psychologist."

"Don't make fun." Jessie's mouth drew into a pout.

"Sorry." Marc leaned forward, resting his chin in his hands in an effort to look sincere. "Please tell me what in the hell it is."

"Children with this condition don't fear strangers. Instead, they tend to be overly friendly or preoccupied with gaining a stranger's attention."

"Dani and Ruby described Amber the same way. The problem is she's not a child." Marc was losing patience with this discussion.

"In many ways, she still is. But when these children become adults, they don't form meaningful, long-term relationships with anyone. They drift." Jessie's eyes were deadly serious.

"What does all this mean to Devin? He's the focus here." Marc was one inch away from snapping.

"It means she may love her mother, Jimmy, or her children, but she's not permanently attached to any of them. It's like short-term memory. She loves the one she's with. Lucky for us, Madeline made a big mistake by putting her in an apartment alone, cutting off Amber's contact. She has no job, family, or friends to anchor her. Today, I'm the one she clings to, but only until someone else comes along."

"Wow, I thought you told me that Amber adored her mother. Madeline *this* and Madeline *that* were the only words to tickle her tongue."

"Yeah, but this time, Amber acted differently. She doted on me, Marc."

He stood up, cleared the table, and slung the plates into the sink, refusing to look his wife in the eye.

"Be careful. You're going to break every dish in the house." Jessie threw her napkin on the table. "What's the matter with you?"

"I'll tell you what the matter is. Somehow, you twisted yourself into being Amber's surrogate mother or guardian or whatever you want to call it. What about our son?"

Tears flooded Jessie's eyes and spilled down her cheeks. "Just because I care about Amber's well-being doesn't mean I don't care about Devin. He's my son too, in case you forgot."

"The girl has no feelings. She's a cold-blooded murderer."

"Wrong. Amber has feelings that run as deep as ours do, but she doesn't know who they belong to. Today, they belonged to me. She told me everything, Marc. She trusted I would keep her secrets. That makes me a manipulator." Jessie looked at Marc, her eyes pleading for understanding. "I'll see this through for Devin's sake, but I hate myself for doing it."

Moving closer, Marc put his arm around Jessie's shoulder. "I know this is hard. This whole business is tearing me up, and I wouldn't hurt you for the world. But here I am, slicing you into little pieces. When you're ready to share Amber with me, I'll listen. Until then, I'll leave you alone. But I can't sympathize with that girl under any circumstances."

He retreated to his office and collapsed in the recliner. Duke would be proud. Marc identified one opponent, and he had no qualms about shedding her blood. He craved a drink so badly that his whole body hurt. *I can make it through one more night without a Beam and water*, he thought until he dozed off. No Beam tonight.

Since Devin made bail and returned home, Marc had slept in the office recliner. Everything he needed was within a few steps, except a change of clothing. He woke at dawn and went to the bedroom closet, careful not to wake his wife. Sometimes, Marc would tiptoe to the edge of the bed to watch her sleep. Her shiny black hair swirled across her pillow like a raven's wing, bringing a lump to his throat.

He skipped his bowl of cereal and went straight to his law office with Ruby's diaries under his arm. He would ask Nancy to read them. She knew this town as well as he did and could pick out passages of importance. He had no stamina to plow through Ruby's musings, but his secretary was keen on that stuff.

"I'll be in the library," Marc said to Nancy after transferring the task of reading the diaries. "Hold any calls and no visitors."

A chuckle escaped Marc's lips as he made his way to the library. Who was he kidding? He had one client, and Ruby couldn't remember whether he was her son or her attorney. Life sucked. He plodded through the afternoon accomplishing nothing.. He couldn't get Jessie off his mind..

The door opened slightly, and Jessie peeked in. "May I speak to you a moment?"

Marc's heart fluttered like a schoolboy's. "How on earth did you get by Nancy?"

"You're not the only one with friends in high places," she laughed. "Besides, you're cute. We're crazy. And I love you. Makes it all worth the risk," The softness of her confession touched him.

"Does this mean . . ."

"It doesn't mean anything except I do genuinely love you. No matter what happens, you need to know that."

"Noted," he said with a forced smile. "Now, what did you wish to discuss? I've got nothing but time."

"Amber."

"Lay it on me."

"First, I want you to understand I find no pleasure in deceiving her. I'll pay the price someday. But in the meantime, I can only worry about Devin. Here are the important points." Jessie slid a notebook across the desk. "Read these."

His eyes dropped to a neat column of handwritten notes. She had covered all the bases. It was up to him to hit the home run.

"I'll call Mr. Kanoske and set up an appointment. Are you ready to go through with this?"

Jessie lifted her head high and folded her hands in her lap. "We have no choice."

28

The trip to Tahlequah had become routine over the past five months, but today everything looked different. The sky was bluer, the mountains higher, and his hopes for Devin's freedom seemed brighter. Kanoske agreed to meet with them at the Waite house this afternoon . . . without Jimmy. Today's meeting offered Marc his last chance to set justice in motion.

The Waite household appeared vacant. An empty driveway and a chicken-free yard troubled Marc. His nerves tingled, and his asthma threatened to flare. Jessie took his hand and gave a gentle squeeze. "Duke will be here. I spoke to him this morning."

Duke rounded the corner by the barn, and Marc welcomed the sight of his Cherokee friend. Kanoske presented an intimidating figure, but Duke had a way of equalizing a man's size.

"Where's Mama Waite and Lisi?" Marc asked out of politeness.

"Shopping in Tulsa. They won't be home for a while." Duke chuckled. "But Mr. Kanoske should be here soon. Let's go inside."

The attorney pulled in before they reached the front door. A stout man of medium height exited a black Chevrolet truck. His stocky frame, clad in a dark-gray suit, reflected an urban flair, except for his brightly colored tie and long braid. He came to represent his Cherokee client in style.

"Duke Waite," Duke said, extending his hand.

"John Kanoske," the attorney answered.

Duke turned toward Marc. "My grandson—"

"We've met."

"And my granddaughter, Jessie."

Kanoske smiled, tipping his head in acknowledgment.

Duke controlled the introductions, making everyone comfortable as he led the party of four to the kitchen.

Per Duke's instructions, Marc sat at the head of the table, with Jessie seated at the end, giving him the honored position. Duke sat opposite Marc, leaving Kanoske surrounded.

"Mr. Kanoske, I—"

"Please, call me John."

Marc cleared his throat and started over. "John, we have some information that might benefit your client, Jimmy."

"I have great respect for your grandfather. The Cherokee Nation is indebted to him for his work with our people, especially in preserving our language. I'm here to honor him and his house. Therefore, I will listen. But my client insists he pulled the trigger, and I have no reason to doubt him. He's up on first-degree charges, and a plea could cut the time he'll serve. Convince me Jimmy's lying before I drop the plea."

"Jimmy's girlfriend, Amber, pulled the trigger. She—not Jimmy—committed the murder," Jessie stated with calm assurance.

"How do you know this?" John asked.

"Amber told me. Would you like to hear her story?"

"As I said, I'm here to listen."

"On the day of the murder, Amber said her mother called her husband to make sure he would be at the farm. David spent a lot of time and money at casinos, and she needed to determine whether he would be home when they arrived. She said her mother told David the kids wanted to store a kitchen table in the barn and would need his help."

"Are you implying that Madeline set up the murder?" John asked, raising his eyebrows.

"I'm not implying anything. This is Amber's story, not mine," Jessie answered.

"Sorry for the interruption." His manner was polite but distant.

"She said David arrived at the farm at about 1:00 p.m. on September 18. They arrived before David, so Jimmy kicked the door down to get in, the one in the garage. When David entered the house, he was madder than hell. He and Jimmy got into a shouting match, and that's when Jimmy shoved him into a chair and tied him up. Amber said she went into the bedroom, found David's gun, and started waving it in David's face, cursing and screaming at him. She said the gun had a hair trigger and went off, killing David. Jimmy told her to wait in the car and that he would take care of everything. He ran to the garage, found the gas can, doused the house and David in gasoline, then set the place on fire. Jimmy drove away in Madeline's old Buick, and Amber fled in David's truck. Amber claimed the shooting was accidental."

Kanoske's expression shifted to guarded interest. "Is there more? Her deposition states that Jimmy held the gun when it went off, and it matches Jimmy's story. What you're telling me is a direct contradiction of her statement."

"They concocted that story to protect her." Marc slapped the table. "I went to the crime scene with David's daughter and gathered several pieces of evidence after the authorities completed their investigation. There are glaring discrepancies when you compare my findings with the crime scene report."

Marc leaned back, weary of recounting the events in his mind for the millionth time. He rubbed his eyes and stretched his hands above his head to ease the tension in his shoulders.

"Let's take a break," Duke said. "Mama Waite baked a Texas sheet cake. I'm in trouble if it's not gone by the time she gets home."

John broke into a wide grin. "I'm down. Her sheet cake is more famous than you are, Duke." John polished off a large piece of the pecan-filled chocolate cake in record time. "Delicious. Worth every minute of the drive here."

Duke's hospitality had broken the tension, and they returned less guarded to the topic at hand.

"Tell me about these discrepancies." Marc's last comment had piqued John's curiosity.

"Let's start with Mrs. Caldwell. I was present during the investigation. Madeline sat in the backyard like a statue, not a tear on her face. Then she took off down the gravel road in her dainty little flats, leaving her car cordoned off at the crime scene. Seems strange to me. And where in the hell was she going? It's miles to a blacktop road, and those shoes weren't made for walking."

John appeared to weigh that before speaking. "May I play devil's advocate? If I represented Mrs. Caldwell, I would tell you that shock and grief create unpredictable behaviors."

Marc grunted. He had thought of that but didn't relish the argument.

"Moving on," Marc said, afraid he had lost momentum. "The crime report states the gun went off at point-blank range. That doesn't fit with waving a gun to scare someone."

"You're grasping at straws. If a gun is fired within three feet, it's considered point-blank. You have no way of knowing if the gun was placed on David's forehead or if it was waved about his head. And you don't know if the shooter intended to scare or kill. Won't hold up. Anything else to add? If not, I need to get on the road to Tahlequah."

John's dismissal irritated him. Marc had one more bullet in his magazine.

"I have footprints from the crime scene that match a woman's size-seven Nike tennis shoe, one identical to a shoe I found in Madeline's burned-out Buick LeSabre."

"Amber admitted she was with Jimmy when the murder took place. What's new there?"

"The footprints were burned into the carpet about fifteen inches from the body. Amber wasn't in the pickup, John. She was dancing over the corpse while it burned."

The shock on John's face gave Marc pleasure. He had managed to break through.

"There was no mention of this in the report." John's arrogance evaporated.

"Exactly."

"Gather your information and come to my office tomorrow at 2:00 p.m.. We'll dive deeper. If you can back up this claim, it's a game changer."

Jessie watched from the kitchen window as John slid into his truck and drove off. She toyed with the curtains briefly, then swiped her finger across the sheet cake for a bite of chocolate frosting.

"What's on your mind?" Marc asked. "You would slap my hands if I picked the icing off a cake."

"Maybe I was wrong about Amber. Maybe she shared propaganda —not secrets. Did she play me to divert guilt from Jimmy?" She paused, waiting for Duke's reaction.

"Could be. At least Devin's name didn't creep in. And if Jimmy's an accomplice rather than the murderer, your son is further removed from the crime." Duke's comment elicited a half smile that faded abruptly.

"What about the tennis shoe?" Jessie asked, grimacing.

"John is ready to listen, but if I produce the shoe, I risk disbarment or jail. Maybe we don't need it. Unless another woman was present, the print on the carpet had to be Amber's."

"Before I forget, Nancy called last night and said Dani needs to talk to you." Jessie ducked her head, feeling guilty she didn't tell Marc sooner.

"I'll call. I need Dani to swing by the lab, pick up the reports, and deliver them here tomorrow. It would push me to roundtrip it to Tulsa and be back by two."

"That's a lot to ask."

"That favor is minor. I want her to take credit for finding the carpet with Amber's burned footprint. She has every legal right to canvass the property. Let her own the chain of evidence."

29

Dani arrived ten minutes late to find Marc pacing in the hall. He needed to ensure she understood what he asked her to do. She listened, nodding agreement on occasion, as he shared his plan.

"I've got this. If memory serves, I rode with you to the farm, let you into the house, and covered each room by your side. I even held the trash bag for you," she said and laughed. "By the way, thanks for taking the samples to the lab for me," she added with a wink.

Dani tucked the document folder under her arm and strode into John's office as if she owned it. Marc watched as she planted beside John and pushed the folder toward him. This girl did not lack confidence.

"Here you go." Her smile lit up the gloomy conference room.

Jimmy's attorney studied the reports, taking the time to digest the results. "It appears our little friend is comfortable close to the fire."

"She stood by and watched him roast. No doubt about it." Marc spat the words like bullets.

"This is huge but might be tricky to introduce. The federal prosecutor's evidence does not include this footprint, and we have a chain-of-custody problem. The prosecutor will have a field day tearing this apart. The court could rule that this evidence has no bearing on

Jimmy's guilt or innocence but pertains to an unknown female. At this point, Amber has no charges."

Marc's face reddened. "At the very least, she's an accessory after the fact. You've got her statement. Why hasn't she been charged?"

"As a general rule, authority over non-tribal members falls to the state, not the Indian tribes. I presented a copy to the local district attorney. The rest is up to him."

Marc knew the answer. JP treated the statement in the same fashion as the evidence from the Buick. Devin and Amber fell under state jurisdiction. Their fate rested with Chief Deputy Davis, whose knees buckled at the sight of Hank.

"Looks like I've wasted your time and mine," Marc said, eyes dull with disappointment.

"Slow down, partner. The court might allow the footprint to be admitted if I turn it over to the forensic team to corroborate your findings. Amber is a witness. If the print is allowed, her pretrial statement is compromised. I can petition the judge to treat her as hostile and lead her testimony. That's where we can score."

"Do you believe your client is innocent?" Duke asked.

"Perhaps," he said and shrugged. "Let's see what happens. Your local prosecutor will be forced to press charges if all goes right at Jimmy's trial. But for now, Amber might speak more freely if she's not lawyered up and ready for a fight."

Marc's friend Ross, a Pawnee County judge, appointed an attorney from Smith & Noble to fill the local DA's position. *Good luck with pressing charges.*

"Marc, hello? Thought we lost you for a minute," John said, jolting him out of his thoughts.

"I'm here. Sort of."

"I'm curious about your son, Devin. What are his charges?"

"Accessory after the fact. My boy faces one to three years if convicted."

"Is he guilty?"

"I don't believe so. All I know is that your client is the key to getting him off."

John stood and walked to the window, overlooking a well-manicured lawn with a bubbling waterfall. He stuck his hands in his pockets and jingled the coins inside. His pensive manner put Marc on edge. The man was about to say something offensive, and Marc braced for the impact.

"There's not a guilty man in prison. They're all innocent, aren't they?"

Marc blew a gasket, Amber be damned. "I am sick and tired of your arrogance and holier-than-thou attitude. If I didn't need your help, I'd whip your ass."

"Stop it!" Jessie screamed, then turned to John. "Please excuse my husband. He's been under a lot of stress. We all have."

Marc's attention riveted on Jessie. *Why is she always apologizing for me?*

"I've had enough," he said as he grabbed his briefcase before making a quick exit.

"What's gotten into you?" Jessie shouted as she chased Marc down the hall.

Marc scowled, angry with himself and his wife. "I'm tired of being the nice guy, the patsy who tries to make everything right for everyone but me. This information could lessen Jimmy's charges, make his attorney look good, and put the real culprits in prison. My thanks? A degrading remark about my son. I'm done." Marc jerked away from his wife.

"You're taking a lot of credit for a bunch of maybes."

Marc's eyes blazed. "I have one more maybe to add to the pile. Maybe you and I aren't meant for each other. I gave up drinking for myself, Jessie. But you've refused to give me any credit."

He reined his anger in. "We've both changed. You dangle your love in front of me, and then jerk it away the moment my actions don't please you. Make up your mind. If our marriage is over, I'll find a better place to sleep than on my office recliner. I can't walk on eggshells anymore."

Jessie looked shocked at his accusations. Marc fidgeted with his watch, praying for a response. None came. Time to walk away.

"Jessie, catch a ride with Duke. Dani, I'll see you tomorrow at 9:00 a.m. sharp. We've got work to do," Marc said over his shoulder as he stormed toward the door.

Duke nodded to Jessie. "Let's go, sis. Ole Buttercup needs milking."

"Grandpa, talk sense into him. He's lost his mind," Jessie pleaded.

"I did," Duke replied with a twisted grin, "and he listened."

"What about me? What am I supposed to do?" Dani asked with a blank expression.

"If I were you, I'd grab a tomahawk and join the war party." Duke strode down the hall with a bounce in his step.

30

Dani lined the kitchen counters with rows of documents in date order but carved out a space at the end for morning treats. The aroma of freshly brewed coffee and a platter of Krispy Kreme doughnuts smelled wonderful to Marc since he had skipped breakfast.

"Help yourself," Dani said. "Cups and plates are in the cabinet by the sink."

He polished off a couple of sugary treats and licked his fingers. Jessie would never permit him to indulge in a billion calories for breakfast at home, which made every bite a sinful, guilty pleasure.

"Ready?" Dani asked. Without waiting for an answer, she attacked the first pile. "Look at this CD. It—"

"Whoa, slow down. Tell me what we're looking at and why."

"Sorry," Dani said and giggled. "I guess I'm anxious to get Grandmother's money back."

"I understand, but tell me exactly what you have and what you think it proves. We'll then color-code the papers so Nancy can process them for exhibit purposes. What's first on the agenda?"

"Okay. First, I have the CDs. After my granddad died, my grandmother put them in her name, and my dad's, so he could cash them if she became incapacitated."

"Very trusting," Marc said, lifting an eyebrow in disapproval.

"That's just it. Grandmother trusted Dad with everything she owned. She had no one else. Dad feared she might make me her guardian and did everything he could to convince her I was too young to manage her affairs. Besides, he had his fancy degree in business."

Marc had seen this often in his practice and knew where it would end. Older people got fleeced by their children.

"Go on."

"I got copies of Grandmother's bank accounts and went through the last five years of transactions. What I found makes me so mad I could spit nails." Dani thumbed through the bank statements and pulled out the month when the CDs were cashed. "A CD for seventy thousand dollars cashed out the same day Madeline made a down payment on the new house. The deposit of the CD into the checking account and the check written for escrow both had Madeline's signature."

Marc examined the deposit slip and the check. Madeline had executed the transactions.

"Dad cashed two CDs for one hundred thousand dollars each and paid the balance on the home. Ten days later, he cashed a sixty-thousand-dollar CD and purchased a new pickup. You get the drift."

"How much did she have left?"

"That totals three hundred and thirty thousand, and she reported four hundred and seventy-five thousand when she applied for assisted living, which should have left one hundred and forty-five. But Dad cashed out ten or fifteen thousand later to cover his gambling, so Grandmother ended up with nothing."

"You discovered this when the assisted living center ran an asset check on her application?" Marc asked.

"Yep. To my way of thinking, Grandmother owns a three-hundred-thousand-dollar home and a spiffy truck."

Marc nodded in agreement, but he knew it would be hard to

wrench a home and transportation from the hands of a widow, especially since David, by Ruby's assignment, owned the CDs. He had a legal right to convert them to cash, regardless of the moral implications.

"Dani, is your dad here?" Ruby called from her bedroom.

"No, it's Marc Whitcomb, our attorney. You remember."

"Attorney? Your dad oversees my business. What do I need an attorney for?"

Dani rolled her eyes and twinkled a smile toward Marc. "Cute, isn't she?"

"You remember me, don't you? You accompanied me on a date to Cain's Ballroom." Ruby moved close to Marc and examined him through narrowed eyes. Her face relaxed.

"Yeah, I remember you. You can't dance. Ha. I go to Cain's Ballroom, and my partner has two left feet." She let out a tiny chuckle and punched him on the shoulder. "Don't worry about it. My husband couldn't dance either."

Dani winked. "I told you she's a corker."

Marc didn't mind being the brunt of Ruby's joke. Her flushed cheeks and sparkling blue eyes touched a soft spot in his heart.

"Allow me to fix you breakfast, Madame." Marc placed a donut on a fancy napkin and poured her a cup of coffee.

"You're funny," she said and then devoured the sugary pastry.

"Marc and I have work to do. Do you want to watch TV in your bedroom or go to Ronda's?"

"Who's Ronda?" Marc whispered.

"A friend down the hall. She watches her on occasion."

"Never mind me. I'll watch TV here." She latched onto a second doughnut and headed down the hall.

"Entertaining, isn't she? By the way, I think she likes you."

"As David or Marc?" They both laughed.

"Have we covered everything on the CDs?" Marc asked.

"No, I have one more thing to show you."

Dani disappeared and returned from her bedroom with a handful of David Caldwell's CDs.

"David kept his CDs and cashed out his mother's?"

"Worse than that. I took these to the bank and asked the president the same thing." Dani shook the papers in Marc's direction. "He turned as pale as a ghost and sent one of the cashiers to pull the files. These are fake copies of my grandmother's certificates. Dad had forgeries made, removed grandmother, and named Madeline beneficiary upon death."

"They're worthless?"

"Yep." Dani flipped the documents onto the table.

"Why would he go through all that trouble if they have no value?"

"Madeline accused Dad of wasting all their money, according to Grandmother. So I think he made these and showed them to Madeline to get her off his back," Dani said, grinning like a cat who snared the rat.

"Where did you get these?"

"Grandmother's bank deposit box. Dad thought he had the only key, so he kept all kinds of stuff there. But he was wrong. Grandmother had a spare, and we cleaned the box out the day they found Dad. I didn't trust Madeline, so we acted fast." Dani's triumphant look said it all. She had bested the devil.

"Wow, this man conned his whole family."

"Especially his wife. Grandmother said they fought like cats and dogs, and he didn't go to the farm to spend weekends. He had moved there to get away from her."

Dani had uncovered a textbook motive for murder: money and greed. She had told him more than once that she thought her grandmother's assets might be tied to her dad's case. JP had kept it simple. He had a confession and an aborted plea deal that ticked all the boxes for Caldwell's death, but didn't scratch the truth.

"May I keep these?" Marc asked, pointing to the forgeries.

"Sure." Dani stepped back for a moment, cocked her head, and grinned impishly. "Makes you think, doesn't it?"

Marc didn't reply, but knew what she meant. Madeline had her prints on the killing.

"Moving on to the deed for the farm. David took the 'dresser-drawer' deed, as you call it, and filed it before your granddad's death. I have a copy, so let's discuss it briefly. Your dad filed the deed prematurely since your grandmother was still living. Do I understand correctly?"

"Yes."

"We have a couple of problems. One, I couldn't find any stipulation directing the deed to be filed after both parents' deaths. On the surface, Tony and Ruby assigned the farm to David, with no time restriction." Marc frowned at the omission.

"Wrong. Granddad wrote 'file upon the death of Tony and Ruby Caldwell' on the blue envelope containing the deed.

"Do you have the envelope?"

"Here." She shoved the envelope across the table.

"It's not attached to the filing document. Your grandmother could have given your dad permission to file whenever she wished."

"But she didn't. Granddad was dying, and Grandmother had just gotten out of the hospital." Dani's voice became screechy, and tears formed in her eyes. "Both were too sick to do such a thing. Believe me."

"I do, but it's not verifiable."

"He paid the farm insurance and taxes out of Grandmother's checking account so she wouldn't catch on. Look at these checks." Dani held the copies out to Marc.

"Your grandmother could have approved," Marc said, his hands spread as if pleading. "It's one person's word against another. And in this case, one is dead, and the other has Alzheimer's."

"I guess there's nothing else to talk about." Dani rose from the table.

"Oh, there's plenty to talk about. I'm taking the case, but I want you to understand the odds are against us."

"Why?" Dani said, tearing up again. "It's clear they stole her money."

"Because Ruby is not a reliable witness. We just covered that," Marc fumed. "She swings in and out of reality. She could testify that she gave David the CDs and the farm, or she could call him a thief. It's anybody's guess."

"I know the truth. I can testify. Have you thought about that?" Dani flipped back at Marc.

His face flushed with frustration. "You have no firsthand knowledge of the conversations your dad had with Ruby. It's just hearsay. Won't be allowed in court."

"You're as weak as Halley." Dani's eyes narrowed in anger.

"Look. Your dad died without a will, so you will receive half the estate minus the house. That deed was held as joint tenants with right of survivorship. That's more than enough to take care of Ruby's needs. If you even got the chance to testify, Madeline's attorneys would slice you into pieces—call you greedy, self-serving. And for the record—Halley was probably wise to refuse this case."

Dani pulled back like a scolded child. "So it's a lost cause."

"Maybe. Maybe not. Let's see how this unfolds. I'll get back to you."

Marc left, cursing his judgment every step of the way, but he would take the chance of being laughed out of court to pierce Madeline's inner sanctum.

31

The idea of moving to the office had plagued Marc since the Tahlequah debacle. It felt like a coward's answer, but with Jimmy's approaching trial and Ruby's lawsuit pending, he didn't have the energy to sort things out. If Jessie wanted a divorce, let her file. Anything would be better than her drill sergeant attitude. Her stony silence while he crept about the house, trying to remain invisible, had to stop. The best solution was to leave.

After work on Monday, Marc went home to pack his clothes, toiletries, sheets, and a pillow. That was minimal baggage after twenty years, he thought, slinging the items in the back seat of the Jeep. He had paid a high price of submission to live in Jessie's world.

Devin ran across the lawn and stuck his head in the driver's window. "Hey, Dad. What are you doing?"

"I'll be staying at the office until all this legal mess is over," Marc answered, wondering if he should tell him the truth. He put the Jeep into park and waited for the next question.

"Because of me?" The pain in his son's eyes hurt.

"You're not the only reason."

"Mom?"

"Yes."

Devin glanced away and back again, scrutinizing Marc with the same melancholy look he used on stray puppies. "We haven't talked since I came home, and I need you to hear what I have to say."

"Sure, son. Come by the office after you have dinner with your mom. No need to upset her by cutting out early."

Marc drove through the alley and lugged his paraphernalia through the back door. Brule would have his marriage debacle out on the street by noon tomorrow, but he didn't want to deal with gossip tonight. A long leather couch would do for a bed, and the bathroom had a small shower for emergencies—not a bad setup unless you like to eat. The library had a tiny refrigerator and a sink in the minibar, but nothing to cook on.

Marc made a quick trip to Venture Foods, purchased a sandwich and chips from the

deli, then returned to a cold, lonely office to wait. He stuffed the ham and cheese in

the fridge and tossed the chips on the counter. His appetite had left him. Thoughts of his family weighed heavily on his mind. Where was his son? He should be here by now. Minutes slowed to a crawl as he sat in quiet solitude for the next two hours.

"Open the door!" Devin shouted as he stood in the alley with arms full of food. "I brought you some ham, scalloped potatoes, salad, and sweet tea to wash it down."

"That's my boy. You have no idea how good that smells. You always did take care of your old man. Thanks, son." For the moment, Marc ditched his loneliness and relished the company of his son and Jessie's delicious cooking.

"Sit down and tell me what we need to discuss. You sounded serious earlier."

"It's not serious, but it's important. Mom relayed Jimmy's statement to you about me being gay. For the record, I'm not."

"It doesn't matter, son," Marc said, waving as if shooing a fly.

"It does matter, but not for the reason you might think. Jimmy was taunting you. He does that sometimes. It's as if he lashes out and draws blood, hurting someone just for the doing of it."

"Why are you telling me this?"

"Jimmy has a mean streak and keeps secrets better than anyone I know. He told me nothing on the trip to Sallisaw, and I didn't pry. But since the murder, it's crossed my mind that Jimmy wanted me to go to the farm to confront Mr. Caldwell and keep Amber out of it. The barn was locked when we got there, and no one was home. I should have pressed him, but I didn't. Trust me, I haven't lied to you since I told you the twins broke the fence instead of me." A boyish grin eclipsed Devin's face, reminding Marc of his son's tender heart.

"Relax. I rank you up there with George Washington and Honest Abe."

Devin chuckled. "I'm sure you do. But seriously, there's something I need to tell you about Jimmy. He and Dani dated before he hooked up with Amber."

Marc spun to face Devin, unable to believe his ears. "The hell you say?" He recalled Jimmy's face when he mentioned Dani's name, but she explained it away, and he bought it.

The blood drained from Devin's face. "Maybe I overstated the relationship. They didn't *date* date. They met a couple of times at Cain's Ballroom. That's all."

"Why did you think it would be important to me?"

"Because when I go to trial, I'll be asked if I know Amber, Madeline, or any family member. I didn't want you blindsided."

"Do you?" Marc's eyes narrowed as he watched Devin's face for traces of lies.

"Amber and Dani are the only two, and Dani doesn't count. I only met her once."

"I'll decide what counts. The stakes are high, my boy, and you are fair game. What about Amber staying in your apartment?"

Devin winced. "Mike Halley made that deal with Mrs. Caldwell. At first, it made me mad, but Amber is a sweet girl. I didn't have the heart to throw her out. Since I wasn't using it, what's the harm?"

Marc's temples throbbed. "Not only is Jimmy your best friend, but you also allowed your attorney to provide a haven for Amber. She murdered her stepfather. Not a good combo, son. You're smarter than that."

Devin stepped toward Marc. "No one's as smart as you are, Dad." A sardonic smile twisted his lips. "Never have been and never will be," he said as he left, slamming the door behind him.

32

"You're here early," Marc said to Nancy on his way to the coffee pot. "My one client must be keeping you busy."

Nancy nodded and continued her morning ritual. She removed her coat, hung it on a peg by the door, then placed her handbag in the bottom left drawer of her desk. Her nimble fingers tucked stray tendrils into the bun at the nape of her neck. Her only nod to vanity was the sparkly brooch pinned to her shoulder. Completing her routine, she directed her attention to Marc.

"I read Ruby's diaries and then tried to document what I could. David and his wife did a number on her and that's not the half of it."

"Yeah, Dani told me."

"You don't understand. Hank and JP helped with some of the shady stuff. I made copies of the important entries."

The revelation didn't surprise him. "Lock the front door and come back to the library."

Marc took Nancy's copies and began reading.

September 19, 2014 – Today is Tony's birthday. Madeline and David don't even remember. David left early, and Madeline shooed me to the bedroom. She doesn't want me to know about the man who comes by when her husband is gone. Ha. That game is centuries old.

I've told David, but he acts like I'm crazy or doesn't care. Oh well, it's his life. Madeline talks like a little mouse, so I can't always understand her, but that man sounds like a boom box. He blabbers at her about buying my farm, thinking she owns it. All I can say is he's chattering to the wrong person. I'm not selling.

"So Madeline is running around on her husband, or at the very least doing business behind his back?" Marc asked.

"Keep reading."

August 22, 2015 – That man came by twice today, so I never set foot out of the bedroom. Every time David's gone, she has a hissy fit about something I've done. She screams at me for being messy if I leave a cup on the counter or take my shoes off in the living room. I feel like a prisoner. She sure acted all sweetie-sweet to me when I first moved in. I offered to pay rent or part of the utilities, but she insisted they didn't want or need any money from me.

August 23, 2015 – Amber came to my room and started hugging me and crying, saying, Don't let my mom and David sell the farm. I pushed her off. That child.

They can't sell my farm?

August 24, 2015 – I got a peek at Madeline's beau. I think his name is Frank. He's a big man with red hair. I hope he didn't see me. I shut the door fast.

August 25, 2015 – David and Madeline had a terrible fight today, and I think it was about me. David shouted, "Mom doesn't have the money to leave." Imagine that. I can't take this anymore. I'm going home.

"That must be about when David dropped her off at the farm, leaving her to fend for herself," Marc said.

"It gets better," Nancy answered, flipping to the next page.

September 6, 2015 – I told David I was going home to the farm. He said he wouldn't take me, so I told him I would call Marie. Man, oh man, that got his attention. I told him I was still his mother and could do what I wanted without his permission.

September 7, 2015 – David brought me to the farm today. All my furniture is gone except for a bed and two chairs. Ha. Guess I'll start over. Hope the old Buick runs.

September 8, 2015 – Picked Marie up, bought groceries, and came home. We couldn't cook without propane, so we sat on the old kitchen chairs and ate ice cream like two old roosting hens. Marie said she would never eat Rocky Road ice cream again. Ha.

"Dani told me this story, and it makes me sick. Too bad I can't file elder abuse charges against a dead man. What else do you have?"

September 17, 2015 – David and Dani got into a screaming match over the phone about my money. She accused him of stealing my money and hung up. He called me, and we went to lunch. He said Dani had it all wrong, and the money had been moved to another account to draw more interest. It seems to me that Madeline and Dani are jealous of how close David and I are, so they make trouble.

"Thanks, Nancy. Leave the diaries with me. I'll take it from here."

"May I say something?" Nancy asked, wringing her hands. "I didn't know the Caldwell family, but David's treatment of his mother is awful. She deserved better. I'll do anything to help her get the money back."

"I'll let Ruby know she has you on her side." Marc shuffled through the remaining copies and then put them aside. When he glanced up, Nancy was standing with her hands folded across her chest, waiting.

"Is there something else?" Marc asked.

"Yes." Nancy bit her lower lip. "You know how I hate gossip, but I think God will forgive me this once. I believe 'Frank' is Hank Walton. There's talk around town about those two being a couple. He's the first person to come to mind with all the talk about the farm. The land joins his, and he's a greedy man."

Marc had not forgotten that Judy, the waitress from Harper's, had reached the same conclusion. Hank would be the match if Madeline's greed had a soulmate.

"These entries are months old. Do you think they became involved before or after David's murder? Think about it carefully. It makes a lot of difference."

Nancy's arms remained locked across her chest, her head held high. "Before. Long before. Hank's wife suspected he was having an affair, and she's been gone two years now."

Talking about Madeline raised Marc's blood pressure.

"For the record, God approves your decision to share with me," Marc said as he patted her hand.

"Hmm. You represent God?" Nancy said and laughed, relaxing a little. "Good to know."

"Okay, I overstated . . . a little. Now, back to work. Call Dani and tell her to make sure she is added as a next friend and attorney-in-fact to the plaintiff list. And don't forget to include David Caldwell's estate by and through its administrator as defendants. Then tell her to have her attorney file the blooming thing this afternoon." Marc smiled. "Not sure how good our chances are, but we can sure gum up the works."

33

Two days had passed since the Tahlequah trip—two days without Jessie and without confronting JP. He had no idea how to fix his marriage, but he would tackle JP today. He dropped by the sheriff's office and caught JP playing on his phone at his desk. Marc walked in and shut the door behind him.

"John Kanoske, Jimmy's attorney, said he delivered a copy of Amber's statement to the DA. Have you brought her in yet?"

"Hold your horses. This matter is between me and the DA. No one mentioned I needed to report to you." JP swiveled in his chair to face the window, signaling that the conversation had ended.

"That's where you are wrong. This matter is between the State of Oklahoma and the perpetrator. If you're not up to the job, I'll keep going up the ladder until I find someone who is."

JP laughed—a loud, shake-the-devil guffaw that sent shocks of anger to the bottom of Marc's toes. "Do you think anyone cares about a murder in Podunk, Oklahoma? Go ahead and talk to the bigwigs. And when you're through, I'll remind them that our little county is underfunded and understaffed. We don't have the money to chase rabbits when we have a confession. I read Amber's statement, and the best I can tell is that she watched her boyfriend lose control and kill her old man. That would make her a witness. We don't usually arrest witnesses, do we?"

"What about breaking and entering?"

"Into her parents' home? Give me a break."

"Jimmy had to have help to drive a Buick and steal David's truck."

"Guess that's where your son comes in." JP tapped his pen on his desk and locked eyes with Marc. "Your son could have copped a plea and gotten twelve months less time served. Thanks to you, he might get more."

Marc assessed JP's cocky assurance. The sheriff had it all figured out, except for one thing: the footprints. Time to spring the trap, as Duke would say.

"What about Amber's footprints?"

"I don't know what you're talking about." The pen tapping stopped, and tiny beads of sweat popped out on his forehead.

"Didn't you cut the carpet samples with footprints and turn them over to the FBI?"

"Yes, I was the first one there and didn't want to take a chance on the footprints getting trampled when everyone started buzzing around." JP clenched his lips together until a white ring formed around his mouth.

"Brilliant work. I assure you, not a single footprint got destroyed."

JP's barrel chest quivered. Marc had hit a nerve but misjudged his opponent. JP flipped on his good-guy demeanor. "No use getting all upset about this. I intended to bring Amber in for questioning . . . as soon as we find her."

"Ask Jimmy's attorney, John Kanoske. Or better yet, ask Madeline's attorney. I assume you know Mike Halley. If you have any trouble locating her, give me a shout." Marc tipped his hat and headed toward the door.

On his walk from the courthouse to his office, Marc passed a small park on Main Street, courtesy of the Ladies' Missionary League. When the old drugstore building burned down, these women swooped in to beautify the gaping hole in a row of brick buildings. The league purchased a wrought iron bench and placed it between the charred walls of the old grocery and hardware store. Jessie spent hours with the ladies "beautifying" the downtown park by painting the old brick. Marc had paid no attention. He had lived in Brule all his life and still didn't know what it looked like. Familiarity blinded him. Tonight, he soaked in every minute detail his mind could absorb.

March was fickle, dropping a blanket of freezing temperatures over the rural town of Brule. The evening air smoothed the day's raw edges as he settled onto the cold metal bench. The closeness of this tiny town comforted and choked him with the same embrace. Small towns were funny. During the thirties, Brule had teemed with horse-drawn buggies on Saturday mornings, but the Dust Bowl blew the farms and the people away. The one stoplight on the corner of Main and Broadway burned out eight years ago, and the loss made little difference. Everyone drove twenty-five miles per hour through town, not because of the speed limit but because they feared they might miss something if they moved too fast.

A semi rolled down Main, loaded with complaining cattle. A string of pickups followed close behind. Marc chuckled. Nothing dainty would do in this rugged country. The people in this godforsaken town did not drive cars; they chose a four-wheel-drive or a dually truck. He drove a Jeep and Jessie a Suburban, though they seldom left the blacktop. Tonight, Brule looked as tired as Marc felt.

He stayed until the light from streetlights pooled on the empty street. Brule went to bed at dark, and he would too. The dry night air and the brisk walk energized him. When he turned onto Broadway, the sight of the sheriff's truck brought him to a dead stop. Two men sat huddled in the front seat. JP couldn't wait to share their encounter with Hank out of the presence of prying eyes. Marc backtracked and headed down the alley to his office, where he collapsed on the couch and put the world on hold until morning.

"Marc, I have John Kanoske on the phone. Will you take the call?" Nancy asked.

The last person on earth Marc wanted to talk to was John Kanoske, but he needed the man.

"Marc, John here. I want to keep you in the loop. I put a bug in the ear of state DA about the slow-walking of Amber Browning's involvement on the local level."

"Great." John's one-eighty surprised him, but he welcomed the turnaround.

"I need your help on Jimmy's behalf. He deserves a fighting chance. Are you game?"

"Yes," Marc gushed.

"Time's getting short. The trial begins on Wednesday. Can you be here on Monday?"

"You bet . . . but let me give you a heads-up. Dani filed a quiet title petition with the courts on Ruby's behalf against Madeline and the Caldwell estate. She'll be madder than a hornet and lawyered up."

"Might work in Jimmy's favor. Monday, then?"

"Monday . . . and thanks."

What a relief. John finally caught the gravity of Amber's story. She might be full of it, but if any nugget of truth existed in her chatter to Jessie, it could make a considerable difference in Jimmy's trial.

At the risk of angering Jessie, Marc called Duke. He needed a place to stay and missed Duke's counsel. Marc's only problem would be dodging Mama Waite's prying questions. His enthusiasm waned. On Tuesday, he would work beside a man he had lambasted last week, which concerned him, but Mama Waite presented the bigger challenge.

Marc arrived in Tahlequah early Monday morning, anxious to share the basis of Ruby's civil suit against Madeline and the estate, which could influence the line of questioning. He and Kanoske spent hours crafting the approach to Amber's testimony in the coming trial. In Marc's mind, the woman was guilty of murder or aiding and abetting. The first could get her life; the latter might be as little as a year of probation.

34

The drive to Duke's house gave Marc ample time to reflect on this morning's preparations. Questions far outnumbered the answers, and he couldn't wait to share with Duke, provided Mama Waite didn't kick him out.

He loved the winding roads that were wrapped between the mountains. Hard gray boulders contrasted sharply with the delicate spring bloom of dogwood trees. The sun rested on the western cliffs, casting shadows across the valley floor. Marc felt a pang of jealousy. Duke lived in paradise but now was not the time to be sentimental. He pushed the pedal to the floor, spinning dust devils behind the wheels of the Jeep as he raced along the dirt road to the Waite home.

Marc spied Duke heading toward the barn.

"Is it time to milk?" Marc called as he ran to catch up with his friend.

"Yes, and today I will teach you to milk Buttercup, Kemosabe." A smile wrinkled Duke's tawny skin.

"Sure. Why not?"

Marc parked his butt on a stool and waited for instructions.

"First, make sure your hands are clean." Duke pointed to a hydrant on the outside corner of the barn.

Marc washed his hands in the cold well water and shook them dry.

"Now, rub your hands together to warm them. If you grab Buttercup's teat with your icy fingers, it won't be the cow that jumps over the moon."

Marc cupped his hands and blew a warm breath across his palms before rubbing them together to generate heat.

"Sit down and take her teat in the palm of your hand and wrap your fingers tightly. Pull down with a gentle squeezing motion."

Marc did as he was told, but nothing happened. He looked at Duke and shrugged. "You want to take over?"

"Nope. Do it again."

On the fourth try, a stream of warm milk hit the bottom of the bucket with a soft clang. Marc smiled. *Not bad*, he thought as he squeezed streams of fresh milk in a steady rhythm.

"It's full." Marc raised the bucket above his head for Duke's inspection. Buttercup, startled by the sudden move, kicked the stool, sending Marc and the milk bucket rolling across the barn floor.

Duke exploded into a belly laugh. "Don't take victory laps until you cross the finish line, Kemosabe. On the bright side, you didn't get kicked in the head."

"Your point?" Marc said, flicking manure off his shirt.

"We should have started with gathering eggs," Duke mumbled as he started toward the house with Marc following.

"What happened to you?" Mama Waite asked, giggling.

Marc glanced down at his pinstriped shirt, plastered to his chest with sticky milk and cow patty stuff. He held an empty bucket in his hand.

"Grab Marc's luggage from the Jeep," Mama Waite directed her husband. "And you," she said, tugging at Marc's elbow, "come in here and take those nasty clothes off."

"You can thank me later, Kemosabe. Mama is much too busy fussing about you to cluck about her spilled milk." The twinkle in Duke's eyes made Marc wonder if the man had set him up.

After a quick shower and a change of clothes, Marc braced to face the family at the dinner table. He wondered whether Jessie had shared the current state of their marriage. He hated losing the Waites in a divorce, especially Duke.

"Jessie tells me you two are fighting." Mama Waite wasted no time clearing the air. "Pass the rolls to Marc, Duke. The man looks like he is starving."

Meals had lost their importance over the last few weeks, and Marc ate only when he remembered, as he continued to lose weight.

"Thanks, and yes, Jessie and I are going through a rough spot." Marc focused on his meal, discouraging further discussion.

"We'll talk later. Eat." Mama Waite had spoken.

Marc took refuge on the front porch after polishing off the huge meal. Spring evenings in the mountain valley were sweet, filling him with a serenity he had never known. A desire to live in this beautiful country tugged at him, but that could never happen after his divorce.

"Penny for your thoughts." Mama Waite moved her rocker close to his.

"This is heaven. I envy you. It's stunning here."

"I will tell Duke. He will find a place for you and Jessie to live when you move here."

"Oh . . . I didn't mean we could move."

"Why not? It's a good thing to live among your people."

After Marc lost his dad, he had no people except for Jessie and his sons.

"When Jessie files for divorce, you'll no longer be my people." That pained Marc to say.

"Jessie will not divorce you. She loves you very much. Both of you are under stress, but it will pass. Give it time."

"When did you start liking me?" Marc teased, hoping to lighten the mood. Instead, Mama Waited grew somber.

"We have needed to talk for a long while. I never disliked you, but I resented Jessie marrying outside the tribe. I've watched my race be diluted, and it breaks my heart. We are a decimated people, not by war but by intermarriage. Yes, I disapproved of your union with my daughter, but that is in the past." Her dark eyes glistened with sincerity.

"I'm not sure I understand everything. I'm sorry for causing you any pain, but I loved—*love* Jessie."

"I know. And I see the affection Duke has for you, too. He is a hard man to win over." Marc's heart skipped a beat. He admired Duke more than he admired any man except his father. "We need you to fight for Jimmy. He is part of my tribe and yours."

Marc felt tears threatening and turned to hide them from Mama.

"I tell you what. We'll poke our fingers and do the blood brother thing later." Mama laughed as she lifted her ample body from the chair and headed indoors. "Right now, I must clear the table. I'm sure my husband didn't."

35

Marc found Kanoske reading emails in this office when he arrived the following morning.

"I got a copy of Madeline's sworn statement. Let me print it and see what her game is," Kanoske said.

The printer spat out two copies, and Kanoske slid one Marc's way. "Skip to paragraph two. That's where the good stuff starts."

On the morning of September 19, 2015, my daughter, Amber Browning, and I took her children to the Mohawk Park Zoo and then to a movie in Tulsa, to keep them busy until we figured out what to do.

We decided that the children should stay with Amber's ex-in-laws until David's murder had been resolved. I enlisted a friend's help in finding an apartment for her since I didn't think it would be wise for her to return to work or stay at my house while all this trial stuff was going on.

I went to the farm on September 20, 2015, at 6:30 a.m. and notified the authorities that I had found my husband's body. And for the record . . .

"That lady is a piece of work. How do you go to the zoo or movies until it's convenient to report on your husband's murder?" Kanoske threw his hands in the air and pushed back from his desk. "We're working with a weird one here."

"Did they charge her with accessory after the fact?" The question seemed silly, but with the Pawnee County DA and his sidekick, JP, on the case, anything could go down.

"They filed, but she's out on bond."

"How about Amber? Any news on her?"

"The DA also brought her in and charged her with second-degree murder and accessory after the fact, but she couldn't make bail, and her mother didn't offer to help. How strange is that?" Kanoske asked.

"Not as strange as you might think. Ruby's lawsuit tied up Madeline's assets. She probably suckered a friend into funding her bail, and Amber is on her own."

Marc walked out of John's office, down the hall, and over to the waterfall in the courtyard. The gurgling flow silenced the white noise in his head, allowing him to think. He felt like a mountain climber who had reached the halfway point of Mount Everest. He had corralled Madeline and Amber, at least for the moment. However, it shouldn't have been that hard. These charges should have fallen into place as naturally as the water tumbling down these rocks. Yet he fought for this moment every step of the way. The second part appeared even harder. The opposition would be more significant, and the stakes would be higher. He had to figure out the pieces that made sense and prove them.

"What's up, Marc?" Kanoske had followed him.

"Nothing about this whole thing is right, not a blooming thing."

"Do you mean how long it took to bring Madeline and Amber up on charges?"

"Yes, but more than that. An innocent man is facing life in prison by choice. Why?"

"And what makes you so sure Jimmy is completely innocent?" Kanoske asked.

"Duke."

John laughed. "I couldn't agree more, but we still must do the homework and convince our man, Jimmy, not to accept a plea, and then pray like hell we can prove his innocence. With a plea, I can get him off with eleven years. If we go to court and lose, it's fifteen years to life for a second-degree conviction. I don't even want to think about a guilty verdict for first degree. We're gambling with his life."

"And if we go to court and win, he goes free." Marc paused. "Kanoske, you've been in this business a long time. Answer a philosophical question for me."

"Sure, if I can."

"Jessie asked me why a crime is worth less punishment if you take a plea rather than being convicted in a court of law. She said it's like our justice system rewards someone for giving up their right to a trial by jury. I stumbled around with an answer, but I'd like to hear your take."

"That's a hard one, and I've struggled with it for years. I think it's a holdover from our Puritan Christian roots. Society demands you admit guilt, accept responsibility, and benefit."

"Kinda goes against our Founding Fathers' position, doesn't it? The defendant is not mandated to admit that he did anything. It's up to the prosecution to prove it." Marc's voice faded to a whisper. "We're screwed if the judge disallows the footprints."

"There's not a snowball's chance in hell those footprints will be admitted in court, but they might trigger Jimmy."

"Is Jimmy on board with a trial rather than a plea?"

"Oh yeah. He's got the notion from someone, and I think that someone is Madeline. He believes if he committed a crime of passion for a good reason, he'll walk. I can't convince him otherwise. I want to knock some sense into him, but if I don't do as he asks, he'll ditch me as his attorney. Crazy, isn't it?"

"You mean Amber's allegation that David molested her children is his defense?"

"That's the one. I don't think a jury will buy that level of 'passion' when the children are not his. We need to prove the gun wasn't in his hand. Since there were no prints on the weapon and the glove in the garage had his DNA, the shooting points to Jimmy . . . unless he wiped the gun clean."

"Footprints," Marc said, pressing his hands together. "Pray for footprints."

"Footprints would be great, but we have a bigger problem with a jury." Kanoske tossed a stone into the fountain. "The odds of getting a jury of Cherokees are slim to none. Our jury will be a bunch of pale-faces, no offense."

"None taken."

The challenge overwhelmed Marc. He understood his son could be called to testify. Devin's fate marched in lockstep with Jimmy's. If one fell, the other would follow. Marc braced for the gates of hell that would open tomorrow morning.

Marc rose at sunrise, too anxious to sleep. He didn't need coffee this morning to spike his energy. The drive through the mountains didn't work its usual magic, but the miles passed unnoticed as he played the what-if game on today's outcome. Before he knew it, he arrived at the courthouse and found a front-row bench near the defendant's table. He had no legal standing to serve as Jimmy's defense attorney, since he was not a member of the Cherokee Nation Bar, but could serve as Kanoske's right-hand man.

Jury selection began, and, as Kanoske predicted, the small pool of tribal citizens offered little hope of a favorable choice. He worked on the process for hours, but the outcome was disappointing. Seven men and five women, two tribal, rounded out the panel of jurists. Marc felt exhausted and could only imagine how Kanoske must feel.

"Join me for a drink?" Marc asked.

"Not tonight. I need to bring my A game tomorrow."

Marc nodded, hiding a smile of relief since he preferred to spend the evening with Duke. He found his friend in the barn milking Buttercup. The old Jersey kept Duke on a schedule as demanding as an alarm clock.

Duke turned with his arm extended, palm up. "Stay back, Kemosabe. I don't want this old cow kicking at me." Duke resumed his milking until the foaming white liquid filled the pail. "Now, come on in."

"Any advice for me today?" Marc asked, not expecting an answer.

"I can tell you what Kanoske needs to accomplish, but he must figure out how. From what you have told me, Jimmy's world revolves around Amber. My gut tells me she is using him, and she must be the one who shatters his obsession with her."

"Kanoske intends to do that with her footprint."

Duke rolled his eyes and went back to cleaning Buttercup's stall.

"I can see that's not what you had in mind." Marc felt he had failed another test.

"Kanoske must break the illusion that she cares for him. Ask about her first marriage. Ask about her job as a stripper. Ask about the call where Madeline quoted Amber saying, 'We did it.' Who's 'we'?"

Duke made perfect sense. Ask Amber to answer questions that will destroy her damsel-in-distress facade and reveal her real love—attention. His advice was spot-on, but the opportunity to quiz Amber didn't exist. She had chosen to take the Fifth.

Marc's stomach knotted when he saw Kanoske pacing the courthouse steps like a cornered animal. He took the steps two at a time, anxious to discover the source of his menacing frown. The ominous furrow of Kanoske's brow meant news—terrible news, if Marc read him right. Not a good start to the first day of Jimmy's trial.

"They have petitioned the court to upgrade the charges. Jimmy is now facing first- and second-degree murder and manslaughter." Kanoske's voice sounded husky.

Marc gasped, "What? Where did that come from?"

"The prosecution intends to weaken our theories of Jimmy's defense. This prosecutor always overcharges to set the tone for the trial and to restrict the defense from using so-called technical defenses. I thought a second degree was an overcharge."

The strategy itself did not surprise Marc, but the fact that they raised the stakes did. The DA must believe there's enough evidence to pursue a first-degree conviction. This was not a great start to a bad day.

"Let's go. Won't get any better standing out here."

The courtroom swarmed like a beehive on a warm summer day as locals anticipated the lurid details of a murder. Marc inched through the buzzing crowd to the front. He glanced around the small room and then toward the double door leading into the hall. Jessie came strolling in, dressed in a bright blue-and-white pinstriped suit with a red rose on her lapel. She looked perfect, as always.

She spotted him, waved, and then plowed through the spectators to join him.

"You look nice," Marc said, fishing for small talk.

Jessie laughed. "You know how important it is for me to look good at a murder trial."

"Thanks for coming. Today might be a tough one, especially if Devin takes the stand. I need moral support." Jessie's smile did not erase the strain between them, but at least she made an appearance. Kanoske, Jimmy, and the prosecutor slipped through the side door and took their assigned battle stations.

"All rise," the bailiff instructed as a hush fell over the room.

"Quite dramatic," Jessie whispered. "Like on TV."

"Shhhh. I don't want the bailiff to escort us out of the courtroom."

Judge Bolton entered the room and assumed the bench. His confident manner overshadowed his slight build and thin face, leaving little doubt about who controlled this court. The business of the trial began.

Kanoske's opening remarks for the defense were impressive, but the fiery lead prosecutor, Mike Mitchell, came to play hardball. His delivery was as intimidating as his bulky six-foot frame. He worked the jury like a master violinist, playing the sad notes of family loss to the crescendo of a brutal murder. The jury sat glued to the performance, as did Marc.

Marc reminded himself that the defendant always sounded guilty until the defense witnesses took the stand. But Jimmy's confession presented an obstacle that would be difficult to overcome. Fortunately, Kanoske held an ace, Jimmy's mother. Marc understood the game about to unfold, but logic couldn't calm his nerves.

Mitchell called JP Davis to the stand to establish the protection of the evidence at the crime scene. JP stuck to his written report, reciting each sentence of the process, almost putting Marc to sleep. He had that report memorized.

Marc snapped to attention when the cross-examination began.

John approached JP, with a slow, deliberate gait. JP shrank with each step.

"Mr. Davis, what was your first action upon arrival at the crime scene?" Kanoske's voice boomed in the small courtroom.

JP's eyes scanned the crowd, landing on Hank. Like magic, his gumption returned.

"Deputy Smith told me Mrs. Caldwell's husband had been murdered and directed me to the living room. I inspected the body and saw a gunshot wound, so I called the FBI." JP leaned back and cupped his hands in his lap, seemingly proud of his answer.

"Is it customary to call the FBI for a murder?" John kept drilling.

"No, but the state has no authority over tribal lands, so I called in the FBI." JP's tone was solid.

"If my calculations are correct, the nearest FBI agency is west of Tulsa, and it would take approximately one hour and thirty minutes for the FBI to arrive. Is that consistent with your estimate?" Kanoske cocked his head and looked at the witness with feigned seriousness.

"Yes."

"How did you occupy the time between your call to the FBI and their arrival?"

"I visited with Mrs. Caldwell. I walked around to make sure . . ." JP hesitated, unsure of where Kanoske was headed.

Kanoske rolled the report and smacked his left palm. "To make sure of what?"

"That no one destroyed the evidence." Little beads of sweat popped out on JP's forehead.

"Help me with this one, Chief. According to the report, the only people on site before the FBI arrived were Mrs. Caldwell, Deputy Smith, and you. Would you like to add anyone to that list?"

"No." JP swallowed hard and reached for his water bottle. He took a slow sip as his eyes searched the courtroom before resting on John.

"Which of the two did you suspect would tamper with the evidence?"

Mitchell cried in a resounding voice, "Objection. Leading the witness. He would have no way of knowing who might tamper with evidence."

"Sustained." Judge Bolton ruled in a muted tone, unfazed by the prosecution's passion.

"Let's circle back," Kanoske said in a smooth baritone. "What did you do to ensure the integrity of the evidence?"

JP shifted from side to side like a trapped mouse. "I cut the footprints out of the carpet and gave them to the FBI agent. I wanted to make sure no one walked over them, you know, before they messed them up."

With the sobriety of a priest, Kanoske answered, "No, I don't know. A little out of the ordinary for crime scene procedures." He tapped his pencil against the table, taking a few moments to let his words sink in. It could be that JP's sloppiness stemmed from stupidity . . . or he deliberately tampered with evidence. Either way, h Kanoske could ask for the evidence to be excluded due to an improper chain of command, but that would put a noose around his own neck. He needed Marc's samples to be admitted into evidence.

"How many carpet samples did you remove?"

"About fifteen." JP shriveled before Marc's eyes as Kanoske squeezed the life out of the little toad.

"How many samples were returned from the lab?"

"I don't know."

"How many holes were cut in the carpet?" Kanoske pressed.

"I don't—"

"Then let me help you. Sixteen carpet samples were removed from the crime scene, and thirteen samples made it to the lab for testing." Kanoske hit the jugular and laid the groundwork to admit fresh evidence—Amber's footprint.

The courtroom erupted in titters as Judge Bolton pounded his gavel.

"Your Honor, I want to introduce the three missing samples into evidence." Kanoske's timing was impeccable.

"I object!" Mitchell screamed.

"In my chambers," the judge directed as he wiped his balding head with a handkerchief. "The jury will take a short recess."

A flurry tore through the courtroom, and a cloud crossed Jimmy's face. He appeared angry with the deviation from his defense and sent a scorching scowl in Marc's direction.

Fifteen minutes later, John emerged from the judge's chambers and hooked a thumbs-up toward Marc.

"He got Amber's footprint admitted." Marc gave Jessie a quick hug. "That man knows how to swing a bat."

"How? Wouldn't that trigger a mistrial?" she asked, entranced, her black hair brushing against her shoulders as she shook her head.

"No. The court has the discretion to allow new evidence at any time, including after the close of evidence . . . even after jury arguments. Still, Kanoske will have to walk a fine line on using it," Marc whispered.

"I now enter into evidence as Exhibit 13-b the three carpet samples. May I resume my questioning of Deputy Sheriff JP Davis, Your Honor?"

"Please take the stand, Deputy Davis." Judge Bolton turned to the bailiff. "There is no need to swear him in. He's still under oath."

Kanoske went on, "This sample showed an imprint of a woman's size-seven Nike tennis shoe, which was taken fifteen inches from the victim's body. Were you aware of the presence of a female at the scene of the murder?"

JP shrugged. "Sure. Amber Browning stated that she was with Jimmy Don Allen at the house." Arrogance oozed from JP as he got a second wind.

"Amber alleged she waited in the pickup after the shooting while Jimmy Allen doused David Caldwell in gasoline and set him on fire. Is that your understanding, Deputy Davis?"

"It is, sir. I can read." JP's friends in the front row snickered with him.

"Then how would her footprints burn into the carpet?"

JP sputtered as he tried to formulate an answer, but Kanoske did not wait for a reply.

"That is all at this time, Your Honor, but I reserve the right to recall the witness."

"You may step down, Deputy. Due to the hour, this court will adjourn and resume at 9:00 a.m. tomorrow." The judge looked weary. His call to allow the footprints might set the stage for a retrial.

"Great start." Marc slapped John on the shoulder. "Ole JP needs to put on his thinking cap and figure out what happened to the missing samples. I bet they're all reeling from his mishandling of evidence."

"Yeah, it went well, but the most I can hope for is to impugn Amber's veracity. Jimmy's still convinced David molested the children, and that alone justifies his death, so he won't lift a finger to point at Amber." Kanoske shook his head and gazed past Marc at the stream of people exiting the courthouse. "Jimmy's prepared to sit in prison for years to protect his girlfriend. I don't think he understands that the sentence could be life."

Marc didn't want to think about Jimmy's fate. Tonight, he would concentrate on Jessie. She didn't linger to visit after court, and Duke might throw him out if she felt uncomfortable with the arrangement at the house.

When Marc arrived, the Waite family had clustered on the front porch. The tribe seldom gathered before dark, sparking Marc's curiosity. Duke had completed his evening chores, and Mama Waite had dinner in the oven. He seemed to be the focus of the powwow.

"Marc, Jessie suggested we all attend Jimmy's trial tomorrow," Duke said, "but it's your call."

Marc glanced at his wife, hovering in the alcove near the door, a faint smile on her lips.

"Jimmy needs moral support. I watched him today. He's confused and scared. Friendly faces might help," Jessie said as Marc approached.

"I would appreciate some friendly faces myself. It's a great idea."

"Will Devin testify?" Jessie asked, concerned.

"I'm not sure. I don't look for the prosecution to call Devin to testify, but who knows?" Marc answered. "He's staying at a hotel in Tahlequah, just in case. I didn't want him stirred up by any talk of the trial."

"That's good advice for all of us. Now let's eat." Mama shooed the pack to the kitchen. "And no trial talk at the table."

"Marc, I moved your things to the den so you can work late. I know how you lawyers are." With a wink, Mama removed the awkwardness of sleeping arrangements.

36

Day two of the trial arrived, and Marc's adrenaline pumped like a boxer on a fight day. He met Kanoske at the courthouse early, ready for action. But he wasn't mentally prepared for the entrance of the ice queen, Bible in hand, heading down the corridor to a private room. A young lawyer, clad in a well-tailored suit and carrying a black briefcase, accompanied Madeline. She had the same placid expression Marc had observed at the crime scene, and her demure attire projected an aura of innocence. Well played. She was a pro.

The courtroom contained two large tables, each surrounded by four chairs. The court reporter finished setting up her gear as the lawyers and court personnel mingled, spouting awkward niceties. Marc studied the body language of the court cast, looking for any weakness to emerge. Duke had taught him much about reading faces, and he intended to put it to use.

Prosecutor Mitchell's face, pinched like a prune, revealed irritation. JP's "oversight" had torn a big hole in his case.

Kanoske, on the other hand, twisted with frustration as he engaged in an animated discourse with his client. And Jimmy sat with his arms across his chest, closed to whatever his attorney had to say, a score for the prosecution.

Marc fidgeted with his glasses as a familiar tightness gripped his chest. *Not today*, he thought. *Not today.* He drifted from the group, grabbed a cup of coffee, and returned to the bench as he watched Kanoske rise from the table and weave through the crowd toward the hallway. Soon, he returned. His dark, tailored suit accentuated his solid build. He looked like Atlas, a man strong enough to hold the weight of the world on his shoulders for an eternity. This statuesque Cherokee warrior mesmerized Marc.

Court resumed. After Judge Bolton's informative statements, Mitchell called his first witness of the day, the prim and proper Madeline Caldwell. Her blonde hair cascaded about her face as she leaned toward her young lawyer, whispered in his ear, and rose slowly.

She glided to the witness stand like a royal approaching her throne—head erect, shoulders back, and a halo of perfection that angels would envy. Marc moaned. This woman played the part of a grieving widow, determined to do what's right, perfectly.

Mitchell began in low-key way. "Mrs. Caldwell, were you offered a plea deal in exchange for your testimony today?"

"No, the case against me was dismissed." A faint blush washed across her fair cheeks, as if embarrassed by the question.

"And why was it dismissed?

"The Pawnee County DA did not find the evidence compelling." She glowed as brightly as her blonde locks.

Marc's jaw dropped. He had no idea that the DA dropped the charges. Madeline's perceived innocence could have a profound impact on the jury.

"Mrs. Caldwell, in your own words, please tell us what happened on the morning of September 18, 2015," Mitchell requested in a well-modulated baritone.

"I phoned David about 10 a.m. to make sure he was at the farm to help Amber unload some furniture she wanted to store in the barn," Madeline said with assurance.

The prosecutor continued. “Did you have any reason to believe he would not be at the farm, as you call it?”

“Yes,” she said and nodded.

“Would you state that reason for the jury?”

“He . . . My husband gambled. Sometimes, he stayed at the casino all night . . . in Tulsa. I wanted to make sure he would be there.” Madeline flashed a demure smile toward the jury.

“And was he at the farm?”

“No, David said he would be back at about 2 p.m. He said he had to go to the bank to take care of something for his mother.”

“Did you have any contact with your daughter, Amber Browning, that morning?” Mitchell asked. “Take your time in answering,” he added.

His kid-glove approach irritated Marc.

“Yes, I called Amber back to tell her when David would be home.”

“Was there anything unusual about the conversation?”

“No.”

“Okay, let’s move to the events on the afternoon of September 18. Again, in your own words.”

“Okay. Well. Amber called me about 2:45 p.m. on September 18, and said, ‘He did it. He killed him.’” Her voice trembled, and her hands visibly shook. “I was at work and didn’t know what to do. She was crying, and I . . . I started crying.” Madeline covered her face and burst into gut-wrenching sobs.

Kanoske lunged from his desk. “Move to strike. Hearsay, Your Honor.”

“Sustained. The court will strike this testimony from the record.” Judge Bolton leaned close to Madeline. “Do you need a moment?”

“No . . . I’m fine,” she sniffed.

The prosecutor nodded encouragement to Madeline. “Continue when you are ready.”

“I told her to meet me in the parking lot by my office. When she arrived, we rented a room for the night at the Camelot Inn. I couldn’t bear to go home.” Tears flowed like waterworks.

“Was Jimmy with her?”

"No . . . I mean, yes. Jimmy dropped Amber off and left." Madeline struggled through her tears.

"What vehicle was Jimmy driving?" Mitchell methodically led his witness.

"My 2005 Buick LeSabre."

"Did you notice anything unusual when they arrived?"

Madeline's eyes were riveted on Mitchell. "Yes, Jimmy had red stains on his shirt." She didn't stutter.

"How about Amber? Did she have stains on her clothing as well?"

"No," she answered, with a touch of defiance.

"Did Amber explain why she was upset?" Mitchell had set up Madeline to point the blame at Jimmy. The adage "Once said, never forgotten" was a tool in every attorney's box.

"Objection. Hearsay." Kanoske's quick reaction blocked Mitchell's move.

"Sustained. The witness will refrain from answering the question," Judge Bolton instructed as he tugged at his mustache.

The prosecutor walked to the table and studied some documents, then resumed his questioning.

"You stated that you and Amber stayed at the Camelot Inn on the night of September 18. What transpired over the weekend before you reported your husband's murder?" Mitchell clearly intended to clean his own closet.

"Amber and I stayed in the room. We didn't even go out to eat. I cried. She cried. We were devastated, but couldn't hide in a hotel room forever. A friend loaned Amber an apartment, and I drove to the farm Monday morning and reported David's death." Her sobs exploded again.

Madeline's sincerity was striking. Either she was innocent or deserved an Emmy for the performance. Mitchell glanced at this witness, clearly pleased.

"I have no more questions for the witness at this time, Your Honor. I reserve the right to recall the witness."

Act One ended. Marc had no idea why the prosecutor called Madeline as a witness. Most of her testimony was hearsay. But the charges against her were dismissed with prejudice; she couldn't be prosecuted if new evidence arose. Perhaps Mitchell sought sympathy from the jury by displaying a widow's innocence and willingness to cooperate. Since the prosecutor had no personal concerns for Madeline, he may have counted on her to sneak in "He did it. He killed him" before the objections, knowing the jury couldn't unhear that statement.

"Your witness, Mr. Kanoske," Judge Bolton said, pointing his gavel at John.

Kanoske's perfect posture, black hair, and rugged features presented a formidable image of strength. Mrs. Caldwell would meet her match. Marc knew firsthand how his attorney friend could dissect a simple statement.

"From your previous testimony, you stated that you talked to Amber twice on the morning in question, once to ask for help unloading the furniture and second to relate the time David would arrive at the farm. Is that correct?"

"Yes."

Kanoske took two steps toward the witness and stopped. "Had Amber stored her belongings in the barn on prior occasions?"

"No," Madeline answered guardedly.

"So for the first time, Amber needed to store furniture at the farm on the day of the murder." Kanoske's implication was direct and to the point.

Madeline looked at Kanoske, hesitated, then answered, "Yes."

"Did Amber have someone with her?"

"I believe Jimmy was with her."

"You believe? Was she alone, or not? Please answer the question." His tone was stern.

"Jimmy was with her," she answered sharply.

"What vehicle were they driving?"

"My Buick."

Two men and a woman seemed like too many people to unload an item that could fit into a midsize car. Marc hoped the jury thought the same way he did. Marc waved a paper at him, then slipped it onto the table. Kanoske stepped close, read the note, then nodded.

Kanoske raised his eyebrows. "Why would Jimmy drive your car?"

"His car was in the shop, so I loaned him mine." Her haughty manner resurfaced.

"Are you aware that your Buick was found at the bottom of a canyon in Hank Walton's pasture near Blackburn?"

"Yes, JP . . . I mean, Deputy Davis told me."

"The car turned up days after the murder. Did you report it missing?"

"No, I figured Jimmy still had it." Madeline squirmed.

Kanoske took a small step forward. "Did it occur to you that the license plate, make, and model would make the search for Jimmy easier, or did you already know the circumstances surrounding the vehicle?"

"Objection. Argumentative." Mitchell shot a menacing glance at Kanoske.

"Sustained," Judge Bolton thundered. "I don't allow this line of questioning in my court."

Kanoske seemed unperturbed. "No more questions at this time, Your Honor. I reserve the right to recall the witness."

Judge Bolton shuffled through a couple of papers, then glanced at the clock. The hour grew late.

"The court will recess until 9:00 a.m. tomorrow. The jury is dismissed."

Marc liked Kanoske's style. He blew the cocky attitude of the prosecutor to smithereens and took control of the witness. Unfortunately, the judge didn't appreciate it as much as he did. Kanoske retreated to the defendant's table and sat down beside Jimmy. The two engaged in what appeared to be a heated conversation. Jimmy shook his head, and Kanoske threw up his hands.

37

"Let's go," Kanoske said as he marched past Marc in the courtroom. "I need coffee."

"I'll meet you at The Grind." The artsy coffee shop provided an excellent retreat for private conversations. High-backed booths, elevator music, and the best designer coffee in town offered the perfect haven for Marc and John to dissect the day's events.

"What do you make out of what happened?" Kanoske asked.

"I've been immersed in this cesspool for months, beginning with my son's problems, and I'm here to tell you that nothing happened the way Madeline is painting it. Unless she's the flying nun, someone gave her a ride on the day she 'discovered' her husband's body, and Amber doesn't have a car. I'd bet my last dollar that *someone* was Hank."

Kanoske stirred his coffee, preoccupied with the swirling liquid. "Well and good, my friend, but that was after the murder. I'll cross on that, but don't expect anything to come of it. No one has accused her of pulling the trigger, and the prosecution is very sympathetic to the pretty widow."

"Try this on. Devin said he and Jimmy went to the farm early on the 18th, just the two of them, to *pick* up a kitchen table for Amber, not *put* furniture in storage. David wasn't home, and Devin had to get back to work."

"So you're saying Jimmy made two trips to the farm that day?" Kanoske's spoon stopped, mid-swirl.

"That's exactly what I'm saying. And remember, Madeline said Amber had never stored furniture in the barn." Marc shoved his coffee cup toward the center of the table to punctuate his thoughts. The hot, steamy liquid splashed over the rim, staining Marc's crisp white shirt. "Damnation. Hand me a napkin."

"Relax. Your shirt is ruined, but you make a great point."

"Yeah, and she thinks we're stupid. A Buick won't hold much, so why would it take two men and a woman to unload it?" Marc's enthusiasm faded.

"I appreciate your take, but my primary focus is on how Jimmy fits in." Kanoske resumed stirring his coffee with a vengeance as if beating the innocent brew would produce an answer.

"As your friend, I need to ask: Have you considered the possibility that your son is lying?" The tinkling in the cup stopped as Kanoske awaited the answer.

"He's not lying. The way I see it, the local authorities have no interest in getting to the bottom of this. I have my suspicions as to why. An easy confession. A convenient accomplice. Voilà. We have a neat wrap on capital murder. Madeline is now a wealthy widow whose boyfriend can buy or marry the farm, and my son is sacrificed for her daughter."

"What about her daughter? You think she pulled the trigger?" Kanoske asked.

"Amber? You bet I do, but she had no reason to kill her stepfather until her mother gave her one. Molesting her children. Her mother tried to set Amber up as an innocent bystander to a murder. She was charged with accessory after the fact, but I bet the sentence is nominal." Marc pushed away from the table as if to distance himself from the ugliness.

"But why would Jimmy want to take the wrap?" John quizzed.

"You know why. Amber's pretty, childlike, and . . . yada yada yada." Marc's hands twirled in circles above his head.

"And she is the love of his life. That 'murder one loves murder two' note made that clear," Kanoske added.

Marc's face relaxed. "You didn't believe his allegation that Devin was the intended recipient?"

"Not for a minute. Jimmy is under the impression he will get off or get a light sentence because the shooting was accidental or in the 'heat of passion' since David allegedly molested Amber's kid. He intends to be her hero."

"Where do *you* think he got this crap?" Marc asked.

"Same place Amber did—Madeline," John replied as he signaled the server for a refill. "You know what amazes me? You can't crack Jimmy. He won't let go."

"There are holes in the story, starting with Madeline's, but juries have a hard time picking up nuances. There will not be an aha moment. Madeline has spun a web like a spider, and Jimmy got trapped." Marc grabbed a packet of Sweet'N Low and dumped it into his coffee.

"For instance?"

"Like I said, Devin and Jimmy went to the farm to retrieve a table for Amber. What's that about? Madeline testified that Amber had never stored furniture at the farm. Besides, that's a two-hour drive, and Devin had to be at work by 10:00 a.m. They left Tulsa and arrived about sunup. Sunrise on September 18 was 7:18 a.m. Hank, a rancher who owns land that joins the Caldwell place, alleges he saw the boys at that time. That's the line that dragged Devin into the mess."

Kanoske leaned toward Marc. "So you think Jimmy tried to drag your boy into the actual murder?"

"That was the original intent, but in my opinion, it fell apart quickly. David was not at home. According to Dani, he was in Tulsa to convince his mother that he did not steal her money. He took her to lunch, drew money out of his account, and gave it to her to 'prove' all was well," Marc said.

"So where does Devin fit in now?"

"Accessory after the fact for giving Jimmy a ride to Sallisaw." Marc slapped both hands on the table in surrender. "You're making my head hurt. Let's order lunch and give it a break."

"It's been my pleasure to make you suffer. What do you recommend from the menu?" Kanoske's smile lightened the mood.

"For you, Counselor, a meatball sub. I'll be having the hero sandwich."

They both laughed, eager to shake the weight of murder. They ate their meals in silence, each preoccupied with the day's events.

"See you in court tomorrow." Kanoske flipped his napkin onto the table. "If you have any earthshaking thoughts, give me a shout." He made a hasty exit, leaving Marc to pick up the tab.

38

The court hummed with anticipation of the day's proceedings. Kanoske and Jimmy had settled in place. Judge Bolton addressed the jury in his usual dry manner and then nodded to lead prosecutor, Mike Mitchell, to present his next witness. The attorney stood and flexed his shoulders like a bull preparing to charge.

"Your Honor, I call Betty Thompson to the stand."

A stocky woman in her late forties, dressed in a white shirt, khaki pants, and sensible shoes, made her way to the front and took her seat.

"Please tell the court your current occupation." Mitchell's brusque approach replaced yesterday's mild-mannered style.

"I am employed as an agent for the Oklahoma State Bureau of Investigation." Her sober demeanor exuded authority.

"And what is the nature of your testimony?"

"I conducted forensic interviews with the children to determine if sexual abuse had occurred."

"I object. Your Honor, may I approach the bench?" Kanoske scrambled to his feet, clearly angry.

"Will the defense and prosecution approach?" Judge Bolton appeared put out with the interruption.

Both attorneys stood at the front of the court in a heated debate. Kanoske had filed a motion in limine seeking to preclude the admission of the testimony of two witnesses, the OSBI agent and the paternal grandmother, arguing that such testimony would include inadmissible hearsay and violate Jimmy's right to confront witnesses —the children. Blocking this line of questioning was crucial to Jimmy's defense since it might discredit his motive for killing Caldwell. Jimmy had told several potential witnesses that David Caldwell had molested Amber's children. If this premise was debunked, Jimmy's defensible motive evaporated.

Marc strained to hear the proceedings without luck. He would have to sweat it out.

"Objection overruled. The witnesses will be allowed a limited opportunity to testify, but I caution the prosecutor to tread carefully. I will not allow a modicum of hearsay in my court. Stick to direct observations and interactions with the children."

Kanoske swallowed a groan. This decision could break the back of Jimmy's "crime of passion" defense.

"You may proceed," the judge said, nodding to the prosecutor.

"Agent Thompson, please tell the court your findings concerning your observations and interactions with the children," Mitchell began.

"Neither child disclosed any abuse by Mr. Caldwell or anyone else," Agent Thompson said with self-assurance.

"No further questions." Mitchell made his point with very few words.

"The defense may question the witness," said the judge.

"No questions, Your Honor." Kanoske had no intention of harping on the damning words. The testimony would only strengthen with cross-examination.

"The prosecution calls Beth Sanders to the stand." Mitchell was on a roll.

A plump, grandmotherly figure took timid steps toward the stand, her discomfort evident.

"State your relationship to the children."

"I am their grandmother on their father's side. I keep the children a lot when Amber is working," Beth answered in a quiet, assured voice.

"How many days a week do you care for the children?"

"Maybe five. It depends."

"Please tell the court your observations concerning your grandchildren's alleged molestation." The prosecutor spoke carefully, in keeping with the judge's directive.

"They never acted out sexually or told me about any abuse." The grandmother's lips quivered. "I think I would have noticed. I try to take real good care of them."

"I'm sure you do, Mrs. Sanders." The prosecutor hesitated and then turned to the bench. "No more questions, Your Honor."

"Would the defense like to cross?"

"No questions," Kanoske replied. Attacking a grandmother would be suicide.

Marc could not take his eyes off Jimmy. The young man deflated like a punctured balloon as he lay his head on the table, visibly crushed by the testimony presented.

"Does the prosecution have any additional witnesses?" the judge asked.

"Yes, Your Honor, I call Devin Whitcomb to the stand."

"Devin Whitcomb will not testify but invokes his Fifth Amendment right against self-incrimination," the judge announced.

Marc had taken the necessary steps to prevent Devin from asserting his privilege before the jury. The trial court erred in advising them that he had invoked his Fifth Amendment rights. This error might provide grounds for reversing Jimmy's sentence, but the immediate effect weakened his defense. Another hill to climb.

"The prosecution rests, Your Honor." Mitchell had wrapped up with a win.

"Mr. Kanoske, I presume you are prepared to call a witness for the defense."

"Yes, Your Honor. I call Mary Thomas to the stand."

"Jimmy's mother?" Jessie asked, her mouth gaping. "What kind of mother testifies against her son?"

"Mary is a defense witness. Hopefully her testimony will help, not hurt."

"But will they believe her?" Jessie asked.

"She doesn't want to go to jail for lying under oath." Marc remained calm. He had seen the witness list and anticipated that she would testify.

Mary's hair, pulled back into a single braid, revealed a handsome Cherokee woman who reminded Marc of his wife. She didn't look at the crowd as she approached the stand, but she held her head high. Her steps were purposeful, anchored in the pride of her people. The bailiff swore her in, and she edged toward her seat.

"Would you state your relationship to the defendant?" John began.

"I am his mother," she answered in a low, throaty voice.

"Mrs. Thomas, may I ask you to speak louder? The court reporter will not be able to hear your answers."

"Yes, sir." Her voice was barely audible.

Great, Marc thought, *the jury won't feel the impact of her testimony if she doesn't speak up.*

"Are you acquainted with Amber Browning?"

"Yes."

"In what fashion?" Kanoske asked.

"She is my son's girlfriend and came to the house with him once."

"How long did your son and Amber date?"

"Not long." She hesitated, weighing her answer. "Maybe a few months."

"Did you have a conversation with your son on September 17, 2015, the night before the Caldwell murder?"

"Yes."

Kanoske stepped closer. "Tell us about it. Take your time and try not to leave anything out."

Mary's composure broke. She fidgeted with a Kleenex and sipped from a bottle of water. Her hands shook; her voice trembled.

"Jimmy called me, very upset. He told me that Mr. Caldwell, Amber's stepfather, had touched her children inappropriately and molested them and rubbed them raw while bathing them."

"Did Jimmy make any other comments?"

"No, he handed his phone to Amber. She told me that Mr. Caldwell would pay and that if she killed her stepfather, she could plead insanity because of what Mr. Caldwell had done to her kids. She also said that her mother was a nurse and could cover up the death by making it look like an accident or a heart attack." Mary's voice rang loud and clear. She had regained her confidence.

Jessie nudged Marc. "That's the same thing Amber said to me." Marc put a finger to his lips to silence his wife. He wanted to hear every word.

"And how did you respond to Amber?" Kanoske asked.

"I told her not to do anything and that she needed to take the children to the emergency room to be examined by a doctor, and to call the police and let them take care of it."

"Did you have any further conversation with your son or Amber?"

"No." Mary puffed up and crossed her arms over her chest. "She hung up on me."

"Have you had any conversations with your son since the murder?"

"Yes. Right before Jimmy turned himself in, he called and said Amber had shot Mr. Caldwell but that he was gonna take the blame."

"Why would he admit to a murder he didn't commit?"

"Because of her." Mary looked like she could spit, but thought better of it. "She twisted Jimmy around her finger."

Mitchell sprang to his feet like a jack-in-the-box. "Objection. Speculation."

"Sustained," Judge Bolton said without looking up.

"No more questions at this time, Your Honor." A faint smile crossed Kanoske's lips. Mary had planted seeds of doubt.

Judge Bolton glanced at the large clock on the wall. "Court will take a short recess until 11:45."

Marc welcomed the short break so he could corner Kanoske, but he searched the crowded corridors to no avail.

"Wait up, Kemosabe." A hand from the crowd clutched his sleeve.

"Duke, just the person I was looking for," Marc said, lying, not lying. At this point, any sounding board would do. "What do you think so far?"

"A mother is a poor option for a strong witness."

The same thought had crossed Marc's mind, but he hoped that paranoia clouded his judgment.

"How so?" Marc sounded anxious.

"The prosecutor will play on bias . . . textbook motherly love. But let's see what arrows your friend has left in his quiver."

Marc's hopes began to topple like a string of dominoes, but he caught himself before the last piece cratered. Kanoske had a solid approach. The main obstacle was Jimmy. If Kanoske failed to convince him not to take the stand, the outcome would be anybody's guess.

"Later." Deflated, Marc returned to the courtroom to find Jessie.

"This note was on my chair when I returned from the restroom." Jessie opened her hand to reveal a neatly folded piece of paper displaying Jimmy's name written in bold letters.

"Did you see who left it?"

"A heavyset woman with blue hair and tattoos. I saw her put something on the chair, but she disappeared before I could talk to her."

The apartment manager.

"Does murder one still love murder two?" Marc read. He wadded the note into a tiny ball and stuffed it into his pocket.

"What on earth does that mean?"

"Amber needs Jimmy to keep his mouth shut. That girl is trying to work her voodoo on him. I think she trusted you to deliver this to Jimmy."

"What about her? She's knee-deep in this," Jessie said, pursing her lips.

"She's bucking for second degree . . . or less if her mother has a say."

A frown furrowed Jessie's brow. "But she doesn't love him, or at least not for long."

Marc shrugged. "Who knows what love is?"

"All rise," cried the bailiff. "Court is now in session."

Mary returned to the stand as Mitchell strolled to the front of the court. As he approached the witness, he turned on his fake "I'm your friend" smile.

"Mary . . . May I call you Mary?"

She stared at the prosecutor as if she had seen a ghost but nodded.

"How many children do you have?"

"Three—two boys and a girl."

"And how old are your children?"

"Jimmy's twenty-six, Nathan is twelve, and Julie is going on eight." Mary squirmed under his questioning.

"Are you married, Mrs. Thomas?"

"Yes."

"Is your husband Jimmy's biological father?"

"No."

Mitchell side-eyed the jury before turning back to the witness. "What is your husband's occupation?"

The question caught Mary off guard. "Well, you see . . . my husband . . . he's in jail."

"How do you support the family? Do you work?" Mitchell cocked an eyebrow.

"I can't afford to work and take care of my family - The children... my mother.... or me."

"Does Jimmy help you with finances?" Mitchell pressed, not letting up.

"He sends some money, so we get by."

"So if Jimmy goes to prison, your livelihood is cut off? Is that right, Mrs. Thomas?"

Jimmy's mother looked conflicted. "It would make things worse, I guess."

Marc groaned. Mitchell led her right where he wanted her to go.

"And Amber . . . You say she and Jimmy have been dating for a few months, and you met her once. Would you describe the relationship that developed with the one meeting as *close*?"

"I don't understand the question." Mary looked confused.

The prosecutor bit his lower lip, then forced a smile in the jury's direction. "Let me rephrase: Do you and Amber confide in each other?"

"No, I don't know her that well, but Amber told me she might kill her stepdad. That's the only time."

"Did you find the conversation strange for two people who don't know each other?" Mitchell's point would be hard to miss.

Mary became agitated. "I only know what she told me."

"Could you have misunderstood what Amber said?"

"I don't think so. Maybe, but I don't think so. I told them to go to the police." Mary began to cry and couldn't stop. "I told them."

"No further questions at this time, Your Honor. I reserve the right to recall the witness."

"Your Honor, I wish to redirect," Kanoske said, hoping to salvage Mary's testimony.

"Save it for after lunch. You may step down, Mrs. Thomas. The court will recess until 2:00 p.m."

Judge Bolton rose and whisked out of the courtroom as the jurors filed out. *Damn it.* Marc hated the interruption of the chain of testimony. Juries notoriously retained the thread better when unbroken.

Marc found Jessie and the rest of the Waite clan. "How about lunch? My treat. I could use some sane company about now."

Marc herded the tribe to a restaurant within walking distance and secured a booth in the far corner.

"I hope Kanoske has a big tomahawk hidden somewhere. Jimmy's mother blew the whole thing when she said, 'Maybe, but I don't think so,'" Duke said from behind his menu.

Marc secretly agreed, but there was no checkmate yet. Marc knew

Kanoske's cross-examination *must* be hell on wheels. So far, Mrs. Thomas had told the jury that Amber, a total stranger, had confided her intent to commit murder, and that she relied upon her son to support her family. Both were damning Jimmy's defense.

By the time Marc returned to the courthouse, the crowd had grown. Like sharks in a feeding frenzy, the spectators smelled blood in the water. Marc did too.

"Your Honor, I want to recall Mrs. Thomas to the stand now." Kanoske smiled at the woman.

Mrs. Thomas walked toward the stand as if going to the gallows. Her usual fair complexion looked ashen, almost sickly. Mitchell's questioning had tattooed a distrust of lawyers on her face. She raised her hand and swore to tell the truth, whatever that may be.

"Mrs. Thomas, you stated in your earlier testimony that Jimmy sends you money. Clarify that statement for me. Do you depend on the money Jimmy sends to support the family?"

"No, my grandmother, Bernice, pays for almost everything. We live in her house on her land. When Jimmy sends money, we can buy extras."

"Thank you. And for the last question: Did you understand Jimmy referred to the shooter as Amber?"

Jimmy's mother nodded emphatically. "Yes, my son said Amber was the shooter."

"I am finished with the witness, Your Honor." Kanoske returned to his seat. Mission accomplished.

"If there are no questions from the prosecution, the witness is dismissed," Judge Bolton said, waving his hand.

"The defense now calls Agent Adkins to the stand." Kanoske was in full stride.

The plump middle-aged man, in practical khaki shirt and pants with clunky shoes, navigated his way to the stand.

"Please state your profession."

"I am an agent with the Cherokee Nation Marshal Service."

"Have you had direct contact with Jimmy?" John asked.

"Yes, I transported the defendant to the jail facility we shared with the county," he answered matter-of-factly.

"Did he make a statement to you during that process?"

"Yes, Allen said Browning killed David Caldwell, and he intended to take the rap. He said she had the gun and came down the hall and shot him." He nodded curtly to reinforce his statement. "That's what he said. He saw her shoot David Caldwell."

"Anything else?"

"He said Amber had the most to lose and that she was the love of his life."

"No more questions." Kanoske had landed the blow he wanted.

Marc smiled. That was the glimmer of hope he needed.

Mitchell, with slicked-back gray hair and a well-tailored suit, moved toward the witness like a lion stalking its prey. He spoke slowly and deliberately, riveting the entire court.

"Agent Adkins, I have searched the documents presented as evidence by the defendant and cannot find my copy of your report."

The agent looked down at his hands folded in his lap, then raised his head, exhaling slowly. "I didn't memorialize the statement."

The gallery of spectators let out a collective sigh. Agent Adkins's testimony was worthless.

The prosecutor faced the jury as he addressed the court. "No more questions."

The agent's oversight could prove fatal.

"Your Honor, I would like to request a recess until tomorrow morning. I need to confer with my client."

"What say you?" the judge asked, pointing his gavel at the prosecutor.

"No objection," Mitchell answered, with the confidence of a man claiming victory.

"The court will recess and resume at 9:00 a.m. tomorrow. The jury is dismissed."

39

"Where to now, Counselor?" Marc asked as he chased Kanoske down the corridor of the courthouse.

"We talk to Jimmy. He wanted to take a stand and tell his side about the alleged molestations, to give a reason for a crime of passion, but after the two ladies testified that no molestation occurred, he might have changed his mind." Kanoske didn't slow down. He was a man about to deliver bad news to his client.

"Closing arguments are next. Jimmy needs to make up his mind." Marc hated the truth of it. "What do you think? Will taking the stand help or hurt?"

"If I land the closing right, he might get a second-degree, which sounds lousy, but the alternative is suicide. If the jury finds one ounce of premeditation in his testimony, Jimmy will come off as a man on a mission to put the old dog out of his misery. That translates into murder one. Jimmy has no business on the stand." Kanoske marched down the hall at a clipped pace, his steps echoing through the old courthouse.

Marc struggled to keep up. The day of reckoning with Jimmy had arrived.

Jimmy sat in the same small meeting room where Marc and Duke had visited him twice before. The only difference was Jimmy's demeanor. He no longer radiated defiance. He had sunk into a defeated, melancholic funk after today's proceedings. The wall he had built between himself and the world crumbled, leaving him humbled by the facts. Elbows on his knees and head in hand, he waited for Kanoske to speak.

"We need to discuss our next move, son."

Jimmy nodded in agreement without looking up.

"Do you still want to take the stand?" John asked.

"And say what? That Amber killed a man, and I lied about it?"

"If that's true, you need to say it."

The dam broke. His face contorted with the pain of betrayal, deceit, and disbelief.

"Do I tell them that Amber went crazy when David denied touching the kids, and she beat him after we tied him up? Do I tell them she got David's gun, put it to his head, and pulled the trigger? Or do I tell them that Amber and I are going to prison because her mother lied?"

Jimmy stood up, shoving his chair to the floor. His face twisted into an ugly knot as he smashed his fist into the wall.

"Do I tell them . . . Do I tell them we were fools?" Sobs sputtered from his quivering lips.

Tears burned in Marc's eyes as he witnessed the truth choke the life out of this young man. His noble endeavor to protect the woman he loved had failed.

"Give me the lay of the land." Jimmy's crying had slowed to broken sobs.

"You want me to lay it bare?" Kanoske asked.

"Yes." Jimmy's voice steadied.

"Okay, let's start with Amber. I'll list the facts. One, she was present at the scene by her own admission. Two, Amber had to participate in tying David to the chair. Three, she tipped your mother off about her intentions. That could escalate to first-degree—"

"All right, I don't want to hear anymore." Jimmy slammed his fist into the wall again. "How much time will she get?"

"I don't have a crystal ball. No one can predict a jury's verdict. Evidence will come out in her trial that we only brushed on here, such as her footprints. But the outcome will not be good. She'll go to prison."

"And me? What about me?"

"Depends. If the jury is cantankerous, you could get first-degree with a life sentence. If I present the best closing of my life and the jury is in a good mood, you might get off with accessory after the fact."

Jimmy's stare burned a hole in the floor.

"What do you think I should do?" Jimmy's sincerity touched Marc.

"Keep your mouth shut and pray. I'll deal with the rest."

Marc and Kanoske slowly walked back to the parking lot. They would spend the night preparing closing arguments, throwing every shred of evidence they could find at a jury. The evidence gave them a fifty-fifty chance, but if Marc had correctly read the jury's reactions, they leaned toward the prosecution.

"What a heartbreaker," Kanoske said, shaking his head. "Jimmy got played. He let Amber con him?"

"You're a little off on your assessment. Amber fell for the same manipulation Jimmy did."

"The mother? So you think Madeline planted the idea of molestation to push Amber to do the hit?"

"Yes, Madeline is street-smart, but I'm not sure we can prove it. Did you catch it when Jimmy said, 'We were fools'? And remember, Madeline told Amber that David had molested the kids."

"Yeah, makes sense. Madeline must have a guardian angel. Any DA worth their salt would have been on her case from the beginning," Kanoske said as they reached the parking lot.

"I'll grab two coffees and meet you at your office. We have a long night in front of us."

Marc needed a break before tackling the job ahead. His son's image kept haunting his thoughts. Devin and Jimmy were the same age, and Devin's trial would begin in three weeks. He would worry about that tomorrow. Tonight, he must concentrate on Jimmy.

John had worked on the closing points throughout the trial, listing every detail chronologically to avoid confusing the jury, but he lacked a convincing emotional plea for the conclusion.

"Man, the testimony about molestation blew my closing away. Without that, there is no justification for a murder of passion. Any ideas?" John asked. His bloodshot eyes looked painful.

"Yes. The question is not whether the allegations against David were true. The real question is: Did Jimmy believe them to be true? If so, the defense remains the same. If not, then a motive needs to be established. What will the prosecution say if the stated motive disappears? Put yourself in their shoes." Marc waited for his friend to respond.

"Money? Valuables? Or a Dodge dually."

"The money David took from his account went into his mother's bank. What about David's necklace and wedding ring? Madeline reported them missing to the insurance agent. What was the estimated value?"

"About fifty-seven hundred for the ring. The Cuban link chain may be seven thousand. Enough to make it worthwhile." Kanoske slid photos of the items across his desk. "Pretty fancy, huh?"

"Then the only attack is to convince the jury that Jimmy believed the allegations to be real. Drive that home all you can. It's weak, but it's all we've got."

Kanoske rehearsed his closing arguments with Marc until the wee hours of the morning, but despite a million tweaks and rewrites, the statement fell short. They hoped at least one juror would believe that Jimmy had been duped, resulting in a hung jury and ending the trial. The prosecution had plucked the wool off Jimmy's defense.

Kanoske spread the papers on his desk, stretched his arms over his head, and yawned. "I'm done for now, pal. Let's call it a night."

"Agreed. And I'm taking the last of the coffee for the drive home."

The late hour and the moonless April night put Marc in a mood he couldn't shake. To some degree, whatever the reason, Jimmy had participated in a murder. The thought that Devin might be guilty, too, clawed at Marc. The two had been such good friends. Had the love for his son blinded him to the truth? His mind played like a broken record until he saw the Waite's porch light twinkling. He wandered into the den, set the alarm, and collapsed into a heap on the sofa.

40

Marc mentally reviewed the courtroom procedures in a countdown to the verdict. The prosecution rested, the defense rested, the prosecutor took the floor for closing arguments, and the final battle began.

"Ladies and gentlemen of the jury, you have before you a young man, by his admission, who committed murder. On the afternoon of September 18, 2015, Jimmy Don Allen drove to the Caldwell ranch with his girlfriend, Amber Browning, to 'confront Mr. Caldwell about molesting Amber's children.' Mr. Allen would have you believe that during this confrontation, he waved a gun at David Caldwell, and in a crazy, emotional tirade, the gun went off accidentally, killing the victim. Then, in a panic, he burned the house and Mr. Caldwell to cover the crime."

Mitchell spoke in a low, dramatic tone, waving his arms as he paced before the jurors. He paused, drew a deep breath, and stared at the jury foreman with laser-sharp eyes.

"As to the accusation that David Caldwell molested Amber Browning's children, I would like to point out that an expert witness and the children's grandmother testified that the allegations were unfounded. The very basis of this supposed crime of passion is false."

Marc winced. The prosecutor hit a nerve. A fake accusation could precipitate a horrendous outcome.

"Manslaughter. Pay attention to that word. Manslaughter is killing a human being without malice aforethought, or in other words, in circumstances that do not amount to murder. The defense would have you believe this young man was on a clear mission to confront the victim and set things straight when the horrible event of murder erupted out of nowhere."

Mitchell threw his hands into the air with a skeptical look. His animated delivery spun a web of drama, leaving the jurors spellbound.

"But I contend the intent was to commit cold-blooded murder and then lie about it. The killing was premeditated. The problem is, ladies and gentlemen, this 'spur-of-the-moment' murder required a lot of planning. Madeline Caldwell testified that she called her husband to determine when he could help her daughter unload a piece of her furniture into the barn, per Amber's request, but . . ." The prosecutor lifted his head and surveyed the jurors, allowing the statement to sink in. "No items of furniture were found.

"The defendant smashed the door leading from the garage into the entry and waited for David to arrive. While waiting, the defendant broke into lockboxes and removed documents, a gun, and other items belonging to David Caldwell. Again, these actions do not indicate a man wanting a peaceful conversation."

Marc studied the jury. Their expressions, as they listened intently, showed agreement with the prosecutor.

"Mr. Caldwell had duct tape strapping him to a chair. Again, not a friendly way to start a conversation. The victim was helpless. He couldn't move." Mitchell stopped, allowing his statement to marinate.

After his dramatic pause, Mitchell resumed. "Let's go to the actual scene of the murder. The state's reported that the bullet entered at point-blank range, which, members of the jury, does not happen unless the gun is very close to the victim when the trigger is pulled."

Mitchell took a slow sip of water, but never took his eyes off the jury, his hook set to reel them in.

"In an accidental shooting, my friends, you call 911. You don't go to the garage with gloves on, grab a gas can, and try to destroy the evidence with an inferno. And let me remind you, the DNA on the gloves and footprints on the carpet belonged to the defendant.

"After the defendant set fire to the house, he drove to a canyon near Blackburn and burned the car he had borrowed from Mrs. Caldwell, which contained bloody clothing reeking of gasoline. He then fled. All the evidence points to premeditation, which requires a verdict of first-degree murder. The jury has a tough decision, and it isn't easy to sentence a young man for such a crime. I appreciate the agony you will endure, but a dead man cries for justice."

Marc shivered. He would have voted guilty after the prosecutor's closing arguments.

Kanoske rose and stood before the impaneled jury. His usual domineering presence seemed muted, as if he feared alienating the trial-weary men and women.

"The young man I represent today is as much a victim as Mr. Caldwell. Please let me explain. Jimmy met Amber a few months before the killing and fell head over heels in love, as young men do. She told Jimmy that David Caldwell had molested her children, and she was angry. Amber's written statement said that she and Jimmy visited David to set the matter straight. Amber confirmed the victim's whereabouts with her mother. Amber, not my client, knew where David's gun and valuables were kept. The footprints burned into the carpet prove that a woman was present when the gun was fired."

Except for the two Cherokee women, the arguments bounced off the jury like a rubber ball. John noticed the renewed attention from the women and directed his remaining statements to them.

"No one entered testimony that indicated my client entertained killing David Caldwell before September 18. My client did not go to the Caldwell farm intending to commit murder. Mrs. Thomas's sworn declaration stated that Jimmy had concerns about the children and had voiced them to her. Mrs. Thomas conducted the balance of the conversation with Amber."

Kanoske's comments resonated with the two women. Marc and

John had discussed the need to educate the jurors about Cherokee customs, and the timing looked right.

"It might interest you that Cherokee women dictated retaliation in blood vengeance to atone for a wrong against the clan and determined the fate of war captives. The Cherokee people no longer practice the nineteenth-century tribal traditions, but to assume that matriarchal influences no longer exist is an error. Amber exerted a strong influence on Jimmy. If Amber accused David Caldwell of molesting her children, Jimmy would develop the same feelings. Even if the accusations against David later proved false, the critical point is that Jimmy believed them to be genuine. He planned to confront David about Amber's concerns."

The Cherokee women nodded approval, pleased with the elevated status Kanoske bestowed.

"I refer you to the testimony of the Cherokee Nation Marshal, where he quotes Jimmy as saying 'Amber had the most to lose' and that Amber 'was the love of his life.' I contend that Amber Browning became enraged when her mother, Madeline Caldwell, told her Mr. Caldwell had molested her children. She killed David, and my client became trapped in a circumstance that spun out of control." Kanoske dropped his hands to his side. "This alone gives rise to reasonable doubt."

Kanoske smiled at the Cherokee ladies before heading back to his seat. Marc knew he had much to overcome and feared he had missed the mark. Mitchell stepped forth, ready for rebuttal.

"Mr. Kanoske made an excellent point about the strength of character and influence of the Cherokee women, but it raises the question —if Amber could influence Jimmy to confront Mr. Caldwell, could she not influence him to kill as well? As to whether Jimmy Don Allen participated in planning a murder, I would have to ask how a glove would be available without a deliberate action plan. That question is one you, as a jury, must decide."

Judge Bolton read the final instructions, and the jury retired to deliberate. Marc hated the waiting and felt a tiny bit of relief when he saw Duke and Jessie standing at the side of the hall.

"Let's grab something to eat at that little place down the street." Duke draped his arm across Marc's shoulder.

Marc welcomed the suggestion. Kanoske would call the moment the jury reached a verdict, and he needed air that didn't reek of the musty, sweaty smell of a courtroom. Marc ordered a club sandwich with tea and settled in to kill the afternoon. Jessie watched him unload six sugar packets into his tea with a disapproving frown but refrained from chastising him. He mouthed a thank you in her direction and managed a weak smile.

Before Marc finished his sandwich, his phone rang. "The jury has a verdict. Better hurry on back."

Marc gulped the remainder of his sandwich and practically ran down the street.

A crowd of spectators milled about the foyer, waiting for the judge, as reporters stood outside vying for the best position to snap pictures. *What a circus*, Marc thought.

Judge Bolton called the court into session after the jury filed in. "Has the jury reached a verdict?"

A tall, spindly gentleman with a halo of hair about his balding head rose. "We have, Your Honor."

The foreman passed the paper to the judge, who then passed it to the court clerk for reading.

"Count one, first-degree murder, premeditation of an action intended to cause serious harm, with an indifference to human life. We find the defendant not guilty."

Marc's heart pounded against his chest like a drum. So far, so good.

"Count two, charges of second-degree murder from actions intended to cause serious harm as a result of an action that shows the defendant had an indifference to human life, and as a result of an act of killing in a state of high emotion. We find the defendant guilty."

The courtroom erupted into a war of approving shouts and disgruntled boos as Judge Bolton slammed his gavel against his bench. "Quiet in the courtroom. The jury has delivered its verdict. Sentencing will be scheduled for the coming week." The judge turned to the jury. "Thank you for your service, ladies and gentlemen. You are dismissed."

The trial ended as quickly as it had begun, leaving an emptiness Marc couldn't explain. No doubt, Jimmy had participated in the death of Mr. Caldwell to the extent that warranted the verdict, but Marc couldn't get his head around the why of the matter. What possessed a twenty-six-year-old to throw his life away? Kanoske took a stab at the reason, and Jimmy got a lesser sentence, but the real reason eluded Marc.

John put his arm around Jimmy's shoulder as the officers handcuffed his client and led him away. This battle had ended, but the war had only begun for Marc. He had Devin to think about, and the unraveling of Jimmy Don Allen put doubts in his mind. Something other than passion had driven Jimmy to do the unthinkable.

Duke and Jessie waited on the courthouse steps for Marc to join them.

"Devin's inferno awaits," Marc said with a half-assed shrug.

"Kenosabe, justice and law should be twins. But today, the law prevailed, and justice became an orphan."

"Not today, Duke. My brain is too fried to unravel a riddle."

Duke nodded. His grandson-in-law's face had lost its color.

"I see," Duke said. "Is there ample time to worry about Devin?"

"No. Three weeks at the most."

"Then we must move now."

"Okay. Meet me at the house and we'll put our heads together." Marc needed to relax in a hot, soothing shower to wash the dirt of the trial from his body before he could tackle Devin's nasty situation.

A warm stream of water poured over him like rain, clearing his mind until thoughts of Madeline Caldwell pushed their way back in. Why did she take the witness stand when it could implicate her as an accessory? The DA dismissed her charges with prejudice, but it was still a fine line.

Thoughts about Jimmy crowded Madeline out of his head. Devin's trial would depend on Jimmy's version of the ride to Sallisaw, and Marc would bet the story could go either way . . . depending on the outcome of Amber's case.

Tension destroyed the peaceful interlude. He slipped into jeans and a T-shirt, ready to make a hard run at his problems.

The smell of Mama's homemade bread and the chattering in the kitchen soothed his weary brain. Why had it taken him so long to appreciate these people?

"I finished the chores, so you're off the hook," Duke teased, and Marc laughed. No one missed his milking skills, especially Buttercup.

"Where's Jessie?" Marc asked, scanning the room.

"She left. Said she had things to do to prepare the twins for graduation," Mama replied.

The wind left Marc's sails. He had hoped Jessie's appearance at the trial meant something, but apparently not. She went home without saying a word.

"I'm heading home in the morning, Duke. If you have any words of wisdom, give them to me now. Otherwise, my next move is to tackle the Pawnee County DA. I want the charges dropped against my son. Devin doesn't hold a candle to the shenanigans Madeline Caldwell pulled, yet the DA gave her a pass. I'm getting in line for that freebie." Marc knew the DA didn't make that decision of his own volition. Someone influenced him, someone who liked to frequent Cain's Ballroom.

"I'd be careful about a direct approach. Go to the source. Find the decision-maker," Duke said. "Any idea who that might be?"

"I have two people in mind: Hank Walton and my attorney friend, Mike Halley."

"Of the two, which is the weaker target?"

Marc remembered Hank's offer to help Devin from their first conversation on the day of the murder. He seemed eager to get involved on Devin's behalf. Mike Halley walked in Hank's shadow. On the other hand, his last run-in with Hank had been less than friendly.

"I'll start with Mike and sound him out. Hank . . . I need a solid plan to corner Hank."

"I'm here if you need me. Now let's eat. Mama has your favorite venison steaks, mashed potatoes, and homemade bread."

Marc pushed back from the table, his belly full of the first home-cooked meal he had enjoyed since Jimmy's trial began. The pleasant family banter, devoid of legalese, filled the room as the final traces of tension slipped away.

"I found a house with twenty acres two miles down the road. It needs some work, but the land is beautiful. The owner is willing to sell. Are you interested?" Duke never spoke without purpose. He said he would find a home near them, and he did. Marc had doubt that he and Jessie would reconcile, but a house near her family would please her.

"I am. Negotiate a fair price and get back with me."

41

Marc spent the drive to Tulsa rehearsing his confrontation with Halley. He intended to hit him head-on and duck when the bullets started flying. By midmorning, the traffic had died down, and the maze of one-way streets offered an easy path to the parking garage. The top floor had several remaining spaces. Marc slid into the first one he found. A fresh spring breeze tousled his hair as he sprinted to the elevator and hit the down arrow. He was prepared to take the first steps toward cleaning up the fiasco that had started years ago.

The grand foyer of the BOK Center glowed in the warmth of vintage chandeliers that hung from the ceiling like earrings on a fancy lady. Art Deco arches and glimmering marble floors paid homage to opulent oil-boom days. Marc had forgotten how important he felt during his tenure with Smith & Noble, but today he carried an air of confidence that was not born of position but of purpose. He must free his son.

The elevator stopped on the eighth floor, and Marc entered the hall. He could see Halley, chair tipped back, feet on his desk, as he cupped a phone to his ear. Without hesitation, he crossed the hall and plopped into a chair.

"What the hell are you doing?" Halley sputtered as he spun around to face Marc.

"You and I need to settle a couple of matters, and I can't think of a better time to do it."

"I'll give you two minutes to state your business. After that, my secretary will call building security to escort you out." Halley placed his finger on the red call button.

"My business will take longer than two minutes, so buzz security now. I'll take up what I have to say with the DA."

Halley's finger hovered, but he made no move. "Speak your piece, but make it quick." He pressed the button as Marc prepared for the worst. "Hold my calls."

Marc's bluff worked.

"I want the charges against Devin dropped."

"You're talking to the wrong person."

"Am I? I believe you influenced the DA to dismiss charges against Madeline Caldwell."

"And why would I do that?" Mike Halley puffed up as he drew away from Marc.

"Maybe because she's a good dancer." Marc winked at his red-faced opponent. "That new floor at Cain's Ballroom is amazing. I swear, you and Mrs. Caldwell could have been Fred and Ginger."

If Halley understood, he didn't let on.

"Blackmail? That's beneath you. Besides, an innocent dance with a friend isn't fodder for blackmail."

"I couldn't agree more. I'm sure Hank appreciated you taking care of his girl. Friendship means a lot to you. I remember how you helped another client years ago. Of course, I took the fall. But, hey, what are friends for?"

Halley didn't flinch. He was a pro at hardball and intelligent enough to sit one out when the reward was small.

"No promises, you understand, but let me see what I can do."

Too easy, Marc thought. *Way too easy.* He decided to press his luck.

"What was the purpose of charging Devin in the first place? The charge of accessory after the fact is very malleable. It can bend either way depending on the DA."

Halley pursed his lips and squinted his eyes before answering. "The Caldwell case needed a prosecutor with, let's say, more expertise."

"You mean one who would dismiss a blatant accessory to a murder suspect?"

Marc caught the drift. He had a reputation for integrity, a commodity not in demand for the Caldwell murder. Halley ranked among the top defense lawyers in the state. He knew how to pull strings and did so for Madeline. But to do so effectively, he had to tie Marc's hands.

"You underestimate your son, Marco. He's caught in a trap between you and Jimmy," Hally said with a bite.

"Are you saying Devin lied to me?"

"Sometimes kids disappoint."

A swarm of ugly thoughts about his son surfaced. *Did Devin help Jimmy?*

"Say what you mean, Halley."

Mike Halley stepped around his desk and engaged Marc face-to-face. "I mean," Halley hissed, "you're cut from the cloth of a father. There's no conspiracy here, buddy. It's all in your head. Blame someone—blame anyone—but leave my boy alone. Devin's innocent, and these sons of bitches are trying to frame him, right?"

Halley had pegged Marc. The underpinnings of Devin's innocence crashed around him.

"You're still the jackass I've known for twenty-five years."

"There you go again. Blaming me for your fall from grace. It's a pity. You could have been one of the greats in this business. The smarts are there, but you're a little too squeamish. And your emotions . . . they squash every logical thought you have like a bug."

Marc held his anger in check. "Save your breath. Help my boy."

"I will, but not for your sake. I have other reasons."

"No step for a stepper. Give me a shout when everything settles. And make it with prejudice. I don't have time to deal with this twice."

Marc stood, ready to leave. He couldn't believe Halley folded, but Devin was incidental to the case, and releasing his son would have little blowback.

"Hold up," Halley said. "I understand Ruby Caldwell has filed suit against Madeline. That needs to go away."

"Not on a bet. Dani presented her case to you first, and you advised her it had no standing. It so happens I agree, but it's her dime, and I need the money."

"Well, I'll be damned. You do have a trace of larceny in your heart, but quash it. Hank is fond of Mrs. Caldwell."

"Tell you what. I'll slow-walk it until the Browning trial is over."

"Not good enough."

"Best I can do. A civil trial against Madeline while Amber's trial is in the process might be a little troublesome, but your past dealings or my son's treatment won't be more than a ripple in your pond. Your choice."

Marc knew he had pushed Halley to the brink and that he might withdraw his offer to get Devin's case dismissed, but he also knew Madeline's dismissal couldn't bear scrutiny. If he called Marc's bluff, Devin would lose. Marc turned and headed to the door without a backward glance. The waiting game began. Halley would contact Hank, and Hank would give the final thumbs up or down. That was how small-town politics worked.

Marc fought the urge to skip back to his car. If his bluff worked, Devin could be free in a matter of days.

Since Marc lived in his office library, his activities went unnoticed. He stayed under the radar the next week to give Hank and his pal Halley a sense of security, but the isolation wore on his nerves. The idea of a Beam and water taunted him for the first time in six months. Finally, the official document arrived. He ripped the seal open with trembling hands. All charges were dropped with prejudice. His son was a free man. His anxiety died in his chest.

Marc jumped into his Jeep and sped to the house to find Devin. The empty driveway dampened Marc's spirits. He grabbed his cell and phoned.

"Where is everybody?" Marc asked.

"Mom and the twins went to Stillwater to finish something with the college." Marc had screwed up again. He had promised Jessie he would be there to help. He swallowed the knot of guilt.

"The charges against you were dropped. Do you know what that means?"

"Yeah, Hank called me. He said he went to bat for me with the DA. That man's been there for me every step of the way." Marc's elation faded to a dull, pitiful ache.

"Yeah, you never know what that man will pull from his hat. Where are you now, son?"

"In Tulsa. I'm meeting Hank at a fancy restaurant to celebrate."

"Enjoy." Marc hung up the phone. How could he tell his son that the man who freed him was the same man who held him in the trap?

Marc grabbed a sandwich from Venture Foods and returned to his makeshift home. Nancy had left for the evening, and he had the whole gloomy place to himself. He listened to his messages as he slipped off his shoes.

"Duke here. The property is yours. Give me a call, and we'll work out the details."

Marc poured himself a ginger ale and ate the cold sub. After he settled into his recliner, he turned on the TV and dialed Duke.

"Mama is so excited about the house. She's wanted Jessie to come home for a lot of years."

"Glad Mama's happy," Marc said with as much enthusiasm as he could muster. "What's the final price?" Marc listened as Duke filled him in. "Great, and I want the deed recorded in Jessie's name. It'll be my anniversary present to her."

Marc tried to imagine Jessie's reaction when he gave her the house. He didn't want her stuck in a little apartment or, worse, the home she wanted to leave. She could return to her family—the people she loved—which made him happy. He dozed off thinking about Jessie and woke up the next morning with a stiff neck.

42

Amber's trial loomed on the horizon. Marc anticipated the same run of witnesses but intended to catch every session. The Pawnee County courthouse looked alive for the first time in years. Most cases centered around drugs, divorce, or domestic abuse. A murder stretched the courtroom's capacity to accommodate the spectators. Nancy begrudgingly arrived early to save Marc a seat near the front. He made a mental note to give her a raise once he got back into the swing of practicing law with real clients.

The cramped courtroom looked tired. The dark stain on the wooden benches had rubbed bare where thousands of butts had sat over the years, and a "Do Not Use" cardboard sign blocked the last row. The air conditioner could not keep up with the unseasonably hot June weather and a hundred bodies stuffed in close quarters. Soon, the room reeked of sweaty people.

A short, balding man dabbed at sweat beads on his forehead as he meandered toward the defense table. He looked uncomfortable in his dark suit and neck-pinching tie. Marc recognized him as Bill Marlow, Halley's underling at Smith & Noble.

Clem Jackson, lead prosecutor, sat at the state's table. He seemed impervious to the stagnant, oppressive sweatbox called a courtroom as he pored over documents, preparing for a surgical dissection of the witness.

Amber, however, looked cool and radiant in a soft green blouse and jeans. Her blonde ponytail danced on her shoulders as she flipped back and forth, conversing with her defense team. She had effortlessly morphed from a streetwise stripper into a Precious Moments cake topper. If the proceedings stressed her, it didn't show.

Judge Ryan rapped his gavel, calling the court into session. Marc took a hard look at the little man on the bench for the first time.. His plump, round face looked too young to handle this trial, and his demeanor backed that assessment. Proceedings of this magnitude might swamp his court.

JURY SELECTION WRAPPED UP, and the state's witnesses began their testimony. Marc had expected a feisty contest, with Halley swinging with both fists and Jackson punching back. Instead, Marlow took the lead. *What the hell is going on?*

"Your Honor, I call Becky McCall to the stand," Jackson announced.

Marc's ears perked up. This witness hadn't testified at Jimmy's trial.

Becky appeared to be about thirty-five years old. Her dark hair, pulled back in a low ponytail, framed her unassuming face and simple attire.

"Please raise your right hand. Do you swear that the testimony you are about to give will be the truth, the whole truth, and nothing but the truth?" the bailiff asked.

"Yes." Becky lowered her eyes and shifted nervously back and forth.

"Please be seated."

All eyes turned to Jackson as he approached the witness.

"Ms. McCall, please tell the court about a conversation you had with Amber Browning concerning the victim, David Caldwell, while incarcerated in the county jail."

She took a quick sip of water and swallowed hard. "Well, one day, a while back, I went up to Amber's cell—we're in the same pod—to borrow a hair tie. She was sitting on the floor, crying. I asked her what was wrong, and Amber said she was afraid she would get the death penalty for killing her stepdad."

Becky looked at Amber and mouthed, "I'm sorry."

"Direct all comments to the court, please," Jackson admonished.

"Yes, sir." The reprimand threw her off balance. "She . . . she . . . that is, Amber said they set the house on fire and that her mother was mad at her because this was supposed to have looked like an accident, and Mr. Caldwell was supposed to die in a fire and not by gunshot. Amber said that if anything happened, Mr. Allen would say he did it, and she would not have to worry about it."

Marc jabbed an elbow into Nancy's side. "I knew it. The witch put a spell on Jimmy and Amber."

Nancy pulled away. "Shh! Judge Ryan is looking at us."

"Objection. Hearsay," Marlow offered with a voice too big for his body.

Jackson glanced at Halley before addressing the judge. "Your Honor, unless the defendant plans on taking the Fifth, this witness's testimony is admissible and does not rise to hearsay."

"Objection overruled," Judge Ryan said tentatively.

"You said 'they.' Can you be more specific?" Jackson continued.

"Her and Jimmy."

"So, Amber and Jimmy went intending to kill Mr. Caldwell, is that correct?"

"Objection. Calls for a conclusion from the witness." Marlow asserted with conviction.

"Sustained," Judge Ryan ruled.

A clamor of whispers and gasps filled the courtroom. The judge rapped his gavel sharply, demanding silence.

"Do you have anything to add concerning your chat with the defendant?" Jackson asked.

"Well, she said, 'I lost it. I had to put the old dog out of his misery.'"

Marc had heard that phrase from three people in the past months: Jimmy, Amber, and . . . Dani.

"I have no more questions, Your Honor." Jackson took his seat, satisfied with the witness.

The prosecution landed a blow that sent the defense team reeling. Halley reclaimed the lead. He approached the witness, stood quietly for a moment, and began in a calm, even tone.

"Were any offers made to you by the state in exchange for testimony?"

"I don't understand the question." Becky plucked at the Kleenex folded in her lap.

"Did the prosecutor tell you they would reduce your sentence if you testified? Does that help?" Halley couldn't resist asserting his superiority, which might hurt him with the jury.

"No."

"The district attorney's office waived the prohibition against probation to allow you into drug court. Isn't that true, Ms. McCall?" Halley said with a dramatic turn toward the jury.

"Objection!" cried Jackson. "The district attorney has already declared there was no deal or arrangement with the witness."

"Sustained." Judge Ryan's irritation with Halley was evident.

"No more questions of the witness, Your Honor." Halley had been cut off at the pass.

As Becky McCall vacated the witness stand, she looked at Amber and shrugged in apology. Amber shot a go-to-hell glance and returned to doodling on scrap paper.

"Our final witness, Madeline Caldwell, will not be testifying. She has invoked the Fifth Amendment. Therefore, the prosecution rests, Your Honor." Jackson returned to his station.

Wow. Mike Halley should be screaming bloody murder. The state court improperly instructed the jury regarding Madeline Caldwell's invocation of her right to remain silent. *A court cannot reveal a Fifth Amendment assertion to the jury because it smacks of concealing damning evidence. What happened to the razor-sharp attorney I knew? The prosecution sucker-punched the defense without a peep of protest.*

"We will hear the defense arguments starting tomorrow at 9:00 a.m. The jury is dismissed, and the court is adjourned."

Marc sprinted down the courthouse steps and across the street to his office. Today's events lifted the confusion that had plagued him since the beginning. He threw his briefcase on the floor in the library, fixed a ginger ale, and shuffled through the clutter on his desk until he found a doodle-free notepad. His thoughts rushed onto the paper like a tsunami. Everything made perfect sense today. Amber pulled the trigger, and Jimmy Don Allen witnessed the murder. Madeline had no interest in her daughter's fate and orchestrated the grand finale. Her testimony at Jimmy's trial had set the stage for her motherly concerns. She had controlled Amber until she procured her own dismissal with prejudice.

Amber remained in jail under the thumb of the illustrious Mike Halley, who happened to be Madeline's new love interest's best friend. *Brilliant*, Marc thought. She got off scot-free from the charges, then boom—she takes the Fifth, reducing any testimony about herself to hearsay status, which is inadmissible in court. Her daughter will rot in prison while Madeline rides into the sunset with Ruby's wealth jingling in her pockets. According to Marc's calculations, Madeline had orchestrated the perfect plan.

He felt sorry for Amber and Jimmy. Like marionettes, Madeline had manipulated these two young people to do her dirty work.

Marc removed his glasses and rubbed his eyes. John Kanoske had said it right. Any DA worth his salt would have brought charges for aiding and abetting. In Marc's opinion, Amber would get a first-degree conviction, no doubt about it. He now understood his opponent in the upcoming Ruby Caldwell civil trial.

43

"John, Marc here. I need your help. Do you have any free time tomorrow?"

"I'm in court all day. Is 5:30 p.m. too late?" John asked.

Marc sped down the road to Tahlequah, his mind turning as fast as his wheels. If he could convince John to come on board, Ruby would have a chance to recover some of her assets. He pulled into the parking lot and walked to the fountain in the courtyard. He needed a moment for the fresh evening air to clear his brain. This Caldwell case had burrowed under his skin and into his gut like a parasite.

His craving for liquor hadn't subsided, but it grew weaker every day. He had spent the last twenty years of his marriage drowning in a sea of Beam and water. He allowed his failures to rule. Marc drew a deep breath, filling his lungs with a resolve at war with surrender. Today, here and now, he swore to renounce his addiction to alcohol and self-pity and fight for all that was dear to him.

"What are you doing, Marco? You look lost." John slapped Marc on the shoulder and sat on the rock ledge of the fountain.

A genuine smile crossed Marc's face.

"Not anymore. I know exactly where I am and where I need to go. But I need your help to get there."

"Let's grab a bite to eat, and you can tell me all about it."

Marc had lived on sandwiches and chips for days, so the ribeye special with loaded baked potato and garden salad at JB's Steakhouse tasted like a feast. He let John talk until he polished off his steak and ordered dessert.

"Have you seen Jimmy since the trial?" Marc asked.

"Once for the sentencing."

"How did he take it?" Marc paused his spoon of peach cobbler midair.

"There's more to the story than the jury heard. Jimmy threw comments about Madeline in my direction that sounded damning."

"For instance?"

"Remember when Jimmy said, 'We were fools'?"

"Yeah."

"At the time, I thought he meant he and Amber acted foolishly, but he was actually referring to someone who had made fools out of them. Am I making sense?" John leaned in. "And I think that someone was Madeline."

"Same here. I talked to Amber in a parking lot by the strip club where she worked. She told me Madeline didn't like to get her hands dirty. Her mother set those two kids up to kill. What do you think?" Marc needed John as a sounding board. If he agreed with Marc, the plan might work.

"Could be." John seemed hesitant to buy in.

"But?"

"The Pawnee County DA filed charges on Madeline for accessory after the fact. Aiding and abetting never entered the picture," John said as he pushed his plate back and rested his elbows on the table. "Are you suggesting the local authorities gave her preferential treatment?"

"Yes."

"That's a tough allegation to prove."

"I don't give a damn about impeaching the local DA or law enforcement. I intend to make sure Ruby's assets are returned to her."

"I know why Duke calls you Kemosabe." John winked and smiled.

"You are a trustworthy scout. A doer of good deeds. A champion of the oppressed. A—"

"I'm serious, so cut the crap." John's comments irritated him.

John's face clouded. "Relax. It wasn't crap. I meant it, and I'm in."

Marc let out a sigh of relief. "I knew I could count on you. Meet me tomorrow morning at Duke's house at nine o'clock sharp, and we'll pay a little visit to Jimmy."

Marc chuckled as he hurried out the door. John could pick up the tab this time.

The Waite clan had turned in for the night, but the porch light burned bright. Marc tiptoed down the hall to the guest room and crashed. Sleep came easily.

Marc woke to the smell of bacon and coffee. Mama loved to cook, and Marc loved to eat—a perfect match. He showered, shaved at lightning speed, and slipped into a T-shirt and jeans. *No need to be starchy today*, he thought, examining himself in the mirror. His weight had dropped to college level, he noticed with pride, but he still had to suck his tummy in to look fit and lean. Age had consequences, he mused, then headed down the hall toward the kitchen. John sat at the head of the table with a plate of hotcakes in front of him.

"I could smell breakfast clear from Sallisaw," John said, digging into the steaming fare.

"Do you have room for an old man? I could help with Jimmy," Duke said as he sipped a hot cup of coffee.

"I wouldn't go without you, but getting you in might take persuasion. Are you willing to sit in the Jeep if we fail?" John asked.

Duke nodded an affirmative.

"Perfect. We'll hit the road as soon as our friend finishes breakfast."

The two-hour trip seemed much longer as Marc wound through the mountainous terrain. His thoughts turned to Jessie as he rolled through the hills. This region of Oklahoma, rooted in raw wilderness, spoke to his senses. Mornings felt fresher and cleaner here. At night, stars poked holes in the black sky and winked at the valley below. Marc knew his wife missed the tranquility of her homeland.

"When's the closing scheduled for Jessie's new home?" Marc asked with a bittersweet taste in his mouth. Like Moses, he couldn't enter the Promised Land.

"The paperwork's done. We're waiting for your signature."

"Will tomorrow work?"

"Sure, I'll call the title company. What time?"

"Shoot for ten. I need to be back home by tomorrow evening."

The three men passed the remainder of the trip lost in private thoughts until they topped the hill leading to the McAlester prison. It stood like a gray fortress of mortar and brick surrounded by ribbons of razor-sharp fencing. Life in this facility was a sentence to hell.

Clearing Duke through channels proved challenging, but his native background opened the door. John, although Cherokee, lacked the tribal ties unique to men of Duke's age.

The staccato click of their footsteps bounced through the corridor as the three made their way down the hall. The jolting slam of serial security gates pushed them farther into the bowels of the dingy prison. The destination presented a much cheerier setting as the men entered a small meeting room.

Jimmy entered the far-left door and walked toward them with a measured gait, no longer defiant.

"Are they treating you okay?" Marc asked. Jimmy stared back with a solemn hangdog glare.

"Jimmy, we need to have a frank discussion about David Caldwell," Duke said.

"Why? The trial's over."

"True. Your trial is over. But you and Amber are not the only people David hurt. We believe he stole from his mother. She needs help to regain her assets. Right now, she's broke and living off her granddaughter's charity." Marc hoped this might appeal to Jimmy's better nature.

"Dani?"

"Yes. Double jeopardy keeps you safe. It won't change your sentence. Can you tell us anything that might help?"

Jimmy tilted his head down, but his eyes remained focused on Marc.

"What's in it for me?" Jimmy asked as he tossed his head back. A touch of the old defiance flashed across his face.

"Peace of mind?" Duke answered.

"Then the answer is no."

"Jimmy, Cherokee men own up to their mistakes, and you made a big one. It's time to make it right," Duke admonished.

"I thought you said you believed I was innocent. Are you a liar?" Jimmy's flippant side surfaced as he spat the words.

"No, I didn't lie. I knew you didn't pull the trigger. Amber did. That is the innocence I spoke of. But when you broke down the door, tied Mr. Caldwell to the chair, and stole his belongings, you participated. Your hands are dirty."

Jimmy's eyes turned to glass, and he swallowed hard. "What about Amber?" A small stream of tears trickled down his cheeks.

"The jury found her guilty of first-degree murder, but she hasn't received her sentence yet." Marc winced with every word. He knew whatever noble purpose existed for Jimmy had long since evaporated. Amber and Jimmy would spend their lives behind bars for a murder based on lies—Madeline's lies.

"Jimmy, listen to me a minute." Duke moved closer to Jimmy and spoke to him like a grandfather. "Your heritage exalts women. I know you wanted to protect Amber the way you watched over your mother, but you've done all you can. It's time to tell everything you know. There's no judge. No jury. You're talking to three men who want justice for an old woman."

Jimmy's tears had stopped, but his eyes were red and swollen. He slumped forward in his chair like a rag doll. His future held one note, despair. Marc wondered how a man in Jimmy's position could care about anyone's fate.

"It's your decision, Jimmy. We'll leave it with you. Call when you've made up your mind." John turned to his companions. "Let's get going."

The three started toward the door. The failure to convince Jimmy to help Ruby left Marc feeling empty.

"What do I have to do?" Jimmy asked.

Marc spun on his heels and hastened back to Jimmy. "You're doing the right thing, son. John will arrange for an extended session as soon as possible."

"What do I have to do?" Jimmy asked again, in a louder voice.

"You will be testifying about Madeline Caldwell in a civil trial. Ruby has filed charges of embezzlement."

"And if I tell the truth, it can't blow back on me?" Jimmy's eyes darted from John to Marc, looking for assurance.

"No, there are laws against double jeopardy. You can't go on trial twice for the same crime," John said to assure him. "We'll be back as soon as we can."

The three men spent the ride home planning the next visit. John had to set up an interview with the prison and review Ruby's case. Marc knew that Jimmy might change his mind if they didn't act fast. The thought that he might learn things about his son he never wanted to know crossed his mind, but he couldn't turn back now.

44

The waiting room in the title office in Sallisaw, with distressed brick walls and ten-foot ceilings, had a nostalgic, musty odor of history. It reminded Marc of his dad's old law office in Brule.

Marc removed the cashier's check from his wallet and studied the front: three hundred and forty thousand dollars. He had worked hard for the last twenty years to save this nest egg for the day he could retire. Today, he would spend the money to secure Jessie's happiness.

He smirked at the irony. Alcohol and indifference had destroyed his marriage, and he had no use for the money. It belonged to Jessie for putting up with him.

The timing was perfect. Duke could give the deed to Jessie when the family comes for twins send-off party next week. That should leave her ample time to plan her move. He would sell the Brule house and . . . *And do what?*

"We're ready for you now, Mr. Whitcomb," a pleasant middle-aged woman announced in a well-modulated voice.

"Please keep the abstract and title in your vault. I could lose both before I make it out the door," Marc said when he had signed the papers. "Duke Waite will pick up the keys this afternoon."

A quick stroke of a pen changed the course of Marc's life, but he refused to dwell on it. Instead, he reached for his phone.

"Nancy, has Madeline Caldwell responded to the interrogatories?"

"Not yet. Do you want me to contact Madeline's lawyer?"

"No, don't do a thing and pray Madeline's lawyer asks for another extension." Marc planned to amend the charges in the civil suit to add murder, and he could do so without court approval until Madeline responded. He prayed that the meeting with Jimmy would come soon.

Marc turned his thoughts to Dani. The phone rang five times before she picked up.

"Dani, are you free tomorrow?"

"Sure, does Grandmother need to be here?"

"Yes." Marc needed to assess Ruby's ability to testify on her behalf.

The rest of the trip home didn't register, as Marc's thoughts returned to Jessie. When the boys headed off to college, and Jessie settled in her new home, maybe he and Jessie could start over. Out of habit, he cruised by the house to catch a glimpse of his family. A light burned in the kitchen, and the Suburban parked in the driveway meant Jessie was home . . . alone. Devin had moved back to Tulsa, and the twins avoided coming home before midnight at all costs. He fought the instinct to drop in as he slowed down for a better look. As much as he missed her, a surprise visit would make things worse—time to go to the office and call it a night.

The lamp in the office library cast dreary shadows across the floor. Marc turned on the TV and collapsed in the recliner. He pulled the lever to full recline and closed his eyes. He would review Ruby's case as soon as he rested for a few minutes.

"Marc? Are you here?" Nancy called outside the door.

"Yes. Yes. I'll be out in a minute."

"Sorry to disturb you, but usually you're up long before I arrive. I was afraid something was wrong."

"Everything's fine. I overslept."

Fuzzy-headed, Marc jumped into the shower. *I'm late. I'm late for a very important date*, spun in his brain. He could hear Jessie reading from *Alice's Adventures in Wonderland*. It had become their family catchphrase when they ran behind. Today, the White Rabbit had nothing on him as he frantically raced about the room.

"I'm heading to the city to see Dani. I'll call later," Marc spouted as he ran out the door.

The stairs to Dani's apartment were no step for a stepper, thought Marc as he took them two at a time. Ruby cracked the door an inch and peeked out with the chain latch still in place.

She squinted for a better look. "What do you want?"

"It's Marc. Cain's Ballroom. Remember?"

"Come in." Ruby took a step back and eyed Marc head to toe. "Looking good. You've lost that spare tire."

"Thank you," Marc said and laughed. "It's good to see you too." Ruby couldn't help the comments that slipped out of her mouth. "Is Dani in?"

Dani stepped from her bedroom with a phone in her hand. She shushed him with a finger. Marc nodded. He could take this opportunity to evaluate Ruby without Dani's influence.

"Ruby, has Dani told you we are suing Madeline to get your money back?"

"She doesn't tell me anything. If I want to know something, I eavesdrop."

"Surely Dani shares what she thinks you need to know."

"Then she must think I'm not entitled to know anything. She hardly speaks to me. When she does, she's mean." Ruth was in a surly mood today.

Did Alzheimer's cause this?

"Is Grandmother telling you how badly I treat her?" Dani asked as she turned off her phone.

Ruby's anger glowed in her cheeks until both turned a rosy red. "I don't have to put up with her in my home." Ruby waved her index finger in Dani's face. "I don't know what she's doing here anyway."

"If I don't watch my step, she will kick me out." Dani tossed a wink and a smile his way. She then took Ruby's hand and guided her toward the hallway. "Marc and I need to visit. How about we find a movie you like?"

"Do we have *Gone with the Wind*?"

"Yep," Dani said as they entered Ruby's bedroom.

Fifteen minutes later, Dani returned and flopped on the couch. "It's getting worse all the time. I don't know how much longer I can do this."

"One of the reasons I stopped by today was to see if Ruby might be able to testify, but I can see the answer is no."

"She might be able to influence the jury—you know, draw sympathy."

"I don't recommend it." Marc waited for an argument, but Dani dismissed him with a shrug.

"The second reason is to inform you of my intentions to add wrongful death for the murder of your dad to the civil suit. Any thoughts?"

"Go for it. I told you my grandmother's money and dad's murder intertwine."

"Jimmy might be willing to testify against Madeline. I'll know soon."

"I don't think that's a good idea." Dani scowled. "What we have should be enough, and there's no telling what he will say to help himself."

Marc found her objection odd. Devin mentioned the two had a brief relationship, but there was no such thing as too much evidence. Could there be more to it?

"Do you have access to determine how David cashed the CDs?"

"I think so. I'll ask. My friend Barbara, who works at the bank, may get it for me. After all, it's Grandmother's money."

"I'm sure it's a cashier's check. See if you can get a copy. Here's why: A bank issues a cashier's check to both parties on the CD, and both must endorse it. If Ruby didn't, we need to find out who did."

"I'll try."

"Okay, I'll get the amendment rolling."

Dani walked Marc to the door and touched his arm as he left. "Make something happen soon, or I'll be as crazy as my grandmother."

What a funny girl, Marc thought as he descended the stairs. *She wants me to believe I have full rein on the case but pulls up on the harness unexpectedly*. Her need to control worried him.

45

"We're set," John said. "Tomorrow morning at nine. I've arranged for a private meeting room. And bring Duke. I went through considerable trouble to get him approved. They usually allow immediate family or attorneys. I assured the officials that Duke was necessary for tribal connections, and I sense Jimmy trusts him more than us."

"I trust Duke more than us too," Marc said and laughed. "I'm not sure where this will lead, but here goes nothing. I would settle for one good thing to come out of this ugly mess."

"Let Jimmy take the wheel. I've learned more from people when you let them tell the story their way."

"Agreed. Do you want to meet at the Waites' and ride together?" Marc asked.

"Sure. Eight o'clock?"

"Perfect."

Although not fancy, the meeting room offered an atmosphere more conducive for conversation. A guard delivered Jimmy and closed the door. He perused the room as if looking for a hiding place, then walked to the chair in the corner. Jimmy had the chiseled features of a proud Cherokee man with high cheekbones, a strong chin, and eyes so dark they looked like tunnels into his soul. He carried himself with dignity, ready to run the gauntlet before him.

Duke's face remained immobile until Jimmy entered and took a seat. He then moved his chair closer to the boy as if to share his strength.

"Jimmy, we're here to listen to your story from beginning to end. We may ask questions, but the story is yours," John said. "Do you need anything before we start? A bathroom break? Drink of water?"

"Got a Coke?" He directed the question to John.

"I didn't forget." John opened his briefcase and produced a soda. "Here. It's not very cold."

"Where do you want me to start?"

"That's up to you," Marc said.

"Amber isn't the bad person you think she is. I want you to know that." Jimmy paused. "She's like a kid. Takes up with anyone, but she doesn't trust most people except me, and I won't tell you anything that could hurt her."

"No one is asking you to betray her, Jimmy. We want to understand." Duke patted Jimmy's knee. "Tell us how you met her."

"Devin and I went to the Gentlemen's Club for my birthday—the first time we've ever been. We drank a couple of beers and shot pool, but the place was crappy. We started to leave when Amber came on stage. I couldn't take my eyes off her . . . and not for the reason you think. Her blonde hair and blue eyes made her look like an angel."

Marc saw Amber in the courtroom during her trial and understood what Jimmy had said. She had a quality of innocence, real or not.

"We waited for her at the back door until she got off work and offered her a ride home."

"Did she take you up on your offer?" Marc hated to butt in, but he wanted to know if she took up with others as she did with him and Jessie.

"Sort of, but that's the funny part. Amber had her mother's car in the parking lot, so she didn't need a ride. She wanted company. I rode with her, and Devin followed us to her apartment."

Jimmy spoke in whispers, wrapped in memories of a happier time.

"Devin went on home, and I stayed. Amber and I talked all night long. Nothing happened. We just talked. Best birthday I've ever had."

"When did you meet her family?" Marc asked.

"We dropped by her folks' house that afternoon. I called in sick and spent the day with Amber. We've been together ever since."

"What was your impression of the family?"

"Amber's stepdad wasn't home, only Madeline and Amber's grandmother. The old lady kept sticking her head out the door and then quickly closing it. That seemed odd to me, but Amber explained it later."

"What did Amber say?" Marc asked.

"She said that her mother and grandmother didn't get along. I think the grandmother's name was Ruby, but I'm not sure. Anyway, she's David's mother, so she's not related to Amber by blood."

"Was Amber close to Ruby?"

"Yeah. It's kinda funny. Once we stopped by, and everyone was gone but Ruby. She and Amber got to laughing and cutting up when Ruby said she wanted to dance. So Amber put on a couple of old records by singers I've never heard of, like Bob Wills and Jimmie Rodgers." Jimmy's face lit up. "I remember that last one because we have the same first name. And they started doing something called the two-step. You should have seen 'em."

For a moment, Jimmy escaped from his prison. His face glowed. Marc melted into melancholy. One simple, senseless act destroyed Jimmy. Marc took a bullet for Halley, and like Jimmy, he paid the price. Same but different.

"Then Ruby seemed . . . How should I put it . . . normal to you?"

"Yeah. I'd call that normal. My grandmother goes to tribal gatherings and dances. I guess that's what old people do." Jimmy shrugged with indifference.

"How about Madeline? What did you think of her?" Marc asked.

"She was a real snob at first. My mother always seemed happy to see me, but Madeline acted as if Amber had put her out when we dropped by. Her house was always perfect, and everything had to be just so. We even had to take our shoes off at the door so we wouldn't track the floor. I hated to go there, but Amber insisted."

"Did Madeline keep Amber's kids?"

"Not that I know of. I don't think Madeline liked kids messing up her stuff." Jimmy shook his head. "The one time we took Amber's kids with us to see Madeline, they had to sit on the couch and not bother anything. We didn't stay long." Jimmy kicked back in his chair. He was beginning to relax with the telling.

"And David? What did you think of him?"

"That man never was around. Amber said he gambled a lot, staying at the casino all night. When he wasn't at the casino, he went to the farm. I think he moved there about a month before the . . ." Jimmy stopped talking. He couldn't say the word "murder." His demeanor changed. The horror of that afternoon shattered the moment. Tears glazed his eyes, and his body shuddered.

Duke stepped in. "Let's take a break, son."

Jimmy sat up straight and looked him in the eye. "No. Keep going."

"Are you saying that David and Madeline separated?" John asked.

"I don't know if they separated, but he was never home."

"But you met him, right?" Marc asked. *Did you kill a man you didn't know?*

"He came to Amber's apartment once and asked her to check on his mom while he was out of town for a few days. I couldn't tell much about him except that he liked to show his money. His wedding ring had a giant diamond, and he wore a gold nugget necklace studded with diamonds."

"How did Amber feel about him?"

"She liked him. The one time I met him, he was friendly. He smiled a lot. I didn't see any problems."

"So when did that change?"

"About the same time that David moved out. Madeline started coming over in the afternoons to see Amber . . . before I got home from work. She said she was lonely and needed to talk." Jimmy frowned.

"When she wanted something, Amber jumped through hoops to please her mother—chapped my ass. Madeline never lifted a finger to help Amber. Her daughter worked as a stripper to support two kids. Did Madeline care? Not a flip." His tawny complexion colored with anger.

Jimmy looked at John. "Any more soda?"

"That's all I had, and I could get my wrist slapped for sneaking that in. How about water?" John offered, extending the bottle in Jimmy's direction.

"Forget it." The chip on Jimmy's shoulder stood a mountain high.

Marc deflected the conversation. Madeline's treatment of Amber festered in Jimmy. Emotional bias would not hold up in court. The account demanded rock-solid accuracy.

"Tell us about the morning of September 18, when you and Devin went to the farm." The mention of his son's name burned like a hot poker.

"Yeah. Right. Well, Devin and I went to confront David about molesting Amber's kids, but he wasn't home."

Marc could hardly breathe. His son had lied to him. Deep down, he knew Devin had lied. They never delivered the furniture Madeline alluded to in her testimony or loaded the table that his son claimed Amber needed. Marc had buried the devastating tidbit and moved on . . . until now. He drew a deep breath and continued.

"Why would Devin accompany you to confront Mr. Caldwell?"

"That's what friends do. I told him everything about it."

"Did you go with the intent to commit . . . to commit murder?" Marc's stammer returned. He began to count as he took deep breaths to calm his anxiety.

Jimmy put his elbows on his knees and stared at the floor. "No, sir. We went to prevent a killing. Talk some sense into David. I thought if Devin and I confronted him, Amber would let it go."

Marc exhaled, relaxing the muscles that had frozen in his chest. He squelched the urge to ask more about Devin, which would have derailed the purpose. Of course, his son would not betray a friend's confidence. Concentrate. He must concentrate.

"Let's backtrack to Madeline. According to a witness who testified at Amber's trial, Madeline planted the idea that David deserved to die. What do you know about that?"

"Plenty. That's all Madeline could talk about. She told Amber she could kill David and make it look like a heart attack."

"She talked freely around you?"

"Hell no. Madeline's smarter than that. But our apartment was small, and the walls were paper-thin. I heard it all."

"That statement puzzles me. If Madeline could knock him off, make it look like an accident, why didn't she? Why did she drag her daughter into it?"

"I know. I didn't understand at first, but I finally got it. Before she and David split, she had talked him into preparing a gift deed for the farm. Dani would inherit half of the estate without that deed if anything happened to him. The only problem was that he took the deed with him when he left. She missed her chance when David took it and moved out."

The puzzle neared completion. If Madeline had acted before the separation, she could have administered the shot while David slept and filed the gift deed herself. Now, she needed help.

"Did you believe that David had molested Amber's kids?"

"Not really. I couldn't imagine David even keeping her kids. He was never home, and the kids never stayed with him. The trouble is, I couldn't convince Amber that her mother played her. Do you know Amber? In ways, she's still a kid herself, especially when it comes to her mother."

Amber's childlike manner had surfaced more than once. Marc had experienced it himself.

"I've met Amber, and you're right. She's a sweet girl who took a wrong turn. It's hard for me to envision her shooting a man and setting him on fire," Marc said.

Jimmy stiffened. "What are you talking about, man? Amber shot her dad, but I did the rest."

"I'm talking about her footprints near the body. She was there."

Marc leaned toward Jimmy. "Look, there's no point in denying Amber—"

"I'm done. Either that man leaves, or I do." Jimmy pointed at Marc. "Out. Now."

"I didn't mean to—" Marc took it one step too far and blew it. Jimmy had a hair-trigger temper when it came to Amber.

"Marc, leave. I'll take it from here." John took Marc's elbow and escorted him toward the door.

Marc jerked free and exploded. "What's his problem?"

Duke grabbed Marc by the shoulders and shook him. "You're smarter than this. Wait in the Jeep."

Marc sat in the sweltering heat with the windows of the Jeep rolled down. This damn Oklahoma weather. How could it be in the nineties when the high three days ago only reached seventy-eight degrees? Add the high humidity of the state's southeastern quarter, and the Jeep became a sauna. He glanced at his watch—one o'clock. He hoped they would break for lunch. He should have anticipated Jimmy's reaction when it came to Amber. His stupidity might have lost Ruby's case. He reclined the seat, leaned back, and closed his eyes, trying to keep his mind from replaying this morning's catastrophe.

"Wake up." Duke slapped the side of the Jeep.

Marc startled into an upright position. His clothes, sticky with sweat, clung to his body. His brain hovered in a fog.

"How did it go?"

"Scoot over," John said. "I'll drive. Do you mind riding in the back, Duke?"

"What's up?" A queasy feeling filled Marc's chest.

"Jimmy had a few things to say that might not go well with you."

"For instance?"

"He said that the female footprints at the scene didn't belong to Amber. She wore sandals."

"Those prints matched the tennis shoes in the trunk of the Buick," Marc shot back.

"Listen, I'm telling you what Jimmy said."

"You believed a liar?"

Duke thumped Marc on the back of the head. "He's not lying. Shut up and listen."

"He also said he didn't find any file boxes, and they didn't steal any jewelry."

Could there have been a third person? "Did you ask if anyone else was with them?"

"Yes, and Jimmy said he and Amber were alone. He also said that everything in his statement was accurate, with one exception—Amber pulled the trigger."

"Madeline. It has to be Madeline. She must have waited until Jimmy and Amber left, then went in and took the deed and jewelry from the lockbox. This little piece of information could seal the deal on Ruby's case. Now to prove it." Marc's face lit up.

"Better check with your lab guy. See if prints can sear into the carpet with a twenty-minute lapse in time." John spoke with a voice of reason that Marc found irritating.

Marc needed to check on more than the footprints. How did the shoe that matched the print end up in a burned-out Buick? Did Madeline go to work that day as she claimed in court?

"Anything else to add?" Marc asked. Jimmy's input might help more than he first thought.

"Two things. One, Devin picked Jimmy up east of Blackburn. They filled up at the convenience store in town. That's when the owner of the store spotted them."

"What's the second thing?"

"Jimmy didn't set the Buick on fire."

Marc hadn't expected that bombshell. His nagging doubts about Devin were laid bare. Where had his son been between eight a.m. and five p.m. on the day of the murder?

46

The twins would have a college launch party tonight and be gone at the end of the week. Jessie would leave soon after. Marc needed Jessie today more than at any time in his life. He drove slowly by the house, seeing the cars packed in the driveway. Duke, Mama, Jessie's dad, and Lisi arrived last night for the blowout. On the far side of the drive, one spot on the grass remained open. He would have hell to pay for parking on the lawn, but he pulled in anyway. The house bubbled with energy as folks mingled, making lighthearted chatter with the boys. Marc slipped in and hugged his sons, aching with pride. He had blinked, and now the kids were grown.

"Marc, I'm glad you made it. The boys kept asking about you all day."

Jessie looked beautiful, her dark hair flowing against a pale-pink blazer. Marc's heart skipped a beat in the light of her smile.

"Wouldn't miss this for the world. You know that." Marc looked about the room. "Where's Devin?"

The smile on his wife's face disappeared. "He's in Houston. He claimed he had an emergency and would make it up to the twins later."

His son's association with Jimmy stank, and Marc feared the investigation might have been the emergency that pulled Devin away.

Marc felt like a stranger in his own home until Mama Waite gave him a bear hug and giggled with excitement.

"Duke gave Jessie an envelope with the deed to her house, but she hasn't opened it yet." Her eyes twinkled in anticipation.

The minute the boys left to meet up with friends, Duke turned to Jessie. "Open it."

Jessie perched on the couch and carefully pried the fancy envelope open. The corners of her mouth quivered and then pinched into a thin line.

"What is this?" she erupted in outrage, shaking the deed in the air.

Jessie's outburst caught Marc off guard. His knees felt weak. He didn't know what had transpired, but her reaction wasn't good.

"Wait," Duke said in desperation, "there's more in the envelope."

Jessie ignored Duke, her hands trembling as she scanned the deed. "Marc, quit making decisions for me." She threw the paper in his face, and they both watched as it fell to the floor.

"No problem, Sergeant Jessie. Even the kids call you—" He had gone too far. Hurt replaced anger. "I'm sorry. I thought it would make you happy."

"Sorry. Sorry. Sorry. You're always sorry. And for the record, I've managed this house and kids for years while you holed up in a bottle. My kingdom may be small, but at least I own it. I can't say the same for you." Jessie's dark-brown eyes were as cutting as her voice.

"Did you ever love me, Jessie?" Marc asked in earnest. "I'm the same man you married years ago."

Jessie reared back, startled by the question. "I . . ."

"Don't bother answering. Keep the house or burn the deed. Your choice, dear lady. I'm done." With a quick nod to a roomful of spectators, Marc turned and stormed out the door.

"Wait!" Duke called after him, but nothing could stop Marc.

The weekend dragged its feet until Monday stomped in. Marc had to bury his troubles with Jessie and get back to work on Ruby's case. Jimmy had alluded to Madeline's influence on Amber, but nothing concrete had surfaced. Today, he must go to the lab and check a few things out with Steve.

The lab had a faint odor of acid that burned Marc's nose. He rang the bell and waited for Steve to emerge from the wall of beakers and pipettes stacked on top of a whirring centrifuge.

"Hello, Whitcomb," Steve called, drying his hands on a paper towel as he approached.

"How do you find anything in this mess?" Marc said and laughed. "And what's that smell?"

"Hydrochloric acid. My hood fan is going out. I need to have it fixed. What's up?"

"I have a question. If a person walked onto a carpet twenty minutes after it had been set on fire with a flammable liquid and the fire had burned out, would their footprints sear into it?"

"That depends on the fire pattern and the saturation of the liquid. I wouldn't rule it out, but there are too many variables to give a definitive answer."

"Okay, let me try another angle. Could the fire have smoldered out and then reignited a second time?"

"Anything's possible. Where are you heading with this?"

"I believe someone entered the house after the murder, and the footprints belong to them."

"Did you bring the sample back?" Steve asked."If so, I'll look at it again."

"It's sitting in an evidence warehouse."

"Then the best we can do is guess, which won't get you far."

"But the two situations I presented are possible?"

"Yes," Steve said as he landed a ten-foot shot into the wastebasket with the wadded-up towel.

"Can you lift fingerprints off the shoe?" Marc had not turned the shoe over to the court for evidence.

"Easy. But unless the fingerprints are on file, you won't be able to identify the owner."

"I'll keep that in mind. Thanks, buddy." Marc turned to leave. "I'll bring the shoe here tomorrow."

"You know these prints can't be used in a trial . . . civil or criminal. The chain of custody is garbage."

Marc rolled his eyes. "I learned that in Law 101. I'm not looking for evidence. I need an edge to understand how deeply a person of interest is involved in David Caldwell's murder. I'll see what I can dig up and holler back at you."

Madeline's prints should be on file since the DA initially filed charges, but Marc preferred to call Dani. Maybe she had something with Madeline's fingerprints on it. Her response threw him.

"What makes you think I would have anything of Madeline's?" Dani snapped. "I hated the bitch, and she hated me."

"I thought you might have an envelope or picture, something she had touched for comparison."

"Comparison to what?"

"Never mind. I'm trying to cover all bases." Marc backed away from the conversation fast.

"I didn't mean to bite your head off, but Grandmother drives me crazy. What am I supposed to do with no money?"

"No problem. Did you get the front and back copies of the cashier's checks?"

"Got 'em right here."

"Look at the backs. Did your dad and your grandmother endorse them?"

"Yes, but . . ." Dani grew silent.

"But what?" Dani's silence was loud.

"That's not Grandmother's signature."

"Are you sure?"

"Positive."

"Could your dad have forged her name?"

"Not likely. Dad was never good at cursive and printed everything, including his name. Whoever forged this knew how to write."

"Madeline?"

"Madeline."

"Unfortunately, our opinions will not hold up in court. Do you have something with her signature on it?"

"Grandmother keeps every card she ever got—birthday, Mother's Day, Christmas—you name it, and she's got it. I'll look through her stash. Surely Madeline signed one of them."

"Look and call me if you find something."

"Marc, I'm sorry I acted hatefully, but you would understand if you walked in my shoes."

"Forget it. Call if you find anything."

Marc chalked Dani's odd behavior up to stress. He had reached a dead end unless Ruby had a treasure trove of signed cards in her dresser drawer. Marc thought it was odd that Dani didn't connect that any card with a signature would also have fingerprints.

47

The constant demands of Ruby's case bogged him down, and Devin's involvement with the Caldwell murder still gnawed at his insides. He wanted the entire mess to disappear. His mind flitted to a world where he and Jessie moved into their new home in Gore and bought a milk cow. Like Duke, he would own a dairy cow and milk her daily. When the sun went down in the evenings, they would sit on the front porch and watch fireflies twinkle in the cool night air. Remodeling might take time, but when they finished . . .

"Marc. Marc. Did you hear me? John is on the phone. Do you want to talk, or are you too busy?" Nancy asked with a hint of sarcasm.

"Sure." Marc frowned and then smiled. "You know I'm on the job twenty-four-seven."

She rolled her eyes and walked out as he picked up the phone.

"John, buddy, what can I do for you?"

"You've got it backward, as usual. I'm going to help you. I went to see Jimmy, and he acted a lot differently. I don't think he likes you," John said with a laugh. "Today, he was calm and rational, as if he finally understood that we needed to know. I'll send you the tape of our conversation."

"No. Give it to Duke, and he'll bring it to me. I'm short on time. I've got five days to pull this together. We go to court on Tuesday. Will Jimmy testify? I put him on the witness list."

"Yes, willingly."

"Thanks. I owe you."

"I know, Kemosabe, and you will pay." John chuckled as he ended the call.

Marc placed a quick call to Dani.

"Find a signature?" Marc asked without niceties.

"I found one that might work."

"I'm on my way to pick it up. If I don't get it to an analyst today, it won't be ready for court."

Marc had an analyst in the wings, but weekend work was not the deal. He arrived at Dani's around three o'clock, picked up the card, and then raced to Broken Arrow. Traffic delays cut the razor-thin timeline to the bone. With card and check copies in hand, he dashed into the analyst's office with fifteen minutes to spare. Lack of time clipped the fingerprint analysis, but the signature held more importance.

"I need the results by Monday."

"I'll do my best." The plump, bald man showed little inclination to rush.

Marc shrugged and walked out. Duke should be here on Saturday. The tape might be enough, but the forgery should cinch the case.

Devin had not returned from Houston, and the last few months of wrestling with his son's problems had drained Marc of his typical resilience. The drive home allowed him to decompress.

Jessie was waiting at the office when he arrived, her foot tapping with impatience. "You're late," she said, making no attempt to hide her irritation. "But I'm not surprised."

Crap. Marc's days were running together. *How could he mess this up?* He and Jessie went to the Admiral Twin in Tulsa on their first date. The retro drive-in would play old favorites, followed by fireworks after the movie. He had begged Jessie to keep up the tradition. She reluctantly agreed. It would be their first *first* "date" in years. He had to fix things between them. After the twins were gone, he feared he would never see her again.

"What's playing?" Marc asked sheepishly, hoping for a Western or war movie.

"*Gone with the Wind.*" Marc detected a touch of retribution in her delivery.

Great. A three-hour chick flick with popcorn.

"Life couldn't be any better," he said, chuckling to himself. He and Jessie had seen this show twice, and he could only remember two lines.

Marc rolled the windows down and placed the speaker on the doorframe. A dry, gentle breeze teased the black tendrils of Jessie's hair. He reached across and brushed them from her face.

"You look beautiful," he said.

Jessie answered with a faint smile, "Care for a soda?"

"Not yet." The conversation felt forced and awkward. He fumbled to find a safe topic. "Are the twins about ready for college?"

Jessie laughed. "I don't know about them, but I'm ready. Thank goodness John is going to Oklahoma State and Robert to the University of Oklahoma. They'll fight one day a year at the Bedlam football game, but peace will reign for the other three hundred and sixty-four days."

The twins were very competitive, like their mother.

"And will you move to Gore when they leave?"

Jessie shrugged. "I'm not sure about anything, Marc. Let's enjoy the movie."

Mr. Peanut danced across the screen, touting the salty treat, followed by a singing Coke—the perfect excuse for Marc to break the uncomfortable mood. "I'm going for a soda and Milk Duds. Want anything?"

"Coke and popcorn," Jessie said. "With extra butter."

Three hours later, Rhett left Scarlett crying on the stairs of their Charleston mansion. He was done with her. For the first time, Marc understood the movie. He, like Scarlett, had selfishly screwed everything up. Could Scarlett win Rhett back? Could he win Jessie?

Fireworks boomed then burst in a black, starless sky, leaving threads of red and gold streaking the darkness like the tentacles of an octopus. The show was spectacular, the evening not so much.

Monday morning arrived with a whole load of disappointment. He placed a call to the handwriting analyst, and the phone rang three times before a recording answered. "You have reached Gil Melton's office. I will be out of the office today. Please leave a message, and I will get back to you as soon as possible."

The little toad didn't mention this last Thursday. Marc left a pleading message and then called Duke.

"I will be there in about an hour," Duke said. "Do I meet you at the office?"

"Yes."

Marc spent the afternoon organizing bank statements chronologically and preparing a diagram tracing the money flow from Ruby's CDs to the home purchase and the truck. Documents in perfect order would not win the case for Ruby. He needed a large hammer to knock a hole in Madeline's defense. He had read her interrogatories. She had a slick answer to every question.

Ruby had added David as an owner, and he didn't need her permission to cash out and deposit proceeds into his bank account. Madeline claimed not to know how he and Ruby conducted business. The innocent-spouse argument dominated the rebuttal of the embezzlement charge. She had a strong defense with one loose thread that could unravel her lies, but Gil Melton was not in this afternoon.

The civil action for wrongful death presented a different problem. Jimmy held the hammer that could drive the final nail into Madeline's coffin. Marc had no idea what John had on tape, but he sure as hell wished Duke would hurry. If Marc failed to wrap his hands around these two pieces of evidence, his chances of winning seemed bleak.

A bell jingled, then the door slammed as heavy footsteps tromped down the hall. Duke had arrived.

"Here you go. I hope that's what you need. John sent two tapes, one about Madeline and the other about Devin."

"Let's play them and find out." Marc's heart pounded with anticipation.

The beginning of the tape sounded garbled.

"I can't understand a word," Duke said, shaking his head. "I'll start over and turn up the volume."

"John Kanoske, attorney at law, with Jimmy Don Allen, July 1, 2016."

"Still garbled," Marc muttered.

"Let it play," Duke said. "It may straighten out."

"I have Jimmy Don Allen with me this afternoon. He has additional information he wishes to share." Silence followed the introduction, then Jimmy began to speak.

"I got mad when we talked before, but I'm over it. I have nothing but time to think, especially about Madeline. Most of what I know about how much she hated David and wanted him dead came from Amber. Madeline was careful not to say much when I was around."

Jimmy stopped talking, and John prodded him. "Go on. Tell them about the day of the murder."

"I was getting to that," Jimmy said, clearing his throat. "On the day Devin and I went to the farm, David wasn't home, so I dropped Devin off at work and returned to my apartment. Madeline was all mad. She had plenty to say then."

"Stop the tape for a minute. I want to close the door."

Once he settled behind his desk, Mark said, "Let'er roll." Jimmy continued to reveal damaging tidbits that could hang Madeline. "This is great stuff." Marc slapped the desk with both hands as the tape trailed to white noise.

John's somber tone broke the whirring interlude. "Marc, Jimmy wants to share some things with you about Devin. I recorded it on a separate tape."

Duke looked across the desk for the go-ahead. Marc nodded weakly in approval.

"Mr. Whitcomb, I want to set the record straight on Devin. He and I have been best friends for a while, and he would do anything for me. I protected him and didn't spill my guts on the way to Sallisaw.

He knows nothing from me about . . . about the whole thing." The tape went silent.

The elder Cherokee's forehead creased with strong disapproval. "Wonder why he said that? Kinda leaves it open."

"Don't make more of it than what it is." Marc clipped his friend with his curt words, doubts shadowing his thoughts.

Nancy cracked the door and peeked in. "I have a Mr. Gil Melton on the phone. Should I transfer his call?"

"Yes."

"Sorry about the late call, but I broke a tooth, and I couldn't wait. Listen, I have my report. You can pick it up this evening before five. I'll have my wife meet you."

"I'll be there." Marc glanced at his watch—2:30 p.m. He might make it if he could navigate the rush hour traffic.

48

The civil case fell under Tulsa's jurisdiction since Ruby was a county resident. The labyrinth of rooms in the Tulsa courthouse flooded Marc with memories of his tenure with Smith & Noble. The courtroom's interior had that seventies look—dark wood benches and tables, white Formica countertops, and gray Berber carpet. It felt cold but unintimidating. Decades had passed since Marc had practiced in these halls, but it felt as fresh as yesterday.

Madeline and Mike Halley sat on the left, and Ruby occupied the right. Dani had ignored his directive to keep Ruby from making an appearance. She believed Ruby would draw sympathy from the judge and jury, but it could backfire. Deep down, Marc feared Ruby would tag him as her son and send the entire hearing down the drain.

Judge Hanson entered as the bailiff called, "All rise."

After a few moments of busy work, the judge peered over his black-framed glasses and announced, "The plaintiff may call their first witness."

Marc moved to the front of the room and nodded. "I call Dani Caldwell to the stand.

"Ms. Caldwell, please state your relationship with the plaintiff, Ruby Caldwell."

"Ruby is my grandmother, but she's more of a mother to me than my biological mom."

"Would you please elaborate on that statement?"

"Well, my mom and dad divorced when I was three, so they dumped me on my grandmother," Dani said, flashing a huge smile at Ruby. "She's the only reason I made it this far. She and my granddad provided my food, clothing, car, and education."

"Your father or mother . . . did they play any role in your childhood?"

"Sure did. Mom played the part of a drunk, and Dad played the part of a self-centered jerk. Is that what you're asking?" Dani lifted her chin in impish defiance. She loved the spotlight, and Marc suspected she relished shooting darts at the people who had tossed her aside.

"Not exactly, but let's continue. Is it fair to say your mother abdicated any role in your upbringing?"

"Very fair. She had no interest." Marc cringed. Dani was a self-propelled bottle rocket.

"And your dad?"

"Not much . . . until granddad got sick."

"How old were you at the time?"

"Twenty-four."

"Never as a child?"

"Sometimes he would drop by to borrow money from my grandmother . . . not to see me."

Halley jumped up like a jack-in-the-box, fist-pounding the table. "Objection, Your Honor. Relevance. What child doesn't have a grievance against their parents?"

"We are establishing a pattern, Your Honor." Marc needed to impugn Madeline's veracity before she took the stand.

"Objection overruled. But keep it brief, Counselor."

"When did the controversy of the deed arise?" Marc cut to the heart of the matter—theft from an elderly parent.

"My dad came to the house when my granddad was dying, and Grandmother was fighting cancer. He took the deed from Granddad's desk and ran out the door with it. I tried to stop him, but he was hell-bent on filing the deed to the farm."

"And that deed was filed before your granddad's death, correct?"

"Yes, and he was not supposed to have the deed until both of my grandparents were dead." Dani glared at Madeline.

"Did your granddad have a will?"

"I thought so, but I can't find one. But I did see where Granddad wrote on the blue jacket for the deed that no one got the farm until they were both dead."

"Did Madeline Caldwell know of this transaction?"

"Objection!" cried Halley. "Requires a conclusion."

"Your Honor, I think you will find it interesting to know the basis of Dani's conclusion." Marc looked forward to this sucker punch.

"Overruled. Proceed," Judge Hanson ruled in monotone.

"Answer the question," Marc directed.

"The day of the funeral . . . the day we buried my granddad; the church prepared a dinner at the farm. So many people were there that I had to get out of the house for a minute. I walked down toward the pasture, and Madeline followed me. When we were out of earshot, she grabbed my shoulder and told me to get all my stuff out. The farm belonged to my dad now, and I was no longer welcome."

"She kicked you off your grandmother's farm?"

"Yes, and I told her we'd see what Grandmother had to say about that." She winked at Ruby.

"And what did Ruby have to say about the situation?"

"Nothing. Dad and Madeline packed her up and took her home with them. Then, out of the blue, they bought a great big home, a new truck, and new furniture . . . you get the drift. And not with Dad's money. He never saved a dime in his life. Gambled away every penny he had." Dani relished every word.

"Did your grandmother give them the money for the purchases?"

"I don't think so, at least not knowingly."

"Objection. Objection. Objection. Your Honor, this has gone way beyond the bounds. Ms. Caldwell could not possibly know her grandmother's intentions."

Without waiting for Judge Hanson, Dani sprang to her feet and began shouting, "I am a next friend of the court for Grandmother and I *can* speak for her. I *know* my dad said old people didn't need money. I *know* my grandmother offered to pay them rent so she could live there. She had no idea she had bought the house for them. I *know*—"

"Will the witness please be seated and remain—" Judge Hanson cried loudly, pointing his gavel at Dani.

She ignored the judge. "I know her account was dry. Every certificate of deposit was gone. I know—"

Judge Hanson slammed his gavel on the bench with unprecedented fury. "Order, order in the court." The buzz died to a gentle roar. "Court will recess until 2:00 p.m. Attorneys for the plaintiff and defense, in my chambers now." This was not the result Marc hoped for.

Mike Halley hurried to follow the judge to his chambers. From the back of the courtroom, Hank Walton's red hair bobbed up and down with excitement like a bobber on choppy water. David's widow sat without expression, a King James Bible on her lap.

Ruby dithered, waving and smiling at the jury as they filed out of the courtroom.

Duke hung back, observing the fiasco unfold. *Today could be a long one*, Marc thought as he hastened to the judge's chambers.

Court resumed at two o'clock. Madeline's attorney had used the recess well.

"Ms. Caldwell, you testified that your grandmother, Ruby, did not know David cashed her CDs. Is that correct?"

"Yes."

"What do you base this statement on?"

"Grandmother has Alzheimer's. She thinks that World War II is still going on. I produced a doctor's diagnosis to prove this."

"Is she aware that she is the plaintiff in a case against her son's widow and his estate?" Halley smirked in the direction of the jury panel.

"I believe so. Grandmother comes and goes from the past to the present. I'm never sure which decade she's in." Dani giggled and glanced at Ruby.

"I know I'm in court to get my money back from that bitch," Ruby stated, slapping her hand on the table as she pointed at Madeline.

"Your Honor, I—" Marc said.

"Hold on, Counselor. I'll handle this." Judge Hanson leaned forward. "Mrs. Caldwell, you cannot speak in court unless called upon as a witness."

Ruby jumped to her feet and took off toward the judge. "I'd be happy to be a witness. Swear me in."

"Sit down, Ruby." Marc grabbed for her wrist and missed. "Your Honor, this—" Marc began, but Judge Hanson's temper had reached critical mass.

"Mr. Whitcomb, keep your client quiet, or I will have her removed from my courtroom."

"May I have a moment, Your Honor?" Marc asked.

Judged Hanson frowned and slammed his gavel with vengeance. "Get a handle on this, Counselor. I won't allow these shenanigans. Court will recess for ten minutes."

"Come with me, Ruby. Duke could use company." Marc handed his unruly client to Duke. "Get a grip on her. She's killing me."

Marc needed to pull a rabbit out of a hat quickly. Ruby wasn't the only one agitated by Dani's insolence, and it could cost him the trial. He had precious few minutes to knock some sense into Dani. "Just answer the questions and show some respect. Cut the flippant crap."

"I'm sorry," Dani whispered. "Seeing Grandmother upsets me. My mistake. I shouldn't have brought her."

"That one's on me. I should have sent her with Duke the moment you two arrived. Just keep your wits about you. It's our last chance," Marc snapped as the judge gaveled the court into session.

"The defendant would like to cross-examine Dani Caldwell." Halley sounded cheerful at the prospect of baiting the witness.

Dani took the stand like a perfect lady.

"Is it possible, Ms. Caldwell, that Ruby gave David permission to cash the CDs and may not remember?"

"Quite possible, and that's elder abuse," Dani answered.

Marc cringed. She had given Halley exactly what he wanted, and didn't stop there.

"My grandmother needed her money to live, but she had no idea how to manage her finances. She trusted my dad. Why would you not trust your son? No one in their right mind would give all their money away and live like a pauper." Dani's eyes flashed with anger, and her ladylike facade evaporated.

"Please limit your answer to the question asked." Judge Hanson smiled with Halley's smug rebuke.

"I did," Dani said weakly. "I did."

"No further questions, Your Honor."

This was not going well. Dani was a lousy witness. She talked too much.

The judge pointed the gavel at Marc. "Counselor, call your next witness."

"Your Honor, I call Gil Melton."

Gil strode to the stand like a pro. He testified regularly and acted at ease in the courtroom.

"Mr. Melton, you analyzed the signatures on the back of two cashier's checks remitted to David and Ruby Caldwell upon cashing CDs. Is that correct?"

"Yes."

"Please tell the court your findings."

"Mr. Caldwell matched his recognized signature. Ruby Caldwell's signature was a forgery."

"Did you compare the signature on the cashier's check to Madeline Caldwell's?"

"Yes, and I found the results inconclusive."

"Would you say there is a likelihood the forgery is by Madeline?" Marc skated on thin ice with this question.

"I would lean toward that conclusion, but again I cannot say with certainty." Another near miss.

"No more questions, Your Honor."

"Defense, your witness."

"No questions, Your Honor."

The defense had taken light hits. Marc didn't deliver a knockout.

"I call Madeline Caldwell to the stand." This was Marc's last hope to score on embezzlement.

"Mrs. Caldwell, did you withdraw three hundred thousand dollars to purchase your current home on June 12, 2014?"

"Yes."

"Were you aware that your husband deposited the same amount into your joint account the day before?"

"Yes."

"Do you know the source of funds for his deposit?"

"Yes, David cashed his CDs from First American Bank." Madeline smiled sweetly, seemingly pleased with her answers.

"Do you know the value of your husband's CDs in round numbers?"

"David told me he had to cash out half to purchase the house. If that's the case, there should be approximately three hundred thousand left."

"Your Honor, may I present these CDs for Mrs. Caldwell's perusal?"

"Approach."

Marc handed the documents to Madeline. "Mrs. Caldwell, are these the CDs you are referring to?"

"Yes."

"And the sum?"

"Three hundred and seventy-five thousand dollars."

"Your Honor, I would like to offer this statement from First American Bank as evidence and request that the bailiff read the contents."

The bailiff began the recitation, "'The certificates of deposit with the following serial numbers were issued to Ruby Caldwell and her son, David Caldwell, who is listed as a joint owner. The certificates of deposit presented, listing David Caldwell as owner and Madeline Caldwell as the POD beneficiary, have no value. They are altered copies of the originals.'"

Madeline's mouth fell open like a fish gasping for air.

"According to bank records, the only money your husband had upon his death was Ruby's final CD worth thirty-six thousand dollars, which David cashed the day before his death." Marc harpooned Madeline with this revelation.

Madeline's face puckered. "I knew about the cash, but you've made a mistake on the CDs. David showed them to me and promised I would have ample money to live on if anything happened to him."

"It appears that your husband deceived you *and* his mother."

"Objection!" Halley bellowed.

"Sustained. The jury will disregard the last statement."

"Let's return to September 18, 2015. Your statement at the time of your husband's death indicated you talked to your daughter by phone around 10:00 a.m. Is that correct?"

"Yes."

"Did you have a conversation with Amber at her apartment earlier that day?"

Madeline shifted to the side and glanced at her attorney.

"I dropped by frequently on my way to work. I don't remember that specific day."

Marc anticipated that Madeline would move to the "I don't remember" stage of testimony, but he needed to get her replies on record.

"Do you recall telling Amber that her stepdad molested the children?"

"Yes," Madeline said and then backed up. "Well, I told her I thought the children acted funny one afternoon after I left them in David's care." Her shoulders slumped, weary with the prying questions.

"Let me repeat the question: Did you tell Amber your husband molested the children?"

"Objection. The witness has answered the question."

"Sustained."

"Did you tell Amber that you could give David a shot to kill him and his death would appear like a heart attack?"

"Absolutely not. Amber and I were watching an episode of

Snapped. You know, the TV show where people snap and commit murder. It's a hokey drama. A nurse on the show killed her husband by injection and claimed he had a heart attack. Amber asked if that was possible, and I said yes." Madeline's features hardened as she stared at Marc.

"Did David prepare a gift deed and name you as beneficiary?"

Madeline struggled to remain calm. Her jaw clenched. "I don't think so."

"I would like to enter Exhibit B 1-25. Mrs. Caldwell, please identify this document for the court."

"It is a . . . gift deed."

"Who is the grantor?" Madeline grimaced. Marc struck a nerve.

"David . . . David Caldwell."

"In Oklahoma, a gift deed does not require a notary. However, two people must witness the signatures. Please read the names of the witnesses."

Madeline's eyes darted to the back of the courtroom. "Hank Walton and JP Davis."

"Did your husband sign the deed?"

"No, but . . . but he told me he would take care of it."

"I'm confused. You stated you didn't think a gift deed existed, but one exists with your signature as grantee and two witnesses. Your husband, the grantor, had not signed the deed. What, pray tell, did the witnesses witness?"

Marc spun on his heels and left Madeline sputtering. He had landed a solid punch. "No more questions at this time, Your Honor."

Marc prayed the jury would connect the dots. David kept the impotent gift deed and the fake CDs in the bank's safety deposit box —the one place safe from Madeline. He dangled these prizes in front of Madeline when he wanted her off his back. Dani had a key to the bank box and found the documents after David's death. Touchdown.

Halley approached Madeline with the deference due a grieving widow.

"Madeline, has your daughter, Amber, ever been evaluated for clinical personality disorders?" Halley avoided the subject of the gift deed, preferring instead to play on the jury's sympathy.

"Yes."

"Please tell the court the findings of the evaluation."

Her brow wrinkled with concern. "She has disinhibited social engagement disorder. She will take up with any stranger. I never could leave her alone for fear she would take up with the wrong people."

"In your experience as her mother, would you say people easily influence her?"

"Yes, Jimmy influenced her to kill my husband." Madeline broke into wild sobs and buried her head in her hands.

"Objection." Marc jumped to his feet. "The witness has no basis upon which to make that claim."

"Your Honor, she has spent a lifetime judging who has influenced her daughter." Halley directed his attention to Madeline. "That's what a mother does."

"Overruled."

Halley at his best, Marc thought as he watched Madeline's dramatic performance. But the deed blew a gaping hole in the defense, and they both knew it.

"No more questions, Your Honor." Halley retreated, somewhat disappointed with his client.

"Your Honor, I call Jimmy Don Allen to the stand." Marc whispered a thank you to his friend, Kanoske, for sending a preliminary tape of Jimmy's proposed testimony for preparation.

Jimmy stood erect and walked to the stand with confidence.

"Tell us about the morning of the murder," Marc said, giving Jimmy latitude to tell his story.

"Devin and I went to see Mr. Caldwell to talk . . . just to talk. Amber went crazy when Madeline told her David had molested the kids, and I couldn't let her come with me. Her dad wasn't home. We hung around for a while, but he never showed." Jimmy ducked his head low but kept his eyes on Marc.

"What did you do when he failed to show?"

"Went back to Tulsa."

"To your apartment?"

"Amber's place."

"Who was present when you returned?"

"Amber and Madeline. And I was mad. I told Amber to stay away from her mother and let me handle this. But the bi—" With a slight nod of the head, Marc discouraged Jimmy's choice of words. "Madeline . . . Madeline and Amber were at the kitchen table, and her mother was doing all the talking."

"Can you relay the conversation between Madeline and Amber?"

Jimmy perked up. "Yeah, she wanted Amber to go to the farm and look for a deed before David came home. No matter what happened, she said to find the deed." Jimmy reached for a bottle of water and took a swig.

"Was David Caldwell at home when you returned later that morning?"

"No, Madeline called and said he would be home about two, so we had about an hour to look around."

"So you kicked the door down?"

"Yes."

"And did you find the deed?"

"Nope."

"What transpired when Mr. Caldwell arrived?"

"Objection, Your Honor. We are not trying a murder case here."

"Sustained."

Marc knew his questions were in overreach territory, but he wanted to needle Madeline in any way he could.

"No more questions at this time, Your Honor."

"The defendant's witness," Judge Hanson said.

Halley slow-walked his way to the witness stand. Marc could see his wheels churning on the best way to smear Jimmy as a convicted felon. Classic law with a Halley twist.

"Mr. Allen, according to the records, you were convicted of accessory to a murder for the part you played in Mr. Caldwell's death. Is that correct?"

"Yes."

"State your relationship with Amber Browning."

"She's my girlfriend." Jimmy couldn't hide the pride in his voice.

"I believe you said she is the love of your life. Is that still the case?"

Jimmy nodded in enthusiastic agreement. "Yes, I would do anything for Amber."

"Would that include lying to set up a basis for appeal?"

Jimmy's eyebrows shot up. "I'm not lying. I don't know what it might take for her to appeal."

"What was your motive behind the killing?"

"I had no motive and no intentions of killing him."

"Two expensive pieces of jewelry went missing from the Caldwell farm. Do you know what became of David's diamond ring and gold chain?"

"No, sir."

"No more questions, Your Honor." Madeline's attorney slammed his notebook closed and looked at the jury as if to say, "There's your answer."

Judge Hanson glanced at the large clock on the wall and pushed his chair back from the bench. "Court is adjourned until 9:00 a.m. tomorrow."

49

"How do you think it's going?" Dani asked, anxious as a puppy in traffic.

"I don't know." Marc's gauge sat on empty. He had fought for months to help Ruby, save his marriage, and secure a grip on his son. Tonight, he must grapple with a different dilemma. Should he call Amber? He had decided not to put her on the stand because she could fire like a loose cannon in any direction. The next reasonable step for the defense would be to call Madeline back to the stand. She would refute what Jimmy said, and the jury would have to choose between a well-groomed widow who spoke softly, or a prisoner. Marc didn't like the odds. He had to take his chances with Amber.

"Let's grab dinner across the street. Grandmother wants to know what happened in court today."

Spending an evening with Dani and Ruby ranked rock bottom on his list, but last place went to sitting alone and waiting. "Sure." He regretted his decision the minute it left his mouth. The nagging urge to down a bourbon and water grew into an overpowering obsession. The dark restaurant had a bar in an adjacent room that lured him with the siren call of a Jim Beam, neat with a splash of barroom ballads.

Duke's hand rested on his shoulder. "There's an empty table in the corner." He gently steered Marc away from the bar.

The four slid into the corner booth and buried their noses in the menu. Marc had no desire to make small talk and didn't need to. Dani dominated the conversation with an animated rendition of how the phony CDs and a gift deed with no signature played in the case. She had found both items in Ruby's safety deposit box, and he couldn't deny their importance.

"Looks like Dani won this case all by herself. What are we paying you for?" Ruby said with a wild laugh and a slap on Marc's back.

"We haven't won yet. We've only given the jury something to think about. You can't rule out that the jury will believe your son was the villain and Madeline is blameless."

Marc did marvel at Dani's ability to produce the right document at precisely the right time.

"What's on the plate for tomorrow?" Duke asked.

"I'm calling Amber to the stand."

"Do you think that's wise?" Dani's assertiveness grew with her wine consumption.

"Yes."

"She could go off like a rocket and ruin our case."

"Or she will break a tie. I've made my decision."

Marc was relieved when he and Duke parted ways with the women. The two men entered the dark house, and Marc hit the sofa with a thud, leaving Duke to fend for himself. Jessie had left for Gore the week after the twins left for college to stay with her folks. After a long talk with her mother, she decided to keep the house. Duke shared that the two of them had plunged into a remodeling project he preferred to avoid. Her excitement about the project made Marc smile. The expense, not so much.

Duke emerged from the kitchen with two tall glasses of iced tea. Marc sipped slowly, relishing the absence of pressure, as he studied his elderly friend.

"I've been meaning to ask you what was in the envelope with the deed. Jessie never looked at it. She was too busy screaming at me."

Duke roared with laughter. "Do you want to know? I wrote the same thing to Lisi sixty years ago when she threatened to leave me. I figured it might work again unless they compared notes. If they put their heads together, you won't be the only one getting a divorce."

"Tell me."

"Okay, I wrote something from my father. I thought Jessie would appreciate it. It goes like this: 'The sun refuses to shine on the face of a fool. Only love can chase the darkness.'" Duke leaned back in the recliner and laughed. "Sounded good at the time."

"It's beautiful."

"I also said, 'I am that fool. My stupidity almost cost me the most precious love in my life. I promise to do whatever it takes to win you back.' I wrote it as if I were you. Not bad, huh? Too bad it didn't work."

"Let me size this up. I confessed to being a stupid fool who promised to obey his wife for the rest of his life. Did I get it right? Did it work with Lisi?"

"Yes. Look at us now. Perfect wedded bliss."

Marc forced a wistful smile.

"Remember, you and Mama Waite are now blood brothers. Maybe she can work some magic." Duke winked.

"Only a few more days of this nasty trial, and I'm heading to Gore to help Jessie with the house."

"Not a good idea, Kemosabe. Give Jessie her space. She needs to sort things out on her own." Duke nudged Marc in a new direction. "So you intend to call Amber tomorrow?"

"Yes, I don't know where we are going, but we are going there tomorrow."

"We ride at sunup, Kemosabe. Better rest your horse." Duke rose and headed up the stairs with Marc close behind. Morning would come much too early, but Marc was ready.

"All rise!" cried the bailiff, and the spectators stood in unison. Judge Hanson issued the usual instructions, and Marc swallowed.

"Your Honor, I call Amber Browning to the stand."

Madeline smiled at her daughter as Amber approached the stand. Halley leaned in and whispered, nodded, and folded his arms across his chest. From the looks of things, Madeline felt confident she could control Amber's testimony.

"Please state your name and your relationship to the defendant."

"Amber Browning. Madeline is my mother."

"Amber, please tell us the events that transpired at your apartment on September 18, 2015."

"What do you want to know?" Amber's question had a tentative quality.

"Did your mother come to your apartment before she went to work?"

"Yes." Her China doll complexion and wheat-colored hair gave her an aura of fragility that alarmed Marc. If he pushed too hard, she could break.

"Was she angry at Jimmy for going to the farm?"

"What exactly do you mean?" Amber whispered, her face twisted in confusion.

"When Jimmy returned and told you David wasn't home, did your mother react?"

"She thought Jimmy was meddling, and Mom doesn't like anyone knowing her business." She chewed on her lower lip as she threw a sideways peek at Madeline.

Madeline stiffened and shook her head to the side. As if by signal, Amber shrank back.

"She wants what is best for me and didn't trust Jimmy."

Madeline relaxed.

"And why didn't she trust Jimmy?"

"Objection. Calls for a conclusion."

"Sustained," Judge Hanson ruled with little interest.

Marc must find a way for Amber to expand on her answers before her mother reined her in.

"Do you trust Jimmy?"

"Yes." A perky smile tipped the corners of her mouth and

dimpled her cheeks. "We write each other notes, you know. I wrote, 'Murder one loves murder two,' and he answered, 'Murder two loves you too.' Isn't that cute?"

Amber spoke with an innocence that jarred Marc. *Did she understand the gravity of killing a man? Putting Amber on the stand could backfire big time if the jury felt I manipulated her. On the other hand, if she tells the truth, the outcome for Madeline would be devastating.*

"Do you trust your mother?"

"I object to this line of questioning." Halley jumped to his feet and stepped forward. The objection reflected a gut reaction to a question he preferred she not answer. "The plaintiff is seeking to influence the jury unduly."

"Your Honor, I need to establish the emotional relationship of the parties engaged in the exchange between Jimmy, Madeline, and Amber."

"Objection overruled. Counselor, keep it brief," Judge Hanson said without a glance at either attorney.

Madeline engaged Amber with an angry, foreboding stare.

"Amber, do you trust your mother?"

Amber sat in a trance, glancing neither left nor right. Marc began to doubt she had heard the question.

"Amber, would you like me to repeat the question?"

"No, I understood the question, and I don't trust my mother." Amber drew a deep breath, lifted her gaze to meet Madeline's, and continued, "She lied to me about my stepdad. David didn't molest my children."

"Why would she lie to you?"

"She wanted him dead." The cold delivery of her words chilled Marc. Amber's ice-blue eyes never wavered from her mother. With her hands clasped tightly in her lap, she sat frozen, and for the first time, she looked formidable. He had touched a deep-seated vein of hatred in his witness.

"Did she tell you this, or is it your conclusion?"

"When my stepdad moved to the farm, my mom said he intended

to cut her off from his money. They fought over money for a long time. She accused him of throwing everything away on gambling, and he told her it wasn't her money to worry about." Amber reached for the glass of water and took a sip, watching her mother over the rim, then paused and looked straight at her mother. Marc feared she wouldn't continue. Then, as suddenly as she had stopped, she began again.

"A man from the bank had called the afternoon before my stepdad died and said he had made the amendments to the beneficiary on his CDs, and that David would need to sign them. That's what set her off."

"Do you know the nature of these amendments?"

"Not really, but Mom said she bet he intended to remove her."

"What happened next?"

"She started up about how David molested my kids. She said if anyone had molested me, she would have killed them." Sadness replaced her steely defiance.

"How did you interpret her statements?"

"She wanted me to kill him and make it look like an accident, like a fire or something."

"Did you go to the farm to kill your stepdad?" Marc asked in a near whisper.

Sadness had given way to defeat. "No, I went to talk to him . . . I didn't even have a gun."

"No more questions at this time, Your Honor."

Halley's turn to cross-examine. He moved close to Amber and screwed his face into an intimidating frown.

"Why have we not heard these allegations from you before, Ms. Browning?"

"Because Mother said she would hire me the best attorneys, and I would get off because of temporary insanity if I kept quiet."

"Hmm. Could it be that these statements are not true, and you wish to hurt your mother?"

"Objection. Leading the witness," Marc bellowed.

"Sustained." The veins on Judge Hanson's forehead bulged as he turned to Halley and pointed his gavel. "Let me remind you, Counselor, law schools teach the consequences of leading a witness in the first course."

A plum-red blush flooded Halley's face. He returned to his desk and pretended to review his notes, but Marc detected a wobble. The judge's rebuke hit him with a karate chop to the knees. Marc remembered the feeling and smiled.

"Ms. Browning, you indicated you do not trust your mother, but you turned to her on the day of the murder. Why is that?"

"Jimmy couldn't help me, and I had no one else."

"No more questions, Your Honor."

The defense had wilted under Amber's testimony. Marc knew it could go either way, but today's win belonged in his column.

"I wish to redirect, Your Honor." Marc walked to the stand. "Did your mother ever mention a gift deed?"

Amber's face looked drawn, but she spoke with steady conviction. "Yes, Mom told me to find a deed and bring it back to her. I think she called it a gift deed."

"Did you find one?"

"I tried, but I couldn't find it."

An ugly look crossed Madeline's face. Hate? Remorse? Marc couldn't tell. She stood up and yelled, "You're a liar, a filthy piece of —" Her screams shattered the sanctity of the courtroom.

"Remove the defendant!" the judge howled, smacking his gavel on the bench.

The few spectators in the courtroom gasped and began buzzing like a swarm of bees.

"Order, order, order!" the judge cried. "I will have order in the court."

The buzz died as quickly as it began.

"Does the prosecution wish to call any more witnesses?"

"No, Your Honor, the prosecution rests."

"The defense may call its witnesses."

"We have no more witnesses, Your Honor. The defense rests."

"Court will recess until tomorrow at 9:00 a.m. At that time, we will hear the closing arguments. The jury is dismissed."

Marc had expected Jimmy's testimony to go well, but had not anticipated a Triple Crown—Jimmy, Amber, and the oh-so-lovely Madeline Caldwell. He wanted to do a victory dance to the office, but Duke held him in check.

50

Nancy had not left for the day, which struck Marc as odd. She always skedaddled at five sharp unless a pending case required overtime.

"You have a visitor." Nancy jerked her head in the direction of the library. "Hank Walton."

"Got it. Send him in." Marc knew the day would come when he and Hank would have to square up the past year's events. He glanced at Nancy. "Would you give Duke a ride to the house?"

"No problem. My car's behind the building, Mr. Waite. Are you ready?" The two disappeared down the hall and out the door, leaving Marc alone in the dark.

As much as Marc hated the timing, he wanted his confrontation with Hank behind him. He opened the door to the library to find Hank stretched out in his recliner, sipping on a root beer.

"Hello, Hank. Make yourself at home. Can I get you something to drink?" Marc asked with a slight edge.

Hank let out a belly laugh. "Sorry, but I didn't know how long you'd be in court, and I couldn't find the real stuff. This root beer ain't bad though. Haven't had one since I was a kid."

"What can I help you with?" Marc moved across the room to his desk.

Hank raised the long-necked amber bottle of soda in a toast. "Here's to you, buddy boy. You were right. I had no idea how conniving Madeline was until today. My apologies to you and your boy."

"A little late for apologies, Hank, but thanks for stopping by."

"Let me say my piece before you boot me out the door." Hank's jovial, boyish manner faded into earnest contrition. "I met Madeline and David when I tried to buy the farm. It joined my place, and I wanted more land since my boy graduated. She agreed, but David would have none of it. According to Madeline, she and David had a real knockdown drag-out fight about it after I left."

"And why is this important to me?" The man sitting in Marc's recliner looked smaller now. Hank had always dominated a room with his over-the-top personality. He wore his wealth with an air of entitlement that buffaloed everyone he met. Marc had been as guilty as the rest. He laughed at Hank's jokes and bent the letter of the law to please him. Today, Hank shrank to the size of an ordinary man.

"It's important because I want you to know I never set out to hurt Devin."

"Why were you passing the Caldwell place so early in the morning? You lied about checking cattle. There's no pasture in October." Marc wanted to call out Hank's lying to his face, to strip him of his power.

"Madeline . . . asked me to keep an eye on the place. She said David usually carried a wad of cash and worried someone might follow him from the casino—you know, rob him. I guess she played me too."

"Sounds like it. How did you persuade JP and the DA to dismiss her charges? You put a heavy thumb on the scales."

"Did you ever talk to Madeline? She's pretty convincing."

"So you bought her story about being so distraught and concerned for her innocent daughter that she made poor decisions. Is that it? Did she cry tears on the Bible and appeal to your manly sense of protection?" Bitterness burned his throat.

"Brule doesn't deal with this stuff every day. We all fell for her story."

"Small-town justice." Marc nodded knowingly. "Damn, Hank. The judge and the jury sit at a back table in Harper's Café, and verdicts come easily over a cup of coffee."

"I'm here to apologize, not to get raked over the coals for an honest mistake. You took a few wrong turns along the way too. You said Jimmy wouldn't kill anyone. You sure missed that call. And I don't remember you protesting when I put my thumb on the scales and got your boy off—with prejudice, by the way."

"Touché. I guess we both believed what we wanted." Marc grew weary of the sparring. He must carry part of the blame himself.

"Go a little easy on JP too. He tries, but he's a local boy whose roots go so deep in this town that he can't be objective." Hank's plea for his friend touched Marc. The king protecting his subject. In a weird way, he seemed honorable at this moment.

"Did he deliberately hide the footprints on the carpet in the washer?" Marc's question surprised both of them.

"No." Hank gazed across Marc's shoulder into the past, then chuckled. "JP barely passed third grade. If you and I hadn't helped him cheat, he would still be in Mrs. Tate's classroom working on math problems during recess. JP is weak and easily manipulated. I think Madeline pushed him. But for the most part, he's not dishonest. We are."

"I suppose you're right. Guilty as charged." Hank made his point. "But I'm putting Brule, with all its dirty laundry, behind me—that includes you, pal. I'll be moving to Gore next month." A genuine smile crossed Marc's face.

"That's near Jessie's old stomping grounds, right?"

"Yes, I'm going into practice with John Kanoske. He's a straight arrow, someone I hope to be like someday."

"Leavin' us, are you?"

"I need a clean break, sunshine, and a milk cow."

Hank raised his eyebrows. "Milk cow?"

Marc rose. "You're nothing to me, Hank, not a friend nor an enemy—which, by the way, is a good thing for you. I wash my hair in the blood of my enemies." Marc laughed at the thought of Duke's words.

51

Marc presented his closing statement, detailing the timeline and events surrounding Madeline's involvement in David's death. With expert precision, he laid out a compelling litany of her sins. Jimmy's testimony overwhelmingly pointed to Madeline's guilt. Jimmy had extracted blood vengeance against the one who had wronged him.

The defense struggled with their closing arguments, which lacked the fire-and-brimstone passion of innocence. The case now rested in the hands of twelve jurors.

The jury panel deliberated for less than two hours before returning a verdict. Marc's heart pounded, and his palms grew sweaty. No one could predict a jury.

Judge Hanson turned and addressed the foreman. "Has the jury reached a verdict?"

"We have, Your Honor."

"Is the decision unanimous?'

"It is, Your Honor."

"Please hand the verdict to the bailiff."

The bailiff presented the papers to the judge, who read them carefully before passing them to the court clerk.

The judge slid the documents across the bench. "The court clerk will now read the verdict."

"Charge One. For the charge of embezzlement in violation of Okla. Stat. Ann. 1451 (B) for unlawfully taking money or property belonging to Ruby Caldwell with the intent to defraud, we find the defendant not guilty."

Ruby yelped and began crying as Dani shot a withering look in Marc's direction. Marc didn't flinch—the critical decision centered on wrongful death.

"Charge Two." The clerk cleared her throat. "For the charge of wrongful death against Madeline Caldwell for knowingly and intentionally causing the death of David Caldwell, the jury finds the defendant guilty."

Ruby lifted her head. "Will I get my farm back?"

"Not exactly, but close. Dani will inherit David's assets. The Slayer Law in Oklahoma does not allow the person who caused the death of another to benefit from that death, so the assets pass to the next in line, which is your granddaughter."

The judge addressed the jury. "I thank the ladies and gentlemen of the jury for their service. Court is adjourned."

"Let's celebrate," Dani said. Her eyes twinkled with excitement as she squeezed Ruby's hand. "We won. It's over."

"We still have to tie up loose ends, but it calls for a celebration—later. Duke and I have work to do."

"Party poopers," Dani teased. "What's so important you can't have a celebratory drink?"

"Moving," Duke said. "We've got an office and a house to pack. We sure could use some help. Any takers?"

"Let's go to Cain's Ballroom iWho needs them." Ruby tugged at Dani's arm. "I'm in the mood to dance."

"Why not?"

Marc watched the two ladies descend the stairs, chattering and giggling like two schoolgirls.

"What a pair," Duke said and laughed. "Makes me appreciate Lisi." He cast a thoughtful look at Marc. "That was quite a performance, Kemosabe. Too bad you're too busy to kick up your heels a little."

Marc winked at his mentor. "I'm not," he said. "But I am choosy about whom I celebrate with. Care to join me?"

"For what?" Duke raised both brows in surprise.

"You'll see. Better call Lisi. We may be a little late getting home." Marc raced to the Jeep with Duke not far behind.

"First stop, the liquor store." Five minutes later, Marc emerged with a brown paper bag under his arm.

Duke frowned at the turn of events. Marc had come too far to backslide now, but he held his tongue.

"Second stop, Dollar General."

"For crying out loud," Duke said. "What in the hell are you up to?"

Marc's cheeks crinkled with amusement. "Patience, my friend. Isn't that what you pounded into my head over this last year?"

"Your show, I guess." Duke was uncomfortable. He hated seeing Marc flame out.

"Seriously, I need your help. I want to go back to Paw Paw Bottom, and I'm not sure I can find it." Marc shot an impish grin at his stoic Indian friend.

An hour later, Marc pulled to the shoulder of the road above the ruins of the intruder settlement. He grabbed the booze and sack from the Dollar General and raced toward the river. Duke wasn't far behind. When he reached the water's edge, he dropped to his knees and began digging with his hands in the soft mud along the bank.

"There," Marc said. "All set." He removed the Jim Beam from the bag, screwed the cap off, and lifted it toward Duke. "Here's to you, for helping me fight the demon in this bottle." With that said, he poured the bourbon into the hole and threw the bottle in after it.

Duke burst out laughing. "You had me worried for a minute."

"Wait. That's not all." Marc drew his wallet from his pocket and began rummaging through cards and receipts. "Aha!" he said, pulling a yellowed business card from the stack and handing it to Duke.

Understanding crept across Duke's face as he stared at the

tattered card, which read, "Smith & Noble Attorneys at Law, Marcus Whitcomb, Associate."

"Why did you keep it?"

"I guess I held on to it to torture myself about all I had lost. But today I bested Halley. Beat him like a drum." Marc pounded on his chest and let out a primal scream. "I'm burying the past—every rotten piece of it." With that, he tossed the worn paper into the muddy hole.

Duke slapped Marc on the shoulder and began kicking dirt over the Beam bottle.

"Stop." Marc grabbed the Dollar General sack, pulled out a package of cookies, and sprinkled them over the bottle. "I never want to eat another Fig Newton as long as I live, either."

"I'm proud of you, son," Duke said after filling the hole and stomping it hard. "But we had better get on the road. Big day ahead of us tomorrow."

"First, we hit Wildhorse BBQ. I'm starving for a pulled-pork sandwich with hotter-than-hell sauce and a large sweet tea to wash it down."

"You're the boss," Duke said as they strolled up the hill.

The exuberance of the afternoon waned as the long drive to Brule stretched late into the night. Marc felt like he had a hangover the next morning, despite not touching a drop of alcohol, and the mess in the office looked daunting.

Piled boxes of books in the hallway created an obstacle course. Duke and Nancy gathered personal items and put them at the end of the line. Marc backed a U-Haul to the back door and began to load.

"I'm never moving again," Marc mumbled as he bent to lift another box.

"What are you complaining about? I'll have to do all the unpacking when we get there," Nancy said. "You're severely challenged in the organizational department."

Marc laughed. "True. Hey, thanks for giving this a shot."

"I couldn't let you go without me," she said. "Besides, I've lived in Brule my whole life. I'll be fifty-three next month, and Brule is all I know. I'm ready for fresh air."

"See you in Gore, Kemosabe," Marc said with a wink.

"Kemosabe?"

"Yep. It means 'trusty scout' in . . . Never mind. Get there as quickly as you can."

The trailer reached capacity by the end of the day, ready for the first trip to his new life. Marc and Duke rose before sunrise in hopes of reaching Gore before the August heat became intolerable. The mountains covered with a thousand shades of summer green had changed. Marc's eyes skimmed the rugged boulders bursting through the earth's crust. He couldn't describe how their strength infused his soul. Like the mountains, he, too, had changed. But until he reached the top peak, he wouldn't rest.

"What are you thinking about?" Duke asked, breaking his spell.

"How hot it will be when I unload these damn boxes." Duke laughed harder than Marc. He had no intention of lifting a hand to unload.

Marc entered the tree-lined drive and wound over the hill toward a two-story home with a tall red-brick chimney, white siding, and black shutters. The architecture looked like a mash-up of colonial and southern plantations.

"What would you call this style?" Marc asked.

"Pioneer homestead style circa 1898."

"Never heard of it. What does that mean?"

"It means the wiring is old, the plumbing is outdated, and the floors are probably uneven."

"A money pit?"

"Yep, but ain't she a beauty." Duke broke into a broad grin.

Marc's anxiety increased as they approached the house. He hadn't seen his wife since the end of July, but she offered to store the boxes from his office until he could find a space to rent. Jessie met them on the front porch that spanned the entire east side of the house. Lisi and Mama stood behind, their hair tied back with bandanas, paint splatters on their clothes.

"Wait until you see it, Marc. It's going to be beautiful. We've finished painting the downstairs and will start upstairs tomorrow." Jessie's babbling was infectious.

Marc walked through each room, noting that the floor slanted slightly to the north and the ceiling had a few cracks.

"Jessie, are you sure"—Marc caught Duke's warning grimace and hesitated—"you don't need more time? It's beautiful, but you don't want to rush it."

"Nonsense. I hope to have the furniture here this weekend." Jessie's enthusiasm fired on all cylinders. "I put shelves up in the spare bedroom. You can unload and reuse the boxes for your things." Sergeant Jessie had reported for duty.

"Look at this." Duke held up three volumes of Ruby's story. Nancy must have packed those by accident.

"Put them in the Jeep so I don't forget. I'll drop them by Dani's apartment tomorrow."

By sunset, Marc's back was ready to call it a day.

"Stop by the house when you're ready. Mama has a roast in the oven, and there's a bed waiting for you. You might as well stay," Duke said as he, Mama, and Lisi climbed into his old truck. Marc watched dust fog the two-rut road leading to the blacktop, leaving him alone with Jessie.

"I'm starving. Are you ready?" Jessie asked.

"Not quite. I brought you something. It's a little housewarming gift. Not much really." Marc walked to the Jeep, removed two folding rockers, and placed them on the east porch.

The musky dampness of the night air crinkled Marc's unruly hair. *I need a haircut*, he thought as he watched fireflies flicker in the ink-black sky. The distance between him and Jessie vanished for a moment, but he knew better than to deceive himself. She had managed quite well without his help. He had become an accessory—not a necessity—in her life.

"Do we have a chance?" Marc asked, his voice rising softly on the gentle breeze.

"I don't know . . . but . . ."

Her reluctance shattered Marc's hope. "I'll catch you tomorrow. You must be tired," he said as he stood to leave.

"Wait. Let me finish." Jessie shivered in the cool night air, her hands tightening around the sleeves of her shirt. "I need to say something that's been weighing on my mind. And I don't need you to fix it or make it okay for me. I just . . . just need to say it."

She looked sad, and Marc sank slowly into the rocker and turned to face her fully. *Is this where it ends?*

Jessie forced her eyes to meet his. "When you were drinking, I thought . . . if I just controlled everything . . . if I held on tightly enough, I could keep us safe, but I was really trying to protect myself." Jessie dropped her gaze, struggling to continue.

Marc desperately wanted to hold her, to make everything all right.

"I think . . . I think I made you feel small. Cornered. Like you were the problem and I was the solution. Sometimes I think you drank to get away from me when I wouldn't let you breathe." Tears welled up in her eyes.

"That was part of it. I remember feeling . . . trapped," he confessed. "Every room had you in it, watching, waiting for me to fail. And yeah . . . some nights the bottle felt like the only door you couldn't close." He turned away from his wife, ashamed to share the ugly truth.

"I'm so sorry, Marc. You were fighting for something huge, and instead of standing beside you, I stood over you and made things worse." Jessie swallowed hard and drew a deep breath. "I needed to say that out loud—take my share of the blame."

"Apology accepted," Marc said in a low whisper. He reached over and covered her hand with his. "But I also know why you did it. You were scared. We both were. Thank you for seeing it . . . for saying it."

Her tears flowed freely as Marc squeezed her hand. An emptiness mixed with relief washed over him.

"Nothing's fixed, but at least we're being honest. Confession is good for the soul, but it's hell on a marriage," he said with a half-laugh. "The real question is: Where do we go from here?"

"I want to go back to the beginning and start over—find *us* again."

"We're different people, sweetie," Marc said.

"Yes, different, but better, and I still love you."

"I've never stopped loving you."

"It's settled, then?" she asked, casting a faint smile his way.

"Yes, settled," Marc said, pulling Jessie into his lap. The tension left his body as he cradled her in his arms. His world felt right again.

"Get your things out of the Jeep and let's go into the house. It's late, and Duke will be here early in the morning."

"Oh, yeah. I had forgotten about your dowry," Marc said with an ornery grin.

"Dowry?"

"The milk cow Duke promised. No cow, no deal."

"It never was about me, was it? It's about my Jersey cow." Jessie swatted his shoulder and giggled as she ran into the house with Marc not far behind.

52

The climb to Dani's apartment challenged the sore muscles in Marc's legs. His right calf began to cramp. He rang the bell and waited. No Ruby. He tried twice before Dani finally cracked the door an inch.

"May I come in?"

"Sure, but watch your step." She tugged to free the latch chain.

"Where's your grandmother?"

"With her sister. We're moving, and she gets in the way trying to help." Dani's tinkling laughter amused Marc. "I have iced tea. Would you like some?"

"Sounds great."

Dani disappeared into the kitchen and returned with two icy tumblers of sweet liquid.

"So how did your grandmother react to the decision?"

"She doesn't understand that I own the land."

"We've still got some work to do. Madeline surrendered the farm without much fuss but will fight like hell for half the house and all the furniture and probably win. The money in David's bank account should be released to you in a couple of weeks, but it won't amount to much—sixteen thousand and some change. That won't last long."

Dani sat cross-legged on the floor, twisting a gold necklace between her fingers. It looked familiar, but Marc struggled to remember where he had seen it.

"Beautiful piece." He pointed to the Cuban link gold chain.

"It's Grandmother's. I borrowed it." She quickly tucked it into the neckline of her T-shirt.

She avoided Marc's eyes as she plucked at imaginary lint on her jeans. *She's lying.* She dodged him like Jimmy did when he lied to Duke. The hair stood up on the back of his neck. He saw that necklace in the photos from the insurance company—the Cuban link chain and the black-diamond ring reported stolen on the day of David Caldwell's murder. Dani squirmed under his gaze. Every fiber of his being wanted to quiz her, but he held his tongue. The Cherokee had cautioned him to say little in situations like this. Your opponents will spill their guts if you give them a chance.

"More tea?" Dani fished for a diversion.

Marc nodded but said nothing. Her navy-blue Nike Air Zoom tennis shoes skimmed across the carpet as she headed to the kitchen. Jimmy had told John that Amber wore sandals, but the sneakers he found in the Buick bore a strong resemblance to the pair Dani had on, except for color—too many coincidences.

"Anything wrong?"

His silence troubled her.

"Nice shoes."

"You can stop the game. I know what you're hinting at."

"Do you care to fill in the blanks?"

Dani's Tinkerbell features hardened into a grotesque caricature of the young woman with a pixie cut and dimples.

"Why not? There's nothing illegal about what I did."

Amber's testimony concerning a call from the bank lingered in the back of his mind. The calls were fake. First American had not placed that call.

Marc pushed his glasses up the bridge of his nose. "The way I figure it, Devin placed the fake call from the bank to push Madeline's buttons."

Dani flashed a mischievous grin. "Yep. And the bitch bit. Devin said she would."

"And you entered the house after the two had left to look for the gift deed. The footprints by your dad's body belonged to you."

"You're very good. Your son said you were, but he came up with the idea of cutting my prints out of the carpet and hiding them in the washer. He's smart like his dad." She smirked. "You did scare me when you went snooping."

Dani hurled Devin's name like a sling blade, but she missed the target. He had grown accustomed to the possibility that his son had been involved in this mess.

"And when Devin went to help Jimmy roll the car into the canyon, he placed your tennis shoes in the trunk. Did he burn the Buick too?"

"Yep. Your son gets credit for that." Dani's smugness did not faze him.

"Great job."

"Good but not great. Madeline will probably keep half of the house. That's one thing Devin couldn't figure out."

"And the gift deed. Had your dad signed it?"

"Yes, but Devin burned it." Dani turned her back on Marc and resumed packing. "Thank goodness Dad left a copy in the safety deposit box before he put his name on it."

"Where will you and Ruby move?"

"Grandmother is in her new home. They had room for her at the Grace Living Center. Since she has no assets, it's free. Me? I'm headed to Houston."

"A little heartless."

"As Devin said, 'Old people don't need money.' I guess I'm like him in that way."

A queasy knot formed in Marc's chest. "I'll let myself out," he muttered, anxious to escape the sickening truth.

Marc descended the three flights of stairs for the last time. The rotten feeling in his stomach made him want to puke. He needed to see Duke more than anyone in the world, but forced himself to drive to Brule and check on the movers before returning to Gore. Marc halted abruptly. He still had the diaries, a tennis shoe, and a good set of fingerprints from a card. A smile crossed his lips.

When he returned to the Waite house, everyone had retired for the evening, but the porch light burned bright in the darkness. Weariness ached in his bones, begging him to surrender, give up, and accept that his son had orchestrated the theft of Ruby's assets.

The old Cherokee met him at the door and studied him as if he were a stranger.

"Let's head to the den." Duke took Marc's arm. "We won't wake anyone back there."

Marc followed, tired yet eager to spew out the day's events. When finished, he knew what he had to do. "Devin conned an old lady, and I intend to right that wrong."

"Just so. But maybe it's time *you* dismiss a trial that's over," Duke said, closing the book on unanswerable questions.

"Not yet." Marc patted his briefcase, holding the three volumes of Ruby's diaries. He suspected Dani had fabricated most of the content. If only he could prove his suspicions . . .

Devin had fooled him, as the others had. The real culprit was his son. Somewhere in the fog of booze, he had lost his boy. Like those damn daffodils, a winter freeze had killed the hope that his son was innocent.

Marc rubbed his eyes in exhaustion. Tonight, he would sleep the sleep of the dead, but tomorrow he would start a new journey, the fight for Ruby. He would wash his hair in the blood of his enemies until justice and law walked as twins.

The End

www.ingramcontent.com/pod-product-compliance
Lightning Source LLC
LaVergne TN
LVHW090554110826
845146LV00001B/117

* 9 7 9 8 2 3 4 0 2 1 2 0 5 *